P9-CBE-323

RAVES FOR A WILDLY ROMANTIC NOVEL OF LOVE AND MONEY BEYOND THE DREAMS OF FANTASY...

"THE SUSPENSE NEVER LETS UP ... Who among us is so bloodless as to disdain a tale of bold heroes, beautiful and treacherous ladies, jungle violence, idealistic sacrifice and hairsbreadth escape? ... The nineteenth century teemed with writers who knew how to turn out a riproarer on demand ... But maybe this is going to change ... First the movies gave us *Star Wars* ... Now in book form comes BLACK ORCHID, a new nineteenth-century adventure ... There is enough verve, thrilling suspense and exotic and dangerous tropical color in this rouser to fuel an old-fashioned steamer halfway up the Amazon ... It's a wow of a set-up ... There's a tense escape and a splendid chase downriver, with no fuel, the ravening jungle all around, and a beautiful hostage bent on sabotage. *Madre mia,* how this book calls out to Hollywood!"

—*Washington Post Book World*

BLACK ORCHID

by NICHOLAS MEYER and
BARRY JAY KAPLAN

A BANTAM BOOK
TORONTO/NEW YORK/LONDON

BLACK ORCHID

*A Bantam Book / published by arrangement with
The Dial Press*

PRINTING HISTORY

*Dial Press edition published October 1977
2nd printing ... December 1977
Bantam edition / November 1978
2nd printing*

ISBN 0-553-11659-2

*Bantam Books are published by Bantam Books, Inc. Its trade-
mark, consisting of the words "Bantam Books" and the por-
trayal of a bantam, is registered in the United States Patent
Office and in other countries. Marca Registrada. Bantam
Books, Inc., 666 Fifth Avenue, New York, New York 10019.*

PRINTED IN THE UNITED STATES OF AMERICA

BLACK ORCHID is based on
historical fact. But it is a story, not a
history. The authors have made free
with events and dates, telescoping time
willy-nilly. Events herein described occur
not as they happened, but as the authors
feel they ought to have happened.

Se non è vero, è ben trovato

For Connie and Michael,
and for Sue. It is very
hard to misinterpret sincerity.
NM

For Knox and Kitty
and for my parents.
BJK

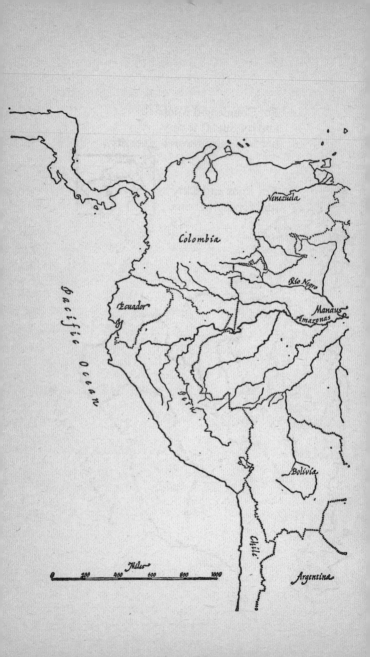

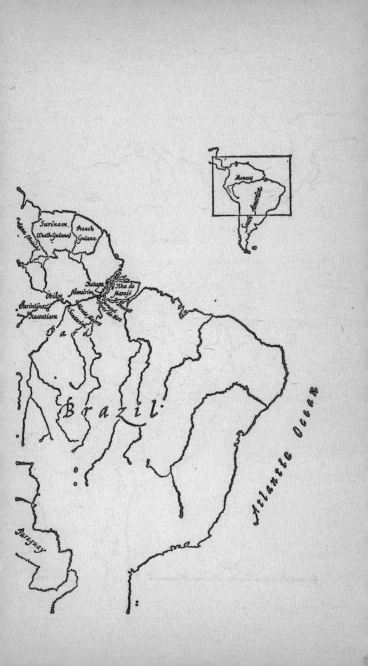

PROLOGUE

Millions of years ago a channel of easy waters joined the Atlantic and Pacific oceans. South America existed as two masses: Venezuela and the Guianas to the north; to the south, the great island of Brazil. The Andes rose from the sea: roaring, foaming, brilliant. After an eon the metamorphosis was complete; the bottom of the Amazon valley had been raised, the waters of the ocean rolled back, and the great Amazon plain formed —the base of the most astonishing river system on the face of the planet.

From the Andes to the sea the gradient of the river is but two hundred feet in two thousand miles, yet the Amazon carries millions of tons of mud and silt into the Atlantic along its thirty-five-hundred mile length. Its drainage basin covers two and a half million square miles. All its tributaries combined disgorge three billion gallons of water into the ocean every minute. Tree trunks and tons of vegetation swept from the Peruvian Andes are found in the ocean four hundred miles east of the mouth of the Amazon; ocean waters six hundred miles from the delta are still stained with its colors.

1

The great river teems with virulent life: the caiman, speckled as if diseased, its enormous snaggle-toothed jaws a bestial smile. The slick gray anaconda, largest snake in the world, four, five, six times longer than a man; before it eats its prey, it squeezes the life from it in indifferent leisure. The piranha, deceptively tiny, traveling in silent, lethal schools, teeth bared, ravenous. Also the *jacare-assu* alligator, formidable in ugliness and diabolism, its baleful stare the inspiration for a basic Indian belief in evil. Catfish fifteen feet long, hairy, their stomachs repositories of human remains.

The jungle that surrounds the Amazon is a storehouse of riches: rough-barked palm and balsa, the nectar and seed of the pomegranate, smooth guava, papaya, coffee trees, and the nut trees used for drugs: the coca, the kola, the curare. Diamonds. Gold. The jungle pants with the riotous eroticism of the colorful frangipani, shimmers with the bell-like lavender garlic vine and the tuberous black velvet gloxinia. There are startling flame vines, tobacco, nightshade and glory, passion flowers in crimson and pink, phenomenal cacti that imitate roses and geese, bougainvillea dropping coy magenta blossoms, cattleya orchids, and odontoglossum, the fragrant pure white Amazon lily.

The scents of flowers and rich dark soil, of dampness, of rankness and too much life; the constant hum of insects, russet moor hens in their reeds, biting flies—black, crane, horse, and deer—bugs that suck blood, flamingoes, dragon- and damselflies, heat-mad spiders, and furry tarantulas. The noises are small ones, muted cacophony—sighs, whispers, rustling—yet they murmur with innuendo. An occasional whistle, an odd rasp, a choke.

The jungle is a presence thunderous as religion, within it possession is indiscriminate. It is only Man, in his infinite vanity, who presumes to rule; who attempts to civilize what is relentlessly savage.

The jungle, deep as time, mocks him.

PART
ONE

❈ 1 ❈

Kincaid surveyed the river. He had floated sar-
cophagi down the Nile, pearls along the Yang-tse,
and aces high on the Mississippi, but he had never
encountered the likes of the Amazon. The Amazon
was longer than the Nile, twelve times the size of
the Mississippi, and the Yang-tse, Kincaid reflected with reluctant admiration, wasn't worthy of
being a tributary.

He chewed on the stub of his cigar, leaned his
tall frame against the railing of the bridge, trying
to discern either bank, and failing. Several days
before, the *Mãe de Deus* had coasted along the
southern side of the island of Marajó, at the mouth
of the river, maneuvering carefully through a series
of channels that ultimately brought her into the
main stream. They had passed several other river
mouths, some nearly as wide as the Amazon itself:
the Tocantins, the Madeira.

Kincaid was tired and couldn't understand why.
At first he ascribed it to the ocean crossing. The
Atlantic was especially unruly this time of year,
particularly outside the Gulf Stream; the long rolling swells had depressed him. But the change from
the steamer to the *Mãe de Deus* had failed to im-

prove his spirits. Another boat; it must be the confinement. Perhaps. Now he had another explanation. He squinted against the sunset and told himself it was the heavy air.

There was something else, unacknowledged but dimly sensed, sapping his strength when he needed it most, for this time nothing less than total success would suffice. Kincaid was counting on this labor to be his last. He'd outlived the average age for men in his peculiar profession and was well aware that the odds were no longer in his favor.

The month previous, Kincaid had returned to London from Hong Kong, where he had helped settle a vicious opium war in a manner that had—as usual—left his methods open to question. He reached England via the China, Arabian, and Mediterranean seas, where he was immediately recruited by the directors of the Royal Geographic Society for employment on the Amazon.

The proposition was an enticing one—enticing enough for Kincaid to plan on retiring when it was over. He'd repacked his bags and trotted round to the British Museum. Sitting in the reading room, surrounded by topographical records, the Amazon seemed to be a river, nothing more. Kincaid had dealt with rivers before, and generally regarded them of little consequence. It was not until now that the true immensity, the simple unprecedented hugeness of the Amazon came home to him.

The days seemed endless and so did the water, yellow and thick as soup, in which not only uprooted trees floated by, but also enormous clumps of dried grass and beds of vegetation that looked as if they'd been someone's harvest, now gone to sea.

The weather was so changeable that the seasons seemed compressed, dreamlike. Each morning the sky was gray, piled-up clouds shot with blue. Then it blackened and poured rain in a steady deafening roar, only to subside in a fine mist that made it seem that London followed them wherever they went. But there was always the heat—relentless, merciless—even when hidden behind a thick layer of clouds and night; so heavy it felt solid.

Islands dotted the river; some were so large they had names: Cotijuba and Tapuoca lay so low they seemed nothing more than green discs floating on the surface. Other islands were overgrown with bizarre jungle trees, crowding each other to the banks, trunks half submerged in the flow. There were varieties of scrub brush, reminding Kincaid of the barbed wire he'd once hitched on a ranch in Montana; behind it were layers of vegetation in shades of lime and moss.

And still more islands, tall and majestic, columnal; others with smooth tawny sand beaches. Some even floated—vast tangles of dislodged jungle—perhaps to take root somewhere else, perhaps to wash to sea. The first officer had shown Kincaid a map of the river, indicating a particular island, a large one, that had moved more than a mile in twelve months.

The islands were often so big, an acre or more, that, standing in the bow of the yacht, Kincaid had difficulty distinguishing the islands from the bank. What looked at first to be successive levels of jungle turned out, upon closer inspection, to be rows of islands lying one behind the other. Some islands rose and fell in the wake of the boat while others were snagged nearer to shore and bobbed as inconsequentially as corks. Kincaid sighed; yes, yes, but let's get on with it.

He wondered with a sinking feeling if it was this kind of impatience that got men killed. When he was young, it had not seemed so. There was something clean and quick and bright in all his deeds, and his actions were precise even when they were dangerous. Now that he was older, the risks seemed greater, life infinitely more precious, and the brightness of his youth had departed, leaving him with the vague intimation that if he did not end this style of life soon, there would be no life left. Perhaps it would be better to quit while he was still ahead.

Longford joined him on the bridge, the two exchanging perfunctory greetings.

He looked like the sort of man most comfortable in a London club; his skin a vague sooty pallor that winced red in the open Brazil sun; sidewhiskers impeccably trimmed and a nose held statically aloft, giving him the perpetual air of having just sniffed something unpleasant.

Longford, who thought of the Royal Geographic as nothing less than an alma mater, had specifically and urgently requested the assignment of Kincaid by the Society. He hadn't seen Kincaid for several years, but had followed his exploits as reported by the newspapers and by rumor. Knowing Kincaid as he did, Longford was inclined to trust the rumors more than the London *Times*. After all, there were some things a paper simply did not print.

On the other hand, the Kincaid who stood next to him on the bridge now was not the man Longford remembered.

Once almost theatrically handsome, with his dark blue eyes, bristly mustache and taut muscularity, Kincaid had been the perfect picture of the stage hero. Upon closer inspection, the mustache proved an unsuccessful attempt to conceal the countenance of an overeager boy. Now, Longford noted, the boy's face and the stage actor's face had been succeeded by a third visage. Longford couldn't quite place the category into which it fit, but there was something unmistakably hang-dog about it. Longford sighed, and put the thought out of his mind—an exercise he had performed several times since the trip began.

"Coffee plantation," he said, pointing to an area along the near bank.

"I can smell the yellow fever from here."

Longford shrugged, not indifferent to the dangers but accepting them. He was perplexed by the weariness and cynicism in Kincaid's tone. The ship's bells sounded in rapid succession. "Hungry?"

Kincaid shook his head no. "I think I'll stay up here awhile."

Longford left him brooding and went below.

Captain Mactavish was dining informally with his crew of eight, all crushed into the tiny mess. They were an odd mixture of Negro, Indian, Portuguese, Spanish, and Italian blood that gave them skin that burned red in sunlight and in moonlight glowed purple. They were talking of monsters that haunted the Indians of the jungle.

"There is one with the feet turned backwards. The *maiturus*."

"A faceless one. Only holes. The horrible *simia-vulpina*."

Their conversation ceased when Longford appeared. The silence was broken by a belch from Mactavish, a signal for them to depart. They filed out silently, carrying their food. Mactavish pushed aside his own meal and produced a second glass for his bottle of Forty Rod, a signal for intimacy. Longford accepted the drink.

"Just wondering about your friend," Mactavish began, his eyes raised to the ceiling as if he could see Kincaid through the deck.

"What about him?" Longford asked, curious that Kincaid had already provoked the curiosity of others. Mactavish narrowed his bloodshot eyes, droll and portentous.

"No offense, now, but are the two of you on the square?"

"Square?"

"Above board . . . on an even keel," Mactavish

sputtered impatiently. "Are you both what you say you are?"

"I'm not sure I follow," Longford persisted, amiably, "but I can tell you Mr. Kincaid is here to collect jungle orchids for the Royal Geographic Society. We—" Longford flushed with what he hoped would be taken for pardonable pride "—we have been involved in similar expeditions for years." Mactavish grunted noncommittally, lulled by the Englishman's gentle voice. "Orchids are all the rage nowadays in England, and quite profitable, as well. Oh, yes, quite profitable," Longford insisted, though no one had contradicted him. "Of course the Royal Geographic is less interested in lucre than in genera and species." He allowed himself a mild titter. "Mr. Kincaid and I have, however, worked for private patrons, fanatics, no less, willing to pay any price to augment their amazing collections." He shook his head. "Orchids. I, myself, find them a bit . . . mmm . . . fanciful."

Mactavish surveyed him dubiously over the rim of his glass. "Profit, you say?"

"Astounding profit. We have just returned from the Far East, despatched by the Van Lieu brothers, Belgian millionaires who've made all of their fortune as commercial nurserymen, if you can credit it. The week before we left London this time, the elder Van Lieu got three thousand pounds for a single plant at auction."

Mactavish stared.

"*Trichoglottis philippinensis brachiata,* commonly referred to as the Black Orchid—common that is if you're ever lucky enough to see one." Longford glanced easily at Mactavish now, satisfied that with this rambling chatter he had dissuaded the man from pursuing Kincaid's credibility. The Captain, indeed, appeared blearily convinced.

"Ah, well, then," he responded vaguely. "I expect I'm not surprised. Black orchids, indeed. This river is full of legends, full of blather, if you take my meaning. The whole thing's named for some women that maybe never even existed."

"You mean the Amazons. Yes, I've read of them. The Green historian Herodotus first described them as the lost tribe of women warriors."

"The only Greek I know did me out of a shirt and gaiters last year in Pará," Mactavish mumbled, well into his third bourbon. "This here I'm speaking of was a Spaniard, name of Orellana. He discovered all this—" A wide gesture sloshed some of the amber liquid. "—the whole river. Then the bloody fool goes and tells his king—"

"That would be Phillip II."

"Whoever . . . about the river and these wild women he'd seen and the king gets this bloody clever idea to call the river after these creatures— had a thing for a skirt, that's sure—and nobody really even knows that they was ever even here."

"Orellana," Longford said. "A sad case. A hero nobody remembers." There was a silence then and Longford realized he was thinking with like sadness of Kincaid.

No one seemed to know precisely where in the States Kincaid was from. He had been paid to fight with the Berbers in the great desert war, and so people had called him a mercenary. When he remained in the desert to learn the ancient art of *panstout*, the designated piling of layers of sand in conjunction with fasting and continence, others branded him an ascetic. Traitor and patriot were labels simultaneously applied, and he appeared to wear both with indifferent equanimity. Gordon had praised him and called him a man of promise, Kitchener had reviled him, women succumbed to him, and Disraeli, on one occasion, had paid him. Few—even Longford, who was an ardent admirer—trusted him. Longford had little doubt that the stories passed around the mess would carry them easily to the city of Manaus, their journey's end, a thousand miles inland from the delta, and several days' time. And as a gentleman's gentleman, he could hardly be expected to tell tales.

Longford bid Mactavish a good evening and returned to his cramped quarters, where he made the best of a small dinner, served him by a swarthy Neopolitan steward who had not, to his knowledge, spoken a single word since Pará. Longford could not blame Kincaid for foregoing the repast. It had not been badly prepared—on the contrary —but he was beginning to become seriously tired of the same food. Dried beef was predominant, braised or in fritters or cooked in a stew; lots of black beans and farina and, of course, delicious coffee, and perhaps some Edam cheese.

After eating, Longford walked to the companionway, passing and nodding to crewmen standing by the exposed engine. They looked up from their round tin bowls (filled with a mixture of rice, mandioca, and meat) but did not smile. They ate with their fingers, or speared their food with pointed wooden sticks.

Topside the moon was rising. Kincaid was still leaning against the bridge railing, Mactavish next to him sharing the bourbon. He gave Longford a small smile and a nod. Everything here was different, strange. Kincaid was glad to have a familiar face nearby. Mactavish did not qualify.

Kincaid, who had lived most of his life among strangers, had suddenly grown tired of it. He passed Longford the bottle, and Longford, to oblige, took a swallow, careful to wipe off the neck before drinking. They watched the moon ascend, white and full, a giant light in the black sky.

The *Mãe de Deus* steered closer to the north bank and they stared at cacao orchards, the golden fruit wildly shining out from green-black leaves, and behind the orchards, the lofty trees of the Amazon forests, rising majestically like mountains in China.

Mactavish looked at his watch, grabbed Kincaid's arm, and pointed to a place on the bank. There was stillness and then a tremendous fluttering roar as a flock of hundreds of small birds rose from the jungle, flew across the river, and disappeared somewhere far on the southern bank.

"Parakeets," Mactavish said. "They cross the river like clockwork. Or maybe clockwork is like the parakeets crossing the river. At any rate, they've been at it ever since I first came here."

For most of the trip the shores were too distant to see clearly, but now Kincaid noticed small boats cruising beside them, huts with cooking fires and some women and children standing in the water, waving.

On another day Mactavish told Kincaid that the only difference on the Amazon between summer and winter was that in winter it rained every day and in summer only every other day. Kincaid smiled at the absurdity and gritted his teeth. Mactavish called his attention to the river's changing color—patterns of yellow, olive, chocolate, mauve, and red that were a combination of reflected sky and shifting silt. He was so familiar with these changes he steered by them.

But it was days later when the steam yacht came to where the Amazon met the Rio Negro that Kincaid received his biggest surprise; he had not expected the line of demarcation between the two rivers to be so sharply visible. In the early morning light the Amazon was pale, flesh-colored, and as clear as if the bottom were only two inches below the surface when actually the water was deep enough to carry ocean liners. The churning waters in the wake of the boat were bubbling pink and light brown, and ahead of them was the Rio Negro, still, ink-black, depthless. As the prow steamed into this blackness, the foam churned up like boiling molasses. One of the crew lowered a bucket over the side and drew up some of the water for Kincaid and Longford to examine; in the

bucket the water was brown with silt, in the hand
it was almost clear. Ahead of them now, the
water was slick as ebony, its surface glassiness
broken only by the surprising leaps of dolphins
who seemed to welcome them to the Rio Negro.

At first its mouth seemed almost as large as the
Amazon's, but this was deceptive. It drained a vast
region of the Amazon valley, but it was only near
the Amazon itself that it so increased in size. High
bluffs of poplar trees stood guard along the banks
so that the *Mãe de Deus* seemed to be steaming
alongside a well-protected fortress. Cacao plantations lined the banks too, familiar sights now to
Kincaid, and again behind them were the dense
forests of palm trees.

The dolphins were still bounding ahead, and as
the boat turned up the Rio Negro Kincaid got his
first glimpse of the city of Manaus. Rising from
the wildness of the jungle on the north bank, shining like a handful of diamonds dropped in a field
of grass, the town sloped up from the river and
covered the hills with a maze of white buildings
roofed in red. And above it was the glittering
opera house at the peak of the highest hill, its tiled
dome roof splattering sunlight over the city. Cathe-
dral spires of blue and gray and black carved
stone pierced the heat waves that shimmered the
sky. As the *Mãe de Deus* came closer, the buildings
near the wharves grew until they clarified—large
business establishments, staid and stately as ones
in London or Washington.

The slips were filled with steamboats, ocean liners, fishing boats, dugout canoes, schooners, all bouncing idly alongside the floating docks. The green and yellow flag of Brazil waved limply atop the Customs House. The Booth Steamship Company flew its own flag, the red cross of Saint Andrew. There were ships of the Italian Liguria Brasiliana and of the Hamburg-American Line, their shields and anchors vivid against the solid fields of the company flags.

"Manaus, Mr. Kincaid," Captain Mactavish remarked superfluously.

"Quite a sight." Kincaid could feel the pulse of faint excitement racing through him. "I don't know if it's the sun or what, but the damn city looks made of gold."

"*Ouro preto,*" Mactavish said in a brogue unaffected by years away from Glasgow. "Black gold is what they call it around here. It's rubber that's the gold. Rubber, sir. Don't know if you orchid fellers know that, but all the rubber in the world floats down this river."

"Is that a fact?"

Mactavish nodded, watching Kincaid closely.

"You'll want to be careful collecting your flowers . . ."

"Orchids."

"Orchids, then. You'll want to be careful collecting them, in that jungle. Back in Pará they were talking about a war."

"War?"

Kincaid looked back at the golden city, properly curious and appreciative and committing every sight to memory.

"Between two of them rubber kings . . ." Mactavish spat over the side. "Those men are so rich . . . Andrew Carnegie looks like a pauper next to them. They live in palaces, nothing less. And they've got their own private armies. You'd best be careful out there. They're bound to be a bit jumpy."

"Thanks for telling me."

Mactavish nodded, concentrating on the wheel, but Kincaid could see he was not finished. "There's yellow fever too, you know. You'll want to carry around a bottle of castor oil. You feel a headache coming on you take a pull on that castor oil. Best stuff there is for yellow fever. Best stuff there is."

"I'll remember that."

Mactavish nodded; he considered it no more than his duty to tell what he knew. He had given up trying to read the riddle of Kincaid. The man's servant had remained inscrutable and liquor hadn't loosened the master's tongue, either. He pointed. "Customs shed coming up."

As Kincaid started below to change his clothes and gather his belongings, Mactavish placed a hand on his shoulder and spoke in hushed, conspiratorial tones. "Even without the fighting you want to watch it here. After Macao, this has got to be the wickedest place on God's earth."

"I'll watch it," Kincaid replied, appropriately

solemn, and continued down the companionway, a creamy grin spreading across his face. Kincaid had sported gleefully in Macao and had a rather intimate tattoo to prove it.

2

The harbor at Manaus had been built with maximum haste to accommodate the constantly accelerating growth of the rubber-rich city. The Amazon was navigable by large freighters only as far as Manaus, a fortuitous circumstance that allowed the rubber and consequently all of the growers to ship the raw cargo from their own docks. The rubber came downriver on smaller vessels from as far away as Peru, steaming a virtual straight line for 2,350 miles. Other steamers cruised up and down the Rio Branco, the Rio Madeira, and the Rio Negro to bring other supplies to the port. The Amazon Steam Navigation Company, built by English capitalists in the 1850s, covered half a million miles of river every year. The Brazilina line had twelve steamers of its own and loaded thirteen thousand tons. Thousands of ships docked at Manaus every year, and as the rubber boom continued, the numbers increased, and the vulgar splendors of the city competed with the real horrors of the jungle.

The docks that supported all of this activity were constructed to allow for the tremendous rise and fall of the only river in the world with a tide.

The planks were already moldering, splintered, and soft; the water that lapped about the pilings was yellow and steaming in the heat.

Kincaid reappeared on deck of the *Mãe de Deus* resplendent in a fresh linen suit that would wilt within the quarter hour, and a soft-brimmed Panama that would get softer until it conformed to one of the three local styles: slouched front, heavily starched by an elegant haberdasher, or dangled carelessly at fingertip. Kincaid checked his time with Captain Mactavish, signaled for Longford, who appeared from his cabin in a gray cutaway, and together they walked down the gangway to the docks.

The number and variety of people at once amazed and amused Kincaid, who retained the airs and attitudes of a perpetual tourist despite, or perhaps because of, having seen almost everything. He watched as Negroes and mulattoes loaded and unloaded the ships, carrying huge boxes of rubber from warehouses on the dock to the holds of the great vessels themselves. From the ships they took bales and bore them back to the docks on their heads. The people were all shades of white, yellow, red, and black.

As master and man joined the swarming throng, Kincaid was reminded of the dazzling and aromatic New Orleans.

Eager, jerky porters in white jackets jostled frantically through the crowd, sticking out their chests to display the insignia of the hotels they worked for, and calling out their names as if hawking a product, not satisfied until they had wrested from someone at least a straw bag and rooster. There was an enormous flow of passengers disembarking from a towering, multileveled ship that reminded Kincaid of a Mississippi steamboat, but in this, a *gaiola*, the passengers swung idly in hammocks like birds in a birthday-cake cage. There were salesmen of every nationality in tight checkered suits, flashing gold teeth and a glad hand at whoever walked past, selling tonics of vanilla and ginger for the nerves, and country boys in the *mate* shirts of the small jungle village on the eager arms of the prostitutes of the river saloons, their teeth filed sharp as a shark's, their flanks sheathed in acid green satin. There were old women in black, their faces a thousand tiny wrinkles in a life map, come to seek someone in the city to take away their pain.

Other tourists milled about, sweating under their stiff celluloid collars and stiff-brimmed boaters, while all around them the laborers jostled them in bare feet, most of them bareheaded, too. The men wore cotton shirts and trousers, the women bright-colored dresses of calico. A Negro man pranced by Kincaid with a huge turtle balanced on his head, the turtle as big as a washtub, kicking lazily, its shell serving as a shade for the man.

They made their way through the crowd, good-naturedly fending off propositions of all sorts, and headed for the Customs House. Kincaid found the

noise and heat and crowd unbearable but familiar.
Thieves were everywhere, their treasures a bizarre
assortment of soaps, powders, and potatoes. Beggars, toothless, ageless, missing limbs, plucked at
his sleeve, insisting he share his wealth. The air
was thick with smells the heat accentuated—rotting fruit, shaved fish, flowers in decay, a smell of
overabundance that assaulted the senses instead of
stimulating them.

Opposite the dock, flanking it and dividing it
from the city itself, were two-story warehouses.
Tattered posters of elections come and gone hung
limply from the walls, the paint was chipped and
peeled, layers revealed other layers once green,
once orange, once blue, a generation's colors. The
windows were broken and dusty, the iron balconies dilapidated, dangerous.

Beneath them, at the point the walls met the
streets, were rows of small concessions selling
fruits, nuts, baskets, handkerchiefs, glass beads, key
rings, run by Indian women in pale cotton dresses
whose demeanor was a pocket of calm in the bus-
tle and noise. On the stone and mud pavement
around them were dockworkers, probably their
husbands or sons, squat, disgruntled, faces seamed
with wear that came from having no time to be
young, dressed in clothes that charted bodily se-
cretion.

Above them all, framing the entire scene, were
the galvanized iron roofs of the rubber warehouses,
glinting and winking in the impossible sun, and

spelling out, in huge white letters that covered almost a quarter of a mile: MANAUS HARBOR LTD.

Kincaid had been told about the city, but at close range he saw it battling to hold off the jungle. There was a sense of undergrowth everywhere, little specks of dirt showing weeds, vines appearing between buildings, flowers staring from cracks in the warehouse walls. It was as if the city were merely something for the jungle to overgrow, like spores on bread in the dark. The heat was moist and rank, a breeding ground for infestation. Kincaid felt an exhalation would produce a palm frond.

Finally, the Customs House loomed before him, a monument to Victoriana. Prefabricated in England and shipped from Liverpool, it had been assembled stone by stone under the careful eye of the same team of British engineers who had designed and supervised the execution of the steam cranes and aerial haulage gear that caused several hundred Indians to be thrown out of work and several dozen importers to beam with pride.

The smug façade of the Customs House whispered good manners but could barely be heard in the incredible din of Manaus. It reminded Kincaid of the one in Bombay, tall, imposing, and majestically out of place. Kincaid smiled at the incongruity, checked to see that Longford was still with him, and entered the formidable edifice.

Inside, the air was cooler for being out of the

sun, but still the humidity hung as heavily as if it might wilt the huge marble columns that supported the roof at intervals of twenty feet. The pillars soared up into dusty reaches where Kincaid saw bats nesting in the elaborate wrought-iron chandeliers. The floors were marble too, as were the walls, but a marble so yellowed with the heat and moisture as to appear sickly, sweating, foul with the disease it carried in the mold that formed at the cornices. It resisted even the lye that was splashed onto it every morning. Large circular desks lined the walls like scalloped edging. Before Kincaid or Longford could move in any direction, they were collared by a hobbling old Indian whom they heard addressed as "boy" and brought to a fat, unsmiling customs official in wilted gabardine and a sweat-stained shirt under a soggy four-in-hand.

While the man inspected his papers, Kincaid watched a procession of impatient Europeans arriving in Manaus for the much-talked-about rubber convention. They were in high spirits, flushed with prospects. Kincaid looked at Longford and turned back to the customs official, who was tapping the papers on his perspiring forehead.

"You are Senhor Harry Kincaid of Brooklyn?"

"That's me," Kincaid replied. The official grunted by way of acknowledgment and looked at Longford's British passport.

"And this belongs to—"

"My valet," Kincaid interrupted.

The official looked up and froze the air with a look of imperiousness worthy of the maitre d' in the main salon of the Grand Hotel in Rio.

"The man has a tongue, does he not? You are Bertram Longford?" He had some difficulty with the pronunciation.

"Of Bristol, yes, sir, that is I." Longford inclined his head in a stiff little bow.

The official studied both passports until it became clear that there was nothing out of order here. He put them down and filled out a form, sighing with disappointment. He received a bonus when he spotted forgeries. "You are here for the rubber convention?"

"Don't know a thing about it."

Kincaid reached into the breast pocket of his white suit and the man jerked his shoulder as though expecting a gun. Kincaid took notice of the skittishness and handed him a piece of paper.

"It's all in this letter from the Royal Geographic Society," he said. "A copy was supposed to be forwarded to Colonel Armando Mendonça and another to the head of the Chamber of Commerce."

The official read the letter carefully and looked up, dazed by the idea of it.

"You propose to collect orchids?"

"That's right. My yacht, the *Mãe de Deus*, is equipped with a hothouse to get them downriver. In Pará they'll be transferred to a steamship for the Atlantic crossing."

The official eyed him skeptically for several moments more, doubtless to impress upon them the seriousness of his position, and then, with a portentous sigh, stamped the passports and returned them gravely.

"Enjoy your stay in Manaus, Senhor Kincaid."

"I'll try." Behind Kincaid, Longford let out a mild sigh of his own. "Oh, yes, one other matter . . . I've got to send a message to the Society—to inform them of my arrival. How do you folk reach the outside world?"

"There is a telegraph office here on the docks," the man replied with a distinct touch of pride. "You can send a cable if you like. Very reliable."

"I see. Thanks again." Kincaid touched his fingers to the brim of his wilting Panama, but the clerk's attention had already been distracted by the next candidate for admission. When Kincaid and Longford turned, they saw the crowd split neatly in half like a melon under a machete, creating an aisle whose boundaries were as clear as if there had been a velvet rope and functionaries with gold-braid epaulets.

Down the very center of this aisle waddled a short, squat man in a voluminous white suit, a string of Indians trailing uncertainly in his wake, to whom he barked incomprehensible commands, accompanying his orders with majestic waftures of his pudgy hands. Kincaid smiled sardonically at the self-importance and looked at Longford, who shook his head in disapproval. The man conferred briefly with the customs official who had just ad-

mitted them, then whirled about almost at once in
search. His eyes alighted on Kincaid and he hurried over, beaming.

"Senhor Kincaid," he breathed and doffed his
Panama as though it were plumed. "Emmanual
Torres, President of the Chamber of Commerce.
It is my privilege to welcome you to Manaus." His
uncertain native retinue regrouped behind him
awkwardly. Torres shrugged, indicating the Indians, the crowd, the Customs House, the heat,
la vie. "I am so sorry."

"Not at all," Kincaid assured him and shook a
moist hand. "You got here in good time. It's been a
long trip."

"You want the bath?" Torres said, more an order
than a suggestion, almost chortling at his own intuition. Abruptly the chortle ceased and he
snapped his fingers at the Indians and pointed to
Kincaid's luggage. His men assembled the pile
and disappeared into the crowd. "The luggage is
gone," Torres concluded, with another grandilo-
quent gesture, ill suited to his hands.

Kincaid restrained an urge to applaud. "Very
good," he said soberly.

Torres smiled at the praise. "If you will accompany me, I will escort you to the Grand Hotel Internacional."

"By all means. Lead on."

Torres spun on his heels, waving his hands to
clear another path for himself, and started out of
the Customs House. Kincaid followed the sweep

of his white suit, and Longford brought up the rear. Outside the sun descended like a weight.

"I'm pleased that you speak English so well," Kincaid shouted over the din of the crowd, lengthening his stride to keep up with Torres, who seemed to know every crack in the sidewalk, every starving peasant, every bit of herb or snakeskin that hung overhead.

"It is nothing," Torres said over his shoulder. "Did you have a pleasant journey?"

"The flies . . ."

"One gets used to them."

Kincaid exchanged another glance with Longford and attempted to stop, but Torres didn't notice. "One moment, please." The President of the Chamber of Commerce halted as though a switch had been thrown, then ducked into a doorway, signaling to Kincaid that he would only be gone for a moment. Kincaid turned to Longford and shrugged.

"Go to the telegraph office and cable the Society," he ordered. "Then tell Captain Mactavish he and his crew can stay in town until we leave. As agreed."

"Very good, sir." Longford bowed and allowed himself to be swallowed up in the crowd. Kincaid waited for Torres in front of a stand piled with watermelons, a baby crawling across his shoes.

"I am sorry to be so long," Torres apologized, as he returned, withdrawing an ornate gold watch from his waistcoat and consulting it, "but the Convention begins tomorrow and my responsibilities are great."

"We're off," Kincaid assured him.

Torres grunted and once again spun off into the crowd, reminding Kincaid of the white rabbit Tenniel had drawn to illustrate *Alice's Adventures in Wonderland*. He hurried to match the man's pace and finally they broke free of the crowd and stood on a wide street that intersected the dock.

Torres looked suddenly exhausted. "My wife uses the carriage today," he informed Kincaid. "We take the streetcar to the hotel."

Kincaid looked skeptical, but in several moments the tracks in the center of the road began to vibrate and clatter. There was a whistle and a streetcar appeared. It seemed to shimmer in the heat, brilliant crimson and blue, and gave off, even from some distance, the distinct odor of electricity, a kind of smoldering greasy smell that had only lately begun to infiltrate some of the larger cities of the world.

The streetcar screeched to a halt in front of them. Torres stepped onto the running board and pulled Kincaid after him; they ascended the narrow steel stairwell to the upper deck. The seats were wooden, painted green and gold so that the overall effect of the streetcar was that of an enormous parrot. But the breeze was wonderful despite the smell and Kincaid leaned back, looking at the city through half-closed eyes while Torres lectured.

Torres informed him, in the manner of a sleepy

tour guide, that the streetcar was built by the John
Stephenson Company of New York and spon-
sored by Charles Ramlett Flint, whose United
States Rubber Company purchased one-fourth of
all the rubber of Manaus. And did Senhor Kincaid
know, he asked rhetorically, that a city even as
large and famous as Boston still made do with
horsecars while in Manaus trams serviced the city's
sixteen miles of tracks, dawn to dusk, right to the
edge of the jungle, electrically? Kincaid allowed
as he did not know and remarked that Torres certainly was civic-minded, certainly was proud of
his city. Torres nodded seriously and explained
that the city of Manaus was largely the creation of
a handful of powerful families—the Mendonças, the
Coutards, the Gonçalves for example—whose great
wealth—founded on the rubber trees—was responsible for the importation (always at enormous
cost) of all that was beautiful, civilized, and refined, here in the midst of the jungle. It was
Kincaid's turn to nod; he'd heard of Colonel
Mendonça, indeed, had come with high hopes of
meeting the man and viewing the world's most
fabulous collection of orchids. Torres cocked his
head sympathetically and clucked his tongue over
the Colonel's recent troubles. He did not elaborate.
Kincaid looked at the starving urchins who ran
alongside the streetcar, skinny arms outstretched,
and wondered what could be troubling the Colonel.

Once away from the docks, the city of Manaus
began to live up to its reputation for beauty and

luxury. The streets widened considerably and were
intersected in perfect perpendicularity by boule-
vards running headlong into the jungle. They were
paved in cobblestones shipped from Portugal at a
cost of twenty cents apiece; it had taken one thousand Indians two years to hand-set them. At corners and at designated intervals along the streets
were electric-lamp standards and near them, in
contrast, impeccably manicured trees: fig, jacaranda, and eucalyptus, imported from Australia for
its sweet scent.

The streetcar had a certain rhythmic whine and
bump, but it fit into the overall pattern of noise.
Carriages passed, pulled by high-stepping Spanish horses. Vultures sat on roofs like gargoyles and
occasionally swooped down to compete for a scrap
of food with the children of the street. Enormous
tiled mansions loomed behind foul-smelling slums
where open cisterns bred fever-carrying mosquitoes. Wafting through the fetid air from the great
houses beyond came the sounds of flutes and cellos
practiced by the children of the rich.

But even where the streets were fine and the
houses stately, the parks well tended and grand,
the artificial lakes stocked with European fish, the
jungle was never absent, its smells trapped in the
city. Kincaid took it all in, the sights, the smells,
the contradictions and the ambiguities, but his im-
pressions were unsorted, random.

Torres had stopped speaking. In repose his face
was alarmingly vacant—knowing everything and

understanding nothing, Kincaid decided. He coughed and reached into his breast pocket.

"Actually, I have a letter of introduction to Colonel Mendonça. From the Royal Geographic." In the near distance he saw the enormous hotel with its crimson banner welcoming the conventioneers.

The mention of either Colonel Mendonça or the Royal Geographic Society woke Torres with a start. He stared at Kincaid, eyes unfocused. When Kincaid returned the stare he noticed the dilated pupils, blindness he had encountered in the opium dens of Shanghai. So that's how it is, he mused.

"I will take you to the opera," Torres crooned softly. "There is nothing in Manaus to compare with the opera. The women are the most beautiful, the most beautiful, the most . . ."

"Right now I could use that hot bath," Kincaid reminded him.

Torres nodded as though the statement were filled with implication and he a master of unearthing the unsaid. "I understand you perfectly well. Fastidious. Like myself." He fingered the wilted linen of his suit and smiled up at Kincaid. "Manaus welcomes you, Senhor Kincaid. Welcome. Welcome."

✳ 3 ✳

Longford had delayed his arrival at the dockside telegraph office, using this time to acquaint himself with as much as possible of the docks and alleys in the vicinity of the *Mãe de Deus*. His gray-striped trousers and gray morning coat would have drawn a second look in London only by those of his acquaintances who knew he was not really in service. But he attracted a bit more attention in Manaus, where most servants were Indian, and he had begun to feel self-conscious.

It was of the utmost importance that attention not be paid him; he was reasonably certain that it would not. Even those who knew him from previous visits to South America (and he had never set foot in Manaus) could scarcely be expected to recognize him in the character of a valet. If the Society had believed for an instant that there was real risk involved, they would have offered the project to another man. And they certainly would not have paired him with Kincaid. Here Longford had to suppress a smile; chaperon, rather than valet, he would have thought an accurate description of his rôle—but that, he reflected (frowning now), was before he'd seen Kincaid again.

Longford's abilities as a botanist came first, of course. Added to that were his former experiences in Brazil and his familiarity with the language, a wife who not only understood the basis of his professional life but encouraged it, a nature that was peaceful, stable, and cool to counter Kincaid's, which tended toward the volatile, and a belief in the betterment of peoples hitherto unrewarded for their efforts or enslaved by their ignorance.

Although the description would have brought a blush of modesty past his muttonchops to his pale cheeks, Bertram Longford was a man who wished to make the world a finer place than it was. Undeniably, he had come to Manaus for just that reason.

He entered the telegraph office, a glass-fronted shack with a counter inside and behind it a very neat clerk in shirtsleeves and garters. On the wall in back of the clerk hung an enormous map of the Amazon punctuated with large red dots that indicated the relay points for the cables. As Longford dictated his message to the clerk, who was nervous to be copying in English, he glanced at the map, pitting the locations of relay points against the ones he'd been supplied with.

"Kincaid party arrived safely, stop. Will commence orchid gathering as soon as possible, stop. Regards, Kincaid." The clerk was behind and Longford slowed down, using the extra time for additional scrutiny of the map. "That's K-I-N-C-A-I-D," he said when the man looked up. "When will that go out?"

The clerk held up a hand to hold Longford's attention and when he finished with the name, looked up, eyes shining, face glistening with triumph well earned. "Right now. Why wait?"

"Why indeed?" Longford echoed, amused.

"Pardon?"

"And when will it arrive?" he asked, sorry he had attempted levity; better to let that rest in Harry's domain.

The clerk shrugged with magnificent righteousness. "What they do in England is beyond my power, but here I can promise you immediate transmission. We are equipped with the finest: a Caton Key, a relay magnet, and a battery of sulphate of copper gravity. Also, the cable has just been fixed."

"Fixed?"

"The river plays tricks," the clerk said, brushing off the possibility that anything could seriously go wrong. "Sometimes it moves—" He touched the telegraph machine, which began tapping metallically, and he smiled in relief. "But today it works."

"Yes, I see it does." Longford tried to appear suitably impressed. His true impression, which was quite unsuitable as far as the clerk was concerned, was that this sort of efficiency was not a good sign; not a good sign at all. Harry would be very displeased.

*   *   *

The hotel suite was empty when Kincaid entered, flushed and exhausted. He dropped a trail of damp white clothes on his way to the bath, not even pausing to look at the furnishing of the sitting room, getting only a peripheral sensation of reds and golds. And he barely blinked at the golden lions whose necks he twisted and from whose jaws his bath water roared, or noticed the hand-laid tile floor, the velvet settee, or the crystal ball lamps of this most sumptuous bathroom. He lowered himself into the water to the accompaniment of a long sigh, then lit a cigar and poured himself a glass of whiskey neat from a cut-glass decanter at the foot of the tub. It was not his custom to bathe without a revolver nearby, but his present rôle demanded subtlety be the better part of anticipation.

He heard the outside door open, and in a moment Longford's serious visage appeared at the threshold.

"I hate this heat," Kincaid commented and sipped his whiskey.

"You'd best get accustomed to it," Longford replied, patting his forehead with the back of his hand.

"I haven't your patience, Professor." He flicked his cigar ash on the floor.

"One must keep up appearances." Longford automatically bent down to brush away the ash.

"What about the telegraph?"

"The cable runs through the riverbed," Long-

ford called back to him, going into the drawing
room of the suite. "Occasionally the river shifts
about and snaps it . . ."

"Always handy to know," Kincaid murmured.
Then he raised his voice. "And the relay points?"

Longford returned to the bathroom preceded by
a large open map, which he held out from his
chest like a tray. "The relay points coincide with
the ones given us." He bent down and spread the
map out on the bathroom floor so Kincaid could
see it without getting out of the tub and traced
the telegraph relay points on the river with a long
searching finger. "Now let's see, there's Itacoatiara,
of course, where our man is. One at Parintins; one
at Santarem and at . . . where is it? I've misplaced
. . . ah, one here at Monte Alegre, then Gurupá
. . . and of course, Pará."

"It seems clear enough," Kincaid grunted,
clenching the cigar with his teeth.

Longford folded the map carefully, but he was
worried; his usually placid face was scored with
lines, and when he spoke his words were both
cautious and cautionary. "It won't be necessary,
will it, do you think?"

"Professor, it probably won't," Kincaid said,
subsiding gratefully into the water. "But I haven't
lived as long as I have without calculating all the
possibilities."

Longford stood, his face settling, and tucked the
map under his arm. Now that he'd gotten the reassurance he'd asked for, he felt free to dispense
advice and instruction. "We'll have to be extremely

circumspect, Harry. This civil war, or whatever it is, has made them all jittery."

Kincaid shrugged. "Our friend Torres is an opium eater, by the way."

"Oh? Well, that's convenient to know, I suppose."

"You're catching on, Professor. Anyway, he's promised to arrange a meeting with Colonel Mendonça. I've got to get his permission to take specimens from his arborium. Or else we'll have to mount a real expedition. One complication I'd like to avoid."

"That is the whole point, isn't it?" Longford was still unnerved by Kincaid's inexplicable lackluster attitude, as if, now that civilization was getting such short shrift, the man was not really going to do all the things that had been agreed upon over civilized sherry and biscuits in the Royal Geographic Society's conference room.

"You're creasing your face for nothing," Kincaid said. "It's all under control." He sighed, leaned back in the tub for one more long immersion, then hauled himself out, whipped a thick towel from another lion's mouth, and stepped onto the tile floor. "The way I figure it, their feud works in our favor. They're all too busy watching each other to pay any attention to us."

There was an uncomfortable silence in which neither Kincaid nor Longford was willing to acknowledge the uncertainty in this statement. Longford took a silk robe and handed it to him. "Here you are, sir."

"Sir?" Kincaid grinned at him over the tip of his cigar. "Don't bury yourself in the part."

"Sorry, it gets confusing."

"And let's have some brandy."

The drawing room had twenty-foot ceilings crawling with curlicues and scrolls, gilt-edged mirrors on every wall, and window hangings of damask and silk. A pair of tufted Turkish leather couches swam in the middle of a set of artfully arranged oak tables sporting potted palms and glass Bordeaux lamps with grapes carved into their globes. A portière whose rope was made of velvet heightened the theatricality of the room. The floral carpets scattered across the lacquered floors looked as if the decorator had fallen while carrying armsful of roses and gardenias. For a moment Kincaid thought he had stepped into an ornate production of *The Bohemian Girl.*

"Are you sure you want a brandy?" Longford asked.

"Why wouldn't I?"

"They charge ten dollars a glass," he explained with respectful awe.

"You're joking."

"No." Longford was deliciously shocked to have surprised his well-traveled friend. "Manaus has the highest rate of inflation in the world. And, I might add, they are quite proud of that fact."

"Order it anyway," Kincaid said, throwing himself into a full recline on the black leather couch and picking up the tasseled dinner menu. "The Royal Geographic is footing the bill. Let them foot." His eyes scanned the menu and he shook his head in dismay.

"Butter from Copenhagen, sauerkraut from Berlin, mortadella from Milan, cauliflower from Brussels . . . doesn't anything *begin* here?"

"Yes, Harry," Longford replied seriously. "One thing."

Kincaid looked over the top of the menu at him and nodded. They were silent, each thinking of the repercussions of a rather small act, a pebble dropped in a lake whose splashed circles would be felt all around the world. "Well . . . let's eat and get to sleep. There are going to be long nights ahead."

* * *

Colonel Mendonça nodded his head in resignation. The stench of the smoldering rubber and burned flesh, as he picked his way through the ruins of the rubber-processing huts, was sickening in a way that went beyond mere smell. There had been human life here, Indians whose fathers had worked for him, and now there was only death and the threat of more.

He was a big man with a hawklike nose that indicated traces of Indian blood. His hands were large, gnarled with veins and calloused from the hardships of his early years that the pampering and manicures could not soften. He gave the impression of tremendous, ageless strength. The rifle dangled in his hands.

As he stood in the clearing, watching men moving bodies and pieces of bodies and charred lumps that could have been more bodies or burnt rubber, he tried to assemble his thoughts and plan what little future he had. A small cough tickled his insides; he covered his mouth with unneeded gentility, but when he drew his hand away, there were flecks of blood on his fingers. He coughed again, harder; his body seemed to shrink inside his flesh and there was quite suddenly the impression, not of strength, but of a monument in decay.

A young Indian on horseback rode up to Colonel Mendonça and dismounted with an agility that the Colonel envied. The rider was Iquitos, so named by Colonel Mendonça when he took the boy from his village. With his straight black hair, worn long in Indian fashion, he made the Colonel think of what his own son might have been. The thought alternately pleased and disquieted him. He had raised Iquitos almost as his own, as much as he dared allow, but the younger man's loyalty would always be short of filial.

The two men stood in the midst of the ruins, looking at the corpses being hauled away in wheelbarrows, and finally faced each other, almost defiant, in a mutual determination to ignore the issues of human cost. The Colonel kept his tone businesslike.

"Well?"

"Besides the factory," Iquitos replied, imitating his timbre, "there were attacks on at least two *estradas* to the north. Eighty men dead or wounded and a hundred trees lost. The toll is inexact. There may have been more attacks. The telegraph is dead, the usual sign. I have runners out now, but it will be at least a week before we know."

The procession of bodies passed them now. The survivors, those who could move without help, walked alongside the wheelbarrows weeping, the women keening, children wailing in pain and bewilderment, men stone-faced. Iquitos was appalled but said nothing.

"This war is costing a fortune," the Colonel observed, with seeming calm.

"Will we retaliate?"

"If we retaliate, *he* retaliates." Mendonça dispassionately considered the alternatives. "Either I throw thirty thousand men into the field against him and we have a real war . . . in which case we lose the harvest . . . or . . . something else . . ." They stood in silence for a moment, viewing the wailing procession. The Colonel saw Iquitos' pained expression and touched him gently. "Come. We have seen this all before." Still Iquitos did not move; the Colonel realized that the anguish went deeper than he thought. "I know," he said, and touched him again. "It accumulates. There is only one thing to do. Coutard must be . . . removed."

Before Iquitos could ask how this might be accomplished, the Colonel was seized as if by a giant claw deep inside him that pulled his body in on itself. The painful gasping cough was the release of the claw and so sudden, so violent that he reached out blindly and stumbled for support against his horse. Iquitos, alarmed, held him and fanned him with his hat.

"You must see the surgeon, *senhor!*"

The Colonel shook his head as the cough subsided.

"What for?" he scowled. "To tell me what I know? Come. We are wasting time."

Iquitos hesitated, but the expression on his master's face contained the same unshakable power that had carried Mendonça from his boyhood in the jungle, the power that had propelled him to become the man he now was, the power that would overcome all enemies save the one that was destroying him from within.

Iquitos helped the old man mount his horse and mounted his own. He stared at the smoldering wreckage, the ruins that had housed his people, and shuddered. A new sensation in his bowels made itself a little more familiar than it had been the day before. For a moment he nursed the idea that the Colonel's illness was eating away at him, too.

"Come!" Mendonça commanded, and wheeling about, he rode off into the jungle.

Iquitos hesitated. Once he had been eager, racing to obey. He looked after the Colonel, looked back at the scene of carnage, looked at the Colonel again as he disappeared into the palm groves. Instead of following, he dismounted, tied his horse to a scorched palm tree, and walked through the remains of the processing huts, his nostrils filled with the stench. For a moment Iquitos' eyes glazed over and he remembered to be thankful that Colonel Mendonça had taken him from this and educated him at the *Casa Grande*. His family had never understood what was valuable about the rubber; to them it was strange and mystical that the trees bled white. Iquitos knew now what gold was, but the Indians who were so feared by the whites knew nothing of it. At first his tribe fought bitterly for their land when the whites invaded to claim the rubber trees. But arrows, chants, and magic paint were not as effective as the organized machinery of the landowners and their mercenaries. And so the Indians were killed for their land, or taken to work on it. They became *seringueiros* to the half-breeds who had risen above that station and who now controlled them. Iquitos remembered his father telling of the white man coming with gifts of food and drink, mirrors and meat and wine, baubles that glittered. And afterward, when the Indians were sated, the white men held rifles on them and told them that since they had accepted the gifts, they had to pay the whites back with rubber.

That was the beginning. Every day the Indians had to walk to the *estradas* and slash the rubber trees to collect the latex and harvest it into the forty-pound *peles* the white man wanted, all to pay back the debt. Food and supplies came from the white man and this meant more debt. Many Indians died horrible deaths by starvation, torture, disease, malnutrition, or simple murder; the half-breeds who ruled them were sadistic and treated them as less than human.

Iquitos' parents were only too glad to give Iquitos to Colonel Mendonça. They did not know what significance their son's face held for the master. Nor, to be truthful, did they speculate. Iquitos, they were told, would be well cared for, and that made one less mouth to feed.

For his part, as he grew older, Iquitos did what he could for his family. He brought them food and spoke on their behalf to the Colonel. As a result, they fared better than the other *seringueiros;* not much, however, for as Iquitos grew, he became aware that mention of his family, his real family, distressed his patron.

Any changeling fantasies nursed by Colonel Mendonça were halted by the knowledge of Iquitos' living parents. The boy could not or would not forget them. At best he learned not to mention them. Mendonça toyed with the idea of sending them away—his domains were as wide as the Iberian peninsula—but he knew what the boy's response would be. Ruefully, he thought: better to have adopted an orphan. But then he had never seen any eyes that reminded him so forcibly of his own.

At twenty, Iquitos knew and understood all the Colonel's thoughts. Early he had learned to do his master's bidding; early he had learned to please him. He had succeeded in separating himself from his real family, persuading himself that their lot was better than the others'. He had even excused

Colonel Mendonça. The man knew little of what went on in his own jungle. How could he be expected to keep track of all the population of his vast domain? How could he know or control the behavior of two thousand overseers?

But now this. Iquitos continued pawing through the rubble, patiently seeking the corpse of his father.

❈ 4 ❈

Emmanual Torres, despite his drugged indulgence of the previous day, was true to his word, and early the next morning appeared at Kincaid's suite in another voluminous white suit, sweating, impatient and anxious to get Kincaid to Colonel Mendonça's house and be off to the Rubber Convention, whose opening ceremonies would begin later in the morning. Kincaid dressed hurriedly with the clumsy assistance of Longford-as-manservant, and joined Torres in the carriage that awaited them, a glass-front landau lacquered black and trimmed in silver, wheels covered with a thin, hard rubber tire, an Indian driver in livery seated high in front. As Torres mounted he muttered something about his wife sitting home and waiting for the carriage, which had to be brought back by ten because there was a shipment of diamonds lately arrived at Rossi-Astinatio Jewelers, and though he was not specific as to what would happen if she were not able to get there, the consequences for him loomed dire. Kincaid settled back against the upholstery, which smelled heavily of whore's perfume—whether Senhora Torres' or the genuine article's he could not tell—and the carriage drove off toward the jungle. It was beginning, Kincaid thought.

From what Kincaid and Longford had been able to learn about Colonel Mendonça, his title validated his past life in the jungle as scrupulously as Cornelius Vanderbilt's "Commodore" pertained to a naval command. The Colonel still grieved that he had been unable to erect a statue of himself on a public building, as Vanderbilt had done on the Grand Central Station in New York. The title was self-appointed and observed by people because, as the Colonel noted, enough money will make people observe anything. Kincaid was perhaps not so cynical as Mendonça, but Kincaid had only seen the world; he had not felt what it was like to own it.

The driver took the carriage along the same road that bore the streetcar, but swerved abruptly away from the riverside of the city as the vehicle neared the jungle. The landau seemed to be heading directly for a wall of trees when there was a sudden break, a flash of white, and they entered the jungle on an avenue of small white stones. Kincaid peered out the side of the carriage. At first he saw nothing but more jungle and the stripe of white that divided it. He was about to ask Torres about Colonel Mendonça's house when he noticed that the side of the road was lined with Indians. Alarmed, he pulled back, but as the carriage passed, the Indians stepped onto the road and wiped it clean of carriage tracks. As they made their way, Kincaid counted eighty-four Indians tending the road.

And then there was the house itself, rising from the jungle, appearing out of place and absurd, embodying the kind of vulgar confidence Kincaid had witnessed around the world in men whose money had come fast and hard. But nowhere had he seen the extent to which that confidence could be taken, or the heights to which that vulgarity could be raised when supported by a bankroll that knew no limits.

"Casa Grande, Senhor Kincaid."

The mansion, for it was nothing less, stood in a clearing; the jungle was forever encroaching and the Indians were forever struggling to keep it at bay. The façade was such a fantastic amalgam of styles that Kincaid felt he had entered a dream that compressed all the palaces and cathedrals in Europe into a single structure. There were Renaissance pilasters, intricate Greek frieze work, Gothic balconies, what looked like Moorish archways, an Italianate ornamental fence that ran around the house with street lamps midway and at each corner. The mansion stood three stories high and sprawled a city block deep, its windows and doors framed in white marble and framed again in contrasting gray, and outlined once more in black so that they seemed to stand away from the façade of the house itself and vibrate.

The white stone drive uncoiled at the entrance and then trailed off again into the jungle. Torres knew everything about the mansion as he had known everything about the city, but indicated no point of view, no opinion, not even that he was impressed by the overwhelming display of wealth. At most he seemed obliquely pleased that the man who stood at the head of Manaus' financial life lived in such a magnificent home; it was right and just, exactly as it should be.

The carriage stopped. Before Kincaid could descend, two servants appeared at the door, one to open it, another to help Kincaid the one step down. He smiled back at Torres, but the man was already absorbed in reading the speech he would be called upon to deliver at the Convention. Kincaid bade him a good day and thanked him. Torres acknowledged this with a limp wave and drove off. Kincaid watched the carriage disappear into the jungle and turned to enter the palace.

Entrance was effected through enormous ground-level doors that Kincaid recognized as copies of the famous Ghiberti "Gates of Paradise" portals to the Baptistery in Florence. The reproductions were not as accurate or artful as those by Barbedienne of Paris, for which Vanderbilt had paid the Prince of Donato $20,000—but for a jungle hut, Kincaid wryly noted, they served. As he reached them, the doors swung open without a sound, manned by two more Indians, these in satin livery, and revealed an immense foyer, the full three stories, with a domed roof of stained glass that cast bizarre images and colors on the walls and floors. The floors were of marble, white, sur-

mounted by a frieze of Medieval figures in low
relief, and dominated by a majestic stairway. Marble wainscoating covered the walls for at least one
full story; at the base jutted benches carved from
the same stone. A sea-green seventh century Tang
vase almost twice Kincaid's height stood between
two of these benches, a live baby palm springing
from it; the vase had once occupied the pink bedchamber of the Maharajah of Jaipur's Rambaugh
Palace.

Colonel Mendonça had tried to secure the decorating services first of the Herter Brothers and then
of Louis Comfort Tiffany, who had recently
formed his own design studio; but neither would
undertake the venture into the jungle. So the Colonel had spent much time inventing the place
himself, relying on a sense of taste, color, and
design that had lavishness as its spiritual force
and ostentation as its muse. Both were faithfully
served.

Another servant, this one in ivory linen and
with the deportment of an English butler, appeared at the foot of the stairs that arched into
the dusky regions of the second story, where fanciful oil paintings of winged creatures predominated, and signaled Kincaid to follow him. Kincaid deposited his wilted straw hat and damp
gloves with the servants who had opened the door,
and quickened his pace to keep up with the butler. The hallways he walked along were wide as
rooms, most of them galleries housing the Colonel's
art collection, which, Kincaid mused, was nothing

if not eclectic. The paintings were huge and hung
so close to each other that no wall space showed
for hundreds of yards, although the ceiling and
the molding were of cast bronze. Statues dotted
the gallery floors, Greek or copies: water nymphs,
satyrs, fishing girls, a slave and a master; they
stared or ignored Kincaid as he passed them. The
paintings, although poorly lit, were an impressive
array of old masters and current European favo-
rites: Meissonier, Bouguereau, Auguste Bonheur,
Detaille, Bierstadt, Outin, Blondel, Turner, Rous-
seau, Diaz, Gustave Doré, Pottenkoffen, Vermeer,
even a Rembrandt relegated to an inferior hanging
position above a coy study of a girl and a lamb
by Esturay and below some vile biblical gore by
the Spanish rage Rubino.

The temperature was hotter than it had been
outside, but it began to cool as the gallery and its
gas lamps ended. The servant paused in front of
six square columns of crimson African marble. On
the other side of the corridor, Kincaid could see a
room that glowed red and gold, an imitation Japa-
nese parlor like those becoming so popular in New
York, and Paris before that: bamboo floors, lac-
quers, and velvet; he could not stare too long
because the ornately carved doors of Colonel Mendonça's study were flung open, the butler disappeared, and Kincaid strode forward to meet the
master of Casa Grande.

The Colonel was seated at a desk in the middle
of a less complicated room: the floor inlaid with
mahogany and bordered with a mosaic of amber

marble, wainscoating of mahogany, rosewood, and mother-of-pearl in an ancient Roman pattern, bookcases and shelves treated in the same manner, and the ceiling set with rows of small oval mirrors. Red leather chairs and couches, in the Chesterfield and Queen Anne styles, were arranged on flat English country rugs. Velvet drapes kept out the light, and *electric* lights on sconces brought it back in. Kincaid sensed that though the Colonel appeared to be allowing him to get his bearings, he was in reality taking his measure, seeing just exactly how well Kincaid withstood this hallucinatory display. Kincaid availed himself of the time to take brief inventory of the Colonel, deciding to disappoint the man and ending the silence with an appreciative, and very American, whistle.

The Colonel did not appear to have heard. He half rose from his chair and gestured with a large hand.

"Sit please."

Kincaid strode twenty feet and sat, sighing involuntarily at the intoxicating smell of fine leather. He found himself almost immediately nervously fingering the Colonel's collection of rich ivory eggs that lay in a lacquered box, displayed on a teakwood stand next to his chair. He imagined he was not the first caller to do so.

The Colonel followed his progress attentively, then looked briefly at the papers on his desk before retrieving one from the pile.

"I believe I recognize my letter of introduction," Kincaid observed.

"From the Royal Geographic Society." Mendonça studied the letter, then regarded his visitor once more. "About the orchids, Mr. Kincaid." He smiled. "I should prefer to call you 'Mister,' yes? 'Senhor' is Brazilian and you are not. It is a courtesy; please take it as such."

His English was hesitant but flawless. Kincaid smiled and inclined his head.

"You wish to view the orchids."

"Ardently. They are said to rival even your collection of art. They will set the standard for my own acquisitions."

The Colonel almost smiled.

"One works and one plays. Do you understand?"

"I think so."

The Colonel hesitated again and consulted the document in his hands.

"You state here that you are particularly interested in the *Brassia*, the *Odontoglossum*, and the *Gongora*."

"Among others, yes. I'll be taking notes, of course, but mostly collecting for study and breeding in England. The hothouses at Kew Gardens are quite sophisticated now."

"As is the hothouse aboard the *Mãe de Deus*," the Colonel supplied softly. "Heated with hot water from the boiler, is it not so?"

Kincaid's turn to almost smile; the Colonel was well informed.

Mendonça sighed. "Collectors have been coming to the Amazon for fifty years, Mr. Kincaid. Some have been respectable men of science, others have simply pillaged the jungle for profit."

"I apologize for the avarice of my predecessors," Kincaid replied. "It need hardly be said that I am not here to plunder prize possessions. I would be happy to show you my list—"

The Colonel held up his hand and Kincaid stopped. Mendonça regarded him with an intensity heretofore absent. Kincaid could see the intelligence suddenly behind his eyes. Abruptly the look vanished. The Colonel smiled, his inventory complete, his decision made.

"You may be free with my collection. Keep a list of the specimens you take. I will compare it with your original when I visit your hothouse before you sail. In addition, I will see to it that you are supplied with as many helpers as you require."

"I won't need many," Kincaid said, perhaps a bit too quickly, for the Colonel paused again. Nevertheless, Kincaid understood clearly: Mendonça took his orchids quite as seriously as the Van Lieus. He refrained from saying another word and the moment of tension passed. A sound behind him helped. Turning, he saw that a young Indian had entered. The Colonel stood up; clearly the interview was over.

"The carriage is ready, Colonel," the Indian said, and flopped down on one of the couches. Kincaid was amazed at this gesture of familiarity but Mendonça appeared to take no notice.

"Iquitos," he said, still in English. "This is Mr. Kincaid. Please see that he is equipped to visit the plantation at his convenience. He is here to collect orchids."

"And, of course, I intend to take in the social side of things." Kincaid rose, winking. "The reputation of Manaus is well known." He risked the vulgarity in the hopes of establishing himself as a harmless American and was gratified to see the Colonel nod with a weary smile. The man seemed to hesitate, unsure how to conclude their business. The Indian came to his rescue.

"You will be late, sir. It has already begun. Coutard—"

"Yes, yes." The Colonel's voice rose and a choke escaped his lips. "Mr. Kincaid"—he gestured more abruptly than he intended—"if you will simply go through those doors, my man will see to it that you are returned to your hotel."

Kincaid bowed, glanced briefly at the Indian, and departed.

The Colonel remained silent a moment, then turned to Iquitos, who waited, impassive.

"An orchid collector," he said. "Harmless. Follow him for a few days, as a matter of course. Don't spend too much time. I need you. Now, more than ever, Iquitos, I need you very badly."

Iquitos nodded and accompanied the Colonel through the gallery and outside, where the Colonel got into a carriage and Iquitos mounted his horse. As the carriage moved off, the Colonel was startled; it had seemed to him only an instant ago that he was talking with the American about the orchids. Where had the moments gone? It had been a long time since the Colonel had taken any notice of his paintings or his house. Not since the fight for his land had begun in earnest.

* * *

Pierre Coutard took a small mirror from the inside pocket of his French-made suit and contemplated his image. He was unhappy with his pallor this morning. He turned to his sister, Mercedes, who was methodically pacing the narrow anteroom of the Chamber of Commerce assembly hall, peering through a lorgnette at the text of the speech she had composed for her brother to deliver to the Rubber Convention. With only minutes to go, her meticulous attention to detail provoked small alterations, made with a gold stylus.

"Am I too pale?"

Mercedes stopped walking and stared at him.

"You are forty years younger than he is. What does it matter how pale you are?" Sometimes she could scarcely believe they came from the same father. Perhaps, she reflected, they didn't.

"It matters to me," Coutard replied, staring at the mirror again. "And it matters to Lisette."

"The opinions of your whores don't interest me at this moment." She looked through the arched window at the clock on the Coutard Bank building, then down the street and nodded to herself. "Not yet. Not yet." She resumed pacing.

"What?" Pierre blotted the sweat from his brow with an embroidered handkerchief. "Are you speaking to me?"

Mercedes shook her head, impatience rising, but she quelled it, breathing deeply, and walked to her brother. "Let me straighten your tie."

"It's this insufferable heat. Linen wilts. What's one to do?"

"You look too much in mirrors, Pierre," she chided with more gentleness than she felt. "Don't you think it's important to know what is going on around you?"

"I know enough," Pierre said. "The crop, the harvest, the yield, the prices . . . When Papa was alive I never had to worry about such things. I had a good time. Now life is such a bore. Do you really think it wise to start before Mendonça arrives?"

"Leave the prices to me," Mercedes counseled, soothing. "And don't worry about Mendonça."

"That's very well for you to say, but I'm the one who must appear in public. I'm the one who must make these infernal speeches. I'm the one who is asked questions I have no interest in answering. Why can't we just spend what Papa left us and let Mendonça have the rest?"

"Never." Mercedes grasped her brother's shoulders, her eyes seeking his. "Listen to me, Pierre. This is of primary importance. If Mendonça wins, we have nothing. No more money for your little Lisette. No more diamond cufflinks, no more trips to Paris, no more—"

"All right, all right," Pierre muttered, disengaging himself from her grasp. "I concede the point. I only mean to say that it's absurd and maddening for Papa to have left me in charge of something so vile as rubber."

Mercedes sighed. "Just because you were educated in Europe, my dear cultivated brother, does not mean that you will be allowed to forget that our father came to the Amazon as a criminal and that he met our mother in—"

"Enough! I can't stand it. How long until I speak?"

Mercedes smiled; the crisis was over. She knew her brother and controlled him the way one controlled a child: by threatening to take away its toys. She looked at him as he gave the final adjustment to his costume.

His physical beauty was admirable: the set of his handsome head, the thickly pomaded black hair, the tight fit of the French suit, even the arch of the eyebrows that she helped him pluck. The same features did not sit quite so prettily on her, though her beauty was a match for any woman's in Manaus. After all, hadn't her mother been the most beautiful Cuban whore in the city? It was rather that beauty did not much matter to Mercedes. It served no practical purpose and she was nothing if not pragmatic; beauty would not get her where she wanted to be. For that she had to develop other aspects of her character.

It never ceased to amaze her that her brother, this harmless shallow dandy, ruled so powerful a

kingdom. What did it matter that she was older
than he and infinitely more capable? It was her
fate to stand behind him, this pretty shell, who
trusted no financial advisers, no military strategists
as he trusted his sister. It was his name that held
their father's land, all his money, and in whose
house her position was no more official than that of
a favored housekeeper. If Pierre should incline to
marry (an unlikely but distinct possibility), she
would be in even worse straits. She would have to
be very careful to pick his wife; a simple girl from
Manaus, perhaps one of his whores—the irony of
that prospect did not escape her—and she would
rule through them both. Their father had not
worked the land for nothing; he had not built an
empire merely to have it squandered, frittered
away, through the disinterest of his own son.

Jacques Coutard's history was illustrious or infamous, depending on one's point of view. A native
of Rouen, he had departed his motherland in 1833,
booking passage on the new steamship of the Brazil Steam Navigation Company. He disembarked
in Manaus as raw as any freebooter, drawn by the
lure of fabulous wealth, easily gained. But the
wealth was not easily gained, and many left or
perished. Coutard, determined to rid himself of the
grinding poverty that was his own bitter inheritance, went to work. He would throw off the stink
of poverty, an odor he could never drive from his
nostrils: it was cabbage soup, stale bread, hard
cheese, and cold dampness. It was the ancient city
of Rouen where the buildings leaned in on each

other in exhaustion; a town proud of having been
the site of Jeanne d'Arc's immolation.

Jacques Coutard had murdered a man in a rage
over a point of history and fled to the new world.
He was in Manaus when the rubber started to pre-
sage profit. He and Colonel Mendonça drank together nightly at Les Couchons Noir, became
friends and accumulated land side by side. It was
a joke that became very serious very quickly. As
production of rubber increased, the demand for
labor did likewise. They stole men from the jungle. Then they stole from each other. Bodies
dotted the rubber *estradas*. Indians were the easiest source of labor and neither Coutard nor Mendonça nor any of the other growing number of
rubber barons was above hiring men to find Indians
to be brought back by force. Coutard, with the
vestiges of a Frenchman's sensitivity, argued that
this method was honored by history; routing
the Indians from their jungle hideouts and giving
them honest labor had been going on for hundreds
of years. Even the Mayor of Pará had organized
manhunts. And of course they were brought—as a
happy afterthought—to Christ. The Church co-
operated, informing the hapless converts that the
sabbath, their one day of rest, fell on every ninth
day.

The years passed in relentless striving. Coutard's fortune grew as his friendship with Mendonça floundered. Each suspected the other—and
with reason. Eventually personal bodyguards became the fashion, though publicly the two men

maintained their show of amity to the last. Each had sense enough to contain the feud, to limit distrust and competition on both sides, lest the sparks of hostility burst into a flame of violence that would consume them both. When Coutard died so unexpectedly, Mendonça had sighed with relief and guilty satisfaction. He would miss his old and familiar enemy, but he felt safe.

It was a short-lived relief. He had not reckoned with Coutard's daughter. Nor could he; he had not made it his business to understand Mercedes' schooling.

It was Jacques Coutard's great personal tragedy that he could not reconcile himself to a female heir. There was no law in Manaus to forbid it; had there been, he could have changed it easily. No, it was an urgent dynastic desire and a tradition of male inheritance to which he succumbed. He had, from the first, enormous confidence in his daughter. She was intelligent, resourceful beyond her years, a willing worker, obsessively interested in land and its management. She was cunning and clearly prepared to be as ruthless as himself. Nevertheless, a woman simply did not rule. No child of hers would ever bear the Coutard name.

His son, on the other hand, lacked almost all Mercedes' abilities. In an effort to lavish upon the boy all the advantages of a classical education (so conspicuously absent in his own history), Pierre had been sent with his mother (whom he adored) to Paris for six months at a time. Each time he returned to Manaus whiter, thinner, and more elegant than before, until at last the jungle had been bred right out of him, leaving Coutard's chosen heir as high-strung and nervous as a lap-dog. Mercedes had stayed behind to keep her father company, to absorb everything he knew about the land, the rubber, the Indians, the money.

Privately, without allowing herself to dwell on the idea, Mercedes missed the European culture and education heaped upon her brother and the other privileged children of the Manaus elite. She missed the clothes and the high life and the gentlemen to court her. The opulent world her father and others had created in Manaus existed in a vacuum; Mercedes was vaguely aware of its comedic components and resented them. Her beauty was largely ignored, or lusted after by brutes who had stayed so long in the jungle that their resumption of society was bound to be—at best—undiscriminating. The men of Manaus were not worthy of her, but she herself was too rough for those whose polish had been bottled in Paris, in London, or in Lisbon. Mercedes was trapped, neither here nor there in the world. When her mother died she received nothing but the burning desire to own all the land she knew was hers by right of conquest. She had lived on it; she had studied it; she knew it. But for a genetic defect it would have been hers.

"Are you ready?" She smiled at Pierre, gently stroking a wayward lock of his hair. She kissed him on each cheek, a familiar ritual, then handed him his speech. "Don't be afraid. Mercedes is here."

* * *

If the Amazon rubber monopoly was not always a civilized business, if it was not always carried out in the higher-toned manner of the Europeans, at least there existed among the rubber kings a fairly rigid set of unspoken rules that served to keep the peace while they progressed through the necessary period of barbarism. Many of these kings were but a single step ahead of their jungle village past. Many were not native Brazilians but Europeans, or North Americans, who had taken the reins of their futures and created the colossal rubber boom, buying up vast tracts of land in the hope that some of it would produce *ouro preto* and not just palm trees, orchids, and snakes.

The power wielded by these men was like that of Oriental potentates. Having no other means to a kingdom but to create one with money, they did so in Manaus and protected it with animal ferocity. It was not merely a financial investment, but a way of life, the seeds of their dreams, the substance of their new identities. To enter the sections of the river that flowed through their land was to court accusations of piracy; blood flowed often in the swift golden current.

One man owned land so vast a steamboat took seven days to cruise the river frontage. Another had an estate yielding five hundred tons of rubber each year. And when labor ran short, a raid on any Indian village provided new workers. Another augmented his supply by corraling five hundred Indian girls for breeding and selecting a small group of studs to do the planting.

In the last decades of the nineteenth century, when business had reached worldwide proportions and Manaus had become a world power, sixth richest city on the face of the earth, the Rubber Exchange was converted into the Chamber of Commerce building. The annual rubber conventions were traditionally inaugurated by Colonel Mendonça and Jacques Coutard—and now, since his father had died three years before, by Pierre Coutard. The men who owned the two largest private estates in the world presided over the yearly meetings, at once mercantile figureheads and absolute monarchs. Each controlled territory the size of Texas.

Behind the ornately carved doors to the newly constructed Rubber Exchange was an auditorium seating several hundred of the men who, by foresight, intuition, or chance of birth, owned rights to land that yielded rubber. At the front of the hall was a raised platform upon which stood a dais occupied by Pierre Coutard, his sister Mercedes, and a phalanx of white-suited men who were there to see that no one approached the siblings without express permission.

As the tall languid figure of Coutard rose and mounted the rostrum, the audience applauded and he bowed graciously, a skill he practiced and enjoyed, and waited with a patient air for the noise to ebb. When it did, he seized the gavel and brought it crashing down.

Silence greeted this punctuation. When he spoke, his voice was as strong and young and clear as he himself appeared to be: cultured, yes, smooth, yes, but commanding. It was the general consensus that though the young man might sport a bit too much he certainly knew what he was talking about.

"Traditionally, as all of you know," he began, "this convention is supposed to be opened jointly by Colonel Mendonça and myself." He looked from left to right and forward again with a helpless smile. "Since the Colonel is not here, however . . ." He paused and turned to receive a note from Mercedes, who sat near him in a high-backed chair. The assemblage murmured with diffuse anticipation: properly dressed gentlemen *manqués*, a sea of white suits, Panana hats sagging, sweat glistening on brows and pates.

"My sister has informed me that Colonel Mendonça may not be in attendance this morning. The Colonel apparently has been detained by a personal matter."

The crowd buzzed in confused response. Mercedes sat bolt upright, perfectly still, a frozen smile of propriety on her features.

"I stand before you alone," Coutard was saying, "to inaugurate this year's convention." The growers, in various stages of conventioneering good spirits, were perplexed. Hats waved erratically, heads jerked from side to side.

Coutard raised his hands to still the confusion and the men began to calm down, to watch him, to listen. He felt the cooperation of the crowd.

"Many of you gentlemen, I know, have heard disquieting rumors since your arrival here—tales of internecine strife between Colonel Mendonça and myself. I would be less than honest if I did not admit to you here and now that the Colonel and I have had our differences." He paused to make way for the good-humored undercurrent of laughter that greeted this remark.

"Colonel Mendonça has been in Manaus longer than I and has his own way of doing things, just as he has done them for so many years, going back to the days when he was a young man and worked side by side with my father. I also have my own way of doing things. It is my belief that traditional methods and policies must give way to modern notions of progress." Here he stopped briefly and consulted the notes Mercedes had prepared. When he began again his voice was raised to an oratorical pitch.

"Let us not forget, gentlemen: it was only one hundred and eighty years ago that rubber was discovered. For one hundred and ten of those years, rubber's only use was to obliterate mistakes in accountants' ledgers." Coutard paused, allowing them time to chuckle. "But today the story of rubber is very different. Rubber, gentlemen, is in demand now as never before, and of its many uses, some will surprise even those of us who supply it. A single factory in the United States makes thirty thousand pairs of overshoes every day. Rubber ties together our bundles, it holds up our trousers and our hose. The combined number of men and boys in France alone who use elastic suspenders is over twenty million. As some of you may know, the use of carriage wheels circumscribed by tires made of rubber is rapidly on the rise. I believe we have in the audience a representative of the Dunlop Corporation, which proposes to specialize in the manufacture of such tires. And last, but not least, gentlemen, there is the hydrogen balloon; wave of the future, practical for the first time, thanks to the perfection of the gutta-percha process, which enables the conquerors of the clouds to travel aloft in perfect safety. Just imagine, gentlemen, how many hundreds of square feet of gutta-percha are employed by a single balloon, such as the one flown with such success last season from Paris to Nice by Félix Nadar."

Coutard, reading from Mercedes' text, not entirely understanding it (and not particularly interested, either), nevertheless, with his flair for the dramatic, succeeded in stirring his listeners to a frenzy.

"And who owns this rubber? Gentlemen, *we* own it! All of it. All the land of rubber is private property. I see representatives here of the Amazonas Company of London. They own ninety thousand acres. And in the back I see the English Rubber Company, owners of one hundred and eighty-two thousand acres and some three hundred thousand rubber trees. Gentlemen, I spoke before of progress. Our business methods must be as modern as tomorrow. I am here to inaugurate this year's convention by proposing that the new export tax on rubber be raised to thirty percent."

A surprised chorus greeted this suggestion—as Mercedes had foretold it would; they were used to the conservatism of Colonel Mendonça—but they liked the sound of thirty percent; and when the time came, they might vote to approve it.

Coutard banged the gavel and held his hands in the air.

"If we work together in a concerted program of selling to the outside world, everyone in this room stands to become a millionaire in the next five years."

This statement was greeted with thunderous applause. A large portion of the crowd rose and gave him an ovation. He allowed it to go on for some moments, smiling broadly at the multitude, then gestured again for silence. It came instantly; they did not want to miss a word.

"Rather than make a long inaugural address, compete with the wonderful rhetoric of the Colonel—and I know my words suffer in comparison to his—I will dispense with further ceremony and allow this convention to turn its attention to the business at hand. It is with great pleasure that I turn the meeting over to Emmanual Torres, head of the Chamber of Commerce, who will itemize this year's crop." He bowed slightly from the waist and received another ovation. He then resumed his seat. Mercedes took his hand and squeezed it, smiling at the still resounding applause. When she felt her brother start to leave, she held his hand fast.

"Not yet."

"I'm hot," Coutard whispered fiercely. "I want to go home. Lisette is waiting."

"In a minute. Let them applaud you. The longer they applaud, the farther in their memories recedes Mendonça. What a pity he couldn't be here to witness your triumph."

"You're lucky he wasn't," Coutard mumbled. "I would never have gotten away with it if he had been here."

"He is old," Mercedes observed.

"He would have strangled me personally, nevertheless." Coutard continued to smile at the applauding men until he saw one face that seemed to burn out at him, and he gasped. "Oh dear God, he's here. I knew we should have waited."

"Who? Where?" Mercedes squinted anxiously but saw only a sea of faces.

"Mendonça. He's standing—"

"Don't look. Don't! You . . . Stand up."

"I can't."

The applause had not yet died, the men still sweated their approval. Coutard could tell from the expression on Mendonça's face that he had heard it all.

"Pierre, they are forgetting Mendonça already.
Now stand up and let them see you. Let *him* see
you."

Coutard hesitated, but he could no longer endure the stare of the Colonel, a look that pierced
directly to his heart and unmanned him. And so
finally, unwillingly, having no other choice but to
bolt, and wishing he were in the soft white arms of
his darling harmless Lisette, he stood and acknowledged the ovation.

Mercedes smiled up at him but she knew he
could not hold up indefinitely. At some point, he
would crack; she would have to be prepared.

*   *   *

The sun threw long shadows across the swirling
black and white tiles of São Sebastião Square.
Monsieur Armand Poincarré had filled his hydrogen balloon, swept out the musty velvet interior of
its suspended basket, and made himself ready for
the business of setting tourists aloft. The balloon
made an imposing silhouette against the sky, huge
sweeps of blue against a field of white, with a
string of red pennants hanging from its circum-
ference. For twenty milreis, Monsieur Poincarré
would take a patron's photograph with an American Optical Company Box Camera against a cloud
and sky backdrop and bring him safely to earth
again. There was, Poincarré knew, always an ele-
ment of hysteria to contend with—ladies fainting,
gentlemen turning pale—but this added to the ex-

citement. If there had been no danger, there would have been no thrill; and no thrill, no people going up.

Although until recently there was never anyone with sufficient reason or interest to check the truth of his story, Monsieur Poincarré insisted he was a direct descendant, on his mother's side, of Étienne Montgolfier, who with his brother Joseph Montgolfier, had invented the hot-air balloon a century earlier. Some citizens of Manaus claimed the story only proved that hot air ran in the family. That first balloon, more than three generations before, had been made of thin paper and cloth, heavily varnished. It was only when a way was found to rubberize silk that the balloon was made leak-proof; and the rubber had come from the very place to which Monsieur Poincarré had brought his balloon and basket several months before.

He adjusted his pince-nez, flipped open an almost-new copy of the scandalous *Les Fleurs du Mal*, and read the lines that had come to remind him of Manaus:

The adored one, naked, knowing my unspoken
    prayer,
Wore only her loud jewels, whose assembled
    blaze
Evoked in her the preening, self-delighted air
Of Moorish concubines in their young palmy
    days.

Monsieur Poincarré rook off his pince-nez and wiped it free of moisture; the passage never failed

to fog the lenses. Some movement across the square
caught his eye, and he replaced the spectacles to
focus on a procession of people pouring from the
Chamber of Commerce building and walking in his
direction. For a moment he thought fortune had
smiled upon his tourist trade, but the procession
looked too determined, too formidable. If his attraction had been more portable he would have
transferred it to a place of safety. As it was he remained while the crowd came at him, finally recognizing, although it gave him no peace, young Pierre
Coutard and his sister leading them. Coutard had
been a guest on the balloon on several occasions
with several different ladies in the recent past; as a
matter of fact, it had been he who had given Poincarré the copy of *Les Fleurs du Mal* fresh from a
bookseller's stall in Montmartre. The young man's
sister had been to see him herself several times
quite recently, pestering him with questions about
his balloon.

Now, to his considerable astonishment and no
small delight, he found his answers to Mademoiselle Coutard's questions being parroted back to
the assemblage gathered about his balloon through
the medium of no less a personage than Monsieur
Coutard.

To the conventioneers, who inspected Poincarré's livelihood with the dispassionate curiosity of
slave traders (pointing out to each other the salient
features: the basket, the velvet interior, and sand-
bag weights, the elaborate system of ropes and
pulleys), Coutard rapidly summarized the history

of ballooning. He began on a seductive note, relating the story of the Parisian lady of dubious reputation, who, in the 1820s, ascended in a car (the technically correct name for the basket, Coutard assured them) with as many as three male customers. Growing serious, he told them of the military uses to which balloons had been put as early as the Battle of Fleurus in 1794, when the French made use of one as an observation post to spy on Austrian troops. As no doubt some of Coutard's listeners knew, balloons had been employed for similar purposes with great success during the American Civil and Franco-Prussian wars, during which latter conflict, they were also used for the transportation of passengers and mail. The British received a share of mention in the lecture, their meteorological research using balloons to study sky light, atmospheric conditions, and electricity being praised in the talk Mercedes had prepared.

Mercedes listened to her brother attentively, noting with satisfaction that his histrionic abilities were helping him to recover his nerve; spotting the Colonel in the audience had been a bad moment for them both, but Pierre was especially sensitive. Mercedes shifted her gaze across the square to the American Bar. She could see the Colonel now, in fact, sitting in the window of the restaurant. A note had been received, asking them to meet him there for lunch, and Mercedes had sent an affirmative reply in Pierre's name. She waited, impatiently now, only half-hearing the conclusion of her speech and its rosy predictions for the future of air travel

thanks to the new gutta percha process. What did
he want, the old man?

It was just past one and Colonel Mendonça was
already exhausted. His nights had been long bouts
of sleeplessness and his days struggles to remain
awake in the heat. The irony was not lost on him,
but, short of conducting business from his bed,
there seemed little he could do to relieve his torpor. The infirmities of age were bearing down on
him just as the need to settle the land battle had
attained urgent proportions. It was typical of this
new phase of his physical disintegration that he be
late enough to the Rubber Convention that the
Coutards could, with equanimity, begin without
him. Respect, which had always been a touch-
and-go affair in the jungles of Manaus, had been
discarded as impractical; strength was all. The Colonel shook his head; he was not yet finished, not
yet. They would not find it quite so simple.

Pink and white orchids floated in a small pool
set in the middle of the table. Scarlet goldfish
swam in languid circles punctuated by abrupt turns
and sudden dashes. The dining room of the American Bar had been cleared by his order with the ex-
ception of Vlubek's Magyar Orchestra. When the
doors were opened and the Coutards entered, the
Colonel rose and stood back from the table. He
greeted them cordially, nodding even to the omni-
present bodyguards.

"Children, you must be famished." He signaled
to the waiter as they sat, addressing them as he

had done fondly a quarter of a century before. The effect of this address was to reduce Coutard immediately to a juvenile relation to the older man. He began babbling at once while his sister watched, intrigued by the gambit.

"I'm sorry to have begun this morning without you, Colonel. The truth—the real truth—was that we didn't think you were coming. Your health had been a subject of anxious discussion recently—"

"Shall we begin with a *bouillon en tasse?*" Mendonça overrode him smoothly. "And when we have dined we will talk. As adults."

Coutard nodded eagerly, ignoring the last thrust because it held no irony for him. Mercedes waited. The *bouillon en tasse* was succeeded by *croquettes de volaille St.-Cloud.* Conversation during this portion of the meal was restricted, as custom dictated, to topics of general and inconsequential interest. Next arrived a *filet de boeuf aux champignons,* which was accompanied on this occasion by *galantine de perdreau aux truffes.* Coutard ate voraciously, his nervousness adding to his appetite. He manipulated his cutlery with a careless dexterity that suggested that he tasted little.

Mercedes noted that Mendonça barely touched his food. He ignored the *chaud-froid de caille à la Richelieu* as if it had not been there, and barely poked at the *aspic de paté de fois gras en bellevue.* He's dying, she thought, with an inward smile of satisfaction. Can't get it down. She elected to mimic his spartan response, dabbling ineffectually at the *canard canvasback rôti* and a *salade de laitue et céleri* as the Colonel wondered if they planned to attend the forthcoming production of *Carmen,* due to open the opera season shortly. A brief but animated disquisition on the subject of that Parisian *succès de scandale* beguiled them through the final sips of a rare Johannisberger wine. The Colonel patted his mouth delicately and ordered coffee. He proffered Coutard a cigar and concealed his distaste when Mercedes asked if she might not smoke as well.

"If you like." He passed one to her, snipping the end neatly, holding the match and studying her while she inhaled. Curious woman.

They leaned back, three well-to-do patrons of an excellent restaurant who had just enjoyed a plentiful repast.

"Now, children. I would like to talk to you about your proposed thirty percent increase of price. It simply will not do."

"Not do for whom?" Coutard interposed. "You saw how favorably it was received. By the time the convention is ended, I will have the votes."

"You may very well have them already," Mendonça conceded. "That is not the point. The point will be the reaction of the outside world to this unconscionable rise in the price of raw *hevea.*"

"But what can they do?" Mercedes found herself objecting. "They must have rubber; they will have to come here to get it still."

"They will not stand for it, *senhorita.* They will take steps. They will use another grade of rubber.

They will switch to Para fine hard, closer to the sea
and cheaper."

"You cannot make gutta-percha from Para fine
hard," Mercedes responded, studying the tip of her
cigar.

Mendonça permitted himself a tolerant smile. It
came to him, quite suddenly, that it was this woman—not her dandified brother, absorbed with the
goldfish—who was waging war against him.

"Senhorita Mercedes, I must tell you candidly
that I do not share your enthusiasm for the future
of the hydrogen balloon. At best, such use of rubber will constitute a sideline of industry—"

"We have plans to build a balloon factory here
in Manaus."

Mendonça saw Coutard turn and stare at his sister. Clearly, he knew nothing about her proposed
balloon factory. Yes, yes, it is she who is the power
behind this wobbly throne.

"Nevertheless. It is my view that the bulk of our
future business will be done in rubber tires for
carriage wheels. Perhaps horseless carriage wheels.
Experiments are already underway. It is rubber on
land, not in the sky, which looks to quadruple our
profits."

"Quadruple!" She could not conceive it.

Mendonça nodded. "There is no need to raise the
export tax; we will profit in volume. And, I may
add, rubber carriage wheels do not require pure
hevea; Para fine hard will do nicely."

"My brother stands firm," Mercedes told him,
trying with increasing difficulty to maintain her

composure. Children, indeed. Mendonça turned to Coutard.

"Your father and I were competitors for many years. We had many difficulties—competitors always do—but we resolved them peacefully. We did not seek to plunge this city and this industry into a civil war. Can I not induce you to see reason?"

Coutard glanced anxiously at his sister, ready to take his cue from her, but she remained expressionless.

"I feel that I have made the right decision," he began haltingly, wishing he were somewhere else. "As I stated in my address, traditional policies must give way to modern notions of progress. We must plan for the future."

Mendonça stared, fighting down an urge to slap his silly face. "Very well. I have spoken my piece. I could not sleep soundly had I not shared with you my views."

There was an awkward pause. Mercedes put down her cigar. "We thank you for a delicious lunch," she said, rising. "And we hope that your health continues to improve. Pierre."

Obediently Coutard rose, and, bowing to the Colonel, swept his sister from the room.

Mendonça resumed his chair and remained a long time, deep in thought. The waiter brought him his accustomed port and he sipped it meditatively. Outside, Poincarré's balloon continued to take conventioneers aloft, two by two, for a look at the future.

The girl is the key, he said to himself. This lunch was expensive, but worth every milreis. A way to undo his ancient knot of enemies had begun to slip gently into his mind.

❊ 5 ❊

The wise and the bitter, though approaching their conclusions from divergent sources, agreed that Manaus had become the expression of aberrant greed and the attenuated imagination of a hopeless *arriviste*.

The Teatro do Amazonas, an opera house whose splendor rivaled that of La Scala, stood at the giddy apotheosis of that folly. It stood, in actuality, at the top of a hill, on the fabled São Sebastião Square, a monument to all that was romantic and foolish; as splendid, in its way, as the Taj Mahal, but the thrust behind its conception and construction was less romantic than ostentatious, tinged with more than a bit of self-love and -congratulation. But to the Latins who ordered it built and the citizens of Manaus who enjoyed its magnificence, the order was toward display; there would be none of the understatement that was creeping into the architecture of New York City, Boston, and Philadelphia.

As if to flaunt human power and resourcefulness in the face of the menacing threat of jungle growth, the opera house was constructed slightly out of scale, larger than life, so that when people approached it at night they appeared to be sucked into its enormity rather than to enter willingly. Each outside stair required two steps to broach its depth, and certain women, following the latest fashion of the hobble skirt, were forced to take as many as six steps from one stair to the next. Despite the inconvenience, these women would no more give up the fashion of the day than they would let lapse their subscription to *Le Matin* or begin printing their dinner menus in Portuguese. The rich of Manaus were Europhiles; hordes of them took an annual voyage across the Atlantic; their children were sent to Paris for schooling just as casually as their linen was sent to Lisbon for laundering.

The things in Europe that eluded them they recreated in Manaus. Hence, the opera house, built at a time when the city was ravaged by poverty on the one hand and on the other, dazzled with the potential of rubber in the Industrial Revolution, all of it coming from their own capacious backyard. The iron framework of the opera house was imported from Glasgow on three ships that had to be gutted and the holds rebuilt to accommodate the girders. The gold and blue tiles covering the dome so that it glistened like coins in the sea numbered almost seventy thousand. They had been wrapped individually in cheesecloth, transported overland from Alsace to Le Havre and stored in a ship designed to suspend the entire cargo section from a series of enormous hammocks, leaving no chance that they would knock against the hull.

A wide winding stairway leading to a terrace, overlooking the swirling patterned tiles of the square, was edged by a white marble balustrade. The coolness of marble in the heat of Manaus made it a favorite material of the rich and the balustrade the favored gathering place to refresh oneself during the entr' actes. Above the terrace was a balcony supporting eight marble columns and above that a second balcony supporting eight smaller marble columns, and above that a semi-circular carving of classical Greek design and Romanesque border, and above that, heavenly, was the shining dome: it was apparent from the size of the opera house that the people of Manaus were publicly, if not profoundly, religious and that they had gratuitously humbled themselves by building a place so grand.

When Senhor Torres extended an invitation to Kincaid for the opening performance of Bizet's *Carmen*, it was received with some enthusiasm. Kincaid had witnessed the opera's infamous premiere at the Opéra Comique in Paris and was interested to see how the rich of Manaus would react to a work whose initial reception, some said, had caused its composer's death not three months later. Another persuasive touch was the lecherous glint in Torres' eye and his veiled promise of fleshly pleasures afterward. After his long Atlantic crossing and his steamy trip upriver, Kincaid felt he deserved a night out.

Besides the Opéra Comique, Kincaid had seen La Scala and the Palais Royal and Covent Garden and the Taj Mahal, so he was not unduly impressed with the Teatro do Amazonas except for the first moment he stood on the terrace of the opera house, surrounded by gentlemen in evening clothes of brittle slashes of black on white and ladies in egret feathers and black velvet, and looked out to see the sight banked, not two miles away, by comical palm trees with heads like ape fists. From the same vantage point, he could see the city spread out on all sides, with the opera house the hub of a wheel the way the Arc de Triomphe was in Paris. Terra cotta roofs burnished gold in the setting sun; tented canvas roofs thin to the point of translucency. And beyond, the eye following a natural downward slope to the floating docks, was the wide expanse of water where the Rio Negro became the Amazon. But beyond that, and behind, and on all sides, the dense tropical jungle held the city like a shiny piece of foil in a grip of fungus and moss.

Torres treated Kincaid like visiting royalty, assuming that Kincaid's acceptance by Colonel Mendonça was testament to his own station. There was little for him to do when it came to the really important work such as the activities of the rubber convention or the dealings of the new Coutard balloon factory or the matters of peace. And so he occupied himself with showing Kincaid the best of himself, avoiding his opium for much of the day so he could officiate at the opera tonight.

A loud Oriental gong sounded and Torres touched his arm. "The first call," he said, smiling so broadly that his eyes disappeared. "We shall wait two minutes, then we shall walk in. We wait, then we walk. As in Europe."

"Just tell me when," Kincaid said, nodding in a great show of seriousness. "I hate making a spectacle of myself."

"Yes, I know," Torres said. "That is the way with the English."

"I'm an American."

"Ah . . . then it is the opposite," Torres concluded, conciliatory to a fault, and led the bemused Kincaid into the foyer where pink marble floors sprouted coral marble pillars and ran along the doorways in dizzying swirls of cream and white and soared around window embrasures in a rose so deep it bled. There seemed, to Kincaid's experienced eye, a clash of styles, not unreminiscent of Casa Grande. Off the foyer were several smaller salons with mahogany and rosewood bars polished sleek as ice. Domenico de Angelis, Italy's leading painter of murals, had made the arduous journey from Padua to Manaus. He left behind several murals of the river and jungle, all disturbingly Paduan, and took home with him a souvenir disease distinctly Brazilian. In corners and next to the brocade settee and chairs carved of jacaranda, which required a dozen men to lift, were trees painfully wrought of bronze and copper, looking at once pathetic and dangerous.

"Five million of your American dollars," Torres declared grandly, beaming with pride as he gestured to the surroundings.

He took Kincaid's arm once again and led him back into the main foyer and up the majestic sweep of the marble stairs to the first balcony level to view the spectacle below.

The men brandished walking sticks and tiny diamond studs set their shirt fronts winking. Diamonds flashed too from the wrists and throats of the women, but there was a lethal beauty here, the harshness of the gems against the vulnerability of pale bluish veins. Even in the palpable heat, the women wore velvet with long trains held up by gold loops. Some wore their hair piled high, set off with tiny velvet bows; others wore feathers at the neck and large perfect pearls; some gowns were beaded and so heavy the women looked exhausted as they climbed the stairs. What skin was visible was powdered white, for the sun was to be avoided at all costs. Any color resulting from exposure constituted an indisputable submission to the vagaries and vulgarities of nature.

Inside the opera house itself, in front of a stage from which Sarah Bernhardt had declaimed the poetry of Racine and been buried to the knees in a thousand gardenias by a gentleman almost as far from his prime as that estimable scribe, all was larger than life, and pinker than heaven. The inside of the dome was a curved ceiling where impossible angels and irrepressible cherubs cavorted on a backdrop of feathery blue. Crystal chandeliers "to symbolize the angels' tears," as Torres said, hung from the ceiling, and the candlepower was enough to illuminate the entire orchestra floor, the stalls, and the four pillared balconies faced in gold leaf.

"You see that woman there?" Torres pointed to a woman wearing a hat festooned with pink ostrich feathers that dripped down her back. "They say she conjugated with half the Russian Navy before marrying and that her husband had to get her out of Moscow because the entire fleet had contracted syphilis and the health authorities were on her trail. Rumor, of course, but . . ." He paused and waved his hand, letting it finish the indictment for him. The woman turned her face and Kincaid saw that it was faintly pockmarked and heavily powdered.

"And that man there, the one with the jade lion's head on his walking stick." Torres inclined his head, less conspicuous than an extended hand.

"A molester of children?" Kincaid suggested helpfully, but Torres hardly heard, so excited was he to tell what he knew.

"A Spaniard; lost all of his money gambling with the king. Came here to Manaus where he continues to gamble. He limps because his mistress goaded him to bet a leg when all his money went, and the fool complied. A pound of flesh . . . you know Shakespeare?"

Kincaid nodded, half afraid, now that he was in the box, that Torres would hold him there, prisoner to the lurid gossip the man exuded.

"That one will remain empty," Torres went on, indicating what looked like a box reserved for royalty: heavy amber-colored drapes hid the rear, a backdrop for four gilt chairs covered in pink satin and twenty unlit pink candles. "It belongs to Colonel Mendonça, but he never uses it. Since his wife died he is not too much for the social life. They say he takes his whores out on that yacht of his, the *Francesca*, and keeps them prisoners for weeks on end. Despite his years the Colonel is amazingly virile. But he never appears here. Oh! Look. The Coutards!"

Kincaid looked, as did most of the audience, as Pierre Coutard and his sister entered their box, next to Colonel Mendonça's. Mercedes was dressed in revealing night blue satin, a matching neckband with a diamond set in the center, a cluster of wisteria blossoms at her waist. Her hair was elaborately curled and knotted at the back of her neck. Kincaid found her attractive in a severe way. Her brother looked as if he never wore anything but white tie and tails. Kincaid had seen a hundred Pierre Coutards at Maxim's; in Manaus they were still something of a rarity. Although the audience did not applaud, they might just as well have, for the amount of attention these two received.

Torres explained, "It was his father who made the fortune but Pierre knows how to spend it. His sister Mercedes—unmarried, and getting on in years. They say she will not marry before her brother. They say she is in love with him herself. It is slightly disgusting, don't you agree?"

Kincaid just looked; he admitted to himself that he found Mercedes Coutard the most attractive woman he'd seen since he had arrived. She was not the most beautiful perhaps, but there was something in the way she seemed to control herself and her situation that impressed him. Kincaid liked his women to be tough-minded and beautiful; one quality without the other never did very much for him. At present, he had very little time for women; none, as a matter of fact. No one could be allowed to come any closer than a polite introduction, especially one that attracted him.

"Look, look!" Torres pulled at his sleeve excitedly and spoke in breathy whispers. "They are lighting the Colonel's box."

While the thirty violins tuned up in the orchestra pit, a servant dressed as a page from the court of Louis XIV appeared in the box with a long taper and proceeded to light the twenty candles. The audience abandoned the Coutards and absorbed this ceremony. The box glowed pink and the servant disappeared behind the amber drapes. A moment later they parted and the Colonel appeared. He nodded to the people in the stalls, who appeared amazed at his presence. Next came a small middle-aged woman with a startled birdlike face wearing a lace shawl over a dress of dark plum-colored taffeta that would have been equally appropriate for a funeral.

"His sister," Torres whispered. "She goes out even less than he does. They say she had a lover once who was a pirate and he left her with a black baby that she—" But Torres was cut off by the next sight, one so evidently unexpected that the audience drew in a collective breath. "Dolores!"

Kincaid regarded the young woman. She was young, twenty perhaps, barely out of girlhood but with a flush of womanhood on her face. Her jet hair was pulled tightly back and parted in the middle, a style dared only by a woman whose face needed no accessories to render it remarkable. Her white dress was simple and sleek, molding the fullness of her body like the curves in melting ivory. The front of it was embroidered with pearls, white ostrich tips, and egret feathers.

"She has been abroad for her education," Torres explained. "Four years ago, she left. I had not thought she would return. A scandal in Paris, a lover perhaps. And now her aunt is here to watch over her. The irony of it! The rich are no better than anyone, Senhor Kincaid; usually worse. It is a lesson I have learned in this life. Look at her, preening like a peacock. She went to a Music Seminary for Ladies in Paris. I ask you, *senhor*, what kind of education does a lady receive in Paris? Only one kind."

Kincaid laughed at Torres' speculations. He had to admit to himself that although Dolores Mendonça was rapturously beautiful, he found her evident vanity as distancing as Torres did. He watched along with the rest of the audience as Colonel Mendonça took his daughter's hand and led her to the side of the box that adjoined the Coutards'. He drew aside the dividing curtain, startling the inhabitants; they had not seen what the rest of the audience had. Coutard stood up reflexively while Mercedes simply lifted her head, surprised. The Colonel spoke a few words, then stood aside and presented Dolores. Coutard bowed, then kissed the hand she had extended in perfect European fashion. Mercedes nodded from her gilt chair.

"Amazing," Torres breathed beside him. "Everyone knows they despise each other. They say the Colonel and Coutard's father each wenched the other's wife so that no one knows whose child is whose. I find the rich impossible to believe as a rule, don't you agree, *senhor?*"

With a crash of cymbals, the wild gypsy music of *Carmen* began and the audience turned its attention to the stage. The overture was as rousing as Kincaid remembered its being when he had witnessed its premiere with the astonishing Celestine Galli-Marié. Kincaid had also seen the Vienna production a year later in which the spoken dialogue had been replaced by Guiraud with recitatives and which this Manaus production seemed to follow, attempting to turn the piece into grand opera. Kincaid hoped that the production would have a Carmen to boast of, although from what he knew of the history of the Teatro do Amazonas, the chances were slim. After the opera house was built, huge sums of money were the bait to lure opera companies from across the seas, but after the disaster in 1872 when nine members of the Guila Raji Company were stricken with yellow fever, no price seemed sufficient to entice the best. It was a scandal that Senhor Torres, as head of the Chamber of Commerce, had tried to hush up as best he could,

but his best was not able to deflect the blows that
the tragedy had hurled Manaus' way. The company now storming its way on stage was a rather
obscure one, the Rura de Montana Company from
Sydney, Australia. It had its attractions, certainly,
most notably in a Carmen as round in form as she
was flat in voice. When she began the "Habañera"
it was quite apparent that a toss of her petticoats
would have to do the work that ill-favored vocal
equipment could not. And the sensual irony in the
lines:

L'amour est enfant de Bohême,
il n'a jamais, jamais connu de loi.
Si tu ne m'aimes pas, je t'aime;
si je t'aime, prends garde à toi!

was dispersed in the inarticulate accents of this
Australian schoolgirl. The aria itself was greeted
with a murmur of familiarity. Bizet had, after all,
adapted it from a well-known Cuban song—hence
its title, which was nowhere alluded to in the
opera. Kincaid turned away from the stage and
found himself smiling in complicity at Dolores
Mendonça. The mezzo's flat notes and broken
French were suddenly less irksome. There was
nothing like a friendly flirtation to pass the time.
Dolores' line of vision encompassed him as she
looked at the stage. Opera glasses were raised to
her eyes, but when Kincaid looked through his he
saw she was focused on him and he smiled even
wider at their game. The girl, pretending to be
flustered, jerked her head away. Kincaid's smile

broadened. In the next moment she turned her attention back to him. For an instant she smiled. He took down his glasses and she did the same. The gesture excited him as much as if she had taken down her hair.

Kincaid decided abruptly that things were looking up. He knew this dalliance was not the sort of thing he could afford, let alone encourage, but the beauty of old Mendonça's daughter grew progressively intoxicating. When he looked again, she was looking at him again. Kincaid's face split into a wide grin. He saluted her with the opera glasses but the gesture was too overt and she turned away, concentrating on the "Seguedilla." Her attempt to appear engrossed did not deceive him. He knew, as surely as if he could read her mind, that she was thinking about him. For the first time in as long as he could remember, the temperature of his blood began to rise. He was glad she'd spent time in Paris; the women there played this game so well. He glanced briefly at Mercedes Coutard, still clinically bemused by her angular perfection, but sensing that such diversions were of no interest to her. He prepared to resume his contemplations of the magnificent Dolores, when his eye was diverted by a peculiar spectacle: an outsized forest iguana wound its way down from the domed ceiling to one of the crystal chandeliers. Its casquelike head jerked amiably from side to side, almost, but not quite, in time with the music; it looked slightly confused by the proceedings and its inadvertent participation in them. Kincaid, fascinated by the phenomenon, which he rightly regarded as one of the unique properties of the Teatro do Amazonas, failed to realize that he was himself an object of scrutiny; Mercedes Coutard, with a discretion for which he would hardly have given her credit, was studying him intently behind the camouflage of her own opera glasses.

The interval arrived; operagoers packed like tobacco into the ovenlike promenade.

The Rura de Montana Company, sensing a general audience lethargy (and perhaps unable to bear the heat under the weight of the period costumes), sped up the last three acts. Kincaid was briefly dismayed by the appearance of live horses in Act IV, but they were evacuated without incident, in time to make way for José's downfall. In the final moments of darkness, he exchanged another glance with Dolores, who smiled as he began tearing his program into long strips. The curtain fell. Kincaid solemnly handed the shreds to Senhor Torres, whose eyes filled with tears of gratitude that the Rura de Montana Company had made it through the night in good health, if not in good voice. The audience, on the other hand, not many social steps removed in origin from the low standing of the characters in the opera, deplored the defective moral sense particularly of the gypsies, and the uncompromising tragic finish, which was out of keeping with the tradition of happy endings associated with the Teatro do Amazonas.

The lights came up. The forest iguana, startled, lost its footing and fell on the white shoulders of a woman in the orchestra floor, whose screams were not drowned out by the applause.

*　　*　　*

"It is no longer enough that the company remain on its feet," Torres whined as he and Kincaid made their way down the stairs to the main floor. "Now they are supposed to sing as well."

Kincaid smiled to himself at Torres' distress. People milled about, all trying to escape the sweltering heat to the outdoors. At the foot of the gigantic opera house steps stood a group of men surrounding a barely visible carriage and shouting out a series of graduating numbers. Kincaid shrugged, restless, his attention only momentarily distracted, his eyes searching the crowd for an evening's diversion. Torres had said something about "afterward," but Kincaid had had quite enough of the man's viperous tongue.

"In all Manaus," Torres was saying, puffed up with the knowledge, "that is the most magnificent carriage. It was owned by Prince Albert of Saxe-Coburg before he married Queen Victoria. He gave it to a penniless cousin to pay off some debts. The cousin prospered and it came to Manaus on an Austrian liner just a few years ago. The man who came with it was a gentleman of the American South, Beauford Post. Senhor Post was once a very rich man, but he is now in reduced circumstances. A fortune gone. A woman from Poland, I think. Some said she was a princess; I said, if she was a princess, what was she doing in Manaus with a *nouveau riche* Yanqui from the South?"

"Isn't everyone in Manaus one of the *nouveau riche?*"

"There are degrees and there are limits, *senhor*. You must live here to know what they are. Senhor Post did not know. He overstepped. So the Polish princess left him and he had nothing but his carriage from Prince Albert. After the opera, it has become the custom for gentlemen to bid for its services for the evening. Senhor Post is also the footman."

Kincaid was surprised the others would allow Senhor Post to remain there as a reminder of what they might themselves become.

"Four hundred!" cried a stentorian voice from the top of the stairs. The crowd of bidders groaned at the sum and looked up to see Pierre Coutard sauntering toward them, waving his white gloves at the carriage, which Kincaid was barely able to glimpse because of the press surrounding it.

Next to Kincaid, Torres drew in his breath sharply; following Coutard at a slower pace, Colonel Mendonça escorted his sister and his daughter, as well as Mercedes Coutard. The families' two sets of bodyguards intermingled and spread the gaping throng on either side of the wide marble steps. Without wasting another moment on his tiresome guide, Kincaid thrust himself through the crowd until he managed to meet the old man at the bottom of the steps.

"A pleasure to see you again, sir."

The Colonel looked about, startled by the voice at his elbow, instinctively eyeing his bodyguards. He drew his daughter close to him and only then, squinting for a moment, did he recognize Kincaid.

"Ah, Mr. Kincaid. The orchids. May I present my daughter Dolores? And my sister, Dona Inês. Ladies, this is Mr. Kincaid, the American orchid collector."

The two women obediently lowered their eyes, and Dolores held out her hand to be kissed, a ceremony Kincaid willingly performed. At close range she was even more breathtaking; there was a creaminess to her that Kincaid could almost taste, a quality of being untouched which he did not usually find appealing. Around them, the crowd of departing operagoers watched the exchange, vastly entertained; royalty in view. Colonel Mendonça appeared not to notice. He might have been conversing with Kincaid in a closet.

"You will come to my house tomorrow. It has been arranged for you to begin your inspection of my collection. If my own schedule permits, I will be happy to discuss it with you." He began to move forward, then hesitated. "Ah, I am remiss. Mr. Kincaid, may I also present Mademoiselle Mercedes and her brother, Pierre Coutard, the son and daughter of my oldest friend."

Kincaid exchanged bows with the languid Coutard, who favored him with a slight inclination of his handsome head, and kissed the black evening glove—the fingers sparkling with diamonds—of the

man's enigmatic sister, who smiled, a bare tugging
of flesh at the corners of her mouth.

"Senhor Kincaid has come to Manaus from London, has he not?"

Kincaid bowed in acknowledgment.

"And I have only just returned from Paris." It
was Dolores who spoke, rolling her eyes with mock
doleur. "Don't you find Manaus provincial and boring after Europe?" she enquired of Kincaid.

"I did, until recently." Kincaid contrived to look
at both ladies as he tossed his bouquet. He was
gratified to discern a blush on Dolores' cheeks and
to hear Mercedes chuckle appreciatively next to him.

Mendonça coughed and shifted his weight from
one foot to the other.

"Mr. Kincaid, we must bid you goodnight. The
air, however warm it may feel, is considerably
chilled after an evening in the opera house. Sus-
ceptibility to yellow fever is greater at such times,
and I must not expose my fragile charges to such
contagion."

He bowed low and moved forward with his company toward his carriage, when Coutard's voice
arrested their progress. The young man had effected a path to the coach whose services he had
purchased so extravagantly, and now held open the
door.

"Colonel Mendonça, it is my pleasure to arrange
for your departure this evening in honor of your
daughter's homecoming."

Kincaid now had the opportunity of actually
viewing the coveted coach. It was entirely covered

in gold leaf, with red leather upholstery in the coachman's box and pink satin in the passengers' compartment. There was a fairy-tale quality to it, so delicate were the wheel spokes, so smooth and almost edible the surface of the gold. Icanthus leaves were sculpted around the windows, small roses around the doors. A bar inside was filled with crystal glasses and decanters of (Kincaid hazarded) cognac and amaretto. There were gold sconces filled with ivory candles, a stream of gardenias hanging from each. Senhor Post, resplendent in coachman's livery, flicked his whip, and two spanking white horses walked the few steps to where Dolores stood. She hesitated, looking first at Coutard, then at Kincaid, and finally at her father, who made a brief show of weighing the offer, then smiled and motioned her to get in.

Colonel Mendonça handed forward his aged sister and followed her into the dreamlike conveyance. As he passed, Kincaid was surprised to note how feebly he moved. When they had first met, Mendonça had appeared the perfect picture of a roughly cut man. Now Kincaid realized with a start that Mendonça was ill and attempting to conceal it. The ruddiness of his complexion was not health but fever.

In another moment, Coutard had raised the steps and closed the door. Kincaid watched Dolores sitting by the window, her face framed by gardenias. She looked quite like the romantic heroine she apparently conceived herself to be. With another flick of the whip, the carriage started off into the night, a golden moth fluttering into the darkness. For sheer melodrama, the entire event supplied what the production of *Carmen* had failed to.

"Four hundred pounds!" Torres exclaimed, materializing once more at Kincaid's elbow and staring after the disappearing coach. "A record price, if I am not mistaken. He is obviously smitten."

"Senhor Torres!"

Torres turned, startled, to see Mercedes Coutard, standing on the bottom step as the crowd dispersed. She waited patiently for him to go to her. Kincaid stood on the curb next to her brother.

"Senhor Torres, my brother has no intention of retiring this early, whereas I am minded to do so. Will you escort me home?"

The question took the fat reprobate by surprise. He glanced longingly over his shoulder at Kincaid, but she tapped her foot imperiously.

"Come, come, *senhor,* don't tell me you would abandon a lady in distress?"

Kincaid listened to Torres' mumbled protestations with a sinking heart; he was about to lose his guide at just the point when he sensed the man would prove most useful.

It was not to be. With Mercedes on his arm, Torres reluctantly tipped his hat to Kincaid and effected a gallant pleasantry about the unexpected honor that would rob him of Kincaid's company, a defect he promised to remedy on another occasion. Kincaid assured him that he envied his good for-

tune, a compliment Mercedes acknowledged by
presenting him once more a gloved hand to kiss
before they sauntered off to her coach.

Kincaid watched as the brougham clattered
across the stones. The steps were now deserted,
the operagoers had departed for their homes or
other amusements. Kincaid turned to survey the
square, and his glance took in Pierre Coutard, who
stood indolently a few feet off, twirling his stick
and grinning at him.

"Deserted?" Coutard asked, solicitously.

"So it appears."

"Have you no plans?"

"No. Have I?"

Coutard's grin broadened.

"My sister," Coutard began, leaning back against
the cushions of the cab and striking a relaxed, intimate tone, "is annoyed with me. Again."

"Whatever for?" Kincaid replied, adopting the
same tone.

Coutard laughed, shrugged and sighed, poking
his booted toe with the end of his stick. "What do
you think of that girl, eh, *senhor?* Splendid creature! A goddess, truly. Who would have thought
the old blunderbuss could father such a thing as
that?"

Kincaid reflected on several unlikely antecedents
he had known, but said nothing.

Presently the young man spoke again. "Not only
is she ravishing, but she breathes the very air of
Paris here in these swamps. The very air! That af-

fectation of innocence!" He plucked his boutonniere and crushed it against his nose before flinging it from the window. "What ecstasy it would be to soil such purity."

Kincaid, who had nursed similar thoughts, concurred silently.

"But," Coutard sighed again and dusted his sleeve of imaginary lint, "it is not to be. My sister would not countenance such an intrigue, not with a Mendonça, heaven forfend. It might upset her plans for the Colonel."

"Plans?"

"Oh, yes, yes," Coutard nodded energetically several times. "Her plans." He looked out the window and chuckled wetly. "We are thrown back on our own devices, my friend. If we cannot enter the portals of heaven, we can march bravely enough through the gates of hell, can we not?"

"To hell it is, then."

6

In addition to the rubber boom and the opera house and the Amazon River and the people of wealth and fashion, Manaus was also famous for its shadier nightlife. Advertisements were run in the daily newspapers that offered "lodgings for gentlemen—French lessons included." This area of the city could be reached by walking up any narrow alley from the docks until Itamarca Street. From there to Epaminondes Avenue, business began at four in the afternoon, and business it was until late the next morning, by which time everyone was either too drunk or too dazed with Turkish opium to care very much whether every *strega* and every lady was paid and accounted for.

The trip into an atmosphere that reeked of unspoken pleasures could not begin at the bottom, for part of the thrill was the descent. And so Coutard began his tour for Kincaid at Hell's Gate on Democracy Square, where the tiny round tables were already filled with wealthy landowners and honorary colonels sipping Cordon Rouge with one hand while Rio Branco cigarettes drooped idly from the other.

Coutard led Kincaid to a back table raised on a small platform, and soon there was a commotion at the door where several gentlemen were tossing uncut emeralds in a path. An ebony carriage drawn by four Spanish stallions had pulled up to Hell's Gate. The door was held open by a gigantic Negro whose near-naked oiled body glistened black as the ebony. No doubt he had been chosen for just that reason. A white hand emerged from the carriage interior and the Negro held it until the owner stepped out, costumed in layers of white feathers, her face dusted white, a mass of orange hair exploding about her head, with the greenest eyes this side of envy. She was barefoot and walked into Hell's Gate over the strewn emeralds as if they did not cut. Blood was on her feet but she seemed not to notice.

The patrons cheered her, urging her to sing, and Coutard explained that the woman was Athéné Moncreux, ex-mistress of a British cabinet minister who had been forced to leave London under threat of scandal. It all might have been a lie, he added; half her appeal was in deception. She had met the enormous Negro while singing in a *she-bim* in Morocco and now was the sensation of Manaus nightlife.

She signaled for the musicians to begin and strolled slowly among the tables, leaving a trail of feathers and heat, her Negro never far behind her. It was common knowledge that he would kill any-one who touched her, although the Negro himself could be purchased for the evening for less than five hundred dollars. Even the gentlemen who were so inclined agreed that the mere knowledge of the Negro's proximity to Athéné, touching her hand every night, contributed to what stirred their loins.

After filling the room with her scent of tuberose and cedar, she turned to the men and sang "Love's Old Sweet Song," the pathos of which was lost on not a man; it would serve to stimulate later pleasures with other ladies.

Although Kincaid was aroused by Athéné herself, he remembered being moved to actual tears when he heard Amy Bellwood sing the same song at Tony Pastor's club in New York. And certainly the girlish Lillie Langtry was prettier, and Sissy Held, nastily coquettish, was more alluring if one did not catch oneself thinking of the rib she'd had removed to make her waist an incredible eighteen inches. It was, Kincaid opined to himself, the dawn of a new era in entertainment.

Athéné's audience was wildly enthusiastic, throwing more emeralds at her feet, shattering magnums of Cordon Rouge against the marble tables for her to continue. Athéné sauntered about and her eyes met Kincaid's. She came at him slowly while the orchestra began a slow vamp to the song she had made famous in Manaus, "You Know the Girl." When she got to his table she stopped and peered at him over a cloud of feathers. In a voice huskier than she'd used before, she sang the opening lines:

You know her face
You know her skin
But you don't know where to begin.

Coutard nudged Kincaid, licking his lips with
vicarious relish, hoping that if Kincaid spoke the
right words, Athéné would be served to them on
toast. Kincaid laughed while the men in the club
shouted encouragement; she had been offered before and none had had her. She leaned down and
put her ear to Kincaid's lips. He whispered just
three words and Athéné jerked back, flustered,
then laughed and Kincaid saw that her teeth were
encrusted with diamonds.

"Take it up with my friend," she said, indicating
the Negro, and Kincaid understood why no one
had had her. Frustrated with the tease, he pulled
Coutard from the table and they left Hell's Gate
as Athéné sang the final bars of the song:

You know her heart
Where her past has been
Still you don't know where to begin.

Coutard chartered another hansom from the
Restaurant Degas, which drove them slowly along
the cobbled streets of open storefronts where the
only thing for sale was women: all ages, sizes,
nationalities, sitting, standing, reclining, crouching,
smiling, shouting, posturing, bantering, mute,
calm, frenzied. The atmosphere was airless, as
though the energy of the solicitation was more in-

tense than anything that followed, as though that
were the thrill.

They stopped at the Viva Mortes bar at the end
of Isamiranda Street, where the walls were black
and strung with death's heads. Coutard assured
him they delivered the finest cocaine in all of
Manaus. It was served on a silver tray, whose pris-
tine elegance contrasted sharply with the yellow
candlelight and sawdust atmosphere of the Viva
Mortes. On the tray was a small silver bowl, lined
in porcelain, no larger than a demitasse, filled with
the white powder, and next to it a tiny silver
spoon. Coutard dipped the spoon in the cocaine,
held it beneath his left nostril while covering his
right, and sniffed several times. He repeated this
action for the right nostril, then handed the tray to
Kincaid. Kincaid inhaled deeply, then sniffed
tentatively. "I've heard that enough of this stuff,
taken in quantity, will deprive a man of his sense
of smell."

"Exactly!" Coutard exulted. "Just the thing to
help one endure this cesspool of a city. I take it
for that reason only." They laughed. "Already my
nose does not smell so well. Do you understand?"

"Not a bit of it," Kincaid said and laughed harder.

From the Viva Mortes, the cab took them
through a darkened area made memorable by its
fetid smells of disease and by the shrieks of infants.
They arrived then at the Chinese Supa on Flores
Street at the very edge of the jungle; an enormous
mango-tree root was the front step. The girls were

Oriental with names like Happy Nights, Miss Bliss, Open Flower, and Tender Blossom. When they entered, the two girls at the entrance sprayed them with the essence of pepper-jasmine and cuirir. The others sat on gentlemen's laps or did the cakewalk with each other. But Kincaid had only time to begin a discovery of a particular girl with greenish-white skin and breath like copper when Coutard pulled him away again, assuring him, with all the heady confidence of cocaine, that he had saved the best for last. So he pushed Kincaid back into the cab, telling the driver to take them to Piamerna Street, to the club called Kiss at the High Life Hotel.

"The price there for a Norwegian virgin is one hundred seventy-five. Dollars," Coutard told him, describing a bargain. "And it is good for the girls too, afterwards."

"Of course," Kincaid said. "If they stayed in Norway they'd still be biting the testicles off reindeer."

"What a way to live," Coutard agreed.

Piamerna Street was totally dark and Coutard had to light matches to find the unmarked door to the High Life Hotel, pronounced "Higgy-Liffey" by the Portuguese. The light inside was smoky and dim, rosy, hot. The girls walked or stood, each in a particular drama with a specific costume to satisfy a special craving. One wore only black-lace lingerie; a small blind boy was polishing her shoes. Another, in red garters, a corset, and spurs, was having her cigar lit by a gentleman holding a flaming stock certificate. Kincaid saw diamond bracelets being passed from man to woman and subtle assents being returned. A man bumped into a servant girl and broke a salt cellar; a woman in flounces above the knee and below the collar drew her price in the spilled salt. It was like looking at an enormous menu, Kincaid thought, and being hungry for all of it.

Coutard sidled up to him, a wreath of blue smoke around his head. In the spirit of opium and good will, he offered to treat Kincaid to one of the hundred-and-seventy-five-dollar Norwegian virgins. He further insisted that Kincaid permit him to choose the girl himself. Kincaid assented and Coutard drifted off.

Kincaid followed a servant to a private room on the second floor that contained, in addition to the standard armoire, dresser, pitcher, towels, and mirrors, a bed shaped like a swan, its tail the headboard, its head and neck guarding the foot. As he undressed and got into its belly, Kincaid wondered if this was the origin of the slang word "swanning." He lay still for a few moments, breathing in the smell of gardenias, when there was a soft knock at the door.

"Come."

Before she even appeared, her feathers preceded her, followed by her flaming orange hair. Kincaid rested on one elbow and watched, fascinated; surprised, to say the least.

"How did Coutard convince you?"

Athéné crossed the room quickly, shedding her feathers until she crouched naked on the sable rug next to the bed, flashing a smile of brilliant diamond teeth.

"Coutard?" She grinned. "Coutard had nothing to do with it."

"Then, why—"

Kincaid interrupted himself, suddenly remembering the three words he'd whispered to her. "You mean I was right?"

"You dare!" She laughed and ran her scarlet nails across his chest, as Kincaid sat up and threw off the blanket. Athéné looked at his exposed nakedness and blushed to her hairline. She came closer to the edge of the bed and reached out a tentative, small white hand to touch the hair on his belly. Kincaid leaned forward and pulled the pins from the coiled red hair until it came loose in his hands like liquid fire.

"Down," he whispered. "Get down."

Athéné kneeled on the floor and opened her mouth, all pretense of shyness gone, and applied herself with considerable lingual dexterity. Kincaid pushed her shoulders gently until she was stretched out on the sable rug below him.

He stared at the pale body, blushing pink at the generously formed breasts. She covered her flaming sex with her hands; Kincaid lifted his foot to urge them away. Relaxing slightly, she reached out to him and he saw tiny beads of perspiration on the red down under her arms. His toes touched

the smooth sex covered with silken curls that might
have been the same rich sable as the blanket. Kincaid knelt between her perfumed legs. He kissed
her and felt her move deep inside like a coil unwinding in irregular undulations.

While his mouth was engaged, he twisted his
body so she might be similarly occupied, but before the connection was completed, the door
opened again.

Coutard's face appeared, mischievous and slightly out of focus. He grinned at the sporting couple
and held up a bottle of champagne. Kincaid
smiled and waved him in, retaining Athéné's attention with a single fingertip. Coutard, dressed in a
white towel, entered, holding the bottle aloft like
a torch and urging someone before him with his
foot. As Kincaid watched, a small figure edged her
way into the room and pressed herself against the
far wall. She was just five feet tall and wrapped in
an enormous silver-fox blanket.

Athéné looked questioningly at Kincaid.

Coutard unceremoniously pulled the cork.
"Champagne?" White foam spurted to the ceiling,
a good deal of it spilling on himself and the silver-
fox blanket.

"It's all right; it's only wine. Here, it's good for
you." Coutard dragged his bundle toward the bed.
Her head was still lowered, her hair in two dark
coils against her ears as she entered the circle of
light from the lamp beside the bed. Kincaid's
curiosity was heightened.

"Here, drink." Coutard held the bottle against her lips and tilted her head back. Kincaid took in a sharp breath.

"How old is she?"

"She says twelve," Coutard replied, appraising the girl carefully. "I think she may be thirteen or fourteen. It's difficult to tell with these Norwegians. Do you mind if we—?" He indicated the empty bed, throwing off his lonely towel and pulling the girl onto the thick down mattress with him.

Kincaid responded, taking the champagne. He offered a swallow to Athéné, whose eyes had rolled up into their sockets. Kincaid's finger had brought her into a private world of her own.

Coutard and the child disappeared into the swan bed, lost to view entirely, their presence made known only by a series of cries, moans, and whimpered exclamations.

Kincaid pulled Athéné down next to him. She lay beside him on the floor, gasping and panting like a racehorse, her body drenched with perspiration, her arms outstretched, fingers flexing convulsively.

"Say it again," she whispered, as Kincaid's face hovered over hers. "Say it for the last time."

"You're a virgin," he whispered. She nodded in frenzied amusement as she drew him to her. The laugh ended in a high-pitched scream.

Above them they were vaguely aware of athletic thrashing on the bed and then Coutard's wail of disappointment.

"Damn! She's not twelve and she's not even a

virgin! Kincaid, I ask you as one man to another: is nothing sacred?"

* * *

Kincaid didn't know where he was, but the cab had obeyed instructions and was still waiting outside the "Higgy-Liffey." Since Coutard was still *engagé* (tearing the house apart to find the genuine article), Kincaid got in and told the driver to take him back to the Grand Hotel. The sun was not yet visible, but the sky had begun to lighten, a gauzy sick yellow beneath gray that promised moist heat for the day. He was exhausted by the night's activities and disagreeably surprised. It was not the sort of exercise that had drained him in the past. On the contrary, when he was younger, such exploits could have been depended upon to have refreshed him mightily. What was lacking? Youthful energy? Or had it been that mindless profligate whose company had so depressed him? Something had. Why, coupling with the notorious Athéné Moncreux, had his mind strayed to thoughts of Dolores Mendonça? He leaned back in the cab, unable to relax because of the bumps in the road, and watched the stray dogs scatter as vultures swooped over the city in the distance. It was their function in Manaus to feast on the mounds of garbage and rotting fish and fruit and help keep the city's diseases in check. He still couldn't countenance the beasts, remembering the ones who'd beat death wings over him when he'd lain half-conscious on a mesa in northern Mexico after being ambushed by a pack of bandits intent on separating him from his horse and boots.

He looked away from them now to the Swiss municipal clock balanced precariously on a column of rose and gray stone atop the Chamber of Commerce building, bleached pink and silver by the dim light, the carvings on the clock's tower as ornate as a Viennese dowager's last birthday cake.

The driver skirted the edges of the city, as the noise of the carriage was prohibited at such an early hour. The smell of rubber was locked in, pressed down by the night's mist and the rising sun, and heat released it like gas from a balloon.

The cab passed two stone buildings that leaned so much toward each other they almost met at the top. Cramped between them was a park, its grass dried yellow, caked with mud, the remains of a stone bench sprouting pale flowers from its cracks. Insects buzzed madly over the bodies of dead lizards. Two stray dogs, ribs showing through matted hair, looked hopelessly at the cab as it passed.

Kincaid turned his head away and closed his eyes until he smelled the pungency of the river. The cab was nearing the docks, passing enormous warehouses that stood open to the street. He asked the driver to stop and peered inside. The warehouses were filled with large, oblong wads of rubber, cured blackish-brown, called *peles*. They were shaped like the smoked hams he'd seen being cured in similar warehouses in Chicago. A breeze or a wave from the river hitting the bulwarks that held up the docks was enough to jiggle the *peles*, and they shivered as if alive.

Behind the warehouses, on the black river itself, Kincaid made out wide gray-brown mats that turned out to be the wads of rubber lashed together to float from the *estradas* downstream to the docks. They covered a surface area of the river as large as several warehouses combined, alive with flies and snakes and rats that jumped from the mats to the warehouses and back in gleeful sport. In the corner of the warehouses were coffin-shaped pine boxes marked for shipment to New York, Liverpool, and Le Havre. Kincaid told the driver to go on; the odor of rubber made him feel sick. He wondered what would happen to these warehouses, to these docks, to Manaus itself, when he had done what he came to do.

*　*　*

Bertram Longford, Englishman, botanist, and valet, had remained awake throughout the night, partially as an exercise in willpower (nocturnal alertness was something he was going to need), and also to make his report. He was reluctant to do this for many reasons, not the least of which was the tiresome necessity of encoding his message.

Finally, at four in the morning, he sat down at the Louis XIV desk in Kincaid's bedroom, took out a pen, put on his silver-rimmed spectacles, and leaned over a blank sheet of hotel stationery.

"Dearest Mother," he began (he had no mother): "I am sorry to have been so long in writing but we have been literally at sea and then a subsequent three weeks opposing the fearsome current of the mighty Amazon. I intended to post you a letter in Pará, informing you of our safe Atlantic crossing but foolishly neglected to prepare one and, as all my exertions were required by Mr. Kincaid in the somewhat cumbersome transfer of our luggage from the steamer to the yacht, I had not the time or the opportunity to dash off even a hasty epistle.

"Our voyage has been uneventful. I might bore you with descriptions of our fellow passengers aboard the *Saxonia* but I know you too well to try your patience with travelogues. Suffice to say my master and I are presently ensconced—as planned —at the Grand Hotel Internacional of this peculiar city, a bustling imitation of civilization, nestled in the heart of trackless wilderness. The people have, with great industry, fought off the natural tendency to torpor—induced, I am certain, by the stultifying heat which renders even thought an effort—and imported or rather I should say carved out for themselves a passable facsimile of a city of some thirty thousand, complete with shops, schools, trams (run by electricity!) and even, I am told, a magnificent opera house.

"If all goes well, my master should begin as-

sembling his orchids within the week. He appears
to be getting his bearings in this strange place,
though I must confess I find him singularly subdued" (Longford underlined this passage thrice),
"and not at all the man I took him to be when I
entered his service." (This, too, was underlined.)
"He seems oddly distracted from the day-to-day
concerns, the sights and sounds he would eagerly
have absorbed (I fancy) in his younger days. Perhaps it is nothing more than the onset of age—
though he cannot be forty-five—which gives him
a melancholy air. I hope and trust that his depres-
sion—I do not know what else to call it—will not
too greatly interfere with his orchid-gathering responsibilities. The Royal Geographic Society, I
have been told (by Mr. Kincaid, himself), is most
particular. He has assured me that orchid trans-
planting is a tricky business" (underlined). "I
earnestly hope that my master will recover something of his former nature, for without it I foresee
a dreary time of it and have the gravest doubts of
his being able to fulfill his obligations."

Here Longford laid aside his pen and, with a
scowl, reread his composition. Then, sighing, he
improvised another two pages in which he defer-
entially asked after his mother's health (describing in considerable detail four lurid complaints)
and then went on to assure her that he would look
up a certain Miss Harris—obviously employed
belowstairs, somewhere in the city, from his text—
and give her the best wishes of her cousin who
lived in Tunbridge Wells. He closed with the af-

fectionate remembrances of a dutiful son toward a doting, if somewhat cantankerous, parent, signed his name, and sealed the letter, feeling cautiously pleased with himself.

He had no sooner completed this task when the door to the suite was unlocked by an unsteady hand and Kincaid shuffled in.

Master and man regarded each other for some moments in silence, each exhausted from trials and tribulations of their own devising.

"The opera must have been a long one," Longford allowed, finally. "How was it?"

"None of the company was lost to yellow fever and that's about the best I can say for it," Kincaid returned. "It was not especially long, but it was followed by a lengthy—" He groped for the right word. "—interview with Athéné Moncreux."

"I've heard of her," Longford admitted, peering over the rims of his glasses.

"You've only heard of part of her," Kincaid began, pulling off his clothes. "The other part is worse. Or better, depending on your point of view." He walked toward his bedroom, his feet like weights tangled in seaweed, then stopped and turned back to Longford.

"How is it that you're awake at this hour? Couldn't sleep?"

"I never tried," Longford said with some pride.

"I'm not sure I follow you."

"I thought I ought to practice staying awake all night. It will come in handy shortly, won't it?"

Kincaid shook his head ruefully. "You mean you

could have slept and you chose to stay awake?
Professor, you amaze me."

"The feeling has always been mutual, Harry."
This was said with more emotion than Longford
intended. There was a silence between them again
during which each man's thoughts inevitably
drifted into the past. Kincaid, afraid of adding
sentimentality to his growing list of vices, cut the
mood short.

"You know, Professor, Captain Mactavish was
wrong about something. Macao is Coney Island
compared to Manaus. See you in the morning."

"It is morning, Harry." Longford indicated the
red glow of the window drape.

Kincaid cursed.

"And I've been invited to call on the old pirate
before noon."

"I'll wake you in a few hours, then, shall I?"

"I hate orchirds," Kincaid said and closed his
door.

*   *   *

Dolores Mendonça sat at her dressing table, staring mournfully into the mirror. Life, she decided,
heaving a theatrical sigh, had played her a rather
nasty trick; it had allowed her to see Paris. No, not
merely to see, but to revel in Paris, to drown in
Paris, to absorb the sights and sounds and ideas of
the most luminous place on earth.

And then life had forced her back to Manaus.
Oh, she didn't deny that she was glad to see her

father; she didn't pretend that she wasn't excited at the prospect of going home and seeing her friends again (and of turning them green with envy at her deportment and accomplishments, she half-acknowledged). But what had been the reality? Her true friends were all now living in Paris. The people and ideas she had left behind four years earlier now appeared hopelessly provincial, and boring. Of what use were her fine lessons, the books she had absorbed, the culture she had assimilated, the fashions she had anticipated? In Manaus, the *haute monde* inevitably trailed behind its Paris counterpart. The opera was a social chore rather than any kind of social or aesthetic joy. No one had heard of Pascal, let alone read him, to say nothing of the newer works that were setting the world on fire—*Madame Bovary*, for example, or the scandalous Zola. And after the initial joy of seeing familiar places and faces, of being clutched in her father's powerful embrace, now had descended a pall, black as doom. Even Manaus' idea of a Frenchman, Pierre Coutard, was, in her eyes, little more than a libertine—and a buffoon, at that. To be sure, she had enjoyed the ride home in the carriage, and felt very like a royal princess on its satin cushions, but the whole vulgarity of its purchase! The man's shameless ostentation!

Here Dolores colored. The first sight of Casa Grande the week before, with its architectural hodgepodge of wedding-cake icing, had filled her with embarrassment; no, shame!

Paris. Paris. Paris.

Dolores sighed and signaled for her maid to help her dress. She felt like the tragic and wonderful Marguerite Gautier in Dumas' *La Dame aux Camélias*, when she says to her maid, "A year ago today at this time we were still sitting around the table singing and laughing. . . . Where are the days when we still laughed?" The scene had caused her to weep at the Theâtre du Vaudeville, and now she understood poor Marguerite so much more clearly. She watched her own maid and toyed with the idea of repeating the speech to her. To have had something, some *joie*, and then, sadly, tragically, to lose it . . . Dolores sighed again. She was well named, she reflected, and wondered if all this sighing might not be the first sign of a cough.

Across the room, absorbed in her needlepoint, Dona Inês paid no attention to the barrage. Dolores' constant companion was among the most insensitive, unsusceptible souls on earth. Heavens, aunt, tatting! This is the nineteenth century, not the middle ages!

It was too horrible. All of it. Her father's fortunes seemed to her suddenly empty and trite. She shooed away her maid with an impatient gesture, finished adjusting the belt on her afternoon dress of lightweight mauve gabardine, slipped on the jacket although it was too hot, and sat down next to the window with a volume of Keats—who cared here that she was able to read him in the original? —and opened it to her favorite poem. He knew her so well, she felt, knew her intimate thoughts and expressed them so perfectly, with such beautiful sadness:

She dwells with Beauty—Beauty that must die;
   And Joy, whose hand is ever at his lips
Bidding adieu; and aching Pleasure nigh,
   Turning to poison while the bee-mouth sips:
Ay, in the very temple of Delight,
   Veil'd Melancholy has her sovran shrine,
     Though seen of none save him whose strenuous
     tongue
Can burst Joy's grape against his palate fine;
   His soul shall taste the sadness of her might,
    And be among her cloudy trophies hung.

Dolores wiped away a silent tear, prepared to sigh again, when the door was opened by her father. He took in the scene with a certain satisfaction: needlepoint and poetry. These, he reflected, were the proper occupations for ladies of good breeding, *not* sitting on podiums before a lot of staring conventioneers. His daughter, certainly, had changed enormously; he sensed, among other things, a subdued aspect which he was not entirely sure boded well. It was utterly uncharacteristic of the girl he had sent abroad for her education four years before, and he could not quite bring himself to believe that such an alteration was either natural or permanent. His sister, on the other hand, returned exactly as she had left: still sour, uncommunicative, and still intent on suffering forever the death of a husband she'd barely known, and whom, if truth be told, she had not even liked. Widowhood suited her personality; he had no doubt that she made a good, if sobering, companion to his daughter.

"Papa!" Dolores jumped up and ran to greet him with a kiss on each cheek, quite French. "Can we go for a drive? Will you take me out? Is there something I may do?"

"Did you enjoy the opera?" he inquired, leading her back to the window and sitting beside her.

"Not as much as the Paris production," she confessed. "Do you know, the ladies smoked cigarettes right on the stage!"

Mendonça, whose views on such things were well known, blanched and regarded his sister.

"I am beginning to think Inês did not look after you properly."

"She's too clever and impulsive for me by half," his sister responded, not looking up from her work.

"Are we to go out?" Dolores persisted, taking his hand.

"I am here to ask you a favor."

"Not a tiresome luncheon with one of your business associates," she begged. "What's the good of playing hostess for them? They can't tell squab from eel."

"Not a luncheon, though it may be tiresome. As I said, it is a favor. I have promised to show Mr. Kincaid, whom you met last night, my orchids. And now I find it is impossible for me to do so."

"And I am to show them to him?"

"I would be grateful if you would. I know you have your reading—" He gestured to the book she held, as if it were a sacred rite she had been performing.

"Of course, Papa," Dolores interrupted disconsolately, but already her mind was racing ahead. She had not forgotten this Mr. Kincaid. She had liked him. He had been to Europe, too, not like the boors who only spent months there to acquire enough polish to impress their neighbors in Manaus, and not like Pierre Coutard, who sought to dazzle her with four hundred pounds. An afternoon with Mr. Kincaid might be just the touch of culture for which she was looking.

"I will get ready," said her aunt, putting away her needlepoint.

Dolores could already feel a sigh coming on.

Kincaid wished he were somewhere else. The solarium was a blindingly bright room whose walls were narrow panels of frosted glass supported by curved cast-iron girders two stories high, so that the glass shot up the walls and loomed overhead. Since the room was bordered on two sides by the jungle, the impression Kincaid had was of being underwater, all foggy greens and murky browns of the trees filtered through the frosted panes.

It was an impression he could do without. His head felt as though an army were marching through it, back and forth on maneuvers. Any sudden turning caused the reverberations of a regiment of feet to throb against his temples. He sat immobile, awaiting the Colonel's pleasure, keeping his eyes on the brilliant white tile floors, along which two tiny white French poodles slipped and slid and tapped telegraphic noises with their nails. To Kincaid it sounded like snare drums. He closed his eyes.

Minutes passed. Finally, with a grunt of determination, Kincaid forced himself to study the list of orchids the Royal Geographic Society had assembled for him. The Latin swam before his vision.

Footsteps approached. Kincaid looked up, prepared to see the craggy old man.

It was Dolores who entered the solarium, followed by her aunt, in black rustling taffeta. The poodles commenced jumping at Dolores' dress, yipping wildly.

"Good morning, Senhor Kincaid." She extended her hand. "I trust you slept well? Pay them no mind, *senhor*. I brought them from Paris and they dote on me."

Kincaid mumbled something about being able to see why, but didn't know if he had made himself audible. The unexpected sight of her, so crisp and brisk and perfect, was worse than the sunlight streaming down, which had the effect of illuminating her like a piece of stained glass from Chartres.

"My father sends you a thousand apologies; his schedule has undergone some alterations, which make it impossible for him to personally conduct you through his collection."

"Shall it be another day, then?" Kincaid strove to

keep the annoyance from his voice. Another day; another delay; inwardly he cursed Mendonça for failing to send a message canceling the appointment. He could have slept off the marching armies.

"Not at all," Dolores was saying with a brilliant smile. "My father has deputized me to be your guide. I importune you to let me show you our magnificent specimens. This does not displease you?"

Even through the fog of his hangover, Kincaid recognized the dripping conceit of the remark. She had not, he realized—headache lifting—forgotten their idle flirtation of the evening before. Now, trapped for a day of orchid-gathering with this woman, Kincaid rued his dalliance with her at the opera house. The one thing he was sure he did not need was a distraction like Dolores Mendonça. And, though it was not a thought he articulated to himself, it was also true that he resented her assurance, her smug satisfaction with her looks and continental education. He determined, dully, to ignore her charms, not to feed her hungry ego. Let her find some other man, some local swain to play with. He would not have his bones bleached white on the altar of her vanity, to say nothing of letting her whims distract him from his purposes.

"I am not at all displeased," he told her, his voice utterly devoid of coquetry, "only impatient to begin."

She narrowed her eyes slightly at this, shrugged mentally, and, presenting her aunt to him again, led them from the solarium, walking at a too rapid pace, seizing a parasol which she flicked against her dress like a riding crop. The doting poodles were left behind, leaping and scratching at the glass walls. Kincaid wondered if their mistress missed Paris half as much as they did.

Outside, a group of Indians carrying Kincaid's equipment for transplantation awaited their pleasure. With Dolores in the lead, the group made its way across an open expanse of lawn where the jungle had been cleared: a croquet field. The outdoor heat was unbearably heavy; Kincaid's temples began to throb again; aftershocks.

On the far side of the manicured lawn, the jungle awaited them. Kincaid at first supposed the girl proposed leading them directly into an impenetrable wall of green, but as they approached the foliage he was startled—and relieved—to see an opening, the beginning of a path. Dolores, turning round, read his mind.

"What you are about to see is not quite the real jungle, *senhor*. This orchid plantation is not thirty years old. Still, I daresay, you will find it wild enough."

"I daresay," muttered Dona Inês, hobbling after her. Kincaid followed suit. Abruptly the green wall engulfed them and all was dark. She was right, he realized, reluctantly admiring; it was quite wild enough. He had been in other jungles, in Africa, mainly, but had never had quite this sense of being overpowered. The trees leaned at all angles. The ground was covered with enormous twisting roots. Huge, thick vines with immense leaves crawled up tree trunks, securely wrapped. Palm leaves forty feet long jutted out like canopies. Banyan trees dripped branches like rain, which rooted and formed new trunks. Occasionally Kincaid noticed a tiny pool of water but it looked less refreshing than diseased, covered with thick layers of slime and hovered over by swarms of mosquitoes. Every once in a while a bit of sun was reflected on a leaf or on a drop of moisture and startled the eye. Otherwise, there was no sun, but a diffused greenish light. There was a quality of the grotesque. Everything was outsized, overlarge; plants lived among other plants in maniacal harmony, feeding off each other, twisted together as if there were not enough room to give each species its own space. The sensation of green everywhere was maddening; the endlessness and sameness began to affect Kincaid's depth perception. A path had been cut and maintained, however, so that walking through the green labyrinth was not difficult. Ahead of him, Dolores was prattling on and he quickened his pace to hear her. She was flirting again, and Kincaid realized with a start that his attitude of diffidence was responsible. She was unaccustomed to it. It intrigued and provoked her more than any forwardness on his part would have done. He toyed with the idea of throwing himself at her feet right there on the jungle floor, shrieking oaths of passion, but decided against it; too much running hot and cold would rattle her hopelessly —himself as well, in all likelihood.

"—My father has promised to clear some of this

and build a tennis court for me. Do you play tennis, *senhor?*"

"I'm afraid not."

"Oh, but you must learn! It is the rage in Paris.
I even bought a new tennis dress from Madame
de Rochas. Now father will have to build the tennis court."

"Miss Mendonça?"

She turned and walked backwards in front of
him, cocking her head as if his question would be
difficult to hear unless she assumed an attitude of
listening. "Yes, Senhor Kincaid?"

"The orchids?"

She hesitated, then turned quickly, petulantly,
and gestured widely with both arms, the parasol
now an arrow. "They are all around you. Shall I
point them out one by one?"

Kincaid looked at the jungle mass on either side
of the path, peering in search. He had never
seen orchids in the wild, only artificially maintained in London's Botanical Gardens and in the
greenhouses of the Royal Geographic. He knew
orchids did not all grow in terra cotta pots or on
ladies' bodices, but how they did grow was rather
unclear to him except from what he had read. But
now that he began to look for them, they seemed
to jump out at him. They were the only spots of
color in the relentless greenery. Suddenly they
were ubiquitous. From a pile of rocks and moss
shot a brilliant spot of red. Lavender and white
petals burst from a mossy growth on a tree trunk.

Orchids sprang from trees that had fallen over. Some had climbed so high they were unreachable, while others were at eye level or lower. Mostly the orchids were nestled in the crook of two branches of a tree in what looked like birds' nests, or they adhered at some point to the trunk, sometimes one flower, one startling bloom; other times dozens of tiny flowers on incredibly long stems appeared to be suspended in mid-air. The roots of the orchids were yards and yards long, twisting snakelike around tree trunks. Mold and moss grew over these roots and the flowers burst out at the end. There was a feeling of strangulation, the tree trunks being the host to the orchid roots.

An enormous iridescent blowfly dove past Kincaid's face as he reached up to cup a startling white flower.

"Cattleya superba" he exclaimed, sniffing with dramatic admiration. "A magnificent specimen." He waved his hand and signaled the waiting Indians. One came forward, dug carefully at the base of the plant so as to obtain sufficient quantity of root, and transplanted the flower, complete with the mossy nest, into one of the leather boxes. When sealed, the box preserved the plant's natural moisture until it could be put in the hothouse on board the *Mãe de Deus*. The moss would die, but that was good; its relation to the orchid was parasitic, draining the plant of water and nutrients.

When the uprooting had been accomplished, the Indian strapped the box to his back, marking it with chalk to indicate it was filled, and rejoined his companions, each of whom carried several similar containers.

Well satisfied with the procedure, Kincaid, without further preamble, plunged into the work, checking his list, marshaling his forces, and ignoring the girl and her aunt, except to ask her questions of a technical nature. Dolores began by resenting this but grudgingly came to admire Kincaid's thoroughness and absorption. She liked his face, had never seen one quite like it before, and was content to watch it. It was seamed and scarred; prematurely aged, branded with secrets and wisdom, she decided. The hours went by; her patience deserted her again and she answered his questions tersely, volunteering no pleasantries or attempts at levity. Really, the man was exasperating.

From a rocky section of jungle Kincaid secured most of the *Cattleya* specimens he had come for: *Cattleya amethystoglossa, granulosa, elongata, forbesii, schilleriana, intermedia;* plus rarer specimens of *Epidendrum atropurpureum, frangrans, cochleatum, ciliare, stamfordianum, ibaguense, Coronatum, Schlechterianum,* and *difforme;* and *Laelia purpurata,* which, Dolores explained, her father was promoting as the national flower of Brazil. Kincaid took this one and handed it to her. She perked up at the gesture and put it behind her ear.

"Do I look like Carmen?" she asked and laughed. Abruptly, the jungle darkened as if the sun above it had literally fallen, and a thunderous booming began. Kincaid was startled, but then the heavy rain hit him, explaining the roar. Dolores, enjoying the excuse, drew him beneath a fern the size of an elephant's ear. For ten minutes they stood beneath the drooping leaves, silent because the noise made speech impossible.

But Dolores knew a language that required no words. She had taken out her fan and the gestures she used to signal with it spoke worlds: she was shy; she was attracted, she was untouched; she was available.

Kincaid had no great difficulty in understanding this language. It alternately amused and infuriated him that she presumed to manipulate him so. But he was neither insensitive nor immune to Dolores, especially standing so close that he had no choice but to inhale her perfume. He stole a glance at Dona Inês, sheltered beneath another elephant's ear, not ten feet away and watching them like a hawk. Why tempt Providence? This child, this woman, this—whatever she was—was the daughter of a father so potent that one word from her or her chaperone might end more than his mission. Kincaid stood next to her, reminding himself of these realities, but her nearness made him dizzy, jumbled his thoughts. She was so close he had only to shift his weight from one foot to the other and their flanks would be touching. He felt himself drowning in her; wanting to drown. In another few seconds . . .

The downpour ceased as abruptly as it had

commenced; a few wedges of sun filtered through
the dripping fronds, celestial and blue as the
moon. A rainbow appeared between two trees.
The sun was a spot of crystal and flame; the silence
was deafening. Dolores studied Kincaid's face,
searching for a clue and only losing herself in the
enigma. Certainly, she told herself, she had met
more handsome men, and it wasn't merely Kincaid's European sophistication that had captured
her imagination and excited her fancy. She felt like
Desdemona and saw in him a kind of Othello, a
warrior who had seen the world, who had tales to
tell, more interesting even than the dandies she
had encountered in the salons of Paris.

And suddenly it seemed to her that he was
responding. His eyes widened as she stared at him,
and she saw golden flecks deep in the pools of
brown. Her heart beat hard, a line of perspiration
broke out on her upper lip. She had read about
this, she knew what this was:

> ... two fair creatures, couchèd side by side
> In deepest grass, beneath the whisp'ring roof
> Of leaves and trembled blossoms, where there
> ran
> A brooklet, scarce espied ...

She leaned towards him slowly, dreaming; she
was dreaming.

"*Dolores!*"

Her eyes opened and she saw her aunt splashing
energetically toward her, almost as though Dona
Inês had abruptly divined her innermost thoughts.

Dolores looked forlornly at Kincaid; without intending it, her flirtation had become—something else.

"It is time to go back," she said, softly; subdued. Kincaid could only nod dumbly and wish it were possible. He signed to the Indians and the party returned to the house. They parted at the solarium; she gave him her hand and he kissed it. Dolores looked at her hand and could still feel the hot imprint of his lips.

"It's been a pleasure," Kincaid told her, and beat a swift retreat down the corridor that led to the front of the house, where his carriage waited to take him and his flowers to the boat. But he wasn't fast enough, Dolores thought, eyes shining, as she watched him go. Her heart was already in the carriage, waiting.

❧ 7 ❧

No sunlight penetrated to the jungle floor, trapped in the fantastic overhang. A silent stream rose from the ground. Silence was broken by the insistent shriekings of birds and howler monkeys, then fell again, tomblike, as Colonel Mendonça traversed his rubber *estradas* on horseback. He rode without apparent direction, crossing streams and swamps, following the lanes of rubber trees. As he had done since he was a young man, the Colonel came here to think.

The rubber trees were strange and fruitful inhabitants of the jungle, their silver bark more like English ash than something that would thrive in the tropics. The tree trunks, ordinarily no bigger around than a man's waist, swelled to grotesque bloated shapes after being tapped. In the hazy morning light the Colonel saw the trees glow as if lit from inside, shooting as high as a hundred feet into the overhang. The flowers that blossomed white in the summer were memory now. The nuts were ripe though, and in the night and early morning he would lie in his bed and listen to them burst with the sharp explosiveness of rifle fire, tossing so many seeds on the jungle floor that as a young man he had gathered enough in one night to fill furrows for over a hundred acres of land.

The Colonel gazed at his trees as he rode, wild things that would take twenty years from seed to tapping. The tally calmed him; there was time yet. There were enough trees and enough rubber to last forever.

He approached a group of *seringueiros* at their day's work and stopped to watch them. They did not speak to him or to each other; their only sound was the clatter of tin cups slung on their belts to gather liquid latex. Each man was dressed similarly in white *mate* shirt, white shorts, hat, and shoes made by a wife or a daughter from dried palm fronds. Across his shoulders, each carried a gourd of lemon water and a long-handled *machadinho* to do the cutting. Colonel Mendonça also supplied each *seringueiro* with the means to protect himself since the fighting had begun: a rifle hung across every back.

Already exhausted by the heat of early morning, the men walked slowly, but they would toil until they had fulfilled their daily quota. The latex had coagulated on the incisions they had made the day before and the beautiful silver bark was scarred and warty, its smooth surface a mass of festering sores. Some of the trees had cups hanging to catch the yellow sap that oozed from closed cuts and would be sold as scrap or second-grade rubber. It was the custom on Colonel Mendonça's *estradas* for the *seringueiros* to reopen these old wounds, slicing into the smooth bark until latex appeared again like an enormous white tear.

The Colonel mused on the fact that these men did not know him; scarcely remarkable, as they had never set eyes on him before. Nor he on them, for that matter. In any case he could not be expected to remember; ten thousand like these— no, *more* than ten thousand—to the north, the east, and the west did his bidding. He had never laid eyes on most of them. Did a king know all his subjects?

Although flies buzzed and parrots shrieked and monkeys whistled and the *machadinhos* made sharp biting noises into the bark of the rubber trees, there was still a quality of silence. The Colonel felt it as the majesty of his land. His thoughts strayed far back to the days when he had been unfettered by the responsibilities of owning it. He had had nothing; he was poor; he starved; and now he had everything. Everything. And all he needed to keep it was to end this war or eliminate Coutard.

He knew how to do it. He had figured it out. The plan was frighteningly simple and yet brilliant as a stroke of lightning. It appalled him, but as he turned the matter over in his mind and forced himself to examine his position, he knew he had no choice. If he would keep his land, the labor and meaning of his life, then he must sacrifice the other.

A shudder wracked his frame, a sob that became a cough.

His thoughts were interrupted by the sound of another horse coming through the brush, rustling and snapping branches. His cough expanded as he reined his mount; he felt as though a *machadinho* had hacked directly into his breast. When he looked up Iquitos was there.

"Are you . . . ?"

The Colonel waved away his concern with a gesture that ended by covering his mouth. When the spasm subsided he faced the Indian squarely in the saddle.

"You had him followed—the Yanqui?"

"He has spent most of the time in his hotel," Iquitos answered, consulting a paper. "He has drunk three decanters' worth of bourbon, though his manservant may have drunk some also."

The Colonel waited impatiently.

"He went to the opera with Torres—that you know—and afterwards accompanied Coutard on a tour of the brothels."

Mendonça scowled. "Go on."

"Afterwards he rode past the docks on the way back to his hotel. He slept a few hours, then came to you, and your daughter showed him the orchids. Would you care for the list of species he transplanted?"

The Colonel shook his head. "He behaved properly with her?"

"Quite properly. Your sister's presence no doubt

had its effect, but in my opinion it was superfluous." Iquitos restrained himself from reporting what he had witnessed of Dolores' behavior. He had not been asked that.

The Colonel leaned against the pommel of his saddle, scrunching the reins in his fists. "Where is he now?"

"He took the orchids to load them onto the boat. Later he will return to the hotel." Iquitos hesitated.

"Well? He seems harmless enough." Iquitos remained silent; his expression darkened. "Very well, keep him under surveillance for a day or two more, if it makes you happy."

Iquitos smiled faintly. "Just to be sure, sir."

Mendonça stared at him, proud of the man he had created. He wanted badly to take Iquitos into his confidence and tell him of the brilliant, the appalling plan, but he did not. When all was said and done, Mendonça trusted no one. And perhaps, as well, he did not want to see the look in the Indian's eyes when he heard. He would know soon enough, at all events.

"You have done well, Iquitos."

Without looking back, the Colonel dug his heels into the flanks of his horse and rode off into the jungle.

*　　*　　*

Though not quite five years old, the *Mãe de Deus* already possessed a checkered and colorful history. She had been designed by Colton Rarefoot of the British firm of Jasper, Rarefoot, and Creel. This firm was not as prestigious as the great George Watson, who was the *ne plus ultra* in steam-yacht design, but the man who commissioned the boat, Sir Edward Cambray, was not as prestigious as, say, the Duke of Westminster. Others, even those men in trade like Singer and Guinness, were building steam yachts in the middle of the nineteenth century. Sir Edward did the best he could and though he had to scrimp on the flourishes and scrollwork, the *Angel of the Seas,* as the boat was originally named, was eminently seaworthy.

Whereas many of the great steam yachts of the era were built as second or third homes, used for long Atlantic crossings or Mediterranean voyages, the *Angel of the Seas* proved to be infinitely more of a good sport. Her size and the careful attention to construction helped a great deal. Her body had been built by Edgewater and Sons, Seacombe, but unlike Lord Tipton, Sir Edward was not interested in a yacht whose steam engines supplemented her sails. A progressive seaman, he eschewed the notion that a ship without sails was like a ship without a rudder. And while most steam yachts were built for luxury, with little effort put forth into developing high power or speed, Sir Edward was interested in both and advised the firm of John Brown and Sons, Clydebank, accordingly. Cornelius Vanderbilt, J. P. Morgan, Jay Gould, and several Astors might not be in a particular hurry to get anywhere, but Sir Edward was.

Thus, at the same time the hull of the *Angel of the Seas* was being hand-sanded at Seacombe, the most advanced developments in the field of steam locomotion were being incorporated into her design at Clydebank. Her engines were masterworks of hand crafting: hand-turned, hand-fitted, hand-polished. In addition, the *Angel of the Seas* boasted a boiler functional up to one hundred and eighty pounds of pressure per square inch, and though she had but one propeller, there were few ships of her size and tonnage who could catch her if her captain threw the stanchions to FULL AHEAD.

Upon completion of her sea trials in early 1872 off the Scottish coast, the *Angel of the Seas*, under Sir Edward's aegis, made a trip around the world, causing heads to turn in the harbors of Bombay, Hong Kong, and San Francisco. A year later she made three successive voyages to the eastern United States and to the West Indies. On the last of these Caribbean sojourns, Sir Edward learned at Trinidad that he had been named to a minor post in the Prime Minister's latest coalition. The position held prospects of advancement and might well serve as a stepping stone to greater triumphs—Home Secretary?—and Sir Edward did not hesitate. He sold the *Angel of the Seas*, his pride and joy, to Pacheco y Riberio, a Brazilian exporter who had made his fortune in not quite legal archaeological digs, and who purchased the craft impulsively as a gift for his wife's mother. Riberio changed the yacht's name to the *Mãe de Deus*, but that was as far as he got. Before leaving Trinidad with his extravagant present, he entered a poker game, where, as the night drew on, it became apparent he was severely overmatched. Before dawn he had lost the *Mãe de Deus* to a vacationing American industrialist, J. C. Forbes, who was himself bankrupt less than two months later. A British creditor of Forbes took the *Mãe de Deus* off his hands at an incredible bargain. An amateur botanist as well as sailor, he gutted the dining salon and refitted the space as a hothouse to store specimens secured from the coasts of France, Portugal, Greece, and North Africa.

A year or so later, a heart condition made it advisable for Forbes' creditor to stay close to home. Being himself a member of the Royal Geographic Society, he generously donated the uniquely qualified vessel to continue her botanical endeavors in the service of that august body. And the Royal Geographic permanently relocated the *Mãe de Deus* in South America, where, under Captain Mactavish and assorted visiting botanists, the ship enjoyed a leisurely life of backwater research.

In the present instance, the duties of the *Mãe de Deus* were to include work of a clandestine character heretofore unexampled in her brief but crowded career. Her great speed, until recently of no great consequence in the eyes of her present owners, abruptly recommended itself as an inval-

uable asset and Kincaid, from London, had given
orders that her engines be retuned, the position
of her ballast checked in the hold, and all other
arrangements deemed necessary to the yacht's op-
timum performance be made. In addition, Longford cabled instructions to Captain Mactavish in
Pará, advising him of certain modifications to be
made in the hothouse. No explanation was given.
If the Society wished the *Mãe de Deus* to carry
banana leaves packed in earth up the Amazon—
like coals to Newcastle, Mactavish thought—it was
the Captain's business to carry them. The banana
leaves were packed as directed.

It was now late afternoon. Longford, on the
boat, had occupied himself as befitted a valet, in
checking his master's accommodations and prepar-
ing a change of clothes for him when he arrived,
dripping from his jungle excursion. The docks were
crowded with boats of all shapes and sizes, the
water sizzled in the heat, murky, brown, thick as
molasses, alive with fish that were nearly phos-
phorescent and flies that buzzed on the surface.
Everywhere Longford looked on shore, something
or someone was for sale. The brightness of the
colors in the heat assaulted the eye and finally,
used to the primmer grays and demurer browns
and quieter sounds of London, he decided to go
below. He was studying Mactavish's river charts
when he heard the tramp of feet overhead.

Rolling up the charts and replacing them carefully, Longford hastened up the companionway to
greet Kincaid, who nodded to him curtly as he

directed his troop of Indian bearers, with their cargo of transplanted orchids. Forming a line down the companionway that led directly to the hothouse, Kincaid supervised the penultimate transplantation of the flowers from their leather carrying pouches into the moist dark hothouse earth, ready to receive them. Longford yearned with a professional's ardor and curiosity to see what had been collected. He was himself no inconsiderable authority on the subject of orchids. But he stifled the impulse to crowd the hothouse with his presence. After all, he was only a valet and had no business gaping at his master's acquisitions. Besides, there would be ample opportunity for examining the flowers after the Indians had left. In fact, he would probably be delegated to uprooting them.

When the last of the pouches had been unloaded, Kincaid assembled the Indians and thanked them in broken Spanish. Since the only tongue they understood was a bastardized regional version of Portuguese, they failed to comprehend a word, but by his smiles and nods they divined that Kincaid was pleased with their work. In addition, Kincaid scribbled a florid note of thanks and handed it to one of them, making it plain beyond all doubt that it was to be delivered to Colonel Mendonça.

"And that is that," Longford remarked, leaning next to Kincaid on the rail and watching the Indians descend the gangway.

"So far so good," Kincaid agreed. "Next time, I'll

see if I can get them to leave the pouches instead of taking them below. That way we won't have to make a continual display of our hothouse, in case they've been ordered to report to anyone. They've seen it; we've got orchids in there." He paused and lit a cigar.

"I've got fresh clothes for you below," Longford informed him.

"Good, I could use a change. But I'll need these again. Have them cleaned."

"Certainly," Longford replied dryly, following him down the companionway.

Kincaid unbuttoned his soggy collar while Longford sat on the edge of his berth and watched the transformation.

"Everything appears to be proceeding smoothly."

Kincaid grunted. "We haven't got to the hard part yet."

There was silence.

"How is our fuel supply?"

"Inadequate, if we were to . . . why do you ask?" Longford felt his throat tightening. "Did something go wrong?"

Kincaid hesitated, thinking about what almost did. "Not a thing, Professor. I just like to cover all my bets."

"We can't refuel yet," Longford protested. "We've only just arrived. People might wonder; it might excite comment."

Kincaid considered this, leaving his clothes in a dank heap where they fell. "All right; we'll be men of leisure. I'm going to have a shower, first." He started out but stopped, seeing that Longford made no move to rise from his position on the edge of the berth, but sat mournfully staring into space.

"Have you ever met Gordon?" Kincaid asked, standing naked at the door to the shower. Longford looked up and shook his head. "Well, I have, as you know. And I can tell you on personal authority that before any sort of action, if the General is nervous, he has two remedies."

Longford said nothing. Kincaid stepped into the shower stall, an ingenious device that sluiced water in a revolving bucketmill and dumped it into a large tub that had its bottom pierced to serve as a drain.

"I'll tell you what they are," Kincaid pursued, grinning. "Perhaps one of them will be of use to you."

"Very well."

"Very well. Before action, General Gordon likes to read the Bible. Don't look so astonished; for all I know it works. It certainly has the effect of calming him. He likes to read the Bible."

Longford smiled reluctantly.

"Then I have ten hours or so to read. What else does Gordon like before action?"

Kincaid's grin broadened. "Little boys."

The water whooshed down.

* * *

At night the jungle air moved in blocks, carrying smells of sweat and sugarcane rum and overripe fruit and roasting coffee, and because there was only darkness for context and nothing to see, the smell of rubber permeated it all with an undertaste of kerosene. Colonel Armando Mendonça sat waiting at his desk, pale beneath the sun ruddiness of his complexion, a quavering looseness about his eyes and mouth that had not been there even a year ago. He wore a heavy brocade robe and silk ascot; both appeared to have outgrown him. He was waiting for his daughter.

He had come to Manaus when it was little more than a straggling settlement from a jungle village also on the banks of the Amazon, but in Peru. He knew the river and the jungle before everything else. His first wife and his son had died hungry, the victims of the climate and Mendonça's poverty. He did not marry again for many years, and when he did so, he had amassed a fortune that made starvation a vague memory. He held a territory twice the size of his closest rival's, half of it laden with rubber trees, and had sixty million American dollars besides. Yet neither land nor gold nor Mendonça's self-proclaimed title could prevent the death of his second wife. She died a few days after giving birth to his only surviving child. He loved the girl from the first, but fatherhood was not natural to him. He did the best he could with the help of his widowed sister, but his influence on his daughter was erratic, distant and forbidding, so preoccupied was he with his own fortunes and those of the city he was creating.

For Manaus, a disorganized and haphazard collection of huts built on the remains of a sixteenth-century Portuguese fort, was becoming a city. Colonel Mendonça sat on committees with State Governor Eduardo Ribeiro and agreed to a twenty percent export tax on every kilo of rubber. Manaus would see four million dollars on that alone. The money began to trickle and then to pour in. Mendonça watched the first street to be widened to one hundred feet and his heart swelled with pride. He nodded his approval to Ribeiro's plan to construct the city on an east-west gridiron and was present at the ceremony that replaced smoky kerosene street lamps with the brand-new incandescent lamps. In late-night suppers at the infamous nightclub called Fer-de-lance, he and Ribeiro and the Frenchman Jacques Coutard and others envisioned a new city and he saw their visions come to be in hospitals and churches and banks of office buildings. In the middle of the century the Colonel smiled when he saw the artist's conception of the Palace of Justice and twelve years later wept as his friend Coutard cut the ribbon at the entrance. He had come to see the Amazon hold the world monopoly on wild rubber—two million square miles, 300 million virgin trees. Every year the world discovered new uses for the magical substance and Manaus was the monopoly.

But something had gone wrong. In the rush to be rich by rubber, thousands of men flooded the town of Manaus every week. The lure of riches was even greater than in the goldfields of California. An American czar of industry had remarked sadly: "I ought to have chose rubber." Greed ate its way through the city and the Colonel's dream of paradise faded. Ribeiro was dead, having swallowed his tongue in a fit of sexual ecstasy; the Colonel's old friend and rival, Jacques Coutard, had died and left all his land and rubber dealings foolishly, sentimentally, to his son Pierre, and Pierre was a wastrel who knew only Polish whores and dinner parties for five hundred. Together with his sister, he had broken the rules of his father's civilization. Still wearing the silk suits and satin manners he had acquired in Paris, young Coutard brought the anarchy of the jungle into the streets and council rooms.

Colonel Mendonça disinclined to trample the son of his friend. It was a costly hesitation and he was dimly aware of its origins. Nevertheless, he hesitated and told himself he was too old to fight (which was not true) and too proud to yield (which was). The dam would not burst while he lived. The power would be shared or all would be destroyed.

Dolores was late. Mendonça could not restrain a smile; no doubt fashionably late. To pass the time, and to nerve himself for the ordeal, he focused his attention again on the papers before him, computing aloud the damage done by the attacks of Coutard's army. Again he estimated the probable costs of future attacks and future retaliation on his part. The figures were astronomical—but not impossible. If only he had the time. But the tickling beginnings of a cough deep in his chest reminded him that he did not.

There was a knock on the study door.

"Come."

She entered, dressed for bed, wearing a lace nightgown from Brussels and a robe of cashmere so fine it showed the eyelets of the lace. She carried a book, her finger marking the page.

"You wished to see me, Papa?"

He nodded heavily, not moving, and waved her to the feathered hammock, strung between the tall open windows of the study, where he usually took his siesta. She walked obediently across the room and flounced into it, waiting until he should choose to speak. The hammock swung back and forth briefly, then settled. Mendonça bent over his calculations again, checking for the last time, reviewing to be quite certain. Then he looked up, saw her looking placidly back, and smiled.

"What do you read?"

"Poetry. Would you like me to read some to you?"

"Later, perhaps."

Another pause. He did not know where or how to begin. "You had a pleasant day?"

"Quite pleasant. Senhor Kincaid is . . ." She searched for the words. "—quite interesting." She smiled. Her father did not return the smile.

"How interesting?"

"Oh." She shrugged and glanced at the ceiling. "It is difficult to say. Interesting." She looked at her father, unable to suppress a giggle that set the hammock in motion, ever so slightly.

The Colonel sat back in his chair and watched her, pleased to observe in her the beauty and spirit of his dead wife. It could have been twenty-five years earlier. It could have been his wife swaying gently in that feathered hammock, humming softly to herself. Outside, behind her, birds rustled the trees and the smell of the earth was rich and heady in the damp night heat—as it had been so many years ago.

"The Yanqui may be in the pay of Coutard," Mendonça hazarded gruffly. Dolores' clear, bell-like laughter made him wince.

"Oh, but you can't think anything of the kind! He is so different from—from all the men I have met since my return. So—European, refined and yet experienced in the ways of—" She caught herself mirrored in her father's steadfast gaze and stopped. "I like him," she concluded lamely.

"Do not like him," Mendonça commanded quietly, rising at last from his chair and walking toward her. "I have other plans for you and they do not include Yanqui adventurers." A terrible and unexpected cough arrested his progress across the room. He staggered back to the desk. Dolores leaped up to go to him but he waved her brusquely away, pulling a handkerchief from the sleeve of his robe and wiping the cold sweat from his face and the blood from his lips.

"Let me ring for tea," she protested, alarmed by the seizure. "And then I will read to you—"

"Be still," he gasped. Her innocence agitated him more than his illness. Moments went by as she stared; all that could be heard besides the distant nighttime sounds of the jungle was the wheezing breath of Armando Mendonça, lord of the Amazon, as he struggled for air.

"The time has come," her father recommended at length, "to deal with Coutard. To fight him will destroy us both . . . and take longer than I will live." This last he added with a little laugh that provoked a new fit of coughing.

Dolores sank back onto the edge of the hammock, her temples pounding. How could she have failed to realize, even to consider the fact of her father's being seriously unwell? The cough—she had grown so accustomed to it since her return (and to his protestations of health). But wasn't it —she now admitted—an excuse for her own selfishness and frivolity, an excuse to ignore, an excuse not to confront a dread reality?

Dolores took a breath and made an effort to gather her wits. Her father was waiting. She knew better now than to nurse his distress. She forced herself instead to stick to the subject. "But they have tried before, those pirates . . ."

"Do not use the word pirate loosely, my dear," the Colonel said, smiling, pleased that she was with him now. "My only claim to legitimacy is simply that I was here first and took most. Like Coutard's father. But young Coutard is more than a pirate. He is greedy. He must not only have my land, he will raise the export tax. He is a blackmailer. But the buyers will not be blackmailed. They will take steps, they will send soldiers, they will find the means to coerce. They are better not provoked. But I cannot make him realize that . . . and my time is running out."

"But—"

"Hear me!" the Colonel shouted, his anger not so much at Coutard as at the specter of death that would most certainly defeat him in any battle. He might win if he played with Coutard, but no matter what happened, he would die. "When I am gone, only you will be left to deal with him and prevent the prices from rising." He stood uncertainly, holding himself erect against the desk. He was a massive man who had shrunk inside his body and now he looked at his healthy young daughter with a mixture of admiration, envy, and grief. "Only you. And look at you! Why did I obey your mother's dying request and send you to Europe when it was here I needed you most? Instead of learning how to rule in my place I have taught you to read" —he gestured clumsily to the hammock where the book remained—"poetry; to be a lady." His words trailed off and he sat down heavily again.

Dolores walked to the window and looked out at the jungle. In the near distance a few candles were lit in her father's greenhouse. There was a peacefulness here she felt slipping away, powerless to prevent its loss.

"But Senhor Kincaid—"

"Forget him. It is impossible."

"I don't understand." She whirled petulantly and faced him. "Coutard is a fool, a country lout in city clothes—Iquitos knows what must be done; he will help me—"

A gnarled hand halted her in midsentence. "When I die, Iquitos will count his life in hours, make no mistake. Coutard *is* a fool, but he is not weak. And he is the pawn of his sister—who is by no means a fool." He ran out of breath and his voice trailed off into a whispered gasp. "Between them, they are not afraid to be ruthless. They are what I was, once." This last was uttered without regret or other emphasis. If he had his strength he would crush them as indifferently as they now proposed to destroy him. "Ruthless," he repeated the word faintly.

Dolores could not bear to look at him or to hear the self-pity and frustration in his words.

"We must be prepared to make sacrifices," he said and tears filled his eyes.

"Sacrifices?" Dolores echoed in a small voice. "What do you mean?"

He began to walk toward her, eyes intent on hers, head nodding slowly, and Dolores felt afraid. The closer he came the more frightened she was, and when he touched her arm she let out an involuntary gasp, as if her flesh had been burned. At that moment, she understood.

❊ 8 ❊

The Royal Geographic Society of Great Britain was nothing if not thorough, Kincaid reflected. It was not its habit to fit out expeditions of exploration in a haphazard or slipshod manner, and it financed and otherwise promoted a number of expeditions. A great many of these endeavors found their way into the headlines of newspapers and the pages of history books; the historic journey of Richard Burton and John Hanning Speke to discover the source of the Nile was typical of the Society in its earnestly inquisitive and, above all, scientific vein. Men of intelligence, dispassionately seeking knowledge.

But there were other expeditions. With the untimely death of the Prince Consort, some of these less than dispassionate facets of the Society gained a dominance in the general proceedings. Not in public, of course; not in the newspapers and history books. The Society retained its image, or did its best to retain it. There was no hint of the influence of Victorian capitalists behind its imposing teak doors, nor of the less savory intrigues and missions that these gentlemen discreetly promoted. When objections were raised—on occasion there were those who voiced scruples—it was sometimes sufficient to point out that the matter in hand had the blessings of Her Majesty.

Kincaid's peculiar project had not been brought to Her Majesty's attention. It had, however, been discussed with the Prince of Wales, and it carried his august seal of approval. An enthusiastic endorsement. Edward had, in point of fact, endorsed the proposal thrice since 1865; the Society had thrice mounted attempts on Manaus, and on the previous two occasions the result had been disaster. In 1866 an attempt was made by a Dutch diplomat—not a professional (and so, reasoned the Society, likely to be above suspicion)—who disappeared without a trace. In the fall of 1871, the Victorian capitalists tried again, this time paying an exorbitant fee to an Irishman, who was in turn betrayed by his native accomplice and summarily executed without trial by the irate citizens of Manaus, whose written and unwritten law, whose one inviolate statute he had attempted to traduce.

In neither case did the Society essay rescue or even acknowledge its participation in events.

It merely tried again, this time employing the services of the controversial Kincaid, sending along its own expert masquerading as his valet, and paving the way ahead as circumspectly as it was able.

It had been thought that the project could not possibly succeed without native assistance. But this essential ingredient to the daring scheme had already brought the Society to grief—at any rate, it had brought a burly Irishman to grief—and thus it was that those involved in planning the third assault on Manaus elected to dispense with Indian help. Logically, the natives stood to benefit from the overthrow of the rubber tyranny, but in practical terms it hadn't worked out that way.

Kincaid, inching his way through the jungle that night, wondered if they had made the right decision.

The entire business, he now realized, stumbling in the dark, was fraught with greater pitfalls than he'd envisioned when he had accepted the job. He could not at the time perceive the true difficulty involved in smuggling his contraband out of the Amazonas, an area over half the size of the United States, with less than one percent of its population. It was simply too much ground with too few to guard it.

Then they had explained to him that the stuff could only be obtained by night and that all roads out of Amazonas led inescapably to the one great highway that could be easily watched: the river. Furthermore, any expedition into the interior could scarcely be made without exciting comment. Whether he and Longford struck off from Pará itself or Manaus, they would need to outfit an expedition, safari-style, and then the inevitable questions would start: an expedition for what? And if, by some good fortune, they did manage to set off without calling extravagant attention to themselves, could they hope to return in a similar state of anonymity? Kincaid doubted it. The experience at the Customs House made plain how jumpy these people were.

And if all that were not enough, he had not been commissioned to seize indifferent specimens, but only the best, pedigreed prime black *hevea*. And since such an expedition had been ruled out, it had to be done here, right around the town, under their very noses. And he'd have to be visible every day, looking as though he were doing something; orchid-collecting.

They crunched along the jungle floor, moving in single file, their equipment getting tangled in mango trees, spiderwebs brushing their faces, leaves and ground occasionally lit up like tin in the moonlight.

Actually, gathering the stuff was not difficult, Longford explained, only strenuous. While the *estradas* were patrolled by sentries, they were expecting—if anything—raids, fire parties intent on noisy destruction. Theft was not a daily preoccupation but an ongoing possibility so much a part of their lives that it was more or less taken for granted, like living at the foot of a volcano. A few casual inquiries on the subject were enough to set Longford's mind at ease. They would have to be careful going in, quiet while they worked, and cautious going out, but if rubber was stolen, the citizens of Amazonas counted on intercepting it elsewhere. And indeed, the Royal Geographic's previous encounters with this touchy question had shown that in this respect—at least to date—those citizens had not misplaced their faith.

Longford led the way, stopping once when a light materialized to their right and waiting until it disappeared from view before proceeding. He led Kincaid crouching beneath low-hanging ferns, crawling under enormous roots, wedging himself past fallen palms. Kincaid found himself cursing steadily as branches swung backward in his face, as flies he couldn't see sat on his nose. Any noise they made was drowned by the nighttime sounds of the jungle, and, eventually, by the erratic *pop* sounds toward which they headed.

"What's that?" Kincaid demanded, holding up his hand.

"That's what we came for," Longford explained, breathless from exertion and excitement. "The rubber pods exploding, jettisoning their seeds after the plant expands in the heat of the day."

Mentally, Kincaid reviewed his price: one hundred pounds sterling for every thousand seeds, or a bonus price: nine thousand pounds for seventy thousand seeds of the finest prime *hevea* and no questions asked.

The popping grew louder in intensity. It sounded like a distant artillery barrage.

"The object is to reach them before they have lain on the ground for more than a minute or two," Longford whispered. "If we don't, moving them ruptures the oil coating and will affect the transplant. On the other hand, Harry, if you gather them up too fast, you'll have too much oil on them —it has to drip off, you see—and they'll turn rancid before we get them home."

Kincaid grunted. "Let's get going."

They scampered about like maniacs in the moonlight, chasing after sounds. It took awhile to become adept at the work; when the pods exploded, the seeds were shot forth as much as thirty-five feet. The labor was backbreaking and did not allow for conversation. Kincaid groveled for his money, telling himself that Markham, who in 1856 had spirited the Cinchona tree from Peru to give the English their own source of quinine, couldn't have endured worse agony than this. The analogy of swine rooting for truffles did not escape him.

Periodically Longford would signal a halt and they would ignore the taunting attacks of the flies while the sentries with their torches, making their rounds, were visible at the edges of the *estrada*.

They had not brought enough water with them to quench their thirst.

Then back to the humiliating task of running hither and yon after the reports from above. Kincaid felt as though he were chasing bullets. In addition, the little dappled brown seeds were slippery to the touch and had to be handled more gently than eggs as they were dropped into the earth-packed banana leaves they had brought in their knapsacks for the purpose.

Seventy thousand seeds: to Kincaid, the task appeared like a labor of Hercules. They would never amass seventy thousand before the season ended, and with it the benevolent poppings in the dark.

At first, when his fist had closed on the precious stuff (*ouro preto*, he reminded himself), he had had to suppress a desire to shout with triumph. Now, as the night wore on and the artillery barrage trailed off in advance of the coming day, Kincaid could scarcely get his breath for running in the damp heat, let alone have any left for exclamations. Also, trying to estimate the speed with which each man worked, they were keeping mental counts of each seed reclaimed. To be safe, Kincaid reflected, to gain the bonus he was after, he must really bring back more than the seventy thousand, for some undoubtedly would turn rancid and perish before their journey's end. Unused to the task, they could go on no longer that night.

Later, depositing their cache in the hothouse on board the *Mãe de Deus*, Kincaid did experience a sort of weary triumph: arduous and monotonous as it had been, the goal was at least visible, something that could actually be held in his hands. In another four hours he would go back into that same detested jungle, gathering orchids. He dismissed the thought with a brusque gesture, pulling a leaf from his hair.

In all, that first night, they took less than five hundred seeds.

Later, their record would improve.

News of a meeting between the two great powers traveled quickly across the grids and alleys of the city. Servants heard it from masters who heard it from dress-makers and tailors who heard it from street vendors and lace suppliers who heard it from dockworkers and fishermen who heard it from servants to the powers in question. The progress of the news was geometric, so midmorning found a vast cross-section of the population gathered on the floating docks for what they presumed to be a momentous occasion.

Anchored several hundred yards offshore was Colonel Mendonça's magnificent steam yacht, the *Francesca*, just over two hundred feet in length, polished brass gleaming in the heavy early sun, sleek and white against the ocher of the river.

The yacht, named in memory of Mendonça's first wife, had been originally commissioned by a Bavarian count who then lost interest in its completion and devoted all his time and energy to the cause of the Franco-Prussian War. The eventual defeat of France failed to revive his interest in the project, and the vessel lay half-completed in the Herreshoff's yards until Colonel Mendonça, bringing his daughter to Europe in 1873 (father and daughter making the grand tour together), spotted her and paid to have her finished. Crispin du Amaral, the scenic artist of the Comédie Française, who had designed the curtain for the opera house in Manaus, was importuned to decorate the interiors. Some say that his refusal signaled the decline of his career; others say that it was a meaningless gesture, for the *Francesca* was decorated with furniture and art objects to rival a small palace and indeed functioned less as a seagoing vessel than a second home.

Prior to this morning's meeting, it had been used

for many other things. Dolores had had an elegant party given in her honor in the main salon at which everyone had been served champagne and swan by Indians sweating in their tight white coats and silk knee breeches. The Colonel had entertained the entire staff of the Fer-de-lance, including the much beloved and notoriously wicked Imelda de Pilaar, who played the flute and other instruments of and for pleasure. Full orchestras imported from London and Berlin had entertained parties of four; a lone violinist from Vienna had once played in the Colonel's stateroom wearing a blindfold and earplugs. Yet never had the *Francesca* been used for such an important occasion as the one for which she was destined today.

Interest on the docks grew high and rumor was spread back in waves. The people who were gathered were the poor, the Indians who worked on the rubber plantations or in the rubber warehouses or on the docks unloading or loading, the small merchants dependent on the rubber industry for their market success, indeed anyone in Manaus who needed the continued good fortune of the rubber industry, anyone with an interest in the affairs of Colonel Mendonça and Pierre Coutard.

A rosewood carriage, pulled by Austrian mares, stopped at the outer edges of the throng and Coutard and Mercedes got out. Before they had taken a step, word of their arrival had spread through the crowd and Emmanual Torres popped from the mass, twisting his straw hat between nervous fingers and darting a white tongue over dry lips, but when he began to speak, Coutard gestured him aside; brother and sister were here on business, not ceremony.

Coutard was dressed in a spotless linen suit, white suède shoes carefully dusted with scented talc, an Irish linen shirt, and a new Panama hat with a dotted yellow band made from the petticoat of his last mistress. Mercedes wore a white linen jacket with padded shoulders, a white shirt and ascot, and a pencil-thin white skirt. Her outfit was daringly masculine for Manaus, but enormously fashionable had she been in the Bois de Boulogne at four-thirty on a Sunday afternoon in spring.

They walked and the crowd of brown-skinned people in mud-colored clothes parted for them. Coutard smiled at how beautiful things looked. Something touched his arm and he was horrified to see Torres' greasy dark fingers on him. He jerked his arm away and snorted in disgust.

"It cannot go on, Monsieur," Torres said breathlessly, hopping sideways to keep up with Coutard's long, impatient strides. "This . . . war between you and Colonel Mendonça . . . people killed by the score . . . rubber burned! The entire city reeks with the stench! With the Rubber Convention here, the whole world will be scandalized by our conduct. They have expressed their concern privately several times. Do we want these foreign merchants to see—?"

"They have no choice," Coutard said abruptly. "They need the rubber and they can get it only here. At any rate, it will all be over soon."

"But Colonel Mendonça will strike back," Torres whined.

"Torres," Coutard said placatingly. "Torres. In a month . . . perhaps in less than a month . . . there will be only one man at the head of the rubber industry in Manaus. Tell that to these foreign merchants you are so worried about."

"With all due respect, Monsieur," Torres said, now walking backward in front of Coutard, parting the crowd for him, "I think you exaggerate the weakness of the Colonel. He is old but he is not senile."

Coutard's confidence was shaken for a moment and he turned to look for his sister. Mercedes was directly behind him and when their eyes met, she stepped up and took her place next to him, her face hard and eager.

"There are three hundred million rubber trees in the Amazon, Senhor Torres, of which man has tapped less than a hundredth of one percent. Why do you worry?"

Torres paled noticeably when Mercedes began to speak, and her question was felt as a threat. He stopped walking and spoke in an oddly melodic whisper.

"It's the heat, you see. When you are young you don't notice it as much. But it is impossible to be an old man in this country. The heat makes you afraid to grow old, afraid you will be sucked of every last ounce of strength. I must shave three times a day in this heat. At my age it becomes difficult to maintain an interest in life."

His legs buckled and he sank to his knees, his arms dangling. Coutard gaped; Mercedes eyed him coldly and dragged her brother through the crowd, away from the sight.

"How can that scum make you nervous?" she whispered. "It's not the heat, you know. He takes opium. It will kill him within the year."

"How do you know?"

"I will see to it."

Coutard said nothing then, content to follow her to the end of the dock, where Colonel Mendonça's launch awaited them. Two of their bodyguards helped them in as the crowd watched. In the launch, Coutard gazed blankly ahead of him, not seeing anything but the blue and brown and red-tipped waves, lost in doubt.

"Mendonça is finished," Mercedes whispered urgently, as she had before and would have to repeat many times again. "Why do you think he sends for us if not to make terms? Why?" Coutard was only capable of a distracted smile; he allowed himself to become absorbed in inspecting his sleeve where Torres had touched him. Silently, Mercedes cursed her womanhood, which forced her to manipulate strings instead of taking charge fully and directly.

Her mood improved as the launch neared the gleaming yacht. As she stepped aboard she found she was ravenously hungry.

"It will be over soon," she said, as they went up the stairs together. "Soon."

When Coutard, his sister, and their bodyguard reached the deck, Mendonça's officers were there to greet them. They were conducted to the main companionway, showed below, and led along the inside corridor of scented maple into the formal library where the Colonel and Iquitos were waiting. The Colonel, also in white, sat in a high-backed chair of blue silk; behind him was a floor-to-ceiling bookcase filled with leather-bound Portuguese editions of Dickens, Thackeray, and most of Trollope. One foot was stretched out, the leg stiff with undiagnosed gout. Iquitos stood near him, slightly behind, also in white. Anticipation was in the air.

After the formalities, and after Coutard and Mercedes had been served cool lime and ice, the Colonel leaned back, interwined his fingers to stop the trembling, and spoke.

"I have decided to be candid, as well as blunt. At our luncheon earlier this week I made the mistake of addressing you as children. Children you are not, unless I am to assume that the brutal assaults and attacks on my men and property are the haphazard work of individuals who do not know how to use or control power." He held up a hand to forestall Mercedes' angry objection. "Please. I am not criticizing. I am myself not guiltless in this"—he spoke the word unwillingly—"this war, but I am prepared to concede that bloodshed and destruction are not improving either of our situations, nor are they helping us to conduct business. Say rather the reverse."

He paused momentarily, half curious to see if either would agree with him, but rather than wait for arguments, he pressed on. "The matter of the export tax is itself symptomatic of those differences between us referred to by Monsieur Coutard in his speech." On the word *his*, Mendonça could not resist a slight, ironic inflection. "As he says, we have our different notions of progress and also of what the future holds for our unique product."

Mercedes allowed herself an audible sigh of boredom. Really, the old man was impossible. Mendonça, if he heard, gave no sign. He placed his thick fingers together before him.

"But the one thing we agree on is this: the stakes are high; too high to trifle over, and, in my opinion, too high to fight over, either." He stopped portentously, leaning forward slightly for emphasis. "I have a proposition to put to you; a proposition which, I believe, can satisfactorily resolve our differences."

Here it comes, Mercedes thought, and bit her cheeks to prevent a smile from leaking out.

"If we can agree, we can decide here, now, together, that only one person will rule in Manaus, and that person will control our combined lands."

The Coutards hesitated. What scenario was this? Iquitos, standing behind Mendonça, did not move, though every fiber of his being was alive and quivering. He thought he knew his master, yet had no idea what was coming. In search for the subtle, he had overlooked the obvious.

Coutard was frightened by the Colonel as a rule, and his bright eyes especially disturbed him at the moment. Unable to return the stare, Coutard fell to eyeing the tip of his shoe. Mercedes ran the possibilities through her mind and discarded them. Still convinced Mendonça was operating on the defensive, she laid a hand casually on her brother's arm, pumping confidence back into him, an invisible transfusion, and waited.

The Colonel rose from his chair, limped heavily to a side door, and opened it.

"Come in, my dear," he said and stood aside. After a moment's pause, Dolores appeared in the doorway, face gleaming and blank, dressed in tiers of white lace to the throat, her black hair coiled and piled high on her head. She looked immediately to her father; their faces wore matching masks, revealing nothing.

Mercedes was offended by the appearance of the Colonel's daughter in the midst of what she assumed was a serious diplomatic confrontation. Coutard rose, delighted. In the broad light of day —usually the worst illumination for a woman, in his experience—the girl looked even more beautiful than she had at the opera. Coutard stared intently as the Colonel advanced a few steps, his daughter lightly touching his arm.

"My daughter, I believe you remember from

the opera?" Mendonça hazarded, removing his hand.

"Of course," Coutard responded automatically.

Dolores inclined her head briefly in the direction of Mercedes, but favored Pierre Coutard with an elaborate curtsy. She erased the painful irony in her eyes before she lifted them again.

"I remember you from long before that," she said in hushed tones. "When we were little your father brought you to my garden parties to play croquet."

"Yes, of course," Coutard repeated dumbly, awed by her beauty and confused by her presence. With a slight motion of his hand, Mendonça signaled Iquitos to bring forth a chair. When Dolores was seated, her father followed suit. Instantly Coutard did likewise. Mercedes, staring, gasped, sensing with dawning comprehension what was about to happen. The knowledge froze her to immobility. The Colonel let the silence hang and regarded the young Frenchman for some moments, his face expressionless.

"Why don't you marry her?"

They gaped. Coutard could say nothing. His mind was incapable of grasping this maneuver or knowing what to make of it. The woman was magnificent. She was being offered him.

At his side, Mercedes' brain reeled. There was a furious pounding in her ears as she forced herself to think how to extricate her brother from this snare. She understood only one thing clearly: this would be a settlement on Mendonça's terms and was at all costs to be avoided. Mercedes aimed at domination, not a cooperative venture.

Other objections exploded in her mind, tumbling about pellmell: What would her own place be if this marriage took place? Dolores was certainly no docile bride she could control; definitely not while her father lived, and perhaps not even when he died. What then? Before she could collect herself to reply, however, the Colonel spoke.

"I propose a merger of our estates, to be controlled jointly during my lifetime; by you and my daughter when I am dead, and by my grandson, your son, when you are gone. No bloodshed."

Before Coutard spoke, he looked once at Mercedes and then quickly turned to Dolores. She looked at him evenly and smiled with the proper modesty and the proper encouragement. The fact that he was getting absolutely everything he wanted, that the Colonel must be a senile old fool, that the daughter was a prize, suddenly struck Coutard as cosmically funny. He laughed aloud, first in his chair, rocking back and forth, his face contorted with mirth, then rising, walking, pacing, stumbling, laughing. No one rose to touch him or quiet him. Mercedes was helpless, frustration like vinegar and molasses on her, heavy and impossible. And still Coutard continued to laugh, in surprise, then defense, delight, astonishment, glee, lust—and most definitely, it became clear, in affirmation.

The Colonel beckoned to Iquitos and gave him his instructions. Impassive, Iquitos looked once at

Coutard and once at Mercedes, and left the cabin. A moment later Coutard's laughter was drowned out by the resounding explosion of the ship's whistle and, a moment after that, by a series of wheezes, toots, bellows, and shrieks as a lineup of other vessels passed on the signal to the population, who received it with much shouting and clapping, delirious in the thought that peace had come at last.

✠ 9 ✠

Kincaid, sweating in the orchid plantation, could hear the boat whistles. They boomed and squeaked across the harbor and into the jungle, but he didn't know what they meant. Crude attempts at questioning his Indian bearers with imprecise sign language only served to convince him that they didn't know either. All of them were left to speculate, which was fine with Kincaid. He had enough on his mind and his body, which ached as though every inch of his skin had been flogged. He was used to physical exertion, he told himself, but hunting orchids by day and chasing after rubber pods at night left little time for his muscles to renew themselves. He consoled himself with the dreary thought that if it went on long enough, he'd probably get used to it; the story of his life.

On arriving at Casa Grande he'd been pleasantly surprised and relieved to find neither Dolores nor her quaint duenna awaiting him; just a simple, handwritten explanation from Mendonça's secretary, Iquitos, that the Indians were at his disposal (and would continue to be), though for

176

the moment, Colonel Mendonça and his family were, alas, not.

A thousand apologies, etcetera, etcetera—Kincaid scanned the Indian's carefully couched phrases of regret. He was far from annoyed. He didn't feel like talking to anyone, nor did the prospect of being polite to the seductive Miss Mendonça exert the slightest appeal. She made him—in contemplation—quite nervous. He sensed, with an intuition born of long experience, that underneath the frivolous, prattling lady of fashion lurked a little hellion; quite a lot for any man to handle, even for one who had her father's permission and approval. Which he did not.

Back to work, Kincaid admonished himself. The jungle dankness was like a second skin that hung veillike over nose and mouth, infested with flies that buzzed and swooped with fanatical persistence. The waving motions of Kincaid's hands became instinctual as they struck up the jungle's own rhythm.

It was not until late in the day, when he returned to the docks, laden with plants for the *Mãe de Deus,* that Kincaid witnessed the city in full eruption of relief and celebration. Intent on depositing his flowers, Kincaid jostled through the crowded streets, too tired for the moment to be curious, ignoring the hubbub and dancing that had already begun. Nothing in Manaus, he told himself, could possibly astonish him.

Back at the hotel, where the rubber conventioneers were cavorting through the lobby to the strains of a lively Strauss polka, Kincaid finally succumbed and pulled the manager aside by the sleeve, shouting in his ear:

"What's going on?"

The man drew back and looked at him, amazement stamped on his perspiring features, his mustache soggy with drink.

"You haven't heard, *senhor?*"

Kincaid shook his head. The manager clapped his hands in ecstasy, jeweled rings glittering in the chandelier light.

"A marriage, my friend, that all the city rejoices in—a wonderful, blessed union of two young people!"

Kincaid made him repeat it. "Does the whole town usually get this convivial when nuptials are announced?"

"But my friend, this is no ordinary wedding! When Dolores Mendonça, daughter of the richest man in all Manaus, chooses a husband, and that husband is Pierre Coutard, owner of even this hotel—" He left the sentence unfinished, startled by Kincaid's expression.

"Is that it? How very—droll." Kincaid nodded and started up the plush carpeted outsized lobby stairs; his thoughts were disorganized. What a match! As he climbed, shoving his way past the merrymakers, he reflected that Dolores, at least, was very likely out of his hair for good, now, with her inconvenient flirtations. And into Coutard's. A lot to handle, he'd been thinking that morning, though he hadn't quite visualized her being tamed by the methods Coutard was likely to employ. He was not entirely sure that out of his hair was where he relished her. Then again, looking at the bright side, he told himself that he wasn't likely to be invited by young Coutard out for another evening's debauch, and perhaps that was just as well.

Walking down the hall to his suite, Kincaid tried to picture them together and failed. The profligate and the virgin; a marriage of convenience. Coutard, after he'd had her, would rejoin his whores in no time. And Dolores? Kincaid wondered what would become of Dolores Mendonça. She wasn't the sort to take things lying down; not while her father was alive, anyway. Or was she? After all, she'd obviously agreed to marry the man and she was no fool. And when her father died? What then?

He unlocked the door.

"What have they all gone mad about?" Longford demanded, as he walked in. He'd been straightening the room, ordering Kincaid's suits.

"A merger, Professor, that's what's being celebrated down there. Nothing more; nothing less."

"I see," Longford said cautiously, when Kincaid had explained.

"It's a blessing," Kincaid decided. "A big event like this—two most powerful families involved and all that—weeks of preparation—it's bound to tie up traffic and generally divert the citizenry."

"And that suits you?"

Kincaid lit a cigar.

"Down to the ground."

* * *

The next two weeks saw the city in a state of constant Carmagnole, but Kincaid and Longford witnessed little of it. They did not see the market stalls furl their tattered awnings closed, their owners dancing to the rising tide of side-street drumming. They did not see the crowds gathered in São Sebastião Square to cheer courting couples as they ascended above the city in Armand Poincarré's balloon or the parade of seamstresses in blinding white that formed a conga line and paralyzed every dress shop in Manaus. They did not see the population of roués and cads bump their hips on the smooth and saucy shanks of the finest Polish whores in town. They did not laugh at the lady in tangerine silk who lost a bet and paid on the green felt of a billiard table while the crowd clicked their teeth in approval. They did not see the fifty-foot afternoon banquet table feeding Manaus' rich while an unseen orchestra played Boccherini in a vain attempt to outdo the samba music in the public park outside. They did not see Emmanual Torres' eyes flutter in a delirious opium haze. They did not see, in the formal recesses of Pierre Coutard's office, the ceremony of paper signing or hear the tense breathing and pounding hearts as first the Colonel, then Coutard, then Do-

lores, put their names to the documents that
would join their lands in peace.

They continued before. Kincaid, bored to misery
with orchids, nevertheless did not fail to appear at
the plantation with his helpers every morning. At
night, it was easier than they dared anticipate to
reach the rubber seeds. No one noticed their late
arrivals and departures. Even the *estrada* sentries
were happy with drink. Kincaid's only worry was
that one of them, holding a lantern, would keel
over and set all of them on fire.

What they did see, one day returning from the
plantation, was the mass jungle funeral for *seringueiros* and processing-hut workers who had been
murdered in attack on Colonel Mendonça's met-
ropolitan *estradas*. The surviving women had spent
their time of mourning stripping bark, softening it
with river water, and wrapping the bodies inside. The corpses were then hung from trees as
high as the mourners could haul them and the men
beat drums night and day to accompany the as-
cent of the souls to heaven.

Longford, much affected by the keening of the
families, said it was shocking of the Coutards—if,
as rumor had it, it had been they—to order such
wanton destruction of human life.

"Don't waste your sympathy on old Mendonça,"
Kincaid forestalled him. "That man has a few
shades of red on his hands, at least."

But he knew what Longford meant and found
himself stiffening as he watched the heartrending
ritual. He'd come to Manaus to do a job, but three

weeks in this depraved section of hell had
changed his mind. Destroying Manaus was going
to be more than a job; it was going to be a pleasure.

That was the night the fireworks had begun.
They were exploding throughout the night sky,
visible from the windows of the hotel suite, and
Kincaid had been trying to get an hour's sleep before departing again for work, when his unsuccessful nap was interrupted by a knock on the door.
When Longford failed to answer it, Kincaid went
to see what it was. Reading the note the Indian
handed him, he reminded himself that nothing in
Manaus could astonish him. Nevertheless, he was.

* * *

Kincaid followed the Indian along the road that
paralleled the river. The Indian carried a torch
that showed the thickness of jungle on either side
of them, the blackness alive with sounds. Every
once in a while a piece of that life would drop
into the light: a howler monkey swooping down
and screaming at the heat of the flame, a mad-
eyed cockatoo appearing, disappearing in a flash
of white; one, two, three enormous butterflies in
succession, their translucency melting in the flame.
Kincaid smelled apricots and earth; it was as if his
lungs were filling with something heavier than air.
Ten yards to his right he heard the sucking sound
of the river, and the wet ground he walked on was
soft and spongy. In the distance he heard laughter,

but the sound was directionless; it could as easily
have come from in front of him as behind, above
as below. If the Indian had not been leading
him, he would have had to stop and wait for daybreak to find his way out of this tangled wildness.

Up ahead he saw a light that might have been
set at a campsite. As they got closer, other people
with torches joined them on the path, coming out
of the jungle mass as though they lived their lives
in waiting for this moment; and yet so bizarre a
sight were they that Kincaid could not imagine
where they lived at all, or how, or who they were.
Except for two men who looked like diamond
hunters the rest were Indians. He could tell by
their faces, by the flat cheeks and delicate wrists
and arms. But he had never seen Indians dressed
this way. The men wore silk pajamas and soft
straw hats such as a gentleman might wear. On
their feet, instead of the accustomed sandals of
palm leaf, were leather shoes highly glossed with
varnish. Their women were dressed in ballgowns,
tattered at the neckline and more at the hem despite the valiant efforts to lift them from the jungle
floor. In the flickering shadows of the torchlight,
Kincaid saw the heavy makeup on their faces,
thick rouge and powder that gave them the aspect
of beauty although the true effect was grotesque;
underneath it, they looked ill. The ground was
muddy; in spots there were pools of fetid water,
and the women trudged on in high heels.

When they reached the lights, it was not a
campsite but a nightclub that looked out over the

Rio Negro. In the murky light of the three-quarter moon, the Amazon glowed in the distance above the wide swath of black. The men and women swooped into the club, kissing the hands of the people already inside. Kincaid looked up at the sign above the door: Il Vatican. He smiled and went inside. The Indian murmured something to him and disappeared into the shadows. The couples had planted their torches in straw sconces along the walls and the more people that came in, the brighter the place became, until the gauzy yellow glow increased to a burning orange that made the movements of the people seem like the tortured dances of hell. How appropriate, Kincaid mused. There was no music, but a man filled a box with nails and shook it with a rhythm so insistent that the couples seemed driven to dance. Their feet dragged and shuffled along the plank floors; when the floor was filled with them, Kincaid could feel the entire club swaying to the nail-box beat as it teetered over the river on palm-trunk pilings.

Why here? Kincaid wondered. Why arrange a meeting here? Of course, it was the perfect place if she didn't want to be seen. The shuffling of the feet was deathly, a death rattle. The dancers' faces loomed in and out of the flickering light; their teeth clicked in rhythm, their flesh shook in paroxysms. Kincaid lowered his eyes to look at his hands, turned them over and over again, the skin white and solid; he flexed; he was alive.

When the Indian finally returned, Kincaid had regained a sense of himself as being necessarily apart from this madness, this nightmare parody of the kind of ballroom society he had seen all over the world. The Indian beckoned with his head, and Kincaid followed him out of the main room, down a long balcony that overlooked the river. The torchlights were reflected as isolated spots of flame, pieces of light that had been tossed out, useless and deranged. And then there was a door beneath which a pale light from a paraffin lamp glowed white and ghastly. The Indian paused, bowed, backed away, was gone. Kincaid paused too and then he entered.

The room appeared to be empty, except for the light. The hair on Kincaid's scalp vibrated. He'd come, dammit; if this was a dream, he'd begun it voluntarily.

"So." Her voice rose from the deep shadows at the far end of the room. All he could see of her was the hem of her black dress resting like an animal at the edge of the white light. He heard her rise, heard the stiff rustle of her dress; he saw her move, the black shiny taffeta coming toward him first, lighting up in sinuous waves of black on black, stealthy as the Rio Negro itself; and finally her face, its unnatural angularity accentuated by her expression—hard and set, beautiful in a remote fashion.

Kincaid realized that he was afraid. He told himself for the hundredth time that he'd had to come. He bowed, and bowing saw the restless clenching and unclenching of her hands. He felt better.

"Sit down, won't you?" she asked, indicating a low bench covered with a sable blanket. Kincaid sat and she sat opposite him, both in the half light. The silence was broken only by the insistent rush of the river and the blurred shuffle of the dancers far away in the dilapidated ballroom. She waited, watching him narrowly. With a sigh, Kincaid drew forth the note.

" 'I must see you on a matter of utmost importance,' " he quoted, " 'signed, M.C.' I cudgeled my brains over that one for forty seconds before I came up with Mercedes Coutard."

"How very clever of you." She took the note and held it leisurely over the paraffin flame. It burned her fingers but she appeared not to notice. He watched her pour two glasses of wine and took the one she passed him.

"Your health."

They might have been sitting in a fashionable restaurant. "And yours."

The glasses clinked and they sipped delicately. Kincaid's patience and his nerves were wearing thin.

"The atmosphere is a trifle heavy, Miss Coutard."

"Do you think so?" she asked in a parody of innocence. "You must call me Mercedes."

"If I must, I must." Kincaid rose and paced the room before turning to face her. "Is this to be a seduction?"

She smiled at him, teeth glinting. "You are rather insolent, I think." Nevertheless, she continued to sip her wine, undisturbed. In the darkness her lip rouge made her lips look black.

"I've been told that before."

"And then she slapped your face?"

Kincaid laughed. "Yes."

"The virtue of a whore is really quite impressive, don't you think?"

"And a lady's?"

"Not so impressive," she said and stood up and took a few slow steps toward him. "And not nearly so much bother."

Kincaid met her in the middle of the room. The light was strongest there and they embraced. The heat of their bodies was indistinguishable from the heat of the evening. The scent they picked up in each other's flesh was the scent of the jungle. When the gunshots rang out, he stopped, alarmed.

"It is nothing," she whispered. "An evening's entertainment. When the dancers are tired the men play music by firing off their revolvers. Listen. You can hear a melody of the different calibers."

Kincaid listened. It was the perfect music to accompany this event. He pulled Mercedes to him again, but she resisted. He looked at her, questioning coquetry at this late date.

"I have a more interesting place to go," she said, pulling him out the door. "No one will disturb us. Come. Come." There was an urgency to her voice and manner that Kincaid felt was not merely amorous. He wondered, but couldn't know; not yet. It

had to be played out. She led him off the balcony
and down a dirt path to the bank of the river. In
the murky light, everything was cast in ancient
bronze; the river carried its own load of anxiety,
and it had also deposited some stray pontoons of
rubber meant for the harbor. They had gotten
tangled in roots and weeds, wedged on the bank.
Kincaid wondered if the grounding of these rafts
was for the purposes he and Mercedes were going
to put them to now, or if it was the mere caprice of
the river. It didn't matter. At this moment, with
the black taffeta rustling as she removed it, nothing else mattered. She lay back on the rubber
barge wearing only her shoes. Kincaid knelt at her
side and removed his coat to put under her
back.

"No. I like to feel the mud."

He tossed the coat aside, then his vest and trousers. As he lowered himself next to her, the sere-
nade of guns began again.

"They're playing our song," he said.

Their lovemaking was brief and fierce, a succession of bites and gasps, each spurred on by the
passion of the other until neither could tell who
had established the pattern; they were past the
point of caring. At the last instant he looked at
the moon over her shoulder. She reared up,
emitted a high thin sound from between her teeth,
and subsided in a series of quick-drawn breaths.
She was covered in mud, got off Kincaid, and
washed her arms and legs in the black river. Kincaid watched, fascinated by the feline attitude of

her movements now that all passion had been spent. He felt a bit as if he'd been robbed, but the feeling was so new to him he could not quite identify what had been stolen. He put it off instead to the jungle and the heat, this heaviness in his chest, this lightness between his legs. Mercedes dressed beside him, then led him back to the little room in which they'd met. When they were seated as they had once been, each with a wineglass, Kincaid could hardly give credence to what had happened. It was as if their lovemaking was contained in a parenthesis between sips of wine.

"I assume you have not done the same with the Mendonça child," she said and lowered her face so that Kincaid could not tell whether she was jealous or simply wanted confirmation of her statement.

"Hardly a child," he said.

"You haven't answered me."

"Did you ask me something?"

"Are you being clever with me, Senhor Kincaid?" Mercedes leaned forward, her head coming into the light. "Cleverness is nothing. I can stamp out cleverness as I would press my thumb to a spider on the wall."

"It sounds to me like you're about to come to the point of our little meeting," Kincaid said. Her tone angered him enough to want to be out of her company, but he knew that she had not asked him here merely for their tryst.

"Impatience. Were you born in April, *senhor*? I have noticed that people born in April are often impatient."

"What do you want, Miss Coutard? You've got my curiosity aroused."

She stood up and walked around the room, as if her thoughts lay strewn in all four corners and she needed to pace in order to pick them up. Finally, she faced him; the light was behind her now. Her face was dark, her eyes darker; behind her the light cast her unkempt hair in a wispy halo. "Would you like to earn a million dollars?"

Kincaid smiled up at her and leaned back, suddenly relaxed. So it was only money; she was not so special after all. Just money. "The usual question now, Miss Coutard, is whom do I have to kill?"

"Just the opposite, *senhor*." She sat down again. "You may have already done it, in fact."

"Then where's my million?"

"You must promise me something first," she said. "You must promise not to ask me why I do or say the things I do. You must promise that or there will be no money. Nothing."

"Not even out of curiosity?" he asked, toying with her now, but Mercedes was not amused.

"There is that cleverness of yours, *senhor*. It will get you in severe trouble one day."

He sighed. "It wouldn't be the first time."

She eyed him curiously then, seeing something in him that she had not seen before, and being quite pleased with how it fit in with what kind of man she needed him to be.

"I want you to marry me, Senhor Kincaid. For this admittedly dubious honor, I will reward you with the sum of a million dollars, on the one condition that you father a son and that upon the boy's birth you disappear. The child will have my name. It will be a Coutard. Kincaid is a name it will never hear. You will disappear."

She paused and looked at him. "Oh, *senhor*, you should see the expression on your face. It is not very clever now."

Kincaid's back hairs went up at the sound of her high-pitched humorless laughter, but what she had offered him was hardly as repulsive as all that.

"Is that what you meant by saying I may have already earned my million?" he asked, and his eyes flickered briefly in the direction of the river.

"I wanted to see if you were . . . possible," she acknowledged with an air at once delicate and businesslike; an interview. "Some men look so good and are so . . ." She ended the sentence with a little shrug of her shoulders, a devastating indictment. "Most I cannot stand to touch me. And after, if I let them, I want to kill them for having seen what they have seen. I do not feel safe." She smiled with deliberate abandon.

Kincaid repressed a shudder; this woman was a bloody scorpion. He forced a smile of dispassionate interest.

"Why me, though? There are hundreds of men in Manaus who are just as possible."

"I've told you; it has to be a certain kind of man, who can excite me. My brother told me about your escapade with Athéné Moncreux. That was quite a feat. I am told she has never given herself to any man. My brother himself was a witness. It excited me very much." Her eyes flashed momentarily as she spoke, but she did not move.

"Am I blushing, Miss Coutard?"

"Why should you blush? A man should be proud of his prowess. A man may be proud of so many things that a woman may not even intimate she knows about."

Kincaid watched her for some moments. She returned his gaze evenly, quite in control of herself once more.

"Supposing my first try isn't a boy?" he asked, just for the sake of seeing how far she'd thought it out.

"Then we will try again—like any married couple. You will live in the lap of luxury for the duration—exclusive of your million, of course."

"Most generous." Something niggled at him. Not that he took any of it seriously—any of it. "Tell me this: how will our child be legitimate with the name Coutard? For that you don't have to marry me."

"His name must be Coutard."

"But if you marry me," Kincaid persisted, "how can the little fellow help but be—"

"It is very simple," she interrupted with a trace of impatience. "You will change your name."

Kincaid stared. "To Coutard."

"But of course." She smiled, radiant at his cleverness.

Kincaid was so boggled by her schemes that he got to his feet and started fumbling excuses. "I'm afraid this is all a bit too sophisticated for me. I've never gotten paid for this sort of thing before. You'll pardon me if I say that being put in the position of whore isn't the most attractive one I can think of for myself."

"Come, come," she responded coolly, ambling over to the door and blocking his exit with her body. "Men buy women all the time—but rarely, *rarely* for such a price." She widened her eyes at him and smiled again, teeth glinting. "Senhor Kincaid, have you never taken money for anything? Never?"

Kincaid stopped and looked down at his hands again. They seemed to be the only things he could see as real, as recognized and remembered. He had come a long way to be here; he felt quite suddenly in that foggy region where old age is puzzled about and then entered. He had called it "tired" before; now he knew it was something else.

"A million dollars," she was saying. "You could stop all of this orchid nonsense."

A million dollars. Suddenly, he saw the whole thing in new perspective. *A million dollars.* Since when did men of his age go chasing across the world picking flowers by day and runting after rubber seeds at night? Was there anything remotely sensible about such goings on? Suddenly the whole rubber scheme seemed like the very height of improbability. Why was he bothering with it? What did it mean to him? Who cared anyway— *really*—what happened to Manaus? It wasn't that much money, certainly not, especially when contrasted with the present offer. And, of late, it hadn't even seemed like much of a challenge. The repercussions were likely the most interesting part, and, all things being equal, he probably wouldn't live to see them, anyhow.

He looked at her; she'd waited patiently, giving him time to figure it out.

"How do I know you'll keep your word?" he demanded. When she didn't answer, he looked into her eyes and saw the hardness there. There was no way he could trust her. She might give him the money, or she might not. She might let him live or she might not. Either way he was in danger for simply having spent this time with her. Then again, there was really no point in saying no to her offer. No point and no way to say no.

"The money must be deposited first, in my name, in a Swiss bank."

"Half," she countered, breathless, but not at all unprepared for his acceptance. Kincaid considered the counterproposal; fair was fair, after all.

"Agreed. Half."

She nodded at nothing, strung like a wire with her success.

"When do we set the date?"

"My brother is getting married soon, as you know," she stated, matter-of-factly. "After that, us."

"Us," Kincaid agreed. In the still night air, the sibilance of the word was like a snake slipping through the underbrush.

10

Telling Longford was going to be a problem. Kincaid winced at the thought. Could he look Longford in the eye and even relate the bizarre proposition—a proposition that even now, as he retraced his footsteps to the hotel, seemed as unlikely as the dream setting in which it had occurred? What would that little Englishman say? Of course he'd offer him a generous portion of the, uh, money. But would that still Longford's qualms? Or his tongue? Kincaid frowned. Probably not. Longford had come to Manaus with a missionary's zeal to right wrongs: break the rubber monopoly, and the growers' stranglehold on the Indians is broken. That was Longford's rationale. And his own? Hadn't he boasted righteously to himself that ruining Manaus was going to be a pleasure?

Anyway, what could Longford do if he refused to fall in with the scheme? Expose him? Would he do that? Could he? Without revealing his own purposes in Manaus? The whole thing was getting stickier by the minute.

Perhaps the wisest course of action was not to tell him; go on with the rubber nonsense and the orchid nonsense as if nothing had happened. Let the thing run its course. The two plans were not incompatible, after all; not mutually exclusive. Up to a point.

Then where had he been tonight, instead of in the jungle alongside Longford, gathering rubber seeds?

Kincaid was just pondering what lie to tell as he rounded the corner of the Grand Hotel Internacional. Looking up, he saw a lone light burning in one of the windows of his suite. Damn. He had hoped Longford was still out, hard at work; obviously he'd come home early, probably piqued that Kincaid had fled the night's labors. He threw away the soggy stub of his cigar and went in.

The night manager was not surprised to see him. Odd comings and goings were the rule at the Grand Hotel to begin with, and the *carnivale* atmosphere that had prevailed since the announcement of the wedding made Kincaid's entrances and exits even less remarkable.

He padded heavily upstairs, trying to look as though he'd been out tomcatting, then realized with a start that it wasn't a particularly difficult role to play.

When he entered their suite, Longford was seated behind the writing table, waiting for him with an inscrutable expression.

"How did it go?" Kincaid began, affecting a casual tone.

"Not too well," said a voice behind him. Kincaid whirled about as the door was closed and locked in back of him. Seated in a chair beside it, a carbine resting easily on his lap, was the Indian Kincaid had seen in Colonel Mendonça's study, who'd spoken so familiarly with the old man; his secretary—what was his name?

"Iquitos is his name," Longford supplied. Kincaid turned around again. "Sorry, Harry." Longford threw out his hands in a helpless gesture.

Kincaid sighed, came into the room, and removed his suit jacket. In the spreading light of day it was a muddy trampled wreck. Nothing surprised him here, he reminded himself.

"What's the situation?" He sat down on the purplish divan and faced the Indian, wondering if it would be necessary to kill him. Such decisions were not an uncommon part of his history.

Iquitos smiled, as if reading his thoughts.

"It wouldn't do any good, sir. If anything happened to me, my men would understand. They have orders to report the matter directly to Colonel Mendonça."

"I see." The man was more clever than he thought. "Well, then. Suppose you tell me where matters stand."

"I've provided you both with some coffee, if you like."

Kincaid saw that indeed he had. Thought it all out, had he?

"That's very kind of you, but no thanks."

"As you like."

Kincaid waited, his mind racing. How much did the Indian know? What did he want? What could they do about it?

"You have been followed, almost continuously
since your arrival in Manaus, Senhor Kincaid—on
my instructions. Please do not take offense at this;
in Manaus, it is not at all unusual for strangers to
be—" He looked at the ceiling in search of the
right word in this language he spoke as a second
tongue "—understood? Yes, understood. It is a common precaution here and Colonel Mendonça directed that I, or someone in my employ, keep you
in view until our curiosity was satisfied. You were
escorted to the opera, to the brothels, to the orchid
plantation every day, and, of course, to the rubber
estradas by night. Colonel Mendonça knows of almost all your activities."

Iquitos paused; his cards were on the table.
Grudgingly, Kincaid had to admit that it was quite
a hand. Nevertheless, an old campaigner, his mind
reviewed the information sorting out the possibilities. Why, for example, had the Indian chosen to
confront them privately instead of simply having
them arrested? Suddenly he heard the sentence
again and his heart gave a little leap.

"Did you say 'almost all' our activities?"

Iquitos allowed the ghost of a smile to play on
his usually impassive features. Kincaid shot a
rapid glance in Longford's direction and took a
breath.

"Perhaps we can come to some sort of arrangement here," he hazarded.

"Perhaps." The Indian's ghostly smile had vanished. Kincaid drew in another sharp breath, as
though he were wading into water that grew chill-

ier with every step; no time for cold feet, he admonished himself.

"I'm in a position to offer you money."

The Indian was cleverly disappointed in the gambit. "You don't have that much money."

Another breath.

"Yes, as a matter of fact, I do. I am in a position to offer you a quarter of a million American dollars."

A quarter to the Indian, a quarter to Longford, Kincaid added and subtracted; his share had suddenly been cut in half and it wasn't even daylight yet. What a world.

Iquitos was looking at him with narrowed eyes, clearly surprised.

"How is it that you possess such a sum?" he demanded, skeptically. "Rubber thieves are soldiers of fortune, mercenaries, generally underpaid, or paid after the fact for their services. Not gentlemen of means."

"Ordinarily speaking, I'd say you were dead right, Iquitos—may I call you Iquitos?—dead right. Ordinarily, I'd say you'd painted me to the life—mercenary, underpaid, and all that." Kincaid undid his collar and tie, making himself thoroughly comfortable for the bargaining session and whetting Iquitos' curiosity. Longford watched, trying to understand what Kincaid was attempting.

"As I say, ordinarily. On the other hand, I've been made an offer this evening that alters the complexion of things considerably. I had already given up the idea of stealing the rubber seeds be-

fore I ever got back here. My only problem was
how to break the news to him—" Kincaid jerked
his head abruptly in the direction of the writing
table where Longford remained seated. "Longford
usually has his heart set on keeping his word,
which is a charming custom, but old-fashioned, in
my opinion, and probably not the style around
Manaus, anyway."

Ignoring Longford's shocked expression, Kincaid
plunged on, relating his encounter with Mercedes
Coutard and her bizarre proposition, which, under
the present surreal circumstances, seemed like the
most normal offer in the world.

"So you see," he concluded, "as a man about to
marry into a rubber-tree fortune, I have scarcely
any vested interest in making off with the seeds.
Say rather the reverse. Now my point is this: a
million dollars is a lot of money. I figure I deserve
half—a finder's fee plus a payment for services
rendered, *but* I'm willing to split the other half
right down the middle between you two. How
does that strike you? Cigar?"

Longford's jaw dropped open as he watched
Kincaid snip each of two cigars, hand one to Iquitos, who smiled quite broadly, shaking his head
from side to side and allowing Kincaid to light the
cigar for him. Kincaid walked over to the silver
coffee urn and poured himself a cup. "Well?" He
dropped in some sugar and stirred it. "I think my
offer is extremely generous."

"Extremely," Iquitos agreed, nodding through

cigar smoke. "But even if you agreed to pay me the entire million it would not be sufficient."

"The *whole* million!" Kincaid exploded, coffee dashing onto the Oriental carpet. "Now you're not being reasonable. The whole million is pretty greedy, Iquitos. I'd kill you before I married her if it was the last thing I did."

"Kill me and it will be the last thing you do," Iquitos reminded him calmly. "The fact is, I don't want your money—" He held up a restraining hand. "—I don't care how much we are talking about."

Kincaid was stumped. It had been going so smoothly. He resumed his seat, the coffee untasted. "Then what do you want?"

"I want you to steal the rubber."

They stared at him.

"I want you to steal the rubber," Iquitos repeated evenly. "I will help you to steal it. I will show you how to steal it and where to steal it. If you don't, I will tell Colonel Mendonça you *have* been stealing it and you will be arrested. It is a capital crime," he added helpfully.

They stared.

"Steal the rubber," Kincaid echoed at last. "You want us to ... Why?"

"That is my affair."

"Oh, no, it isn't." Kincaid rose, animated again. "You know our game; if we go through with this, we've got to know yours. You're Mendonça's factotum. How do we know we're not being set up so we can be shot on the job—save everyone here the trouble of a formal trial? I believe that's what happened the last two times."

The Indian hesitated. "Very well. Come with me." He turned to Longford. "You stay here."

Kincaid nodded, resumed his coat. "What about Mercedes Coutard?"

The ghostly smile again. "That's your problem."

*　　*　　*

The sun was a sliver of gray along the far banks of the Amazon as Kincaid and Iquitos set out for the jungle. Along narrow alleyways, dockworkers passed them on their way to work; fruit and vegetable stalls unfurled their tattered awnings; children dashed from doorways as if propelled.

They clung to the shadows as the streets became less populated and the stalls fewer until the smell of the jungle was so thick Kincaid felt as if his tongue was covered in moss. The small stone huts were ending, the cobbled streets had become soft and loamy. Ahead was the dense foliage that the early sun had not yet made clear.

Then they were on Colonel Mendonça's property not far from one of the *estradas* that had suffered under the attack of Coutard's men several weeks before. As they passed through a clearing, the sun's first oblique rays cast a sheen on charred ground. In the distance was a series of huts and a stream near it, gurgling down the hill, falling over rocks on its way to the Amazon. Kincaid thought the scene rather picturesque, the huts ñeat and compact, a mixture of what appeared to be straw and hardened mud. As he drew nearer, his impression changed.

Vile smells assailed his ñostrils—rotting food, the sores of illness and jungle dankness whose source would be forever a mystery to him. A halo of flies and wasps buzzed frantically about each hut, which, upon closer view, looked as if the children of the community had been allowed to play with their own feces to create mock dwellings in which their families somehow, madly, were consenting to live. Palm leaves, past the brown stages of drying, now gray with fungus, served as roofing, but there was no protection from the flies that even managed to burrow holes in the mud, not content merely to infect the people with disease when they were outside, but demonstrating their omnipotence by being everywhere, gods of the forest.

Iquitos looked back at Kincaid as they approached one particular hut, and beckoned him inside. Kincaid nodded, then shook his head; he did not know what to say or do. He felt the Indian punishing him and apologizing for it simultaneously. Inside the air was heavy and still, the odor of the jungle more powerful for being contained. Kincaid caught glimpses of people, lumps beneath rags, eyes staring, huge, frightened, and he looked away. The mud floor was strewn with hay but the moisture came from underground. The windows were simply holes left in the mud, uncovered but for peeled strips of palm bark. Save for a piece of sheeting on a small area of the floor, the room was without furniture. Finally Kincaid had to look at the people. Two small children sat silent, staring at him, naked and streaked with mud. In the corner stood two more children, older, eight or nine, clinging to the skirts of their mother.

"My family," the Indian informed him tonelessly. "My brothers and sisters and my mother. My father was one of those killed in Coutard's last raid. Colonel Mendonça found me as a small boy and took me into his house. He even gave me a new name. I was born Ceara Zampano; he called me Iquitos. He gave me an education. Perhaps too much. My family followed me here. It was *sêca*, dry where we lived. In Northern Brazil there are terrible droughts. My family had to leave. I thought conditions here would improve. I thought *he* would improve them. But all he improved was his own fortune. Indian labor is cheap. The Indians are beaten down, poorly paid. You see how they live. No *estrada* is better than another. Coutard is as bad as Mendonça. Sometimes I come here at night and the old men sit around the fire and talk of their wild young days of freedom in the jungle. The young men listen. I listen. But we do not speak. They are not our memories. I cannot be as patient and docile as my father. He was a patient man; he thought his freedom would come someday. But he waited too long. And this is what he lived in and what he left behind. It is impossible to live here, and yet my family does it. They are treated like dogs because they look like dogs.

And act like dogs. But they are not dogs. They are men in kennels. If I had been treated as they are treated, I would be as one of them."

Iquitos walked through a doorway, beckoning Kincaid. Beyond the first room were several smaller ones, equally dark, the smell inconceivably foul. The furnishing of one of the rooms was four hammocks; the other contained a circle of stones and the charred remains of last night's fire. A knife lay beside the stones; a scrawny yellow hen hobbled in, behind her a goat whose coat was half eaten by maggots.

Kincaid opened his hands to Iquitos, in helpless compassion. The Indian stalked from the hut. Kincaid found him sitting at the base of a tree under the curious eyes of his brother and sister. He raised his eyes as Kincaid approached.

"If Colonel Mendonça must be destroyed to end the suffering of my family, so be it." He had had this argument with himself many times before, but Kincaid sensed that affection for the Colonel was tearing him apart.

"But without the rubber, what—"

"Brazil is filled with natural resources!" Iquitos jumped up impatiently. "There is sugar and there is coffee and here, these nuts, very rich with oil. My people will survive better without the rubber kings. Greed has made them madmen."

The same argument Longford advanced to justify their actions. Kincaid wanted to voice his agreement but held back, sensing the Indian might find such empathy hypocritical coming from a man of his stamp. They sat in a heavy silence as people from the other huts came out to begin their day.

The men went off to the *estradas* with their machetes and tin cups, the women occupied themselves setting fires and cooking beans for the smaller children. Kincaid could see Iquitos' pride in his people and his rage at their galling subjugation.

His mother appeared from inside the hut carrying what looked to Kincaid like a gourd but whose surface was more that of a tree. She placed the gourd on a plank of rotted wood and picked up a machete. She touched the blade with her hand and for a moment her eyes glazed as if trying to remember the husband who had wielded it until only a month before. Abruptly then, she lifted the machete and brought it down on the gourd. The gourd split open with a neat click and out poured scores of nuts, clustered together like tiny brown pearls. Iquitos laughed and so did his mother. The abundance was a wonder, Kincaid realized, a wonder and a grace, and he had the laughter to take with him from the jungle.

Kincaid laughed at himself, too. He could just picture himself on a soapbox in Hyde Park carrying on about the poor Indians in Brazil. No, he knew himself a little better than that. What he wanted was to get out of this alive, and it was only too clear that if he didn't throw in with the Indian, he would die in the jungle. As for Mercedes Coutard, Kincaid had to laugh again and shake his head; the whole thing was turning into a farce.

The only unfunny thing about it was Mlle. Coutard herself; cross her, he mused, and the falling house of cards would break his neck just as surely as the sun rose in the morning. The thing to do, he decided, was go aboard the *Mãe de Deus* and find out exactly how many seeds they had amassed and how many more they'd need before they could leave at a profit. Every hour spent in this madhouse was making him giddier with fright. The rendezvous with Iquitos was arranged and Kincaid departed.

As he made his way back toward the docks, the stalls had opened and the Indians called to him, offering their wares.

There were fish, cut up or whole, slapped on stone slabs. Some stalls carried livestock, although how live was a matter of opinion, for the hens looked sick and the rabbits cramped and comatose. An old man grabbed Kincaid's hand and poured rough flour into it. "*Farinha de mandioca*," he said, nodding, incantatory, and gestured for Kincaid to taste it: sawdust. At another stall a sickly boy of eight or nine was being pawed by a nervous monkey. Behind him were ten caged monkeys, shrieking for release; next to them were more cages with parrots and cockatoos hysterical and gay in bright reds, blues, and yellows.

Hands grabbed at him, at his coattails; with some difficulty Kincaid managed to make it through the gauntlet without having bought anything and with all the clothes still on his back. The *Mãe de Deus* lay docked at the far end of the slip, and he watched it bob gently in the wake of a passing steamer filled with a new load of passengers from Rio or Pará or the mountains, all crowded along the railing, eyes and mouth agape at the strange port, the floating docks and obvious opulence, all in the middle of nowhere.

Once on board, he went immediately below and found Longford in the hothouse with pad and pencil in hand.

"I thought I'd best take stock of our progress."

"My idea exactly. Something tells me our days are numbered." Kincaid stripped off his jacket in the stifling heat and took down a box of seeds.

"What's his game?" Longford asked, trying to appear calm.

"Same as yours. Philanthropy."

"Seriously?"

"Quite seriously. I have to admit he's got a point."

It was sweaty, dirty work; the hothouse had to be kept at one hundred and ten degrees at all times or the seedlings would harden and die. And they had to be wrapped in banana leaves and soil to retain their natural moisture. Each packet now had to be opened—and quickly closed—and the seeds inside counted. They exchanged numbers and nothing else until they were finished, the packets resealed and replaced on the hothouse shelves.

"Another week should do it at our present rate, in my estimation," said Longford, looking up from his calculations.

"We don't have a week, Professor. We may have only days before this thing blows up in our faces.

Include the Indian in your computations; with his help it should go faster."

"Ah, yes, I'd forgotten that." More scribbling. "Say four or five days, then."

"Say four. What about fuel?"

"That's a bit tricky. We're half full, but I don't think we dare call attention to ourselves by ordering coal, do you? Everyone and his brother appears to take an interest in our movements."

"All right." Kincaid started to light a cigar, then realized. "Sorry. I'll wait till we're outside."

Longford remembered something, too. "This arrived after you left the hotel," he said, handing it over. The envelope, rimmed in gold, proved to be an invitation from Pierre Coutard to a costume ball two days hence in honor of his engagement to Dolores Mendonça.

"Costume?" Longford asked, reading it over his shoulder. "Do they think it's the eighteenth century here?"

"Evidently. I'm told they have them all the time." Kincaid set down the engraved cardboard and sat, thinking. "I'd better go," he decided. "This gracious invitation is sure to have come from Miss Coutard, who doubtless intends keeping a proprietary eye on her investment, as well as building our romance to the point where our engagement comes as no surprise. If I don't show up there are bound to be questions, and questions are the one thing we don't need at the moment."

Longford grunted his assent. Kincaid was suddenly depressed. The Mercedes plan had not been one of his finer moments; and he did not at all relish the prospect of once more seeing the delectable Miss Mendonça.

"If only we could fly like birds when the time came," Longford mused aloud.

"If only," Kincaid concurred, which reminded him of something. He sat in silence while Longford watched, studying him.

"I say, Harry." He coughed, looking rather embarrassed.

Kincaid looked up. "Yes?"

"About that—" Longford flushed uncomfortably. "—about that woman and her offer. Did you ever seriously intend to—to go through with it?"

Kincaid looked at him without expression.

"Professor, what would you have done in my place? What would you do if someone offered you a million dollars?"

Longford's flush deepened and he scratched his head, a gesture he never permitted himself, either in or out of his character as valet.

"It's a great deal of money," he allowed, stealing a glance at Kincaid.

"A very great deal, don't delude yourself."

"I don't know—it's not for me to judge—" he faltered.

"Exactly." Kincaid stood up and put an arm on his shoulder. "I never gave it a moment's serious thought."

* * *

Despite the tourists who had disembarked from the steamer and were now crowding the docks, Kincaid was able to find a small carriage and driver, and they made their way slowly through the narrow streets until they burst free at São Sebastião Square, where Kincaid paid the man and hopped out. He walked across the square, keeping his eye on the dwindling line of people eager for a ride in Monsieur Poincarré's hydrogen balloon. Ever since the rubber conventioneers had been apprised of the wonders of this contrivance, it had rarely been empty, but Poincarré greeted Kincaid as though he were the first customer of the day.

"A view of the city, monsieur?" he said, gesturing to his property. "Only twenty milreis. And for thirty you—"

Kincaid held up his hand to stop the patter; he had already decided to go aloft. "A view of the city? How did you know that's exactly what I wanted?" He approached the balloon warily, looked inside the basket, looked under it, gave it a little kick. "Safe?"

"Monsieur!" Poincarré protested, looking at the other people in line, hand over his heart, a gesture of hurt and astonishment. "Do I seem the sort of man who takes life for granted? Just do not smoke, and you will be all right. One spark . . . poof!"

Kincaid smiled grimly and climbed into the basket, while Poincarré busied himself in adjusting the pull of the winches that released and reclaimed the balloon, humming all the while. Kincaid watched this procedure attentively. Finished, the man held out his hand for the twenty milreis.

"Could this fly over the jungle?" Kincaid asked.

"It never has," Monsieur Poincarré admitted. "It could."

"Could it go as fast as a steam yacht?"

"Faster," Poincarré boasted. "It does not have to follow the river."

"A good point," Kincaid observed, and paid the man.

"You know," the Frenchman told him, smiling as he watched his palm grow green, "the first creatures ever to fly by man-made craft were in a balloon like this; a sheep, a rooster, and a duck." He began to turn the winch, allowing the balloon to rise in a jerky, erratic rhythm.

"You follow in a grand tradition, monsieur!" he called, as the balloon climbed higher and higher.

Kincaid nodded, though he had not heard, and sat down on one of the velvet seats until the dual winches had unwound the basket a hundred feet above the ground. There was a pair of field glasses chained to the seat and he lifted them to his eyes, scanning the city with more purpose than Monsieur Poincarré's usual customers. He adjusted the glasses to focus on the docks and finally found what he was looking for: Mendonça's steam yacht, the *Francesca*. His eyes raked her from stem to stern, impressed with her grandeur. He put the glasses down, took a notebook from his pocket, and scribbled furiously, rocking from side to side as the breezes moved the balloon with chunky grace.

When he was done he called down to Poincarré, who was so occupied with *Le Matin* that he did not hear. Kincaid called again, shrugged, then sat down, leaned back on the velvet seat and for a few brief moments was more idle than he'd been in months. Only five days, he told himself. No, four. As it turned out, both estimates were wrong.

11

Without question, Dolores Mendonça viewed herself as a heroine of romance. It was, she reflected, perhaps the only way to maintain her sanity. Rather than confront the reality of her ill-sorted match to Pierre Coutard, it was easier to think of herself as cast in the role of unfortunate Emma Bovary, destined for the wrong husband, nurturing within her fevered imagination a wild prince who would carry her away from banality. Her aunt had discovered her reading the book and threw it into the fire before she had learned how the story ended. Yes, she likened herself to Emma. The reality would come soon enough.

Dolores' apartments on the second floor of her *Casa Grande* included a bedroom lined in azure watered silk and furnished in a masculine set of cedarwood pieces sent from Maples of London, and a bathroom of mauve and ocher tiles with a porcelain tub, whose dolphins' mouths poured forth gushes of hot and cold water. Her dressing room was based on a plan that the moguls of India used to cool their palaces. One wall of the dressing room had been removed, so that the room was open to the park that surrounded the house. Along

the top of the open wall ran a perforated tube
through which water was sent to drip down long
strands of scented grass. Whenever there was even
the faintest breeze, the room was filled with cool,
moist, scented air.

Dolores had installed a blue silk chaise longue,
an ebony dressing table inlaid with ivory, and an
ancient Chinese screen. It was here that she was
dressing for her engagement ball. The theme of the
ball was royal costuming, a flexible motif that could
be stretched as far as money and imagination
would allow. As it was an engagement ball, no
masks would be worn.

The last few weeks had been a confusing whirl-
wind for Dolores. She had returned to Manaus reluctantly, plotting, on the voyage home, stratagems
that would enable her to return to Europe and the
life she had found so stimulating there. She had
not expected to become engaged, although she was
of an age and had been reared in a society where
made matches were by no means uncommon.
Nevertheless, she was astonished. She did not
dream of disobeying her remote and austere father,
who in return for her fidelity had indulged her
every whim; and she was obliged to admit that
Pierre Coutard was at least handsome. She had always found him handsome. He did not, however,
improve on closer acquaintance. He was no more
intelligent than he had been as a child; indeed, he
seemed to her to be a child yet. She had despised
him as a child, playing croquet with him at garden
parties, and she found him now insipid and vul-

gar as an adult, his European affectations a grotesque approximation of the real thing. Also, he
frightened her. She sensed beneath his idle and
petulant exterior a very real store of cruelty. At
best he was insensitive and she had no illusions
about how and where he amused himself. It would
be an alliance, not a marriage as she had come to
view marriage. He would bed her when he felt like
it. She would endeavor to produce and raise his
children.

In the midst of these unpleasant considerations,
there had been a week of fittings for new clothes,
then another week of grand dinners and dances
where she was the center of attention, as she'd always wanted to be. How ironic. And everywhere
she turned, the leering face of her future husband
confronted her.

Where, oh, where was her shining prince? She
knew all too well, but it had been weeks since her
day in the orchid plantation with Kincaid. Could
she have really fallen in love? Was it possible for
her affections to be so quickly given? And why not?
she answered herself. How long did it take Juliet
to pledge herself to Romeo? Kincaid. Kincaid. His
very name conjured up mystery and romance. He
looked so much the hero, tall, straight-backed,
deep lines of worry and sadness in his face. Perhaps even tragedy; perhaps he had seen tragedy, a
loved one dead, murdered, withered by disease, a
small child left behind . . . no, she did not like the
idea of Kincaid having a child. But tragic, yes, she

could see him as profound and infinitely sad. Even his age attracted her. A man of experience. Strong shoulders and a gentle heart. She would read to him from Keats. He would tell her about life. Othello and Desdemona.

She would not read to him from Keats, she reminded herself. She would not read to him at all, or see him ever again, in all likelihood. It was, she sighed, her fate. And probably for the best. If she saw him again it would be indescribably difficult to go through with her marriage, which caused her a stab of pain below the heart every time she let her mind stray to it.

Instead she occupied herself in getting ready for the ball. It was a distraction to concentrate on her costume and coiffure, and besides, Dolores (who saw no inconsistency in the matter) had no intention of appearing anything less than splendid tonight. And so, instead of weeping, which would have ruined her face, she carefully attended to it: delicate powder, a dab of kohl over each eye and a spot of rouge on each cheek—not too much or Inês would intercept her, before she got into the carriage, and make her wipe it off.

Dolores surveyed herself critically in the mirror. Her hair was pulled off her face, an invariable rule in view of the symmetrical perfection of her features, but this evening she had relented and allowed a few wisps to stray onto her forehead, carefully arranged, to be sure; the rest was piled high in rows of curls, then dripped down to her shoulders

in more curls; diamond hoops hung from her ears.
To crown the whole, a voluptuous jet orchid from
her father's prize collection was clipped to the top
of the curls with a pair of identical diamond
brooches. She compared her own image with the
one in the magazine from which she had copied
her hairstyle. This edition of *Harper's Bazaar* took
two months to wend its way to Manaus from New
York, and she hoped the style was not already
passé. But then the woman in the picture wasn't
wearing a black orchid.

"Antoinette!"

Dolores' maid, in Manaus by way of a Paris or-
phanage and a New Orleans brothel, stood near the
door, holding the fresh chemise, recently removed
from the kitchen ice box. She helped her mistress
slip it past the fragile coiffure. The chemise had
been fitted at Madame Eglitère's in Manaus, executed of sheer batiste and handkerchief linen in
Alceste's of Paris, and trimmed in lace in Berne. It
was cool and exciting on Dolores' skin, as were the
lisle stockings, which followed.

Then the rest of her underthings, before the costume. Antoinette advanced, brandishing the corset
with as much distaste as if it had been a dismembered torso. Antoinette, years past her prime, had
evolved into a puritan and disdained artifice of any
kind. The corset pulled Dolores straight from below her breasts to her hip bones and laced tightly
in back. Some women of fashion were laced so
tightly they slowly bled their way directly to ane-

mia and spells of fainting. Her waist was nipped, her hips needlessly fleshed out with goosedown deceivers; then the flare of petticoats, a woven wire hoop and dust ruffles, and she was ready for the dress.

Tonight she would appear as Ondine, in a gown of sea-green silk with lavender and rose waterlilies embroidered on the skirt amid long sea grasses of multishaded green beads. Over her hair would be a stiff veil of colorless tulle adorned with diamond stars and moons and sprinkled with silver dust. Except for her earrings she would wear no jewelry but for a large diamond in the shape of a star, hanging from her throat, and a few drops of jade and aquamarine to simulate water.

"Ready." She reached up her arms in unconscious supplication, and Antoinette lowered the dress carefully over her head. She entered it with a kind of grateful sigh.

There was a knock on the door.

"*Entrez.*"

Dona Inês appeared, garbed—fittingly, her niece thought—as a nun.

"The carriage is ready, Dolores. Your father is downstairs. We are late. What have you got on your cheeks?"

"Nothing, I'm flushed, that is all. I'll be down in a minute."

Her aunt nodded and withdrew.

"How do I look?" Dolores demanded of Antoinette when the door had closed. The two of them, Antoinette on her knees, straightened the gown, stared at themselves in the full-length gilt mirror. Dolores didn't need to be told.

In the carriage they rode silently, each occupied with random but solitary thoughts. Sitting between her father and his sister, Dolores felt little inclined to talk. It wasn't merely that their silence rebuffed her before she could speak; she felt the world closing in on her like the shell of the coach they rode in. She was a prisoner sitting there between them. They were guarding her. The carriage was a carriage no longer but a tumbril bearing her to execution. She shuddered at the direction her thoughts had taken, eyed the brass door knobs as they glinted beneath passing street lamps, and suppressed a mad desire to leap for those knobs, fling open the doors, and make a dash for freedom and her own life.

Even a playful dash, she amended, collecting her emotions. In all the excitement of the past few weeks, Dolores suddenly realized she could not recollect having had any fun, enjoying herself. She was a girl of natural high spirits and the solemnity of her wedding celebrations—even the rites and fêtes that were supposed to be gay—seemed weighed down with tradition, lacking any spontaneity or life at all. Very well, but if her marriage was not to be spontaneous, it seemed the least life could grant her was some real laughter before the knot was tied.

She stole a glance at her father, stern and upright in his fur and armor—Richard the Lionhearted—half expecting him to have read her thoughts. He seemed, instead, preoccupied by his own; his bushy graying brows were drawn together in concentration. When he became aware of her looking at him, he smiled as though recollecting himself and touched her gloved arm.

"You look lovely," he told her in a low voice. She heard the faint rasping in his chest, but so far this evening the cough had not made its dreaded appearance.

"Too much rouge," Dona Inês contributed, but Dolores had long ago perfected the art of ignoring her. She continued to peruse her father's craggy features. She respected him for not prettying up the issue of her marriage, paying hypocritical homage to the nonexistent virtues of her husband-to-be. He did not patronize her by trying to convince her the match would make her happy. At least she approached the wedding with no illusions but her own willful fantasies. Cold comfort for a bride on her wedding night, when the time came. She straightened the seams of her stifling shoulder-length black silk gloves.

The sight of Coutard's mansion at the end of the half-mile private drive, its hundred windows ablaze, astonished Dolores and filled her with unexpected delight. She had not seen the building since playing hide-and-seek with the Coutard children, scampering in and out of the kitchens and pantries when she was twelve years old. Its appearance, taken for granted at the time, meant nothing to her. Now it was different.

"Papa!" she exclaimed, clutching his hand as they approached the imposing *porte cochére*. "It's Petit Trianon!"

Petit Trianon it was, down to the last gilded ceiling—only it was larger. Dolores didn't know whether to laugh or cry. She gazed, dumbstruck with recognition at the architectural feat of Jacques Coutard, as a liveried footman handed her down from the carriage. The replica was perfect, only too large, and the disproportion served, in her view, to vulgarize the entire effect. Still, she found herself wondering, as she took her father's arm, what it would be like to take charge of such an establishment. How many servants were there? Briefly, the notion of being mistress of such a place as this excited her, titillated her imagination and sense of fun. What a showplace she'd make of it! What a salon she'd run! No matter that her marriage had no meaning; that wasn't uncommon, after all. Look at her friend Denise on the Rue St. Honore. She'd see to it that society around the world would flock to—

And then she remembered Mercedes, who stood at the top of the ballroom stairs, waiting to greet her, a polite smile of welcome frozen on her features. She was costumed as a huntress, real tiger skin draped ingeniously over red satin; a quiver of arrows was slung across her back and in place of a

peaked cap there was a crown of diamonds that
looked as if a great bird had alighted on her head
and crystallized there. Dolores would never be
mistress here. The titillation died stillborn.

Coutard welcomed her with a lingering kiss on
her glove. He was resplendent as Casanova in hose
and doublet of purple velvet encrusted with jewels
and a powdered wig covering his slick black hair.
Dolores found herself blocking him from her con-
sciousness as she did her aunt and turning her attention instead to the ballroom below and her
guests. Dancing had already begun, and although
Dolores was decorously early for this event in her
honor, a hundred or so couples had preceded her.
On the dance floor below was a swirling, jiggling,
shifting mass of diamonds, satin, and brocade; ice
shaped into swans and forming their own pools of
water; Norse flames imported for the occasion to
drip their brilliant red flowers in long vines from
the ornately carved balconies that overlooked the
main floor. Orchids were frozen in sculptures of
pale blue ice. Behind the ice stood several dozen
servants with palm leaves, fanning the cooled air
into the ballroom and over the dancers. In keeping
with the costumed requirements of the night, the
guests had arrayed themselves variously as Madame de Pompadour, Cardinal Richelieu, King
Henry VIII, even Jeanne d'Arc, in addition to more
anonymous monks and abbesses, court jesters and
princesses, troubadours and a daring street girl or
two.

"May I place my name at the top of your card?"
pleaded a voice at her elbow. Without waiting for
permission, Coutard proceeded to inscribe himself
for the *valse générale* and the latest New York
rage, the Hobby Horse Quadrille.

As Coutard led Dolores down the thirty-five
steps, past thirty-five motionless footmen in blue,
the guests ceased dancing and applauded the
handsome couple. Dolores allowed herself to be
swept into her fiancé's rigid arms and whirled with
mechanical grace about the floor.

The Hobby Horse Quadrille was succeeded by
the Alice in Wonderland Quadrille, which was in
turn supplanted by the first waltz of the evening,
regarded as slightly daring in Manaus. Dolores,
who felt she had little to lose, waltzed a great deal,
drank some vintage champagne and waltzed some
more. Her card was soon filled to overflowing. She
had more champagne. The evening drew on; more
guests arrived, to be received by Colonel Mendonça, Dona Inês, and Mercedes, who acted as
hostess here, Dolores noted sourly. The ice began
to melt, the temperature to rise, and Dolores, holding yet another glass of champagne, began to look
about her, squinting slightly now, as she determined to make comparisons between this fête and
those of similar caliber she had known in Europe.

She began by observing the women. No expense
had been spared, she noted, no artifice or subter-
fuge ignored that would make them ravishing for
the night. While the effect might not necessarily

survive a close inspection, in the aggregate, she had to admit, it was stunning. Dolores knew these women well, not as individuals, but knew their counterparts in Paris and from the summer she spent in Rome; women who lived for the Season, for the galas and fétes and balls. As the time for a particular rite approached, the elation made them giddy; the arrangements for hair, jewels, and gowns assumed an importance in their daily routines that utterly overshadowed any other duties or responsibilities. Every effort was made to keep *au courant* with the latest European fashions, though inevitably Manaus lagged behind by a good six months. Nevertheless, assembled by the hundreds at their best and lit by two thousand gilt candles in a ballroom such as this, they combined to produce a genuine sense of splendor.

So much for the women, Dolores concluded, setting down her glass a little harder than she'd intended. The men? She renewed her survey. The men ran to the thin side, as if—she decided— gnawing at their insides was a necessary protection against the diseases carried in foreign objects entering their bodies. They led with their heads, more animallike than their wives cared to acknowledge.

And while the women were the arbiters of taste, it was the men whose energy and wiles supplied the vast resources needed to cull that taste and style from wives, who, for the most part, were not to the manor born, but who were of desperate necessity quick studies. Dolores smiled. She would

see to it that Coutard kept her well supplied with
the resources she required. On the whole, she
pitied them all, the women especially, now that
she came to think of it; their postures and their
ambitions appeared particularly ludicrous and provincial.

For their children, especially for their daughters,
they hoped for marriages to European royalty, and
in the last decades of the nineteenth century there
were several princes and dukes to be had, even
more barons and earls, and an actual plethora of
counts, whose titles were all that recommended
them. These were men whose family fortunes had
been lost, the seats of their crests made virtually
nonexistent, the power of their titles vanished except insofar as a social-minded mother might see fit
to purchase one as a wedding present for her
daughter. Many of these marriages were arranged
during annual trips to Europe, often without the
bride-to-be present to interrupt her mother's flirtation. Many of the brides were handsome only in
the cut of their dowry; many of the grooms, often
handsomer, were dissolute and depraved, debtors
and spenders, and sometimes far worse. Tears and
boudoir scandals were rampant. In the end it became difficult to determine which party had used
which.

This particular train of thought was leading Dolores into areas she blearily felt it was better to
avoid. Something about these reflections was familiar to her, trod on immediate territory, and she

was happy to banish the unwelcome ideas by stepping into the arms of her next partner and whirling energetically to the strains of yet another waltz.

It was then that she saw him, standing at the head of the broad steps to the dance floor, eschewing costume, but wearing instead an impeccably tailored evening suit, holding white gloves, a dark walking cane, and an evening cape with a lining of crimson silk like an open wound which he handed with the gloves and stick to the servant before descending the stairs.

Dolores stopped dancing and gaped, her eyes blinking rapidly in an attempt to focus. Without any explanation to her astonished partner, she glided uncertainly across the floor by herself, weaving in and out among the dancers, in an effort to meet Kincaid at the receiving line at the bottom of the steps.

She was too late, arriving only in time to watch him kissing Mercedes' hand.

"You're not in costume, Senhor Kincaid," she heard her future sister-in-law protest with a slight giggle.

"Oh, but I am," Kincaid countered, not letting go of her hand. "I'm here disguised as a gentleman."

And with that, as Dolores watched, helpless, her shining prince put his arm familiarly around Mercedes' waist and began to dance with her. Her own partner, meantime, had located her once more and stood there, ready to oblige. Absently she held out her arms to him and completed the waltz, dancing automatically, her head twisted round in one constant direction, so as to watch them.

She had to admit they danced well together, the shapely huntress and the gentleman. She knew—it required no great intuition or perception to realize —that Mercedes Coutard envied and loathed her, and took little trouble to hide the fact. Thus far, Dolores had borne this jealous enmity with the same indifference she had displayed to the prospect of her own impending marriage.

Now, however, slightly dizzy and watching her tragic hero in the arms of a rival, Dolores was pricked for the first time in her life, the first time she could recall, with the queasy feelings of jealousy and rage—the one attacking her stomach and the other stinging her eyes. She returned Mercedes' hatred with interest, deriving no satisfaction by remembering the description of jealousy in Shakespeare—"the green-eyed monster, which doth mock the meat it feeds on." Suddenly, Dolores' emotions were not those recalled from or experienced in books, but the painful reality. She stared at her guests and sometime friends with disbelief, knees shaking.

When the waltz had ended, she fanned herself vigorously, wishing she had not drunk so much champagne, and examined her card, dismayed to find it clogged with names that wobbled before her eyes.

Foggily forcing herself to concentrate, Dolores leaned on the back of one of the motionless footmen, clutching her pencil tightly in a gloved hand and altering her card, ruthlessly eliminating candidates for polkas, reels, and waltzes and shakily forging Kincaid's name where the others had been.

She sat out the next dance, collecting her wits and examining her reflection in one of the tall French windows, rearranging the curls on her forehead slightly and making quite sure that the stings she had felt in her eyes hadn't succeeded in swelling them any.

Satisfied, she sought out Kincaid when the music had ceased again. He was talking with her father, something about orchids and various methods of crossbreeding. Heart pounding, knees trembling, she managed to tap him lightly on the shoulder with her fan.

"Senhor Kincaid." She hoped her voice was not as shaky as her limbs. "I believe this is our waltz," and she waved her card quickly past his face before tucking it back into her fan. Kincaid's features creased in momentary confusion as he bowed and took her arm.

"How could I forget?" he murmured. "Ondine looks ravishing tonight."

He knew! she squealed to herself. He knew she was Ondine, a subtlety thus far lost on all the guests tonight. In Dolores' uncertain state, Kincaid's observation was the mystical connection that proved the stars had meant them for one another.

It didn't hurt that he was a superb dancer. Dolores felt herself floating in his arms, looking into his sad face and thinking of nothing else in the world but him. She could not feel her feet touch the ground. She had never been so happy.

"I love you," she told him, without preamble or epilogue. He blanched in surprise, then recovered; he realized she'd been drinking. "You think it is because I have had champagne," she went on clairvoyantly, smiling, "but that isn't so. I have loved you since the day you began your orchid gathering; perhaps even from the night before at the opera."

"Really?" His head turned away briefly.

"Yes, really and truly. You are the only man I have ever met who truly understands me. You love Paris as I do—"

"Yes."

"And orchids . . ."

"Yes."

"Would you like the one in my hair? It's priceless —a special gift for a special night." She reached up as they danced to pluck it for him from beneath her tulle veil, but Kincaid recaptured her hand, looking anxiously around again.

"I don't think that's a good idea. It's extremely generous but I'd hate to ruin the ensemble. You'll give me another one someday."

He put her through an effortless reverse before she could reply. When the waltz was over, they glided to a stop and her head was spinning. In her exalted state it took some moments for her to grasp the fact that he was leaving, shaking hands with Richard Coeur de Lion, bowing low over the Mother Abbess' hand, then holding the sultry huntress' with a disturbing familiarity.

"You are not leaving so soon?" the huntress protested, eyes shining, wet lips parted in a provocatively intimate smile.

"I'm afraid I must." He bent over her hand again and Dolores was certain he squeezed it.

It was inconceivable, she thought, rooted to the spot, dumbly allowing him to mumble his farewells to her. Mercedes, she allowed, was more than attractive, but the sensibility! the romantic rapport—! *Palm to palm is holy palmer's kiss.*

"Don't go," she begged, knowing no shame now, only her own desperate desires. She preferred him here with her, even in the presence of her successful rival.

"I must."

"We'll meet again?"

He couldn't or wouldn't answer, his eyes avoiding hers: her heart leapt out to him with the knowledge; he loved her. It made no difference what she had seen. He loved her.

"Goodnight, Miss Mendonça—and all felicitations."

As in a dream she watched him climb the steps and retrieve his things.

"Aha," Casanova exclaimed at her side, seizing her card. "This dance is mine."

"It is not," she protested. She couldn't take her eyes from the departing figure.

"Yes it is," Casanova insisted and tore the card in shreds, letting the pieces flutter to the floor.

Dolores followed him woodenly through the giddy steps of the *galop*. It simply wasn't fair. It drove her wild to think of Mercedes in Kincaid's embrace, laughing with him, no doubt at her; all her life a poor caged bird. About to be more caged than ever, she realized, looking at Coutard's sweating face and wild blue eyes. Why couldn't she ever think of him as Pierre?

No, she decided, quite calmly as she danced, her head still spinning. This was not the end. She would see Kincaid again. She would see him now; she would—if only as her last madcap prank or protest—deliver an orchid to him as promised.

Dancing, and a little the worse for wine, her mind functioned with a lucidity that pleasantly astonished her. It was simple enough; the question was: did she remember sufficiently the kitchen and pantries where she had played hide-and-seek so many years ago?

It might have gone no further than that, idle planning, had not an event occurred at that moment that coincided perfectly with her scheme; a miracle, no less.

In São Sebastião Square, Armand Poincarré's balloon had escaped its moorings and rose majestically into the night air, illumined by a fortuitous burst of fireworks. The guests, astonished and bemused, converged at the huge French windows to admire the sight and speculate on its probable cause.

Dolores seized the opportunity to escape her fiancé's embrace and rushed to her aunt's side. Her aunt was absorbed, like everyone else, watching the ascending balloon.

"Aunt, it's so hot and stuffy," she sighed. "I have a migraine, I am sure. What shall I do?"

Dona Inês, in her abbess' habit, turned reluctantly to her niece, peering myopically for a brief perusal.

"Do?" she repeated, vaguely. "But the night is young. You cannot leave. It is your engagement party."

"I do not wish to leave," Dolores assured her, smiling bravely. "Only—"

"Go upstairs and one of the maids will lay out a bed for you and give you some eau de cologne for your temples. Cousin Teresa is asleep there already. Too much to drink, the little scamp."

Dolores started to feign a protest, but her aunt cut her off.

"I shall explain to your father. These soirées are too much for a young girl. In my day—" She interrupted herself impatiently. "Go upstairs and lie down. Return to us when you feel stronger."

"Thank you, aunt." Dolores dropped her a perfunctory curtsy and started for the stairs.

Once in the foyer she ignored the curved steps to the first floor and its bedrooms filled with inebriated or exhausted females, and followed a servant with empty champagne glasses down the backstairs she had used as a child, arriving in the scullery. She got lost several times and had to ask directions, but her mischievous air of open complicity easily allayed the suspicions of several dozen French chefs and their assistants, who pointed her way to the stable entrance where the carriages waited on the gravel drive. She mumbled something about having left her reticule and giggled at the oversight.

In another moment, she had stepped into the cool evening air. Free.

❈ 12 ❈

The escapade almost ended before it began; Tomáz, the coachman, hesitated taking Dolores alone to the hotel. He had received no instructions from the Colonel and seldom moved one of his carriages without them. Dolores cajoled him. He had known her since she was a little girl and had never been able to resist her playful, insistent wiles. He had smuggled candy to her when it was forbidden and shared a hundred like conspiratorial intimacies. Dolores found him taking refreshment with some of the other drivers and told him it involved a practical joke on her bridegroom. Tomáz, heady with sangria the Coutards had provided the waiting coachmen, did not understand the tale too clearly or question it too closely. It was enough that his little lady was up to some mischief. He held open the door for her and performed the office of the footman, lowering and raising the three steps, before climbing into the box and unwinding the reins from the whip stand.

Dolores, tingling with her own ingenuity, proceeded to embellish her escape by draping her Spanish shawl out one of the open windows and over the distinctive M emblazoned on the carriage door; her father's self-proclaimed coat of arms. Folded on the seat beside her was Inês' lap blanket, which her niece employed for the same purpose on the other door. She sat back on the comfortable cushions with an exhalation of satisfaction. Should anyone glimpse the big black carriage passing beneath the street lamps, it would be difficult to identify.

She sat up with a sudden start, remembering. In his murmured farewells, Kincaid had said something about having to work with the orchids on board his boat.

"Tomáz! Tomáz!" She rapped on the ceiling and ordered him to take her to the docks.

"But—"

"Do as I say, Tomáz—for me?" She blew him a kiss through the open trap and smiled brilliantly up at him. "It is all for a joke."

Tomáz sighed. Her little kisses had paid for various trifling infamies since she was five. Obediently, he changed directions.

Sitting back again, well pleased with herself, Dolores reached into her hair and extracted the flower. "*Trichoglottis philippinensis brachiata*," she intoned slowly, practicing the sound of the words, and set the dark blossom carefully in her lap.

The docks were still and deep black, shadows of shadows, the moon fuzzed at the edges, left to molder in the fog above the jungle heat. In scattered spots a fire sparked; there was the fleeting smell of fish cooking, spices sharp to cut the brine that preserved the little meat the peasants could afford; drums sounded, light, far away, and coming on the wind like an afterthought. And surrounding them all was the sense of the river, an immense blackness, a pulse that throbbed with sometimes fanciful, sometimes hideous life, a scent both brisk and rank.

The floating city around her, the lanes of river traffic, were ablaze with their grotesque, travestied version of Society. A *gaiola* and its hundreds of hammocks on two tiers was a hotel of strangers laughing lightly and anonymously; houseboat rafts spun in the current, their laundry flapping like arms; the silence parted for the startled bleating of goats that sounded like the cry of children over the water.

When the carriage reached the *Mãe de Deus*, Dolores was hot and chilled, breathless and excited. But any doubts she may have had were left to swirl in the fog. Tomáz resisted leaving but finally gave way to the headstrong young woman and turned the carriage toward home.

As Dolores ascended the gangway with a rush, the sudden danger of being aboard, unknown, left her paralyzed and she broke the silence with her own voice.

"Is anyone here?" she called, the sound frightening her. She spun about, hoping that if she was not heard immediately she would be able to surprise him. The river lapped at the sides of the boat as if hungry for its flesh. Dolores glanced once more about the deck and, seeing no one, entered the open door of the companionway. She hesitated at the top step, listening for the sound of voices or footfalls but hearing only the now-muted sounds of dock life. Gathering her dress, she descended the companionway; when she reached bottom she let go of the gown; the sound of its silken crash was volcanic.

"Hello?" Her voice cracked now with the tension she and the silence had created together. She tried to laugh, tossing her head, and with bravado replacing fear, walked down the passageway that was lit with low-burning kerosene lamps. There were several doorways on either side, and with a dimming precision of purpose, Dolores opened the first one she reached.

At first glance it seemed alive with something, something hot and breathy, and she backed off, but when her eyes accustomed themselves to the dark she saw that the little pulses were the tiny pinpoints of moonlight on hundreds of orchids.

But something was wrong. They had been plucked, ripped to die. The effect was physically repulsive to her and she felt a sweet sickness rise in her throat. Something monstrous was happening, she felt, backing away from the dying orchids that covered the floor of the cabin like their own funeral wreath. The sight sobered her, unexpectedly, but not enough. Why were they here? Why had they not been transplanted correctly? Perhaps he had gathered too many to fit in the hothouse, she thought. The explanation was dimly unsatisfying.

As she made her way down the passage, the boat

rocked, more prey to the vagaries of the river than
her father's massive yacht, and her arms grasped
the bulkheads for balance. In an open doorway to
her left, amidships, a huge hole exposed the engine, dark metal gleaming like a black pearl. She
rushed past with a vague sensation of physical danger, of being sucked in and chewed up by the
workings. Her skirts swished, a ghostly voice: she
turned, startled; no one.

At the end of the passageway was a door that
was not only closed but chained and padlocked.
She studied it for some moments, puzzled, feeling
like Alice in the peculiar book she had read some
years before, and then turned her attention to the
open cabin opposite. By its appointments and
heavy walnut interior, it seemed to belong to the
captain, but its contents perplexed her. In one corner was a stack of Martini rifles and pistols resting
on boxes of ammunition. Next to this were gallons
of paint and paint-brushes. What for? She still
could not erase the dreamlike sensation that had
overtaken her from the moment she stepped
aboard. She attempted to shrug it off literally, and
began to walk outside when she saw a ring of
keys on the desk. More *Alice in Wonderland*. She
reached for them, her head turned to the passageway; she hesitated, listening to the silence.

Then she was out, a swirl of skirts, the keys
clenched tightly in a gloved hand. As she tried one
key after another, she had the odd and frightening
premonition that she was about to be present at her

own execution. The key fit. She sighed, turned back to look at the still-empty passageway that gleamed a dull yellow, and opened the door.

For the moment before her eyes could see in the dark, she thought she had entered a dream of the jungle. The smell in the cabin was dank and moist, heavy with the promise of soil, ripe with rich, oily earth. The heat was strong and vital and laden with jungle moisture, and Dolores realized this must be the hothouse that Kincaid had spoken of so proudly. But if it was the hothouse, why were the orchids dying forward?

She entered the cabin and closed the door partway, taking a kerosene lamp from its wall holder and following its flame as it cast gargantuan grasping shadows across the bulkheads. Throughout the heated room, stacked in neat piles, were boxes made of oily banana leaves, each box filled with soil and bearing a white card as its label. She leaned down, brought the lamp closer, and read the labels: *panciflora, spruceana, rigidfolia, discolor, notida, membranacea, lutea, benthamiana, guayanensis, hevea brasiliensis.* With growing comprehension, she began ripping at the banana leaves, soil falling on her silk dress like summer rain on terra-cotta roofs. And finally, in the palm of her hand, lay the answer to a question she had never asked: the seeds that showed the entire orchid extravaganza had been a lie.

"Interesting?"

Dolores whirled around, her hand opening, the seeds scattering like pellets in the wind. Kincaid stood in the doorway, dressed in twill trousers, boots, and a heavy shirt, another box of rubber seeds in his arms.

For a moment neither of them moved, surprise locking their limbs, rooting them to the spot. She stared, looking at him as if she had never seen him before, her mind abruptly clear of alcohol. She said the first thing that came into her head: "And I told you I loved you."

"You were tipsy," he offered, helpfully, more casually than he had intended.

"I said I loved you," she repeated. "You led me on, you encouraged me."

He looked surprised. "I? I did no such thing. Oh, I admit I found you attractive—very attractive, in fact. I still do. But led you on? Be honest, I've avoided you like the plague since our little— whatever it was—in your father's orchid plantation, when you threw yourself at me. I haven't even seen you until tonight, and when I saw how the wind was blowing I turned around and fled. All the rest is your own fancy."

"*Liar!*" She stamped her foot in rage directed at herself. The accusation was insufferable because she knew it was true. She looked wildly around the confined space for some kind of help, wanting to do something with her hands, then realizing: absurdly she still clutched the orchid. She threw it from her as though it were contaminated.

"It wasn't me." She couldn't stop speaking her thoughts. "It was never me."

Kincaid picked up the flower. "For me?" He

sighed, clearly at a loss, trying to get his own brain to function. "You must know how sorry I am this happened. I—"

"*Save your breath,*" she yelled hoarsely. "I will—" She stopped in midsentence, the threat incomplete as Longford entered, carrying more seeds. Seeing Dolores, he almost dropped the box with an unintelligible oath and looked at Kincaid, bewildered.

"You'll never get away," Dolores said, instantly interpreting the look, almost laughing. Near hysteria, betrayal made her suddenly bold; terrifying. "They will kill you for this. Men have tried it before. All sorts of men, and they all failed."

"That's why they sent me," Kincaid told her, unconscious of any conceit in this remark, stating a fact. As he spoke, he extricated a long piece of rope from beneath one of the boxes. "The Royal Geographic Society . . . that part is true . . . they want to grow their own rubber . . . the price was going too high. Would you mind removing one of your gloves?"

She watched, fascinated, as he moved toward her. Dumbly she let him take an arm and extend it; passively allowed him to peel off the glove. She could not believe they had arrived at this point.

Kincaid spoke to Longford over his shoulder. "We're going to have to leave. Now."

"But the crew!"

"No time to collect them. They'll have to take their chances. Get these seeds stacked and cast off.

The first thing we have to do is stop at the telegraph office."

Longford hesitated, overcome, like Dolores, with the sense of events happening too fast, reeling out of control. As he left the hothouse, he caught a glimpse of Kincaid, impatient and harried, and of Dolores, squared off as if in combat, angry and intense.

When Longford had gone, Kincaid flicked the rope and advanced on her again.

"Hands behind your back."

Her eyes opened wide, unbelieving. As he raised the rope she lunged past him into the darkness. Silently then, only harsh breaths and grunts, Kincaid grabbed her, forced her arms behind her, and tied her wrists with deft expertise. Her chest heaved with the effort to fight him, loose strands of hair fell across her face; the prize orchid was trampled underfoot.

"I'm sorry this had to happen."

"You're sorry?" she echoed wildly over her shoulder. "You are not sorry. You are a—" words failed her "—a cad," she concluded ludicrously.

Kincaid gently put his hand over her mouth, felt her body squirm and writhe against him as he reached for the silk glove and carefully wrapped it around her protesting lips.

"I *am* sorry," he said, and this time, though he was sincere, he was also a bit amused to see her so helpless. Her eyes were wide and darting, as if she could escape imprisonment through sight alone.

"Please believe me," he continued, and saw her
eyes widen further, now in astonishment. He
turned to see Iquitos standing in the doorway,
bare-chested, gleaming and brown, holding another box of seeds and a flaming candle that lit up
his own startled features. Kincaid could feel the
electricity of the interchange between Dolores and
this Indian whom she had thought of as a mechanical extension of her father's will. She struggled in
her bonds, making sharp guttural sounds behind
the glove.

"I'm certain the two of you have a lot to talk
about," Kincaid said, restraining her when she tried
to lunge at Iquitos. "Some other time." He dragged
her across the cabin, sat her down in a chair, then
tied her to it. "I'm sorry about this too, but I've got
to leave you here for now."

Dolores let forth with a powerful kick to his
shin, cutting him off in midapology. Her eyes
blinked wildly, pinpoints of candlelight spitting
fury. Kincaid shrugged, rubbed his leg, and left the
hothouse cabin with Iquitos, locking it after him,
leaving her alone in the dark. Flies buzzed around
her face, and for the first time in her life she was
made aware of how present they were, for she
could not use her hands in the automatic gesture of
brushing them away. Somehow it was this piece of
misfortune that pushed her to the edge of panic;
hot flashes, cold sweat, shaking. But strangely her
mind was clear; now that the worst had happened
. . . or had it? She wondered. Would he come back

once the boat was underway? She had never known a man before, and to be forced . . . Again she struggled against her bonds and again they defied her. Her father would not let this happen; she was sure. She would be missed and it would be soon. Kincaid would be strung up in São Sebastião Square.

She concentrated on this vision, repeating it over and over like an incantation, insisting upon it to avoid thinking that there might be something wrong with the picture. Kincaid, the scheming Yanqui, deserved to be strung up; of that she had little doubt.

But a voice behind her mind or beneath it told her he was taking her away from Pierre Coutard. He was saving her. The idea would have confused her if she had stopped her chant, her litany: He will be strung up.

She sighed, near tears; it was out of her hands as nothing had ever been before.

* * *

Kincaid, Iquitos, and Longford stood in the engine room, silently acknowledging their difficulties as they fueled the boiler. There was no way they could remain in Manaus. Even if Dolores were not missed this evening, which was unlikely, there was still no guarantee that the crew and Captain Mactavish could be found. Remembering his own experience with Manaus nightlife, Kincaid knew how easy it was to get lost in the smoke of opium, and the headiness of French perfume. They had to leave. Now.

Once a head of steam was raised, all three shoveling coal furiously, Iquitos ran topside and jumped to the dock. Years aboard the *Francesca* had taught him about steam yachts. Quickly he threw off the four ropes that secured the vessel, coiling them over his hand and elbow and throwing them over the railings. He climbed back aboard and cut loose the gangway before racing to the wheelhouse, where he opened the throttle as gently as if caressing a baby's arm. The *Mãe de Deus* moved forward from the slip, away from the floating dock, a small yellow light visible in the wheelhouse, disembodied, a fleck of gold on the black river.

River traffic at this time of night was not heavy, but as long as the *Mãe de Deus* remained in the area of the docks there was no question but that she would be seen. There was nothing suspicious about the boat; people were used to the sight of her and no one but the four on board knew anything of her very special cargo. But there was no doubt that her departure differed radically from what had been planned. She was supposed to have left in broad daylight, with Senhor Torres' hearty blessings, and cruised downriver to Pará without trouble or interference from anyone. At Pará she would have effected a rendezvous from the dreadnought *H.M.S. Achilles*—also equipped for the occasion with a functioning hothouse—which would carry them in safety back to England. Enlisting a dreadnought had been Kincaid's idea. He felt safer having the warship waiting for them with her protective guns. To Longford it was ludicrous and he had argued for a Cunarder.

Now all that was changed.

After Iquitos pulled the boat out of its berth, he guided her farther out on the river, holding the wheel steady against the powerful tug of the current. He watched in silence as his home receded in the blackness, a floating city, and wondered when or if he would see it again.

Kincaid went to his cabin while Longford stripped the canvas cover from the dinghy and lowered the small boat into the water. Kincaid returned topside with a small sack of tools slung over his shoulder; they clanked fitfully as he got into the dinghy. Iquitos left the wheel and stood next to Longford by the rail, watching him.

"If I'm not back in fifteen minutes," Kincaid ordered, adjusting the flat oars in their locks, "you're on your own. Whatever you do, don't slacken speed."

"You'll make it, Harry." Longford smiled tightly.

"Fifteen minutes, Professor," Kincaid repeated, then turned to Iquitos. "There isn't anything floating around in the water this time of year that I should know about?"

"No piranha, if that is what you mean," Iquitos replied. "They stay much further upriver until the rains come, and then they—"

"That's all I wanted to know." Kincaid pushed

the dinghy from the boat. "I'd hate to come back without a vital limb."

In another moment he was cloaked in darkness, a light behind him on the *Mãe de Deus* and a hundred yards in front of him the scattered lights of the docks. Rowing as fast as he could while still retaining a smooth surface to the water, Kincaid pulled into one of the narrow muddy channels at the docks. He stood up to make sure he was in the right lane to reach the telegraph office, then sat again and maneuvered among the boats that made this area of the city a community unto itself: long, narrow canoes of hollowed treetrunks that canted left and right under an unevenly distributed wealth of bananas; tiny one-room houseboats with roofs of shaggy palm fronds or terra-cotta tiles fitted with dried mud; some were attached to rafts made of planks filched from under the docks themselves; most were on platforms of watersoaked logs lashed together with chains or rough hemp. Fires burned in some of them in braziers or on small piles of bricks, but most were dark, the people asleep in the discomfort of the damp, mosquito-infested air. Kincaid saw people stirring in a few of the houseboats that were stores and a few others that were brothels. A prostitute wearing only a cotton blouse ripped at the shoulder displayed herself with an enervation that made him turn away.

In its advertisements the telegraph office boasted of maintaining a twenty-four hour service. This, Kincaid discovered, leaving the dinghy lashed underneath the dock and ascending the dilapidated steps to the office, was a fiction. He was obliged to pound on the door and shout for some time before the operator, who was theoretically on duty, turned up the lamps and unlocked the door. From his distracted but wide-awake manner, and from the way he pulled at his trousers in a hasty effort to buckle them and tuck in his shirttails, Kincaid deduced that he had been interrupted *in flagrante delicto*. Of course. This was Manaus.

"I wish to send a telegram," he stated, entering hurriedly and taking up a form from the counter.

"I did not think you came here to buy boots," the clerk agreed, eyeing his half-open bedroom door. He watched, with ill-concealed impatience, as Kincaid scribbled his message.

"You wish it to go out now?" he enquired.

"That's the general idea." Kincaid handed it to him.

He read it once silently to himself, his lips moving with the words, and then out loud. " 'Orchids blooming sooner than expected. Make preparations.' " He looked up. "That is correct?"

"Correct. I'm in a bit of a rush."

The clerk sat down at the key and unlocked the sender, turning knobs and grunting. He was in a hurry, too.

"Where does this go?"

"Itacoatiara."

The man nodded, drumming his fingers as he waited for the machine to warm up. Kincaid leaned against the counter casually and resisted the temptation to look at his watch.

"Four milreis, *senhor.*"

Kincaid plunked the coins down and watched as the operator clacked out the message. There was a pause, then the machine clicked to life of its own volition.

"Message received."

"Many thanks. Goodnight."

"Goodnight." The man followed him to the door, locking it the moment he was through it and turning off the gas.

Kincaid stumbled down the steps, pulling off his shirt and boots with frantic haste, and got back into the dinghy, glad for the darkness as camouflage. He cursed it, too, for he could not run his hands over every slimy piling to find what he wanted. The thought that all this was Dolores' fault suddenly struck him, and he cursed her under his breath. He cursed Mercedes, too, for good measure; the thought of his missing million galled him as he struck a match and peered about during the flare, looking for the cable.

For the brief instant of intense light, the underside of the dock was a haunting specter, an underworld—stark black pilings in milky green water, beyond them blackness and the sounds of skittish rodent life. The match died; he lit another and this time saw the piling that supported the cable. He rowed the dinghy to it, touched the piling with tentative fingers, feeling the wet slippery algae adhered to the rotting wood, then making contact with the thick cable itself. He lit another match and saw that the cable had been wrapped in copper tubing, that it came from a hole in the floor of the telegraph office above and wound down into the water, where it went on submerged to the next relay point downriver.

Kincaid studied the tubing until the flame burned his finger, then extricated a small saw from his bag of tools and with no hesitation now, because there was little time left, lowered himself into the warm, foul-smelling water, and using one hand to steady himself against the piling, his legs wrapped around it to give him leverage, he began to saw through the cable under the water.

The job was easier than he thought, easier than he had dared hope. Something brushed his bare foot. He jerked away. The thing stuck, nipping, and a sick feeling gripped his stomach. He reached down into the water, fingers tentatively crawling along his own leg, the nip getting tighter, and touched bristly fur. He jerked his hand away but whatever it was let go of him. He heard a splashing sound as it swam away, and he went back to the cable, working faster now, his ears cocked for any sound, his feet pulled close to his body.

When he had finally sawed through, he lifted himself back into the dinghy with relief. Then, checking his chronometer, he sawed through the cable again, this time above the waterline. Kincaid was so pleased with this bit of inspiration that he actually laughed out loud.

As he turned the dinghy around and headed for the *Mãe de Deus*, he tried not to think of what would happen if they left without him. He rowed furiously, the laughter worn off, his mind racked with all the ways he might have saved time; if the current had been in his direction, if the saw had been sharper, if he hadn't been bitten, if he hadn't cut the cable twice, if he'd told Longford twenty minutes instead of fifteen, if the operator had not been making love.

He pulled out of the lane of boats and into the open river, catching a glimpse of the wheelhouse light on the *Mãe de Deus* as he glanced over his shoulder. He breathed a long sigh of relief and doubled his efforts. Not to make it in time now, when he had seen her lights, would be the kind of grim irony that only served in the retelling.

His back ached, his arms felt as though he were pulling the oars through lava, his feet were jammed up into the gunwales for leverage, pin-pricked with pain. His head was pitched forward, straining at the neck. He didn't turn around, and when he heard the sound of the engines he didn't know whether they signaled abandonment or salvation. He took no time more to think but continued to row and hope.

"Harry!" A sharp whisper, oddly intimate on this vast expanse of water, and he felt his whole body relax, the taut wire simply pulled out, leaving him limp. There was the sound of the boathook hitting the dinghy, then he was being pulled until it collided gently with the *Mãe de Deus*. No one spoke until he and the dinghy were securely back on board.

"What took you so long?" Longford demanded

irritably. "It's been twenty minutes. We very nearly left."

Kincaid shrugged. "Very nearly doesn't count, Professor."

"Did you cut it?" Iquitos demanded, helping him on with his shirt. Kincaid nodded heavily.

"Twice. Once for them to find . . . and once to drive them mad." He grinned.

Longford started to expostulate but Kincaid cut him off; time was wasting. After a frozen moment, all three returned to business. Iquitos ran to the wheelhouse, opened the throttle to FULL AHEAD, and guided the craft into the main channel, arching a three-mile course that would bring them due east. As the boat gathered speed, Kincaid lit the gas searchlight. The brilliant beam illumined a murky wedge of water. The *Mãe de Deus* raced after it.

* * *

The boat started to move in earnest, shuddering with every revolution of her screw. Dolores, roped, gagged with her own silk glove, jumped as though a jolt of electricity had shot through her body. She struggled furiously with the ropes, strained, twisted her head and body to loosen the hold, but Kincaid had done his job well. Was this another role for her to play? she wondered. Jeanne d'Arc at the stake? It was all too real, this movement on the water; she longed to be a little girl with her father's protection. But she knew that until he came for her, she would have to defend herself and his empire.

The temperature in the hothouse cabin was unbearable; she thought it a fitting irony that the seeds of her father's destruction lay all about her and there was nothing she could do either to warn him or subvert his enemies. By the time she heard the footsteps coming toward the cabin she had ceased struggling; as they stopped just outside the door, she determined to keep her pride and her silence, never to beg, not even to ask.

"What are we going to do with her, Harry? Put her ashore?"

Delores could clearly make out the formal, precise manner of the man, a typically priggish Englishman, she decided. The next voice was Kincaid's, unmistakably American. Whatever music had she heard in it?

"Put her ashore? Where? Someplace deserted? A hothouse blossom like that? She wouldn't last an hour in the jungle. And if we set her ashore at a village, she'll tell them the whole thing. There's only one thing I can think of . . . At least it would be merciful."

In the darkness of the hothouse the scent of her own fear was powerful; she jerked her head violently but the glove remained tight.

"Put her out of her misery right here and now. Don't look so shocked, Professor. We're dead men if we're caught. She said so herself."

"No, no, I absolutely forbid it."

Sweat poured down her forehead, flies zoomed

into her ears, but she was at an absolute peak of clear intelligence, poised at the edge of her skin.

"We're here for the rubber," the Professor went on, and Dolores was thrilled to hear a note of sensible pleading in his voice. "We're not here to kill people. The Royal Geographic Society could not possibly countenance such an action. Why don't we simply keep her on board for a while?" Dolores' energy was almost depleted by this speech and she was let down by the weakness of the final plea.

"Keep her!" Kincaid said, scoffing, unbelieving, and she hated him even more to think that not three hours since, she had known ecstasy in his arms; the very thought made her nauseous behind the glove. "No, no, no. She'd only get in the way. We'd always be guarding her."

"I'll take full responsibility." The Englishman's voice rang clearly, and it suddenly struck Dolores that they were quite aware that she could hear them, quite aware how loud their voices were. Now that she thought of it, why hadn't they decided all of this before they reached the cabin? Unless they were trying to frighten her. "She'll have to earn her keep," the Englishman was saying. As panic ebbed, her rage grew, steaming white and hot, a quiet steel fury that narrowed her eyes. "Maybe she could cook."

"Well, all right," Kincaid said, with what Dolores now recognized as a very theatrical sigh. "As long as she cooks and makes herself useful, I'll let her live."

She heard the key being fitted into the lock and

straightened up in the chair, trying to look as neat in bondage as possible, thinking with enraged speed that they were fools to believe that they could frighten her into being grateful for her life. Cowards, she thought, as a slash of light fell upon her from the open door. If I were them, I would have cut my throat.

When Kincaid appeared, he found her in a posture of fetching docility. She raised her head a bit, eyes lowered demurely, and he was embarrassed at the lengths to which they'd gone. He remembered the sight of her, next to him in the rain beneath the giant fern in her father's plantation, lush and exotic as the orchids that surrounded her. Seeing her now, bound and gagged, trussed up in the dark, filled him with guilt.

"Now look," he commenced with a faintly desperate air she now found amusing, "we've decided to untie you and we're going to leave you unharmed for the moment." He paused to emphasize the conditions of her freedom and began to untie the ropes, speaking calmly and in great earnest all the while. "Any trouble from you and we'll have to take drastic steps. Is that understood?" He craned his neck to peer at her face and she nodded. Docile, he thought, feeling guilty at the fear he'd instilled, and continued untying her. "You'll have to make yourself useful around here for the time being and eventually we'll set you ashore. Is that fair?" Again he paused, and again she nodded. He stood up then, flipped away the rope, and untied the glove from around her mouth. "All right?"

He watched patiently, pained, as she rubbed her pale delicate wrists and the smudged, bruised-looking mouth that he had to admit looked even more lush for the swelling. She looked up at him, her eyes blinking, and he felt sorry for her and for the ridiculous notions that had brought her here. Now it was not a game; even he did not know the next move.

The next move was a shriek and she leapt at him, brandishing ten painted fingernails and the strength of unleashed rage.

"Lord!" Kincaid was surprised, and his body responded automatically. He saw his own right hand ball into a fist and make a neat connection with the point of her outthrust chin. The part of him that was watching this event was shocked at the shock on her face, its silly yielding smile, and he bent double to catch her at the waist before she hit the cabin floor. "I knew that wouldn't work."

"The young lady is neither a fool nor a coward," Longford agreed, grudgingly, then added with sardonic humor, "But it was a clean blow, Harry. Self-defense."

"Let's put her in the fo'c'sle," Kincaid grumbled, swinging her limp body through the door and down the passageway. Longford moved behind, lamp aloft, then sidled himself in front to open the door. "She can't do any damage here. I don't want her anywhere near the seeds."

Kincaid looked around for a place to set her down. The crew's berths were hard wood, their thin mattresses rolled up to prevent mildew. Some parts of the river were so rank and fertile that fungus grew even on exposed skin, which had to be washed with diluted lye every morning and night. Kincaid set her down gently among the hundreds of dying orchids.

"I guess she'll be all right. Come on. We've got a lot to do."

Longford nodded and departed, leaving Kincaid alone with her. He hesitated, looking at Dolores awash in the blossoms. One tonguelike petal touched her bruised lips. He stepped toward her and brushed it away. He noted, as he turned to leave, that there was something truly obscene about those flowers with their strange roots that took sustenance right from the moisture-laden air.

They were off.

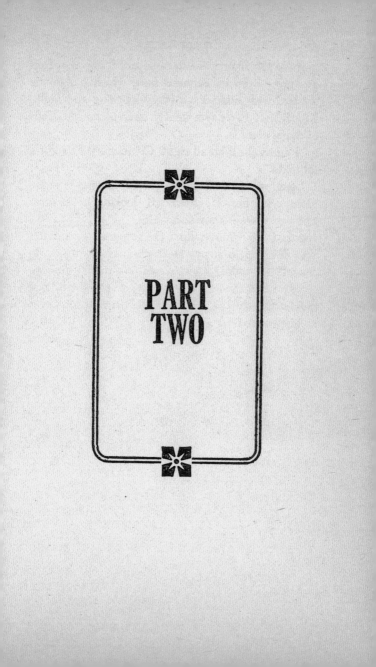

PART
TWO

PART
TWO

❊ 13 ❊

Colonel Mendonça was well pleased. At one o'clock, the majordomo had rapped his staff three times and announced supper in the greenhouse. Almost immediately, guests began ascending the grand staircase in a stately procession. They were pleasantly tired, pleasantly drunk, pleasantly hungry, and perspiring freely. Costumes were dark with sweat in places, or torn from dancing, but all in all the assemblage contrived to look remarkably fit. Indeed, some of the younger couples disdained to quit the ballroom in the majestic rush for food, but followed their host and hostess, who led them through the currently popular Ticklish Water Polka. Mendonça watched his future son-in-law with something very like disgust and shook his head. Rarely had he met so complete and utter a wastrel. A flicker of doubt crossed his mind at the thought of Dolores married to this popinjay, but he banished it; he had never asked her for anything, until now. He was thinking of the future; not just his; not merely hers. The future.

Mendonça spun on his heel and climbed the grand staircase in the wake of the others. He moved slowly; it was past his bedtime.

Slabs of slate formed the winding path to the greenhouse, illuminated by a system of ignited gas jets buried at the path's border, flaming like tiny blue flowers. The way was peopled by guests in transit, some ambling down the walk, others seated in conversation on marble benches in small enclosed glades, lace fans fluttering.

The greenhouse itself was a miracle of inventiveness, glass panes alternating with isinglass for controlling specific densities of solar energy, all in a domed interior that had its exact duplicate on the other side of the mansion, housing a tennis court instead of flowers. Coutard's father had built it to rival Mendonça's orchid plantation when he saw how such a pastime added to his friend's prestige. But orchids either bored him or else the slavishness of such imitation made him self-conscious, and his collection had branched out to include an eclectic variety of flora from all over the Amazon basin.

Tonight while the merrymakers had been dancing, a hundred servants had been at work arranging oilcloth paths over the dirt floors of the greenhouse and erecting long tables on them. When the guests arrived they walked into an Eden, fronted by a huge buffet containing every delicacy from Strasbourg goose-liver paté to *marron glacé*. The revelers entered with gasps of awe and appreciation; so much more amusing than the formal *salle à manager!*

Mendonça nodded in reluctant approval; whatever his private opinion of the man, it was evident

Coutard took the marriage as seriously as he, and accordingly had spared no effort.

But where was Dolores? The question popped quite unexpectedly into his mind. He realized that walking to the greenhouse, he had fully anticipated seeing her presiding; he was quite certain he had not left her in the ballroom. It was Mercedes Coutard who had been dancing with her brother.

As if to confirm his observation, Coutard appeared in the greenhouse doorway, breathless, his white loose eighteenth-century-style blouse open to the waist, displaying his splendid torso, his peruke askew from dancing. He was quite happy, loud, and drunk.

"Where is Dolores?" he cried exultantly, looking wildly about at the diners. "Where is my little bride-to-be? I want to dance with her."

He lurched forward a step, clinging to a wisteria vine. Mercedes tried to take his arm, but he snatched it away and stumbled among the flowers.

"I want my bride. I want my little Dolores. I want my dowry, my treaty of alliance. Where is she?" His uncertain steps led him to Mendonça. "Where's my property?" he breathed into the old man's face. Mendonça smiled thinly.

"Not yours quite yet," he reminded him, resisting the impulse to kill him on the spot. Instead he pushed him gently aside and left him rocking on his heels, his head subsiding amid the *Bauhinia purpureae*. "Inês, where is Dolores?"

The Abbess squinted up at her brother. She, too,

had refreshed herself this warm evening with chilled Dom Perignon.

"Where is she?" she echoed, startled by a straightforward question at this time of night. She placed a hand across her forehead beneath her starched coif.

"Inês!"

"Upstairs," the Abbess remembered with relief and triumph. "I sent her upstairs to lie down. She had the migraine."

"When?"

"When?" The elderly woman furrowed her brow in renewed concentration. It suddenly struck her that "when" had been some time ago.

While Coutard led his company in a series of toasts, which culminated in the guests' hurling their glasses at the rare flowers, Mendonça dispatched a servant to fetch his daughter. The man returned with the news that she was not to be found. When Coutard stumbled over a second time and demanded to see his bride, Mendonça, reddening, was obliged to admit he did not know where she was.

"She probably fell asleep, somewhere, that is all," he said. "She is not used to so much wine."

Coutard nodded, belched, and staggered off.

More servants were dispatched. An extensive if cursory search of the likely rooms was made. No Dolores. By this time, Mercedes had interested herself in the project. She had no particular idea what Dolores' absence portended, but she was a woman alert to every opportunity. Under the pretense of being helpful—and with a very real curiosity—she participated in the organization of the search.

Rather improbably, a servant reported having seen Dolores some time ago in the kitchens. His observation—so unlikely—was ignored until a half-hour later, when another servant was found who said the same thing.

Mercedes, Inês, Mendonça, and Coutard—the latter unsteady on his legs, but still mumbling about dancing with his bride—now proceeded to the kitchens, where several cooks confirmed Dolores' appearance and pointed them to the stables.

Tomáz, the coachman, was found, questioned, and broke down. She had told him it was for a joke, he sobbed.

"Where did you take her?" Mendonça asked, trying to keep the rage from his voice; information first, punishment later.

"To the docks to surprise the Yanqui, the orchid man—" Broken phrases; Tomáz looked from one to the other of his interlocutors. "It was for a joke—"

"Joke!" Coutard tugged off his peruke and hurled it to the ground, livid, red, changing colors like a prism. "Not even our wedding and already I am a cuckold! Joke!" He started for the unfortunate coachman, but Mendonça stopped him. The action brought on the beginning of the cough.

"Cuckold?" he gasped, leaning against the carriage wheel. "What are you saying, *senhor?* You heard him—it was some kind of prank. How dare you imply that my daughter—" He was overcome and stood there, hacking, desperate for breath.

Mercedes interceded on his behalf. She had good reason to know the coachman's story was true; Kincaid was in her pocket. He would never have been so foolish as to contract a liaison with Dolores. He had too much to lose.

"Come, gentlemen, you are both being hasty. I am sure there is an explanation for this. Did you not tell us, Colonel Mendonça, that Dolores was helping the Yanqui with his orchids? Come, come, this is too simple to lose our tempers over."

"But why did she leave without telling anyone?" Coutard demanded in a nasal whine, stamping his feet on the gravel.

"I suggest we go to the boat and find her." Mercedes adopted a soothing tone. The possibilities here were mushrooming into fantastic proportions, but until she had more information, she would play the conciliator. "Let us go to the boat," she repeated. "That way everyone will be satisfied. Pierre, you mustn't be angry. Young girls about to be married oftentimes act very strangely."

"That is very true," Inês volunteered enthusiastically. "I recall—"

Mendonça whirled on her and she trailed off, cowering before his wrath. "I have nothing to say to you," he told her between clenched teeth. Turning, he pulled open the carriage door as if to tear it from its hinges. The Coutards got in after him and the awkward trio departed, leaving the old woman sobbing on the kitchen steps.

*   *   *

In the carriage there was nothing to say. Coutard stared at the window, furious and sullen; it was ludicrous, absurd for him to have to leave his own party—his *engagement ball!*—to chase off into the night after his wayward fiancée. The very thought made him grind his teeth. He hated, above all things, to be ridiculous.

Across from him, Colonel Mendonça sat in abstracted reverie, his open palm resting against his mouth, whether to contain his cough or his words, it was impossible to tell. He tried to keep his mind a blank. There was bound to be an explanation; he would wait for it. For the present, she was his daughter; his obedient daughter. He had no wish to consider her in any other terms. When he looked at Mercedes, seated next to her brother, she smiled encouragingly, as if to reassure him.

The carriage rushed through streets and narrow alleys, the clatter of horses' hooves drowning out the insistent shuffle of Indians bound early for the marketplace, slippers on stone. The Colonel parted the fluted window drapes and saw them, palm-leaf baskets in hand, faces muddy and secretive as the river, their heads lolling from side to side in sleepy protest.

It had been many years since he had come into

contact with the peasants and he realized how alien he had become. When he looked at them, at the flat broad faces so like his own, at the hair black and smooth and so like his own, he felt as if ghosts of himself had materialized. They dressed in bright colors in imitation of the parrots and toucans and macaws of their jungle, and the strips of light sliding into the alleys made them flash like fireworks.

The carriage took them across Astiliana Boulevard and past the glittering windows of Michaelino and Belugii. Only the week previous, Mendonça reflected, he had purchased a diamond ring there —Dolores' wedding present.

What had she done?

They heard the clatter of another carriage, heard the hoarse vendor's cry of "Ice! Ice!" Mendonça rapped the ceiling and told Tomáz to go faster.

They arrived at the docks and the coachman drove them to the same spot. The boat was gone. Mendonça shouted at him: Was he absolutely sure this was where he had brought her? Was he sure the boat was here? Even as he asked, Mendonça knew the answer; the abandoned gangway sat like a bridge to nowhere. It was at that moment, seeing the empty space, filling it in his mind with the vast expanse of the night and the river, that Colonel Armando Mendonça began to understand despair; it had been a long time since he had not known what to do. Now, feelings of shame and ruin closed in on him like pincers and squeezed.

Coutard walked in small circles, his body shaking in paroxysms of rage, trembling uncontrollably.

"So this is the way of your daughter's honor!" he screamed at the night. "To elope! To run off with the Yanqui! *The slut!* Well, *senhor,* much good may your alliance do you now! Much good may all the precious pieces of paper we have put our names to do you now!" And on in the same vein, for his imagination was not lively.

Mercedes stood absolutely still, looking at nothing, seeing nothing. She had misjudged the Yanqui. He had betrayed her. Whether it was the spurning of herself or her money, whether it was her lacerated pride or her mislaid plans that now consumed her, she could not have said with certainty. Without saying a word to her brother or to the Colonel, Mercedes turned and walked the length of the pier to the telegraph office; the boat would be stopped. They would be brought back. Kincaid would die.

Neither man missed her. Coutard continued his pacing and his muttering. Mendonça walked toward the empty space left by the *Mãe de Deus,* staring at the truncated gangway, trying to feel the presence of his daughter, but only recalling his new-found despair.

He drew his cloak closer, wrapping himself tighter and tighter, but he seemed to have no body heat at all. He was colder than the poorest man, colder than he'd been as a boy, colder than when his first wife and son had died in the river, and he knew that he was recognizing death. He choked; his body heaved to accommodate the shock; for a terrified instant he feared he would fling himself into the black water. The pier pilings were soft and wormy, but the Colonel sat down, his back to the city he had helped create, facing instead the emptiness of what lay before him, embodied in the dense mysteries of the Rio Negro.

He thought back to certain decisions he had made in his life; none had been made in the burning heat of rage or conceit, yet he knew now he was not defending his daughter's honor nor even concerned with her loss, but with himself and his own honor. All the things he had rationed to honor had been done in name only; at bottom, he realized now, alone, abandoned of hope and unprotected by the empire of power and possession he'd built to fortify his weaknesses, it had all been for himself.

He had to preserve his land; it was all that he knew. And he did love his daughter; the feelings were not fiction and vanity. Had she spoiled herself? Ruined him? He could not believe it was possible. There was, somewhere, an explanation. Was she even with the Yanqui? Had he. . . ?

There was a large warehouse whose front doors were painted with *MENDONÇA* but open now so that only the *ME* was visible. The Colonel watched column after column of men lug brownish mattresses of raw rubber to the scale at the edge of the docks, next to a freighter bound for Marseilles. He found himself multiplying the number in order to give himself an idea of how much he owned. His mind was occupied with figures that stretched the width of his mind, and then he looked up, aware suddenly that dawn had come, that the city had awakened, that there were flies buzzing on the oblique rays of the sun.

"The cable has been cut," said Mercedes, tonelessly. He twisted around, disoriented; she stood in back of him, a telegram in her hand. "The Yanqui was the last man to send."

Coutard snatched the paper. "'Orchids blooming sooner than expected. Make preparations.'" He looked from one to the other. "What does it mean?"

Mercedes ignored him and faced the Colonel. "This went out at midnight. The line went dead sometime afterward. No doubt the Yanqui cut the cable. The message is obviously some sort of code."

Mendonça looked at her, hope growing in his face, if not for his daughter, then perhaps for his honor.

"Can she have been abducted by him?" He rose stiffly. "Does he intend holding her for ransom?"

"Did he abduct her from my house?" Coutard snorted contemptuously. "Abducted? You have been reading the lady novelists. She has betrayed you; she has betrayed me, and humiliated—"

"Be still," his sister interrupted, the familiar authoritative tone turning off his voice like a tap. She followed Mendonça back toward the carriage, her brother tagging petulantly behind. Mercedes was lost in thought; there was something about all this that disturbed her in ways she had not begun to fathom. The line was cut. How to stop them? Almost at once she thought of her pet project: Poincarré's balloon would do the job. And then she remembered the balloon's untimely escape and how amused her guests had been at the sight. Mercedes pursed her lips primly; yes, she had badly misjudged Kincaid.

"Get rich! Get rich!" The cry sounded from the dock, the lottery seller beginning his day's work. The voices of other street vendors joined in, counterpointing the piston and steam action of the boats, the iron clanking tin that advertised the tinsmith, the flugelhorn for the Viennese tailor, the shrill piping of breath on bamboo blown to attract a sweet tooth to the cake seller.

Other sellers began walking by them, holding aloft their items of specialty: emerald-green caique parrots, turtles and chickens, pineapples and mangoes, wads of rubber on men's shoulders, and in pine boxes beads, shells, rice and corn, armloads of fresh flowers and sour-smelling meats preserved in brine.

"Come." Mendonça stood by the carriage door, holding it open. "This is no place to talk. Whatever has happened to my daughter affects me at least as much as you, *senhor,* I daresay. Let us discuss the matter privately. Our presence here will simply excite undue comment."

Woodenly, Coutard moved to obey him when his foot on the carriage step was arrested in its progress by a commotion at the far end of the big dock. People of all sorts were converging there, straining for a look at the water.

Mendonça exchanged a puzzled glance of enquiry with Mercedes and abruptly turned, pulling and shoving his way through the crowd without pretense of ceremony. Mercedes followed, no less eager, and Coutard, exhausted with dancing, drink and desertion, unwillingly brought up the rear.

What they saw, when they had finally succeeded in forcing their way through the press, was almost religious in splendor, a miracle of the river. Floating on the water, where the Amazon met the Rio Negro, were thousands of orchids. The cool orange-gray light of the early morning made the petals all colors of translucency against the obsidian of the river.

Voices next to them and behind them exchanged astonished explanations, sibilant with speculative wonder. Coutard blinked at the panoply of blossoms in the early light, white orchids on the black water; dazzling and distracting. Behind them the crowd had closed in again, collectively stupefied by the spectacle.

Mendonça stared at the flowers, knowing instinctively what they meant—unsure only how it was that he knew. He had to force his mind to produce the logical connecting links in the chain of reasoning: Kincaid had thrown the orchids overboard; it had not occurred to him (or he had not believed) they would float backward. He had not come for orchids. He had not come for Dolores. He had come for—

"He's taken the rubber." Mercedes read his mind.

Mendonça nodded.

"What? What are you talking about?" Coutard demanded. "This is only a—"

"The rubber," the Colonel repeated, and then repeated the words again and again, as if greeting the news of the return of a dream. "You fool!" he screamed at Coutard, defying him to remain ignorant. "He's taken seeds!"

Mercedes clamped her brother's arm, her fingers so white bone appeared to be glowing through the skin. A pulse throbbed in her neck. The pressure of her finger conveyed the meaning to Coutard, who stood numb with shock, unused to lessons learned in public and in pain.

But the Colonel was bravely, immensely alive, spinning in place, charging the crowd to part for him as he forced his way back to the carriage and climbed atop it with the energy of a young man.

"Citizens," he cried, holding up his hands for silence, "our city depends upon your speed. If the rubber thieves escape, the jungle will grow over our homes!"

Then he began issuing commands. The crowd, until now a hydra-headed creature, devoid of coordination and unity, listened and congealed into one man. They knew the Colonel and obeyed his orders. They understood perfectly; the stakes had been explained to them in their cradles. They raced to implement his commands. Workmen were dispatched to repair the broken cable, others questioned the dock residents for a description of the *Mãe de Deus*, prepared to circulate it. When

the cable was fixed, Mendonça would contact the
Brazilian Navy and alert their gunboats to intercept
the contraband and apprehend the thieves. A mes-
senger was dispatched to Casa Grande for the Colonel's factotum, Iquitos.

Mercedes, for the moment, put aside her personal enmity for Kincaid and for the Colonel. She
climbed into the carriage next to him and seconded
his instructions. The boilers on board the *Francesca*
were ordered fired. Every man with a boat was incorporated into the armada of pursuit.

"Who knows what the Yanqui's boat looks like?"

Mercedes' eye scanned the throng that swayed
like corn in the wind; a break in the uniformity
occurred, a jostling forward until a young French
sailor was propelled from the mass and stumbled
toward the carriage, shouting up at her.

"It was pure white from stem to stern! Ninety-
five feet, high in the water, perhaps five feet below
the waterline—"

"It will be lower now," someone bellowed.

The boy was told to report to Mendonça in the
telegraph office. Mercedes turned and saw the silhouette of her brother, stranded and bewildered
against the whitening sky. A tremor traveled across
her stomach in staggered undulations, but whether
in hatred or desire, she could no longer tell. And
she hadn't time to wonder.

The telegraph office was a scene of confusion.
The line, supposedly repaired, was still dead and
consternation reigned. Only Mendonça seemed
capable of understanding and of making decisions.

"They've cut it more than once, that is all, but they cannot have reached into the riverbed. That means it is near the office. Behind. Around the pier. Underneath." He grabbed the lapels of the man nearest him, almost lifting him off the ground. "You take some men. You find it. Quickly."

He hurled the man away, used up, and found him replaced in his line of vision almost instantly with the young French sailor, a tiny blue and red flag on his whites and an absurd glow on his cheeks.

"It was pure white . . ."

There was a flurry at the door, the crowd parting, silencing the sailor and allowing for the entrance of Mercedes and a Scotsman with a face of fear and anger to match his red hair.

"The Yanqui must have gone in a hurry," Mercedes told Mendonça with wry contempt, indicating the Scot. "This is the Captain of the *Mãe de Deus*. He says the crew are all on shore."

The Colonel looked at Mactavish for a moment so pregnant with rage the very air was galvanized. The moment splintered when the Colonel slapped Mactavish with the back of his hand, a diamond from Michaelino and Belugii making a neat slice across his cheek where the blood, shocked, appeared, waiting.

"He came for the rubber," the Colonel began with dungeon calm.

"Not to my knowledge, Colonel," Mactavish said, pleading, as he wiped the blood from his face with a whore's handkerchief. "Orchids, he told us. Orchids."

The Colonel was about to strike again, but sensed the man was telling the truth. His body gave itself up to a cough as if rage had been the medicine. He grabbed Mactavish's arm for support.

"I want a detailed description of the *Mãe de Deus*," he gasped. "How fast she can go, how much fuel is on board, and how many men it takes to handle her. If you do not tell me the truth I will tear out your throat."

There was a scuffling to his right and the Colonel saw a flash of white being shoved out of the telegraph office into the crowd and heard a piping voice.

"It was pure white . . ."

Mendonça pulled Mactavish along, forcing his way through the crowd, the Coutards at his heels. Outside, a bizarre flotilla was plowing through the bed of floating orchids. The high, narrow bark canoes so common to the harbor led the way out, then clung close to the banks, their wide blades ungainly. Behind them were larger canoes, suggested in design by an old Portuguese captain's memory of a Hong Kong *sampan*, square-sailed and jittery. They managed to maneuver deftly alongside enormous rusted oil tankers from Russia and Galicia and a once-glorious steamer turned river tramp on its way to Rio de Janeiro. A timber carrier recently unloaded of its cargo joined the canoes, square prow sucking up its self-created waves. And behind them came other boats, yachts of varying size and importance of ownership, a three-tiered *gaiola* whose immensity would make it useless in a race but whose spirit cheered the feistier. And behind them all, late in starting but plowing through the center of the mass of boats on a river of orchids, was the *Francesca* in a high-bowed steaming rage. As it passed the sharp line of demarcation where the Rio Negro met the Amazon, their black and yellow waters foaming in swarthy combat, the *Francesca* was everything victory should be.

❈ 14 ❈

Dawn had already torn a jagged orange line across the gray horizon when Kincaid, slick with sweat, came out of the engine room. He made his way toward the wheelhouse, where Iquitos had had the watch during the night, wiping his body with his shirt and glad for the relatively cool river air. Then he was slapping his neck and arms in the ritual dance of the Amazon, swatting flies. When the *Mãe de Deus* had navigated the inky waters of the Rio Negro, it had been free of the beastly pests; the chemical composition of the silt at the Rio Negro's bottom, filtering its way through the water itself, caused that river to be almost free of flies. But once past that line from the black of the Negro to the bright, clear yellow of the Amazon, man waged a constant battle against the tiny, almost invisible *pium* and the relentless bloodlust of the *matuca*.

Kincaid breathed deeply, watching the river lapping alongside the boat in foamy tongues.

When he was offered his commission he read what books there were about the Amazon: Daltrey's *Amazon Odyssey* and the companion piece published several years later, *Daltrey in the Jungle,* a reminiscence of the seventeenth-century explorer by the man who'd served as the second mate on his ship. He also read *The River of No Return,* a first-person account of a brutal attack by an Indian tribe on a party of Jesuit missionaries. But nothing in these books, not the florid descriptions of the wildlife nor the lurid descriptions of the city life nor the torrid descriptions of life in the jungle, had prepared him for the overwhelming vastness of the Amazon. Even Longford's reminiscences on the subject were ultimately insufficient: one had to see it for one's self.

When he had passed through the narrows that separate the southern point of Marajó Island from the mainland, he envisioned the journey as no further than a trip from New York City's harbor to Montauk Point at the eastern tip of Long Island. He was not far off except he did not go far enough; the scale was quite different, the river was hundreds of miles wide at its mouth and it was fitting that the Equator entered Brazil at this particular spot. Early geologists speculated that the Amazon had once divided South America into two enormous islands until the Andes rose in eons of cataclysm and sealed off the western end, after which it poured two hundred and fifty million cubic meters of fresh water into the Atlantic every hour. Early explorers called it Mar Dulce, the Sweet Sea; Brazilians called it the Sea River; the Indians called it River of Life, River of Death, for it was generous and it was merciless. Kincaid glanced at it, shaking his head, and his eye was startled by a flash of gold as a fish approached the surface and darted down again.

By the time he reached the wheelhouse, the early morning mist had lain a film on his body. Iquitos smiled wearily, each man silently acknowledging the other's fatigue. Kincaid checked the charts and pointed to a spot on the map. Iquitos nodded; they would reach Itacoatiara in eight or nine hours, in time to pick up their supplies under the cover of failing light, and to slit the cable again. And from there to Parintins on the Tapajos River and from there . . . his mind's journey ended vaguely, in the same mist they traveled on now, the same river, the same jungle.

Sleep was a gift denied them, snatched fitfully here and there; a full crew was needed to man a boat the size of the *Mãe de Deus*. Kincaid would not say it aloud, but he didn't know if they would make it.

He paused to light a cigar before dipping his brush into a can of paint. He glanced at the length of the *Mãe de Deus*, groaned audibly between clenched teeth, and looked over the side to see what progress Longford had made.

"One hundred and five feet. That's port and starboard and doesn't include the superstructure, Professor."

Longford smiled with grim amusement and dipped his own brush, stilling conversation. To himself he reflected that it was a good thing Kincaid had planned as thoroughly as he did. Back at the hotel he'd said that all this probably wouldn't be necessary. Now that it had proved otherwise, he was grateful he'd checked on the cable relay points, that paint and brushes were ready for use. Still, it would be a job. They had a very short time in which to do something that required considerably longer. And though they were well stocked when it came to paint and brushes, they were woefully lacking in food and fuel. Luckily—or perhaps it was not luck, Longford thought, again remembering how well Kincaid planned—their first relay point at the Itacoatiara telegraph station was holding a supply of provisions for them. Kincaid had not foreseen their hasty departure, but he had provided for it, nevertheless.

Sanguine about their arrangements, Longford urged Kincaid to share some food with the girl. Kincaid turned to consult with Iquitos and was astonished to find him staring at the water astern, open-mouthed.

"What the devil is that?" Longford wondered, pointing in the same direction. Kincaid followed his finger. Stretching into the fog was an unbroken trail of orchids floating on the dun-colored water. With an inarticulate cry, Iquitos released the wheel and bounded from the wheelhouse.

Kincaid followed, calling to Longford to take the helm, and raced down the companionway, along the passageway to the bow. Iquitos had run to the fo'c'sle, was fumbling madly with the key to the lock. He finally forced it, the door banging open, bounding shut, open again, everyone startled.

Dolores whirled about from the starboard porthole, frightened and triumphant: the fo'c'sle was almost completely devoid of orchids. Iquitos sagged against the bulkhead in despair, but Kincaid remained confused, although the sight of Dolores in one of the crew's white uniforms, loose cotton pants and a cotton shirt tight about the chest, was almost enough to bring a smile to his face.

"What are you worried about?" he asked. "No one's going to see them. They'll just float downstream with us." He waved his hand to indicate how meaningless the action was. Dolores uttered a short, dry laugh.

Iquitos groaned. "You do not understand. They will flow *upstream.*"

Kincaid felt a tickle of doubt but knew the Indian was mistaken. "There isn't a river in the world that reverses itself and flows upstream." He waited for Iquitos to agree and explain his own error, but the Indian only shook his head and Dolores laughed again, a sound with more menace than glee.

"The Amazon is not like any river in the world, Senhor Kincaid," she said, with the pride of a mother. "It has a tide."

"A tide?" There was a pounding in his ears. "Even the Great Lakes don't have a tide!" But the words trailed off.

"The Amazon is bigger than all your Great Lakes put together," the Indian said. Kincaid shook his head, remembering the floating docks. Rivers flowed from a source to a larger body of water, they flowed in one direction, they had currents,

they flooded. One thing they did not do was heed
the pull of the moon. Except the Amazon. He
turned to Dolores just in time to see her drop another orchid out the porthole. He didn't like being
made a fool.

"Go ahead and kill me!" Dolores said, fearless.
"You are a dead man, no matter what you do. And
you!" She turned to the Indian, her mouth dis-
torted in disgust, and spat. "Judas! My father made
you everything. He took you from the jungle and
he taught you! He treated you like a son and you
repay him with this!" Tears ran down her cheeks,
but she was not crying. Kincaid perceived that he
had underestimated her.

Iquitos did not erupt at this accusation; rather it
seemed to calm him. He wanted Dolores to confront him, needed her contempt as an excuse to
explain himself.

"It is true, your father has treated me well. But
that does not excuse what he and the Coutards
have done to the tribes. I am a gesture, *senhorita,* a
sop to your father's conscience."

"My father's conscience is clear," Dolores said.
"It is yours which is filled with guilt."

"My people are slaves," Iquitos replied quietly.
"For a long time I hoped that your father would
change in the way he treated the Indians. I hoped
I might change him." He shrugged. "But now it is
too late; even if he wished it, it is too late." He said
this last with the sadness that apologized for his
actions and the regret that he could behave no
other way.

Dolores turned her back on him, her face drawn and tired in the morning light. She stared numbly at her gown in the corner of the cabin, its silk waterlilies eviscerated, drained of their blood in the pale light. Iquitos moved hesitantly toward her.

"Your father has not long to live, *senhorita*. When he dies Coutard will make the situation worse. Your father knows this, yet he planned for you to marry this man and perpetuate the system of injustice. I could not allow this to happen."

"*You* could not allow it!" Dolores' back was stiff and tense, lit by a sudden shaft of light as the sun shot through the porthole. The quaver in her voice did not match the force of her words. "And do you think to do your people good by destroying the rubber monopoly?"

Like a spectator at a tennis match, Kincaid swiveled his attention to Iquitos, dazedly awaiting his reply. The Indian's strength and resolution were almost depleted. Facing the daughter of his foster father and moving farther and farther from the only home he had known, he had begun to be appalled by the enormity of his act, its theoretical consequences thirty years hence suddenly intangible and unreal. He swallowed and spoke almost as if by rote.

"The only way the *grandes homens* will develop other industries is if they are forced to do so. They never will, not while rubber is the cheapest and the easiest, not while monopoly is another word for slavery."

"Yes, you have learned your lessons well; education did much for you," Dolores countered in a voice dripping with sarcasm. She turned from looking out the porthole and surveyed him with contempt. "And you do this with the Royal Geographic Society! And this pirate, this hired thief!" She jerked her head abruptly in Kincaid's direction. "Do you think he cares what becomes of the tribes? He is nothing but a mercenary. His fine manners from Europe mean nothing. His morality comes from the brothel. He uses fancy words only to deceive."

Kincaid sighed and looked apologetically at Iquitos. Daylight was getting stronger, burning off the fog, washing their faces fever red.

"The first round goes to you," he told Dolores and picked up the last orchid. "*Cattleya labiata*," he muttered, tracing the furled lavender petals across his lips. Then he tossed it out the porthole, where it served as the final punctuation of the long and dangerous message that floated upriver to Manaus.

* * *

For much of its length, the Amazon has no banks. Its dense jungle vegetation abuts the river. But this is often deceptive, for in other areas of the flood plains the banks are protected by unseen, impenetrable tangles of matted vegetation, often based on the wandering, twisted roots of the mangrove tree. Boats that wandered into this area and survived reported a tentacular forest as tangled as a web.

The *Mãe de Deus*, because it could not be very

far ahead of those in pursuit, stayed out of the main
channel and skirted the southern bank. The combination of Longford's botanical knowledge, Iquitos'
native expertise, and Kincaid's aplomb was enough
to keep them safe. They hoped.

The sun was up full and blazing, the damp fertile
smell of the jungle washing over the boat. Along the
bank, jutting out in irregular rocklike formations,
were deposits of the red clay that was used for the
roofs of many Manaus homes and that gave the river
its peculiar mahogany color, the land bleeding into
the water. Mourning or celebrating it in shrill
bursts were parrots, toucans, and wild turkeys
peering myopically into the river from high
branches in the overhang.

Dolores, not trusted to her own devices, sat inside the shade deck, a makeshift area where tattered canvas was stretched taut across bamboo
poles. Her expression was disgruntled, frustration
and anger high. Not far from her, Kincaid crouched
at the funnel, a can of gold paint in one hand, a
small brush in the other and a look of concentration on his face as he studied a book balanced on
one knee. The *Mãe de Deus* was now no longer
pure white, but the impure green of the military.
Floating in such calm water, it seemed to belong
more to the jungle than the river.

Dolores left the shade deck and walked to the
funnel where Kincaid worked. She watched. He
ignored her.

"And what is that supposed to be?"

Kincaid bent down again and added a swift neat

stroke of gold. "As you may know, the Amazon is an international waterway, open to the shipping of all nations and patrolled by gunboats of the Brazilian navy." He checked the book in his hand, comparing the insignia on its page to the copy he'd painted on the funnel. "We are now the gunboat *São Paulo, in* the Brazilian navy." He paused again to admire his work, then took in the almost transformed boat with a sweeping glance, sighing. "Of course we're three feet too short and we haven't any deck guns..."

Longford came on deck then, balancing a tray of sandwiches in front of him like a tribal offering, absurdly pleased that he'd been able to direct his scientific zeal to practical use in the galley. Kincaid smiled at him and took a sandwich from the tray; Dolores took one with a desultory nod; Longford walked to the railing and handed one down to Iquitos, who was still painting the hull. Kincaid, sandwich in hand, went around to the other side of the funnel to duplicate the insignia of the *São Paulo*. Dolores followed, sneering.

"That insignia will only fool the anteaters."

Kincaid bit into his sandwich and dipped brush to paint. "You'd be surprised. From a distance I'd say we look pretty convincing ... as long as we don't bump into a real gunboat ... and I think we're staying too close to shore for that."

Dolores shook her head; to give in to the smugness she saw in him would be intolerable; to yield to his assurance of her abduction, his attempt to ruin her father, his successful escape, would be unbearable. She bit into her sandwich and her mouth was sour. She stood up and threw the sandwich overboard.

No one spoke although everyone noticed; the sun seemed raw and the flies frantic. Iquitos, who had just come on deck, went to the wheelhouse for more paint, then disappeared angrily over the port side. Longford went below, back to the galley.

"You shouldn't have done that," Kincaid told her, but Dolores was well into her mood of rebellion. If she could not escape, she could at least make their escape and her abduction as difficult as possible.

"Are you running out of food?" she asked with a cutting laugh. "You will have to stop and hunt, or fish. And then you will lose time."

"But first we could stop feeding you," Kincaid said and saw her confidence ebb just a bit. "That would stretch our supplies for a day or so. Have you ever seen anyone starve to death, Miss Mendonça? Their tongues turn black. I've seen it—on the streets of Manaus."

Dolores turned her back to him and stared at the river. She was being placed on the defensive and couldn't see why. She was not a thief; she was not abducting anyone. And yet he made her feel guilty.

"Every city in the world has its beggars," she responded in a choked voice.

"Not every city in the world is as rich as yours," he countered, not really angry but impatient with this spoiled, selfish girl who seemed to be more than she allowed herself to show. He moved to the railing to check on Iquitos' progress and spoke to

Dolores over his shoulder. "Not every city in the world could do something about it. That's the real crime of Manaus—to say nothing of an economy built on slavery."

"My father freed his slaves years ago!" she cried.

"Tell that to him—" Kincaid gestured over the side to Iquitos. He returned to the funnel and his replications of the naval insignia. His seeming disinterest in this discussion—a conversation in which she found herself defending her entire life—was more than she could bear.

"So you are a moralist, after all," she noted. "How noble!"

Kincaid peered around the funnel at her, then resumed his forgery with a little sigh.

"I don't fool myself, Miss Mendonça." His voice was calm, almost mournful, with more feeling in it than she had yet heard. "I'm just as you described me and not worth a damn. What don't *you* fool yourself about?"

She thought of slapping him, but the gesture died in her mind and she spun around and walked away; hot tears filled her eyes.

Walking through the passageway to the fo'c'sle, she passed the galley and saw Longford polishing glasses that humidity refused to let dry. She stopped and went in, each acknowledging the other's presence but remaining suspicious; they tested the silence as if it had a taste.

"Thank you for my sandwich," Dolores began hesitantly, ready to pull back. "You are a professor?"

"Botany," Longford replied and they smiled at each other without much joy or trust.

Dolores reached for one of the sandwiches and took a bite, making a great show now of savoring it. "You have been to Brazil before?"

"Yes, actually, a number of times," Longford replied, putting down the glass he was polishing, shrugging helplessly at the impossibility and irrelevance of his task. "South American flora is my particular field. Heavens, we've not begun to discover what mysteries are here, much less catalogue them. I worked with Father Gropius at the Jesuit mission near Marajó."

"And Senhor Kincaid?" she asked without thinking. They both knew the question was less casual than she might have wished it to sound. Dolores waved her hand in a gesture meant to lessen the impact and Longford was discreet enough to draw no attention either to the question or the gesture.

"Harry and I have both worked for the Royal Geographic Society before," he said, adding in a conspiratorial tone, "Harry is their court of last resort."

Dolores looked up as if vision could penetrate the structure of the boat and pierce into Kincaid's soul above deck. "I can see why," she said, but her grimness contained a degree of encouragement that Longford did not fail to notice and he spoke with relish.

"No, I don't think you can," he replied, laughing a bit self-consciously, embarrasssed at some of the recollections flashing through his mind. "Harry's specialty is freeing slaves. In the Congo. In China. That sort of thing. He claims his father was with Brown at Harper's Ferry, says it runs in the blood. Of course, he's a terrific liar so one can't really be sure."

Longford laughed self-consciously again. Dolores thought the man wise and sensible in certain areas, but decided he liked Kincaid just a bit too injudiciously for his own good. It would not happen to her; she understood something now of romantic illusions and physical attraction. But it would not happen to her.

Below them the engine heaved like thunder underfoot and both Dolores and Longford were made aware of the steady forward movement of the *Mãe de Deus*. Longford looked away guiltily and Dolores involuntarily pressed her hands to her ears. With each shuddering, she was being carried further away from her home. Following Kincaid in rags to the ends of the earth might once have been her dearest wish. How Fate loved a jest. Could she have foreseen, in her wildest flights of fancy, the turnabout situation in which she presently found herself; where the man she had been convinced she loved—hero, prince, poet—proved a faithless soldier of fortune who worshipped nothing more aesthetic than a golden calf? The fact that he had spirited her away from a detestable marriage only served to compound her confusion and her sense of shame. It was not Coutard to whom she had proved false (she had no illusions of being true to that idiot), but her father. If she had obeyed him as a dutiful daughter she would not have placed him in the untenable position he doubtless occupied at the moment.

One thing was certain: this knowledge would not allow her to succumb to Harry Kincaid. Even allowing for her romantic disposition, she assured herself, she was not capable of that irony.

❈ 15 ❈

From a distance the river appeared littered with the garbage of an ill-planned meal. The motley array of boats, no two alike, similar only in their capacity to remain afloat, was an awesome spectacle.

But awesomeness was to be the order of the day, just as it had been since the beginning of the rubber boom. The men in the boats knew only too well what would happen to them if the Yanqui and his English accomplice were not caught; the barons would be reduced to dealing in the more easily harvestable but inferior grade of wild rubber, Peruvian slab; money would be worth less and less, and, unable to sustain its gargantuan rate of inflation, Manaus would be unable to maintain the life to which it was accustomed. In short, the kings would lose their kingdoms; without the enormous profits in rubber, the poverty that followed would be—like everything else—awesome.

The ramshackle armada poured on every ounce of steam and every inch of sail. In addition to simply overtaking the pirates, each man had some thought of the reward that would be his should his ship reach the renegades first. Not only would he be credited with saving the city; there was also the

Colonel's abducted daughter, whose safe return would surely not go unrecognized by the Colonel himself. The mere thought of Colonel Mendonça's gratitude spun dizzy fantasies in the heads of those who thought about such things.

Visions of the Colonel's generosity, however, did not enable any one boat to overtake the Colonel's own craft. The *Francesca* forged ahead at a speed none could emulate, save perhaps the one she was pursuing.

"I've done some calculating," Mendonça told the Coutards. The massive activity astern was almost totally unfelt under the brass and glass shade deck where the Colonel was studying a series of charts laid out before him. Servants in short white jackets shifted about on the deck just forward, signaling their availability with precise semaphorics. Mercedes, sitting motionless in her deck chair, set down her empty champagne glass and looked over at the old man. She had to admire his stamina.

"They have at most a seven-, perhaps an eight-hour lead," the Colonel informed her, poring over his computations. He was far less disturbed now that he was in pursuit; the very sense of moving forward in space gave him the illusion of leaving something behind in time. "The *Mãe de Deus* is faster than anything in Manaus, including the *Francesca*." He laughed shortly. "The Yanqui planned well." He pursed his lips; if only they had been able to locate Iquitos in time to sail; he felt ill at ease somehow without him.

Coutard spun impatiently off the teak railing,

walked over to where Mendonça sat, and glanced without comprehension at the paper the Colonel handed him. "It's hopeless," he proclaimed with melancholy rage. "If they are faster than we and they have an eight-hour start, how can we possibly hope to—"

"We have several advantages," the Colonel said, snatching back the figures to write some new ones. "We know the river; he does not. We have a full fuel supply; according to Captain Mactavish, he does not. We have a crew; his is still in Manaus."

He looked up at Coutard and Mercedes, nodding from one to the other. Despair was behind him now, but it had weakened him in the very place he'd needed to be strongest. He shook the maps and put them down, searching for more reasons to convince them and himself that they would win. "And Dolores will try to slow him down. It is obvious that it was she who threw the orchids overboard." He smiled now at Coutard, but the Colonel would never forgive his future son-in-law for having doubted Dolores and for having borne witness to his own doubts. "So you see, you were wrong about my daughter."

"Not necessarily. The Yanqui might have thrown them overboard if they were in the way. He might not have anticipated their floating back to us."

Mendonça stiffened at the insult, ready to reply, then decided it wasn't worth the effort. These things could be attended to later.

Coutard turned away, resuming his gloomy vigil by the rail. When had things become so serious?

he wondered dully. His mind, his spirit was still someplace on the dance floor; he was marrying into everything he could wish; it had all been perfect. And now, thanks to a conniving Yanqui, he was threatened with extinction and compelled to take part in a wild goose chase. And, unacknowledged, there was his bitter resentment of Kincaid; Kincaid, whom he had personally introduced to the finest brothels in Manaus, and now this hostile ingratitude. Coutard couldn't tell if it was the girl or the theft that angered him most. It used to be so simple with women and land; you bedded the women and bled the land. Other men's blood, of course. Now, all at once, there appeared the prospect of killing for the women and grabbing in desperation for the land. Somewhere, in the midst of all this, lurked the idea that Colonel Mendonça was responsible as well. If he hadn't proposed his daughter as Coutard's wife—but then, things being what they were, Kincaid would probably have taken the rubber anyway. Nevertheless, he harbored rancor toward the Colonel. Toward them all, including his meddlesome sister, who thought she was one of the Borgias. The only thing that could stir Coutard, that he would admit to, was a slight to something he identified as his good name. He stared at the rushing water below him, his mute rage gnawing as steadily as the German engine that propelled the *Francesca*.

Mercedes remained silent and rigid in her chair, neither hearing nor seeing their discussion. In a private world of her own devising, she thought only of Kincaid and her betrayal. The girl counted for nothing; the rubber would be retrieved—but Kincaid! Kincaid would have to pay. Mercedes closed her eyes and luxuriated in fantasies of revenge. She could picture him now, up ahead on the river somewhere, sweating, shoveling coal for dear life, exhausted, stinking, his panic growing as he saw his supplies of fuel shrinking. She saw him antlike, scurrying back and forth, running from the helm to the engine room in a frantic effort to multiply himself into a crew of sufficient size to run a hundred-foot steam yacht. She squirmed with pleasure. Yes, Kincaid would pay. She smiled at the sunlight; he was paying already.

She leaned back in her chair, arranged the tiger skin of last night's costume, and signaled a servant for another bucket of champagne on ice. The *Francesca* was one of the first steam yachts to sport an ice-making plant. Sixty pounds of ice a day was barely enough to chill the champagne, of course, but for the moment she would take full advantage of it. She wanted to be sipping from a goblet when they found Kincaid. She wanted to be giggling at the bubbles going down when they cut his throat.

* * *

Kincaid stood at the wheel, alert for signs of Itacoatiara, for soon after was the telegraph relay station where they would collect their supplies. It was late afternoon and the ritual rain had fallen, leaving in its wake a mist on the water that would become steaming fog by nightfall. He felt as in a dream, his conscious mind reaching into the mist, but never going beyond it. A native canoe edged into his vision, then disappeared into a flurry of water and mist, boiling. A flare burned somewhere in the distance, on shore, perhaps, inaccessible, silent, strangely removed from the reality of where he was. The engine whirred and bolted with a dependable, noisy persistence, familiar as the wheeze of an old bellows. Lacy reflections evolved and disappeared. The air was warm but looked cold; the river gnats came in swarms, tiny as moisture, and when Kincaid wiped his forehead his palm came away greasy and gray with their deaths.

He spun the wheel and headed briefly to port. The mist parted and he saw the shore as clearly as a stage setting. Small clusters of huts stood at the water's edge, balanced like grasshoppers on enormous stilts, clumsily cantilevered as a precaution against the temperamental rise and fall of the river. Most of the huts were fronted with porches from which were strung enormous fish, fish that looked larger than any river fish he had ever seen. He turned a curious eye to Longford.

"Sharks, if you can credit it, Harry. Swordfish, too. Sawfish, tarpon. You can find ocean fish as far as two thousand miles up. Never knew another river like it. I once saw a group of Indian fishermen in Pará haul in a catfish nine feet long and in the same net an electric eel that threw a charge so powerful it turned a barrel to cinders and knocked three grown men off their feet."

Kincaid swung to starboard and the boat straightened out, the huts sucked back into the mist. He and Longford fell into the silence that this river limbo seemed to demand.

The hours passed slowly. The mist lifted entirely at one point and the sun streamed down, a sultry orange, for the last time that day. The waters of the Amazon lapped a turgid yellow against its banks where trees a hundred feet tall cast monstrous shadows over the water. Palm fronds fanned out like umbrellas. Some trees were covered with flowers; a clump of violets large as a haystack teetered on top of a royal palm; behind and surrounding it were trunks ascending into a field of buttercups as dazzlingly bright in the sun as the roof of some enormous golden dream palace.

Then the sun faded and the mists closed in again, heavier than before. Iquitos left the engine room and entered the wheelhouse, pointing downriver to the beginnings of a few scattered clearings. As the *Mãe de Deus* drew nearer, Kincaid glimpsed small huts and gardens, the huts fashioned of poles and palm leaves, shaded by orange trees. Babies played in the mud; parents stood, watching the boats go by. Kincaid turned away.

A few miles beyond these clearings they approached the floating market of Itacoatiara. Iquitos pointed out their luck in not arriving during the low-water stages, when everything settled down in the mud. Now the docks and houseboats floated and people walked along them quite as easily as if they were streets. Most were grass huts on log rafts, and Kincaid saw that everything was for sale. The city itself lay behind the floating market, but could not be seen from the boat.

A few miles below the market and the town, Kincaid, his vision circumscribed by swirling fog, almost rammed the overturned ferry that was their marker for the telegraph station. He swung hastily to starboard and stopped engines, shouting for the anchor to be dropped.

Longford and Iquitos paid out the chain. Together they unlashed and lowered the dinghy. The air was thick now that they had stopped, heavy and vaporous, the hiss of heat inescapable. A sulfurous film veiled the setting sun, giving them a last view of it, the color of rancid butter.

From the jungle came awakening night sounds, isolated, startled, and shrill. Sand flies bit Kincaid's hands and neck; he swatted vigorously, knowing what the swelling would be. Mercedes would have been pleased; the Amazon and its horrors were slowly encroaching on his nerve.

Kincaid and Iquitos climbed into the dinghy, ready to shove off. Longford leaned over the side and coughed, clearing his throat several times. Kincaid looked up at him.

"What is it, Professor?"

"Harry . . . Harry, I do think something must be done about the young lady."

"I agree." Kincaid took out the oars. "Watch her like a hawk."

The dinghy, painted the same pale green as the

hull, took on a yellowish tinge as it moved through the water. It was as if the entire world had been dipped in liquid bronze. There was something about the uncompromising nature of this metallic rot that seemed unutterably brave and pure to Kincaid, at the same time that its relentlessness stifled and sickened him.

They rowed in silence, each manning an oar. All was still but for the giggling ripples on the yellow water, the diminishing labored breath of the *Mãe de Deus'* boiler, and an occasional cry from the jungle.

Longford watched until the dinghy had been swallowed up in smoke, then went below and found Dolores in the galley, staring forlornly out the porthole, though there was nothing to see. In the moment before she saw him, he sensed her aloneness, and the fact of her abduction seemed not merely a nuisance but a pity and a crime.

She turned and saw him and came toward him meekly, willingly; he felt guilty, he liked her better in combat than acquiescence. They went out the door and down the passageway to the bow. Inside the fo'c'sle, Dolores resumed her position at the porthole. Longford stood at the door, fumbling for the key.

"It's just until we're on our way again," he explained apologetically.

"I understand." The matter-of-factness of her tone shot brine into his guilt. He wished he could say something to comfort her, but knew better. He cleared his throat uncomfortably and backed out, realizing when he had closed the door that Iquitos had burst the lock. It didn't matter. He moved off down the passageway and sat at the foot of the companionway, ready to intercept her if she tried to leave.

Dolores let out a deep breath when he was gone, one she'd been holding since he'd come into the galley. Acquiescence was the last attitude she would strike, but for a protective pose it would do very nicely. And while it was worn, she would be suspected of nothing. Yes, she thought, let them think I grieve, suppose me pitiable, believe me harmless.

She scoured the fo'c'sle as she had done the first time she had been locked there and discovered the orchids. But the cabin had been searched again and there was nothing but an abandoned guitar and the heap of her gown.

Her hand plucked a string; she danced jittery fingers across the silk waterlilies. Were it not for the heat and the sense that everything, all the elements of sky and river, were part of a shared despair, she might have laughed. Harry Kincaid, she thought, and stilled her laugh again.

* * *

They had not gone three hundred yards into the jungle when they heard the sound. Kincaid thought at first it was the chattering of a monkey, or the tapping of a woodpecker, but knew as they drew nearer that it was nothing of the kind. It was the metallic clatter of the telegraph key.

Kincaid reached over and pulled Iquitos back, dragging him down into the brush.

"Wait a minute; that's the bloody key." He slumped to the ground, trying to think, a fingernail straying into his mouth as he wished for a cigar. "I can't understand it. He had specific orders to shut down when he got my message. Nothing to be transmitted upstream or down." He turned to Iquitos. "Do you read Morse?"

The Indian shook his head. Kincaid commenced feeling very uneasy. If there hadn't been food or fuel waiting for them at the station, he would just as soon have cut the cable on its way to the water and gone back to the *Mãe de Deus*. He sighed.

"Something's gone wrong. Let's keep going, but get us off this path. I don't want anyone to see us coming."

Iquitos nodded and commenced a detour, Kincaid following. They fought their way through dense tangles of vines and leaves and hanging branches and clusters of flowers. Kincaid moved apprehensively, straining his ears. He patted the knife he had stuck in his belt; small reassurance at the moment, but all he had. He would have given worlds to understand the dots and dashes.

The clacking got louder. It seemed to Kincaid to be just beyond the next tree, then the next, then just past that overhang of banana leaves, beyond that row of banyan, then the cacao. Iquitos stopped and peered through the vines in front of him; his body twitched in surprise and he motioned gently for Kincaid to stop. Kincaid looked cautiously through the vines into a clearing where the telegraph office stood, a thatched-roof hut that the operator also lived in. The wires, he noted, surprised, ran outside the hut through the front door. When he followed them with his eye, he saw what Iquitos had seen.

The telegraph operator was buried up to his waist in the ground, his chest riddled with arrows, the telegraph key strapped to his head, clattering away like a grief-stricken animal keening over the death of its mate. Empty boxes that had obviously contained their food and fuel supply lay strewn about the clearing. Some provisions were stuck to tree limbs in the jungle just beyond, like strange new vegetation.

Kincaid felt Iquitos pulling at his sleeve but before he allowed himself to be led back he ran headlong into the clearing and ripped the telegraph from the man's head. The head lolled back in what looked like a smile of gratitude. Kincaid could not move. Iquitos ran up to him, took the knife from his belt and cut the cable, stilling the noise. The action and the silence roused Kincaid. He closed the man's eyes and ran back to the jungle.

* * *

The fall of night on the river was as imperceptible in its descent as the fall of a foul mood. In the wheelhouse of the *Mãe de Deus*, Kincaid and Iquitos watched the lights of another village wink at them to port. Kincaid switched off the searchlight that had guided their way for the past hour and steered into the desolate half-light cast by a dour moon.

"What happened?" He asked the question matter-of-factly, lighting a cigar, calm now that it was over and they were under way again.

Iquitos was silent for a moment. "The isolation of these telegraph operators is almost total," he said, finally, his voice disembodied in the darkness. "They live most of the year alone. A strange breed of men. Outcasts, some. Convicts. Men with something to hide or men who cannot live among other men. Their lives are in constant danger. And not only from the jungle. There are . . ." he hesitated, ". . . Indians who cannot tolerate the presence of these telegraph operators. Mostly they are nomadic tribes, starved, half-crazed, without land or home or food. They would kill the operators for a loaf of bread. And yet, the operator is glad to see them. Sometimes they are the only people he sees for months at a time. The Indians come to the clearing and the operator holds his rifle at them. This is how they keep each other company. There was one man who would bathe in the river and send a round of rifle fire into the air to frighten the Indians away. Of course, he would lose half his ammunition this way. The Indians cut his throat besides. Such incidents are not uncommon, only in our case . . ." he trailed off, "unfortunate."

"They took everything he had," Kincaid muttered. "All the food and coal he was holding for us."

"They probably did not know what the coal was. As we came back I saw pieces scattered on the ground." Iquitos laughed ruefully, shaking his head. "My people. They probably tried to eat it."

Kincaid bit down on the cigar. "Wonderful," he murmured. "Simply wonderful."

Iquitos left the wheelhouse without another word and stretched out full on the foredeck, eyes closed, hands behind his head, the blood of revolution and regret pounding in his chest. There had been a moment in the jungle, just that one moment of actually cutting the cable, when he felt that to do this was a literal and physical severing of his ties with his own past. To take the knife and slice the cable was to do more than cut the source of communication between villages; it was to end the connection between what he was and what he would be.

He tried to concentrate on the rhythm of the river, on the night sounds of tree frogs and howler monkeys and the incessant buzz of insects, but he could not shake his mind free of questions. He was reminded of a legend he had heard as a small boy, that the moon was an Indian warrior who had gone against tribal law and spent eternity exiled from his people. It was his unhappy face that could be seen on the moon as he mourned his endless journey.

Iquitos opened his eyes wide and watched the steam pour from the funnel that loomed above him; the evaporation into the air was like his own past. He tried to rest, tried to store up his energy for the time soon when he would have to spell Longford at the boiler.

* * *

Below, in the engine room, Longford checked the gauges to be sure of maintaining the proper levels of pressure. Kincaid came in with a tray of food and left some on the boiler housing. They exchanged a glance that acknowledged the fuel situation, but neither cared to discuss what would soon enough present itself as a major problem. Longford sighed, breathed deeply of the heat-laden air, and continued to shovel coal into the fiery yawn of the boiler.

Kincaid continued down the passageway to the fo'c'sle. He felt reasonably safe. They had not tied her, but there was no necessity for rope: The cabin had been searched and any implement of potential malice had been removed. In any event, he was armed. He nudged the door open with his hip, his hands busy with the tray and the kerosene lamp. The cabin was dark and smelled faintly sweet, the hazy memory of roses and vanilla, or gardenia, perhaps. He held the lamp aloft and in the flickering light caught a glimpse of something in front of him that shone pink and white and then he heard her voice, a low caress on the air, her lips making moist sounds of entreaty.

"Do not stand on ceremony, Senhor Kincaid," she said, pausing just long enough to hear him breathe. "Close the door."

Kincaid hesitated, the picture of her burning into his eyes. She sat at the small table beneath the porthole wearing the silk ball gown in which she had boarded the boat, hair pulled back and piled high. In the heat she looked cool, in the closeness she seemed to carry a freshness of her own device. Kincaid's first impulse was one of suspicion, but he kicked shut the door; the air closed in, accentuating the fact of their isolation.

"What is all this?"

"Let me have the lamp," Dolores replied, reaching out her hand. In the dim, flickering light, Kincaid thought he could distinguish the fluttering of pale blue veins in her temple. Her jewelry winked at him.

"You're up to something." He did not move closer.

Dolores stood, the silk making the sound of cymbals in the distance, waves on the shore brought inland on a sea breeze. "You have a suspicious mind. I like that." She moved toward him; the gown seemed to have a life of its own, undulating in apposition to the body that wore it. As she came closer, Kincaid detected a fine film of perspiration on her shoulders; the smell of gardenias pulsed over him. He knew what she was doing; exactly.

"I don't believe you for a minute," he said.

"Why should you?" She shrugged, her bare shoulders falling diffidently, and she stopped, the gown rustling to its own pause. In the lamplight he saw the white edge of anger rising in her eyes. He put the tray of food on the floor and planted the lamp in a rusted wall sconce. The light gleamed on her shoulder, her skin was flushed at the neck, at the cheek, her fingers clasped the satin, the sweat leaving maplike creases. She was breathless, nearly faint with her own daring. His shadow crept up the front of her gown, casting the pale waterlilies into dusky blush.

Dolores reached down and took the guitar by the neck. Kincaid watched her as closely as if they were about to duel and she had drawn her sword first. She leaned back against the table and ran her fingers across the guitar strings, picking out a melody that sent a shiver across his back. She looked up at him from beneath glistening hooded lids.

The guitar strings plucked out the opening bars of Bizet's "Habañera." Dolores looked up from the instrument. "Carmen has a cassia flower in the corner of her mouth. She glances at Don José. She wants him. He is cool." She hesitated a moment, fingers hovering above the strings as she looked at him, daring him to stop her.

Kincaid knew her, knew her in the palms of his hands, in his chest, his groin; knew her and smelled fear; saw through the whole preposterous charade. But he watched, turned to stone, as she began.

Her voice was soft, husky, but pleasant, and she
sang without taking her eyes from him, without so
much as blinking.

> *L'amour est enfant de Bohême,*
> *il n'a jamais, jamais connu de loi.*
> *Si tu ne m'aimes pas, je t'aime;*
> *si je t'aime, prends garde à toi!*

Kincaid's mouth was on hers; she yielded, then
resisted, but her eyes were closed and she dreamed
for a moment that they were in her father's orchid
plantation and none of the rest had happened; then
her eyes snapped open and she looked at Kincaid's
face in the flutter-eyed flush of burgeoning passion
and her resolve returned. She resisted no longer;
the guitar slid to the floor, making a slicing sound
against the silk.

Kincaid leaned away, but his lips brushed hers
as he spoke with a surprising intimacy. "Why were
you so sure I'd make love to you?"

Dolores looked past him, eyes hard, voice tender
behind set lips. "Why were you so sure I wouldn't
let you?"

His teeth nipped at her earlobe and she cried
out, not in pain. She looked him full in the face,
surprised at her own coldness and not caring about
her reluctance to continue to the end. His nails
touched her skin and she moaned.

Kincaid knew he was drowning. His last thoughts,
like those of a drowning man, were attempts at co-

herency, overcome by sheer sensation. He had ruined her father and knew she would try to ruin him in return; had tried already. He would not give himself fully to this woman; she could not possibly give herself to him. They were enemies. His last thought, before complete inundation, was that he knew better.

❊ 16 ❊

As the pursuit of the *Mãe de Deus* lengthened in time, so did the armada behind the *Francesca*. Boats of all sizes stretched for miles, like a gigantic necklace of unmatched beads on a sagging string. What had begun as a high-spirited adventure, rich in confidence, a chase military in precision, had evolved into an emotion-laden, exhausting trial with the forces of weather, river, and time conspiring to beat them down.

Rumors and reports filtered back from the *Francesca* along the straggling line of boats, much altered by the time the last canoe received them. Optimism was transmogrified into euphoria; as easily did pessimism become imminent success. They comforted themselves as best they could by a constant and detailed enumeration of the odds against the success of Kincaid's mission:

Let's assume the *Mãe de Deus* outruns us all, they said—and that is impossible what with her meager crew and insufficient fuel supply—but let's assume, how could the rubber seeds survive an Atlantic crossing? Impossible, was what they said.

And even if possible, the climate in England was all wrong. It could never support the rubber plants.

And supposing the English could somehow reproduce the climatic and soil conditions, the jungle was bigger than all of England, than all of Europe, for that matter. It would be thirty years before the crop would even mature. They could cross the Atlantic themselves and destroy the trees.

And for a few moments there would be silence on the river until the speculations would begin again. They wanted to agree, to find solace in consensus, but doubts and fears surrounded them despite their confidence, and they continued down the river, unresolved and uncertain, exhausted, their imaginations unable to conceive of what would really happen if by some chance the Yanqui actually did it, actually got away with the seeds.

It began to rain. This occasioned no great alarm, at first. It usually rained once a day toward evening —sometimes for as little as fifteen minutes; other times for upward of an hour.

But today the rain did not stop. More than the daily quota, the rain proved to be the onset of the kind of relentless tropical downpours that were so much more frequent and terrible in winter than now. Storms such as these were known to flood the valley so high that only the tops of trees could be seen. The *Francesca* and her ragtag retinue were trapped in the freak deluge.

It had begun when the *Francesca* and her convoy sailed into a fierce white calm, the islands of the Amazon spread out in a neatly ascending plane in front of them, turning from green to black as the sky piled up thicknesses of white clouds, gray clouds, and deeply, deeply beyond them, the thickest black ash clouds, unseen now, the background in high relief.

Many sounds were shut off, the animals responding with instinctive awe to the whiteness and the calm. In its potential for violence, the calm was like the arrival of the end of the world. When the roar came, directionless, it was like a death rattle.

A rending scream of blue lightning; a wave, a roar, and the roar became rain and exploded in the sky; the sky exploded, the sensation that the earth itself was shattering. The river throbbed and swelled, carrying the boats into the storm, melding with the sky so that people went belowdecks to avoid being squeezed between the two.

Mendonça and Mercedes Coutard retreated to the *Francesca*'s dining room, a cabin half below the waterline, amidships. The room was furnished with surprising simplicity in freshly scrubbed *itelya* wood and subtle archways designed by the master of "the disappearing angle," architect and engineer Cyril Cornfell. Mendonça and Mercedes sat in silence at the long table, drinking late-afternoon cups of tea and staring out of the portholes at the immensity of the storm. Fruits of the river's uprootings floated by, a dance of hysteria, flooded forests, an island with a lone tree and a donkey tied to it. They had in common their watching; perhaps a little more. Both of them, so disparate in age and temperament, loved the river and understood it.

The dining-room door was thrown open and Coutard, sopping wet, pushed his way past a steward and slammed it shut.

"First half speed and now a total halt! You will never catch them at this rate!"

Mendonça looked slowly up from his plate of cheese and cocked his head with a sympathetic but exasperated air; he was dealing with a child. "You want to proceed in this? How?"

Coutard opened his mouth to answer, but words did not come—there were no thoughts to provoke them. In a helpless rage he turned to his sister, his eyes imploring her to take his part.

"The rain will have slowed them down as well, my dear."

"That's not what the Captain says," Coutard retorted, bitterly triumphant. "He says that five hours downriver it may not be raining at all."

Mercedes shrugged, discomfited, but she was not yet prepared to become the enemy of Colonel Mendonça. Not while on his yacht; not until she was in complete control; not until she had had her revenge. "I had no idea you took such an interest, dear."

"Kindly omit the sarcasm; it doesn't suit you." Coutard turned on the Colonel, who had watched the exchange with polite interest. "Don't you want to catch him and find what rôle your daughter has played in this . . . this fiasco?"

Mendonça colored.

"Colonel Mendonça," Mercedes interposed, hastily, "is there no way we can make progress while it rains?"

The Colonel could not take his eyes off Coutard.

"Another time, another place, *senhor* . . ."

"Yes, yes, yes," Mercedes said, fanning herself with blue crow feathers. "If I am not mistaken, we have been over this ground before. Pierre. Be patient."

The Colonel held in his anger and bitterness and disappointment and was seized by a heaving that forced blood into his mouth. Thunder coiled and unsprung the sky. The wind shrilled rain in lashes against the port side of the *Francesca*. The river rose majestically, terribly. The yacht shuddered at the beating.

"Very well," Mendonça said finally, "we will ride the current to Itacoatiara and check the cables there. I expect they have cut them again," he added, pressing a hand to his mouth to staunch the blood. He rang for the steward.

The torrential rain still slowed them considerably, and some of the smaller canoes had so filled with water that the owners had to paddle frantically for shore, fighting their way across the current with long rafting poles. In rain as violent as this, the bamboo poles were often the sole source of navigation, oars being useless.

The river rose and continued to rise; streams that had idled were swollen into murderous torrents, cascading into the river, creating swirls and eddies, a ravaging series of crosscurrents and whirlpools, making direct headway impossible. Mud was everywhere. Vines clung to the boats that came too close to shore, and many were grounded. Panic set in as boats were lost and owners drowned.

* * *

At Itacoatiara they stopped, and Mendonça went ashore with part of his crew to the telegraph office. The Coutards waited impatiently in the dining room; he continued pacing. It was all clear to him now; he understood the stakes. She sat across from him in a fan-backed chair, fiddling nervously with the rattan. Coutard stopped abruptly and faced her.

"Did you know the *Mãe de Deus* carries a gas searchlight?" he demanded, his tone accusatory. "I did. That miserable Scot told me. She doesn't lose the time in the dark that we do."

"Then perhaps they will get away." She studied him carefully before going on. "They have the light; the weather is good downstream; they are faster, cleverer. I think we need hardly wager that our stop at Itacoatiara is foolish. The line will be dead, the cable buried or thrown into the water where we would spend hours searching for it. And it will be the same at Parintins, and Obidos, at—"

"Enough!" He clapped his hands to his ears to shut out the disaster. She stopped speaking with a little shrug. He took his hands away slowly. For a moment all that could be heard was the rain pounding evenly on deck.

"What will he do with them?"

Again she shrugged. "It depends. If he was sent he will take them to whoever sent him—the British, most likely; they have tried before, as you know. Perhaps he is in business for himself. In that case he will sell them to the highest bidder."

"And then?"

"They will be planted somewhere. India, perhaps. The climate is right there, I think. You know, of course, he had a native accomplice. It would have been impossible otherwise."

"The Colonel says no," Coutard murmured, repeating without listening to himself. His face was pale with self-pity in the glow of the lamps.

"The Colonel is an old man. He sees what he wishes to see and believes what he wishes to believe. The Yanqui was with us last night. Who released the balloon?"

Coutard looked at his sister, his face suddenly pulled down, contorted in pain and grief. "And because of this blasted rain we shall never catch them!"

With a bust of energy Mercedes moved from her chair and pressed herself to her brother's side. Her hands gripped his shoulders, and when he looked at her it was as if complementary forces were at work, the reflection of strength and weakness completing the whole.

"We shall catch them," Mercedes whispered, soothing, cooing, stroking his hair. It was a litany, an assurance of well-being. "They will need fuel. They must stop each time they cut the cable." Her face moved closer; flame flickered in her eyes. "We

will catch them. We will catch them." Her voice
was low, breathy, almost no voice at all; her fingers curled into her brother's hair. "And when we
do . . . you will leave everything to me. Everything."

Mendonça entered and the brother and sister
jumped apart, surprised. The Colonel felt like an
intruder.

"The cables have been cut again," he said, looking sideways at them, as if at a reflection that
showed a subtle distortion he had never noticed
before. "We will not stop to check them again." He
did not mention the arrow-riddled body.

"Very good," Coutard said, and Mercedes
nodded. Something in the way the Colonel was
looking at her made her feel she had lost something.

*   *   *

The moon rose across the porthole like an eye
opening in surprise. Dolores and Kincaid watched
in silence until it became its own shattered reflection in the river and heard the utter melancholy of
the *mãe da lua*, mother of the moon, as it sang its
four plaintive notes of a broken heart.

They were flesh to flesh on one of the narrow
berths, their clothes in a sighing heap on the floor.
The moonlight touched their bodies in tiny whorls,
as if pearls had been dropped in necks and shoulders, breasts and hips. He was lost in her scent, his
face buried in the smooth down of her neck. He

ran his tongue over the crown of her ear. She had been regaling him with tales of her student days in Paris—nothing quite so colorful as the stories of Henri Murger. Dolores, more prosaically, had been enrolled at the fashionable Ecole de Ste.-Thérèse.

"And what," Kincaid wondered, "would they say about all this, at Ste.-Thérèse?"

She edged still closer to him, her arm dangling carelessly off the side of the bed, as if trailing in the waters of an alien sea. "The Mother Superior was inclined to view all my activities as evidence of high spirits."

Kincaid lifted his head and laughed. "I'm not disposed to argue with her about that, but this was your first time. Were you always such a good student?"

"I have more fun when I am not so good." She put her hand on his chest, pushed herself up from the bed, then ambled lazily to the porthole in the darkness, humming and exuding gardenia.

He stretched back to look at her body, shades of blue and white in the moon.

"Would you think it strange to hear me recite in Latin?" She looked at him with a schoolgirl shyness that contrasted with the exposed womanliness of her body.

"It wouldn't be as strange as you might think," Kincaid replied. "I've known women who'd . . . well, never mind that. Go ahead. Give me some Latin. I'm fascinated."

Dolores turned to him, hands clasped obediently

behind her back, shoulders straight, a toying smile on her lips. *"Quis custodiet ipsos custodes?"*

"Which means?"

"'Who will guard the guards?'" she said, as emotionlessly as if she'd been translating red pens and blue pencils, and drew Kincaid's pistol from behind her back, holding it steadily and quite determinedly at his chest.

Kincaid sat up, pulling the thin blanket to him, suddenly embarrassed, as though the pistol demanded modesty. In the next instant he saw how ludicrous that was and threw the blanket off. "Come on," he said, smiling and reaching his arms to her. "Come back to bed."

Dolores shook her head and the gun remained steady. "There are certain positions one must assume—in order that one may assume certain positions—" She indicated herself and the gun.

"I don't believe you."

"Yes, you do."

"But—"

"No time for regrets, I'm afraid." She cut off the beginnings of a whine and gestured jerkily with the pistol. "On your belly, *senhor*. Quickly!"

He hesitated, staring wildly at her, making noises in his throat. She waved the pistol at him, cocked it; he flung himself down on the bed. Keeping her hand steady, Dolores lit the lamp, then retrieved the uniform she'd worn before assuming the gown, and donned it once more. Dolores looked out of the porthole once as if to check for her father, then waved the gun again. On the distant shore she saw the lights of another village.

"Call Iquitos and the Professor," she ordered briskly. "Tell them you want them right away." Kincaid looked at her, caught her eye, but did not move or speak. They both waited, and then Dolores fired the gun.

In the wheelhouse, Longford and Iquitos ducked, then peered out over the railings. Iquitos crept to the wheel and lashed it to keep them on course. He reached for one of the Martini rifles. Longford held his arm and signaled for him to be quiet. In the silence, above the engine hum, was Kincaid's voice calling them. They looked at each other, confused, and left the wheelhouse on the run.

Kincaid was picking splinters out of his hair as a result of the shot, which had buried itself in the bulkhead above him. He tossed each piece of wood at Dolores and saved the last as a toothpick. "May I at least put on my trousers?" he asked with exaggerated insouciance.

"Be my guest," she replied in kind, flourishing the gun like a rapier and keeping part of her attention on the door to the fo'c'sle while Kincaid, muttering, resumed his clothes.

"I don't understand you," he sighed.

"This is hardly the issue."

"You didn't want to marry that fop; don't tell me you wanted to marry him." He leaned over intensely. "You're ruining your own escape." She said nothing, her forehead creased in thought. He ventured a step toward her. "It was *me* you wanted—and got."

Dolores was becoming confused when running footsteps pounded closer. She checked her balance, her stance, the light, and Kincaid—hero of unfinished romances. The door burst open; she waved the pistol at them.

"Try to touch the ceiling, gentlemen."

Iquitos and Longford were startled, almost laughed, but when they saw Kincaid buttoning the last of the buttons on his trousers, they knew Dolores had become someone whose gunpoint commands could not be taken lightly. Longford actually did feel his fingertips brushing the ceiling of the fo'c'sle; he had an absurd desire to tell Dolores of this but kept it to himself.

"There has been a change in plans," she informed her prisoners. "First we will unload your cargo. Into the river."

Upriver the rains had begun and the water meeting water began its swells, and the current shifted, sped up, angered and blustery. Downriver felt the forward front of the squall, the river changing temperament. The untended wheel of the *Mãe de Deus* slipped its lashing and performed a slow pirouette to the current's command.

Kincaid was sure she meant what she said; as sure as he'd been that she would not have pulled the trigger on his revolver. She continued to amaze him, but he had to stall; time was the only friend he had. "Dump the cargo? In the middle of the night?"

"Do not play with me, Senhor Kincaid," she snapped, totally in control. "After we rid the ship of these unnecessary rubber seeds we will turn around and go back to Itacoatiara. Now let us go." She jerked the gun and lifted her chin, as though both were connected to the same reflex.

The massive sway of the river continued to toy with the *Mãe de Deus*, moving it to port, to starboard, in no discernible pattern, control belonging to the current. The searchlight cast its beam on the water in murky arcs, illuminating a mossy section of jungle, a stretch of beach, a startled panther come to drink by the margin.

Dolores stood a fair distance away as Kincaid reluctantly unlocked the door to the hothouse cabin. She knew that she was contending with determined men. These three had bargained their lives as collateral for the success of their mission. For this reason they were dangerous. She held the gun very firmly, and with more assurance than she felt.

"Quickly!" she ordered Kincaid as he dawdled with the lock, her voice breaking.

Kincaid nodded but pretended to tremble, and the key kept missing the hole. He wondered what was happening to the *Mãe de Deus;* wondered if Dolores noticed the change in the ship's attitude. He opened the door and Dolores peered in, satisfied the seeds were still there. The scent of rich

soil and banana leaves on the steamy heat of the
hothouse was sweet and slightly sickening. She
motioned to Longford and Iquitos, and each entered the cabin and came out holding a box of the
precious seeds. Kincaid reached in for a box, and
all three men formed a line and began to file past
Dolores down the passageway.

The river, after spinning the *Mãe de Deus* ran-
domly, in a half circle, so that bow was stern and
stern bow, now turned bow to port. The pirouette
ended abruptly as the stern rammed the bank of
the river, the shock jolting the entire yacht.

The passageway tilted. Rubber seeds, soil, and
banana-leaf wrappings flew into the air, suspended momentarily, defying gravity, then
splashed against the walls and slid down to the
floor along with Iquitos, Longford, Dolores, and
Kincaid. Kincaid landed on top of Dolores and
extricated the gun from her grasp. She recovered
quickly enough to bite his wrist. He ignored the
pain and, hoisting her into the air, ran down the
passageway to the galley, where he dumped her
like a sack of meal, and rushed out, locking the
door and leaving her in a rage. As he ran back up
the passageway, he heard her banging furiously on
the door.

Longford and Iquitos had already replaced the
seeds and the three men went topside to see what
had happened.

Iquitos turned the searchlight on the mudbank.
The situation proved rather more serious than they
had suspected. Some of the mud was dried and

showed clear evidence of turtle and alligator tracks. An enormous rock was sunk not far from the boat, its watermark well above the ooze. It was this that was the most distressing, for it might mean that the surrounding water was too shallow for them to float or push themselves out into. It was even impossible to tell whether this was the riverbank itself or one of the thousands of islands in the Amazon. Vegetation, as far as they could see, was limited to one small piece of scrub brush that looked anything but heartening. There was no wood anywhere; they could not even refuel where they were stuck.

The bank onto which they had been thrust was thick with ravenous insects, all of them outsized.

Kincaid cursed, slapping himself absently. "Welcome to the Amazon. Centipedes a foot long; spiders as big as birds; beetles—" He slapped a tiny fly that had bitten him sharply, drawing blood.

"The *matuca*," Iquitos said.

"This whole thing is her doing," Kincaid muttered, surveying the catastrophe. "Everything is her doing."

"Come, Harry, it can't be entirely her fault. You must have allowed her to take you—uh—off guard."

Kincaid stared at him.

"It isn't her fault the lashing slipped on the wheel," Iquitos pointed out.

"A good thing it did," Kincaid responded, "or our cargo would be feeding the river turtles by now." He pulled a cigar out of his case and took a savage bite out of the one end, only to discover it was the wrong one. He held it up to Longford as though it were further proof of Dolores' treachery.

"You have to see her point of view," Longford said, waving the cigar away in a soothing gesture of conciliation. "After all, Harry, she came on board only to see you. She's troubled."

"Troubled?" Kincaid echoed incredulously, flinging the cigar into the mud, where it stood up like a signpost to infamy. "My good man, her troubles haven't even begun." Kincaid lit another cigar; the tip glowed and there seemed to be some peacefulness in the glow. He collected himself in the smoke.

"What shall we do, Harry? Start the engines?"

Kincaid didn't answer for a moment but when he did, Longford knew his patience had been vindicated. "No, that's completely out. We don't have any way of knowing what junk is wedged around the propeller, and we can't take the chance of twisting it." He paused, considering a new idea. "If we were lighter, we might float up and break out. If it's not a floating island we're on, which is a remote but distinct possibility."

Longford recognized Kincaid's speculative voice but jumped at the idea, pulling it along to see how far it could stretch. "What have we got that would make a difference if we threw it overboard? The furniture? We can't lose the anchor. Break up the dinghy? We might raise the draft by one or two feet. Might that prove sufficient?"

"I can think of about a hundred and five pounds that would make a definite difference."

"Now, Harry—"

"Iquitos, shine the light on me and I'll go get wet and muddy." He clambered over the railing; just as he was about to drop down onto the bank, Longford screamed out his name. Kincaid gripped hard and looked down; in the illumination from the searchlight he saw the grisly sight of a family of alligators, a slimy green and brown, eyes rolling in delirium, and the enormous jaws that could take a man's leg off.

He scrambled back on deck and jabbed a boat-hook down into the mud to see if he could thwack them away. When one of the alligators ate the hook, he pulled up the stump and looked at it curiously, gloomily convinced that he was in a place where the resources he'd garnered or invested in the past were now of minimal use.

Iquitos turned off the light and came to the railing, and the three men stared at the alligators. Iquitos looked away. "We could get rid of some of the rubber . . ."

Kincaid's face burned white in the shadows as he whirled, the stump of the hook gripped in an angry fist. "Not a seed! Not one bloody seed! We aren't going to lose so much as one bloody seed on this trip . . . unless we lose them all . . . and that won't happen until I'm only an arm hanging out of one of those ugly jaws!"

After this outburst, the vestiges of which floated over the river and startled the relative night quiet,

Kincaid calmed. He drew deeply on his cigar. The ash glowed with a kind of resignation.

"They will use this time to gain on us," Iquitos observed quietly.

"Maybe. Maybe not. One thing's sure: the *Francesca* does not have a searchlight." He looked at the sky; the moon was still up. "All right." He stood. "No seeds, but everything else that isn't nailed down. Two piles. One for noncombustible material we won't want again: the other for stuff we may find ourselves throwing in the boiler when the time comes. We'll put the dinghy in the water and put all of our second pile in the dinghy, which would make it slightly easier to recover. Everything else goes over. Use your imaginations."

Everything else did go over. No more instructions were necessary. They worked feverishly for many hours as the moon disappeared. Soon the boat took on the appearance of having survived an explosion: mattresses, chairs, panes of glass, sheets, shirts, shoes, boxes, ropes, the polished wood paneling of the Captain's cabin, the wood berths from the fo'c'sle, and more were spewn everywhere. The dinghy was soon loaded to the gunwales and they had to throw potential fuel into the water or on shore, where the alligators walked dreamily over the carnage, one perched halfway on a small bureau, a tail covered in pillow feathers. They seemed totally unafraid of a human presence. Below, Kincaid took time to improvise a new lock on the fo'c'sle door and returned Dolores to her original place of confinement. He did his best not to look at her. For her part, she couldn't help studying him. She had beaten him, she knew. Why did he persist? From the fo'c'sle she could hear them struggling, and even watched as they tore apart the crew's berths. She wanted to ask, but he would think she was taunting him, and Dolores didn't see herself as that kind of victor.

* * *

The three men sat on the deck, exhausted, their bodies glistening with sweat, and took inventory. They had dispensed with everything and the boat hadn't moved. Perhaps the time had come to try firing at the alligators and pushing from the bank, Longford mused. Iquitos took up a rifle and aimed at the beasts, ready to let loose a volley, when Kincaid grabbed his arm.

"Listen." They stood still and heard, as in a memory of something from long ago, the faint sound of an engine.

"A freighter?" Longford wondered.

"Douse the lights!" Kincaid ran below, blowing out wicks and turning off gas as he made his way toward the fo'c'sle. Iquitos raced to the wheelhouse and cut the searchlight. Before Kincaid could unlock the fo'c'sle door, Dolores, who had recognized the sound as well, began to scream. As he entered and threw himself on her, she turned to face him, gleefully screaming again. Kincaid was not in a ceremonious mood. He grabbed her about the waist, she kicked back at him, cutting his shins with her heels, but he managed to gag her again and secure her hands behind her back, fastening her to one of the bulkheads.

He raced back on deck, grabbing his binoculars, and stood on the bridge watching with Iquitos and Longford. In the near distance the sound of the engine was getting louder. Suddenly, as if emerging from a dream, a string of lights appeared out of the fog that lay low on the river. Kincaid brought the glasses to his eyes and saw a sleek white prow piercing the mist, riding high in the water.

"The *Francesca*," Iquitos murmured beside him, in a tone of wonder and fear. "I know her engines."

"Right you are."

"Can they see us, Harry, do you think?"

"I don't think so. Let's be thankful we had sufficient green paint." A smile spread across Kincaid's face as he removed the binoculars. "Now this presents an interesting possibility. Do you play chess, Professor?"

"This is hardly the moment for games, Harry."

"I wouldn't have thought so, either," Kincaid said, "but we're playing one, like it or not. You've heard of castling your rook?"

Longford stared at him blankly, the sound of the *Francesca*'s advancing engines thudding clearly across the expanse of water. Then he too smiled. This was more like the Kincaid he used to know. "What about later?"

Kincaid shrugged. Later was a problem for

another day. "The main thing will be to see them before they see us." He turned to Iquitos, who had been trying to follow the conversation. "We'll let them pass us," he explained. "Not that we have much choice. In effect, we will be pursuing them."

"But how will *we* get by her?" Iquitos posed the same question Longford had asked.

"That isn't our most pressing problem," Kincaid reminded him dryly. "We've got to be out of here by daybreak. We have no idea who's following the *Francesca,* or how far behind they are."

This point was made lightly enough, but Kincaid knew it was a real danger. Caught between a rock and a very hard place, he reflected, taking up the binoculars again. Across the water the majestic string of lights boomed past. Below, faintly, in the fo'c'sle, Dolores' muffled cries could be heard.

"No doubt about it," Kincaid admitted grudgingly, as the boat began to get smaller. "She's a beauty."

"The *Francesca?*" Longford asked. Kincaid turned and smiled sourly at him, handing over the binoculars.

"Where's the celebrated Amazon tide, now that we need it?"

Kincaid took the watch, trying to make himself comfortable on deck, with a rifle in his lap and the *matucas* going after his drying sweat. The stars were clear and glassy, the waning moon a smudge of white; he watched the glow of his cigar swell and subside like the tide with each inhalation.

There was moisture on his face, heavier than dew, and he snorted mildly to think that in addition to everything else, it had begun to rain.

Suddenly there was a scraping sound at the stern. Kincaid remained where he was but hoisted the rifle from his lap. He peered into the darkness but saw nothing. And then a strangely shaped black shadow was flying through the air, and before he could shoot or decide not to, it landed on him, hairy and sharp. A shiver traveled over his body but the shadow turned out to be a small howler monkey with a face like a startled child and long thin arms that wrapped gratefully around Kincaid's neck. *"Buenas noches, amigo,"* he said, "where'd you come from? Looking to get out of the rain? Come on."

He stood up, the monkey on his shoulder, and continued his nightlong vigil from the wheelhouse.

❈ 17 ❈

Apart from a few moments of sleep stolen guiltily from his watch, Kincaid remained alert throughout the night, aware as at no other time of the infinite changes that time wrung from each moment. He tried to watch and listen and smell everything, but would suddenly become conscious that he had not been awake. The sky went through a succession of progressively less-dense darknesses, to lighter gray, to light without color, to thin, translucent strips of orange and yellow and white light until the concentration of the sun itself could be seen as a red glow. Pink clouds skimmed up from the horizon, making blacker silhouettes of the jungle, then burst open so that the full sun spread pure color in washes across the treetops and in shafts to the jungle floor.

The chill and dampness of the night air began to lose its tenacious cling, though shreds of it could be seen around the trees, evanescing in the sun's rays. The birds awoke and signaled as much, the forest dove calling out in successive repetitions, a woodpecker tapping a morning message, a group of toucans screeching like peddlers.

Not long after the first cries had been heard,

Iquitos and Longford appeared on deck carrying coffee, Edam cheese, and stale bread to the wheel-house for Kincaid. The monkey, which had kept him company all night, was still perched on Kincaid's shoulder and snatched at the sandwich. The boat rocked slightly when Longford passed the coffee, and some of it spilled over the edges of the cup. Kincaid smiled and indicated their peculiar list.

"It rained some here last night," he informed them. "If there's a storm upriver, there may be some flooding later that'll serve to float us free. You can see the water level's higher than when we stopped here last evening." He gestured with the coffee cup. Iquitos observed that it was a bit early in the season for a really big rain.

Then Longford noticed. "Who's that?" he demanded, pointing at the monkey.

"May I present Carmen, Professor Longford?" Kincaid pulled in his neck to stare the monkey in the face; the monkey's hand picked at his ear. "I named her so I wouldn't forget a certain song." The monkey leapt from his shoulder to Longford's and grabbed at more food.

"It's all right," Kincaid said. "She's probably hungry."

Longford made a disapproving look and gave the monkey back to him. "If she eats your sandwich and my sandwich, what do you and I eat?" He looked up at Kincaid. "We're out of food, Harry. And almost out of fuel."

Kincaid nodded, and leaned forward, looking blankly at the jungle.

"There's nothing we can do now but wait. We're definitely rising. I suggest we gather in the dinghy and its cargo."

The time went very slowly, accentuated by the increasing heat. A small herd of cattle came to graze at the marsh grass on the rise above them, where the inhabitants of the area had planted quick-growing crops that would not be lost to floods. The alligators stared at them, dull yellow eyes full of unambiguous malevolence.

It was past eight when they felt the first tremor. In the next hour the boat went through distinct rockings, lifted and set down again, accompanied by the progressively louder and more insistent sucking sound of mud loosening beneath and around the hull.

Iquitos went out to the railing and watched, jumping up suddenly and waving his arms to Kincaid and Longford. "We're free!" he shouted exultantly.

Inside the wheelhouse Kincaid took the news with quiet joy, turning immediately to work. When Iquitos came running in, Kincaid ordered him to man the wheel at dead slow ahead, then jumped down the companionway, the monkey clinging fearfully to his neck. The alligators crawled up the bank, away from the encroaching waters. Before he even reached the engine room, the *Mãe de Deus* began to drift off the mudbank, carried without control along the current.

Kincaid soon heard that the engines only groaned at the effort of trying to turn the propeller through the mud. He listened, strained to hear the whirr of freedom and when it didn't come, threw the stanchions to FULL STOP.

The brass speaking tube was hot to the touch, and he held it between reluctant fingers as he called through to Iquitos in the wheelhouse.

"Save it! I'm coming up. We're snagged."

Kincaid ran down the passageway and bounded topside. When he got to the wheelhouse he took over for Iquitos at the helm. His efforts there to dislodge the rudder met with some constrained success. The *Mãe de Deus* continued to float sluggishly with the current that was rich with red clay.

"The rudder's caught a little, too," Kincaid said before anyone could call them lucky. "But our real problem is the screw. I've got to go down there and pull the junk off." He took off his shirt and walked outside to the railing.

"I'm afraid you can't do that, Harry." Longford stared down at the water, vexed now that they were almost free and had run into another obstacle. "The rains that freed us are a bit of a mixed blessing," he explained, and directed Kincaid's attention to darting shadows beneath the water.

"Piranha?" Kincaid asked, the name maniacally gay.

"The high water brings them down from up the river. You get in there and you won't last five minutes."

Kincaid looked into the river, imagining beasts,

disconcerted when the fish proved small as perch. He'd heard enough stories about what piranha could do when they massed. "How do you tell if they're—?"

"They're always hungry."

Iquitos joined them at the railing, and after a respectful pause in which he deferred to the other two to come up with a solution, he offered one of his own.

"There is a native method for fording cattle across the smaller rivers plagued by piranha," he said, staring at the fish, wondering how they were chosen to have devil in their souls.

"How dangerous?" Kincaid asked.

"I have seen it work perfectly," Iquitos said, then looked at him with difficulty. "I have seen it fail."

Kincaid nodded. "Let's go."

"You can't, Harry," Longford protested.

But no one had a better idea.

* * *

The jungle crept to the edge of the riverbank, layer upon layer of vegetation, choking, stultifying in the heat, a bell jar, airless and moist. The umbrella of the treetops was thick, and little sun penetrated the clustered foliage of palm and jacaranda, but the humidity was just bearable. The place was infested with life: shrieking *guarabis*, skittering, shrill parakeets, frogs that roared and trilled in chorus, hissing beetles, birds that moaned, others that laughed, others that imitated the grunts of wild boars. Entering the jungle and these sounds was awakening into one's own nightmare.

Animals peered down from their overhead homes in treetops, arboreal dwellers that never touched the ground, monkeys and sloths who found water collected in pools in the tops of palm trees or in the calyxes of large flowering plants. A spider monkey careered madly from branch to branch like a furred black bird.

But no animal of the jungle could match the tapir, hoglike and hairy, with an elephant's trunk, the bulging walleyes of a rhinoceros, a horse's shaggy mane. A shaft of sunlight attracted one near the riverbank at which the *Mãe de Deus* had dropped anchor. It was large; easily four hundred pounds, as long as a horse, on squat half-legs. It stood in the shaft of light and seemed to be dreaming.

Kincaid fired from behind a bamboo tree and the tapir's head jerked back. Dark blood gushed from a hole near the neck, dream pierced by pain, as it started running wildly through the undergrowth. Kincaid and Iquitos followed, hopping, tripping, Kincaid cursing himself for not felling the beast with a single bullet. Iquitos had said that shooting would be a risk. It would startle the jungle animals for miles around, and if the shot was not accurate there would be little hope for a second try. The proper way to catch the tapir would have been to dig a pit and lure the animal over it, but there was no time for that. A lasso could also be used, but there was no space for one.

And the tapir was charging as if ravenously hungry and pursuing food, barreling through bushes, trampling small trees. The two men followed, breathless, finding themselves circling back toward the river, and suddenly they heard an enormous splash and frightened bleating. The tapir had accidentally hit the river and now, deep brown and blackish in color, snout above water, it pulled itself out and collapsed on the muddy bank.

Kincaid and Iquitos hauled the dead tapir through the ooze and dragged it into the dinghy. They rowed back to the boat with the bleeding carcass half over the gunwale, its blood still warm. The scent of it must have been incredibly powerful, for Kincaid could see the muddy darting figures of the piranha following them.

They lashed the dinghy to the stern of the *Mãe de Deus*, and Longford sighed with relief. Kincaid eyed the tapir with faint revulsion, and went below to his cabin to change his clothes. He looked down the passageway to the darkened fo'c'sle and his anger flared. If she had not seduced him and held them all at gunpoint, they would never have gotten stuck, and he would not have to do what he was about to do to free the propeller shaft of mud and roots. She was desperate and her desperation made her ruthless; Kincaid knew that she and he were a perfect match, and in a corner of his mind he was afraid of her unpredictability and her fearlessness because he knew it was so like his own. If they were not careful, or at the very least judicious, they could end up killing each other.

He emerged on deck a few minutes later in latex gloves and boots, his heavy twill trousers, and a crewman's tightly knit sweater. Longford tried not to notice his nervousness and occupied himself with the rope that he had prepared. Kincaid knotted it about his waist and watched the other end flutter in Longford's skittish fingers as he tied it over the rail. Longford handed him a knife and he tucked it into his belt.

Iquitos called out to them from the dinghy and Kincaid, shielding his eyes from the merciless sun, called back. "Shouldn't you be further off?"

"If I move too far," Iquitos shouted, "we won't be sure of attracting all the fish in the immediate vicinity."

Kincaid nodded, muttering to himself, "Wouldn't want to miss any," and positioned himself on the rail, one foot waving in the air above the water. "How long have I got?"

"Perhaps two minutes," the Indian responded.

Kincaid muttered softly and the sun blinded him again. "Well, no time like the present, I always say. Go ahead."

Iquitos nodded and with the sharpened end of a bamboo arrow, slit the tapir's stomach and dumped the animal over the side of the dinghy. One piranha actually leapt into the air and had already sunk its razor teeth into the tapir's belly when it hit the water.

The piranha were bad. The Indians looked upon them as the curse of the river gods, worse than the monstrous, ugly, but ultimately stupid *jacareassu* or some of the other smaller alligators, more lethal and hideous than the anaconda. The piranha, though only a foot long, would not need its brothers for courage; it would attack alone and the smell of blood would draw thousands of others to the feast. It had the face of a drug-induced hallucination, the face of bottomless, nameless fear with an enormous mouth and under-slung jaw, all ferocity and bloodlust. The instant the tapir's shadow appeared on the water, the piranha, already massed and waiting, their instincts alerting them, gathered together, making the water a solid mass of sly green-black bodies and pointed gray teeth. At the splash there was a flurry of murderous activity and the water foamed pink, flecks of scarlet flying through the air and dotting the sides of the dinghy and the brown flesh of Iquitos' arms.

Kincaid looked, fascinated and repelled, then hurriedly lowered himself into the water, making as little splash as possible, so as not to draw attention his way. As Iquitos rowed back to the boat, Kincaid breathed deeply three times, held the third breath, and plunged underwater, pulling himself swiftly toward the propeller shaft. He glanced at the turmoil behind him, the whirling mass of flesh that was a tapir only a moment before being ripped to shreds by scores of the frantic piranha. He had only two minutes, two minutes before the air in his lungs gave out, two minutes

before the piranha would be looking for dessert.
The propeller shaft was thick with reeds and roots
and mud; Kincaid took out his knife and began
hacking away and trying not to notice the tiny
pieces of the tapir's pinkish innards that occasionally drifted in front of his face.

Above the waterline, Dolores saw the tapir being devoured by the piranha. She had never witnessed such carnage, yet did not turn away but
watched with avid interest. The meaning of the
event was clear for she had heard some of the talk
and seen the tapir being hauled into the dinghy
at the riverbank. If the *Mãe de Deus* were to
get underway again, free, Kincaid's chances of
success were multiplied. The *Francesca* had no
idea of their whereabouts. Let her charge
down the river till her boiler burst, she would
never overtake the *Mãe de Deus* now. It was up
to her, once more, to help her father and atone for
her disobedience. Dolores closed her eyes. Seduction had worked, but not well enough. This time
she needed something larger, stronger, less of
the flesh of the body than of the body of the boat.
The fo'c'sle had been searched, she'd done so herself and uncovered nothing that could be of any
use to her. But she searched again, feeling her
way now because the illumination from the kerosene was dim. Her head jerked up. She looked at
the kerosene lamp and smiled tentatively as if she
had just spotted someone and was not yet sure she
recognized who it was. The lamp drew her, her

shadow growing on the wall, along with an idea for her own sort of carnage.

Kincaid's chest was constricted and at the same time that he was aware only of hacking away at the last thick root that enchained the propeller shaft, he was also aware that any second he would die. He kicked off from the curved hull of the boat and hit his head, then scrambled up to the surface, gasping for air, splashing despite his earlier resolve not to do so.

"Finished?" Longford called down, but Kincaid wasted no time answering; he'd seen the work the piranha had done on the tapir, half its flesh and insides gone, bone gleaming in the dull murky blue water. He dived under again and attached one arm to the propeller while the other hacked and pulled at the root, his movements less methodical now than frantic, the water slowing him down, dreamlike, soundless.

He looked at the foaming bloody debacle a few yards away and saw what he had feared: The obscenely naked skeleton of the enormous tapir was drifting, sinking slowly to the bottom of the river in gradually descending arcs. The piranha were held in position for an instant, and in that instant Kincaid's knife finally freed the propeller shaft. He scrambled for the surface again, but the piranha had seen him or smelled him. However they knew he was there, they were coming at him, a wall of pointed teeth, of malevolent staring eyes.

His pant leg was caught on the propeller, but then the rope around his waist was given an enormous jolt and he found himself being dragged to the surface. In a nightmarish flash he was sure he heard the clicking of teeth. He broke the surface, saw sun and sky, but his gasping relief turned to a scream of pain.

As Longford and Iquitos hauled him from the water they could see two piranha attached to Kincaid's leg by their teeth. Blood poured from the punctures, soaking his trousers, and the water beneath him was a foaming, churning mass of yawning blood-flecked fish.

The monkey scampered to Kincaid and nestled on his shoulders. He patted it absently and peeled his trousers away from the spot where the piranha had sunk their teeth; the marks were a nasty series of tiny punctures, all oozing blood. The piranha that had done the work lay flapping on the deck. Kincaid stared at them, unable to suppress a shudder.

"I knew Brazil was going to make a lasting impression." He sat back and let forth an uproarious, hysterical whoop of relief: They were on their way again! Longford permitted himself a smile of satisfaction that bordered on a grin, and Iquitos acknowledged the feat by shaking Kincaid's hand.

Later, Kincaid could never remember who had first noticed the smoke and whether they heard Dolores screaming first or afterward.

At first they simply stared and listened to the

screams. When Kincaid staggered to his feet, smoke was already pouring from the bow of the ship in irregular gushes, like the hot breath of a mythical beast.

He tossed the monkey off his neck before he rushed forward, down the companionway, smoke pouring upward. He ripped off the tail of his shirt and held it over his nose and mouth as he made his way half blind to the fo'c'sle. Licks of flame poked out from beneath the door, sending black darts along the walls and floor.

Kincaid's lungs were hot and the protection on his face did little to keep the smoke out, so he lunged at the door, eschewing lock and key, and lunged again and again until it burst open. A rush of smoke enveloped him and he spun away from it, but heard Dolores choking and felt his way along the floor until he found her, half conscious, crouching in the farthest corner away from the flames, directly underneath the porthole. He scooped her into his arms; whatever her plan had been, it had all happened too quickly.

Stumbling, blinded by the smoke, his arms straining, he tripped back to the companionway, made it to the deck and dropped Dolores, falling beside her, gasping for air. Longford and Iquitos ran by, carrying buckets of water, and ran out again in a few moments to refill the buckets and charge back down. Smoke continued to belch from the passageway, but after several more trips it began to thin until it was no more than a few wisps.

Kincaid stood up, fell against the rail, and looked out at the water. He remembered what he'd said to Captain Mactavish when they began their trip up the Amazon to Manaus: Quite a nice little river. And when he saw Manaus he'd said that it was quite a nice little town. As Kincaid fingered the piranha bites on his leg and looked at the singed hair and blackened skin on his arms, he tried to find the humor in his present situation, but failed.

A quick inventory of the *Mãe de Deus* itself, however, did much to restore his equanimity. There had been more smoke than fire; the propeller and rudder had been freed; the precious rubber seeds (barring the three packages—totaling nearly a thousand seeds—split when they had crashed) remained unaffected by any of the disasters Dolores had arranged.

The first item on the revised agenda, Kincaid decided, upon completing his inspection, was a full head of steam. Either Longford or Iquitos must have been thinking the same thing, because the boat heaved with the first healthy turn of the engine, a puff of pure white steam shot out of the funnel. Using all the energy he had left, Kincaid returned to the wheelhouse.

The sun baked him and the air was humid and dense. He guided the boat as close to shore and shade as possible and kept a watchful eye on the mangroves, to avoid the invidious tangle of their underwater roots. In many spots the jungle was so dense there was a solid wall of green, and it seemed hardly able to contain all its vegetation, for trees and bushes had spilled over the edge and hung in the water. Red bauxite covered miles of bank, reddening the water like the bloodletting of a prehistoric monster.

When his nerves had quieted, Kincaid lashed the wheel, making sure there would be no repetition of last night's debacle, and went below to wash and change his clothes. The fire had reached his cabin too, blackening and weakening the bulkhead, but he was too tired to care. When he opened the door he saw Dolores stretched out on his berth, her face blackened, her clothes charred, being ministered to by a concerned Longford.

"You might have killed yourself, you know," the Professor said with avuncular chiding as he dabbed a wet compress across her face.

"I wasn't trying to kill myself," Dolores retorted, sullenly eyeing Kincaid. "I was trying to kill him."

Longford turned and shrugged, slightly apologetic. "Smoke inhalation, mainly," he explained. "She'll be all right."

Kincaid stared at the two of them, then looked down at himself, at the piranha bites, the torn and burned clothes, the soot-blackened skin, trying to encompass all the absurdities in one glance. "*She'll* be all right?"

"Now, Harry—" Longford began, but Dolores was not afraid of Kincaid's temper.

"What are you going to do?" She sat up and thrust her chin tauntingly at him. "Hit me again? Why don't you just put a bullet through my brain

and save everyone this trouble?" She was perched
on her knees on the bunk, ignoring Longford's
entreaties to lie down. Kincaid loomed over her,
black-faced; in their physical and emotional attitudes, they were perfect mirrors.

"What in hell do you want?"

"My father's rubber seeds!"

"Never!"

"Never is a long time for a man who has seven
hundred miles of Amazon still to go!"

Longford put a restraining hand on each of
them, forcing Dolores to sit on the bed and Kincaid to back away to a neutral corner of the
cabin.

"Please! Nothing is to be accomplished by
screaming. You must rest. Both of you."

Dolores sat and suffered Longford's fussy atten-
tions, satisfied that she had let Kincaid know exactly with whom he was dealing. Kincaid stood
in the corner, muttering to himself, annoyed, impatient, tired, and angry; he didn't know if he
had room for so many different feelings.

"We've got Parintins coming up within the hour,
Professor. We have to get food and we need wood
for the boiler. And you want me to rest." He shook
his head in consternation and walked slowly out
the door, then stopped, spun around, and pointed
a quivering finger at Dolores. "*And you can go to
hell!*"

"*Only to see you!*" she screamed back, and the
quickness of her rejoinder only served to further
infuriate him. He turned away again, paused, his

shoulder muscles tightening, then smashed his fist into the fire-weakened bulkhead, which collapsed into charcoal and ash at his feet. He turned to look back at her, his eyes narrowing, then walked out the door. There was another crash in the passageway and Dolores could not restrain a smile of triumph.

"You know," Longford observed, I believe you've reached him."

*   *   *

The *Mãe de Deus,* underway again, maintained maximum speed, her boilers now supplied with parts of the ship itself, in an attempt to augment her dwindling reserves of coal. Kincaid's plans were fuzzy, but top speed was a must. He had no idea how many boats were searching for him in the wake of the *Francesca,* or how far behind they were. It was essential to put some distance between them. Catching up with the *Francesca* appeared less likely for the moment than falling back into the arms of a Navy gunboat. Pará was another matter. If the *Francesca* got there first, they would never be able to transfer the rubber to the *Achilles*—which, in any event, was not due in port before the fifteenth, which left them hopelessly ahead of schedule. They would be trapped on the Amazon with a cargo too hot to unload and a hostage too volatile to control unless they killed her. Somehow, Kincaid couldn't picture that alternative.

Iquitos took the helm; Kincaid sat in the bow, hypnotized by the foaming water, trying to make some decisions. The river ahead was smooth as steel, but with a translucency that made it seem as if it were being lit from its depths. The bank loomed on the right, high as a city; slim-trunked palms a hundred feet high, thousands of them, branchless, ending in tassels of leaves that waved sinuously in the warm damp breeze. Other palms grew closer to the ground, in bunches, rough-barked, loaded with coconuts. Many of the trees were covered in vines, silver-gray in color, creeping along from tree to tree, wrapped tight; it would be impossible to put an axe through. And every once in a while something of startling beauty would interrupt the mass of green foliage; orchids or the swift flight of a parrot; dead ferns that had dried and sprinkled the trees silver and gold with their dust.

The sun went down, turning the river deep copper; the sky seemed to congeal, milky blue to a murky, nearly tangible purple. A scent of decay rose from the jungle as a familiar mist settled on the night. Farther ahead to starboard was a town called Parintins, its buildings brightly colored, ranged on hills overlooking the river; black men worked on the narrow docks; singing could be heard, wafted toward them on a slight breeze. As darkness came over the river and the jungle, the *Mãe de Deus* passed another village, one whose lights were pale yellow slugs that made the place look as if it were under the spell of disease.

"Harry? Harry?" He opened his eyes and saw Longford bending over him, a steaming cup in his hand. "Tea?" Kincaid sat up, his body tied in knots of pain. The air was chilly with mist.

"How long have I been out?" He took the cup and sipped gratefully.

"A few hours. We decided you needed it." Kincaid nodded heavily in agreement. "Last of the tea, I'm afraid."

"Give me a minute to get my bearings and I'll take the wheel. Anything left to eat?"

"Not much."

"What about her?"

"Subdued for the moment." Longford smiled in the gathering dark. "See you in the wheelhouse." He gave Kincaid's shoulder a squeeze and moved off. Kincaid sipped more tea; in the dark the smell of their fuel seemed to predominate, even in the bow. He lit a cigar, hoping no one would interrupt him. His thoughts strayed to the girl locked below. She had changed. What had happened to the spoiled child with her pretentious Continental affectations? He had to smile; back in Manaus he'd suspected that underneath all those artificial manners lurked a genuine hellcat. Kincaid heaved a reluctant sigh and got to his feet. In any circumstances but these—but then, in what circumstances but these could he have seen the real Dolores Mendonça? The cigar hissed when it hit the river. Kincaid entered the wheelhouse and nodded to Iquitos. The Indian offered to stay at the helm; Kincaid kept him silent company.

Fog came at them like greedy hands reaching out for favors and embraced them. The air became thick and heavy; breathing was something one had to concentrate on. Two or three times they pierced the fog and broke into a patch of clear air that was, by comparison, chilled.

An hour passed; then another. The fog had closed in tightly about them; they felt as though they were contained within a giant silver fist; they had to slow down.

"What's that?"

Ahead of them the fog parted for seconds. Kincaid had just time to make out the words: *Francesca. Manaus.*

"Stop engines," he hissed into the speaking tube.

Iquitos snuffed out the searchlight.

"Now get below and stop her noise. I don't want her recognizing her father's boat again." The Indian nodded and headed for the companionway, squeezing past Longford in the companionway. He started to ask what had happened, but Kincaid silenced him, a finger over his lips, and pointed. Longford had just time to see the stern of the *Francesca* disappear into another fog bank.

"I almost buggered her," Kincaid chuckled softly, watching the running lights wink out. "It's a wonder they didn't see us."

"Or hear us."

Kincaid shook his head. "Their own engines are too loud for that."

Longford peered into the white. "I don't understand. How can we have caught up with her? She must have stopped for some reason."

"Either that or she's been standing still in this pea soup. In any case, it looks as though our luck has begun to change."

He spun the wheel hard to starboard and waited. Minutes passed. The sound of the *Francesca*'s engines faded into silence. Kincaid blew through the speaker tube and set the engines to AHEAD SLOW. Iquitos whistled back his confirmation.

"Aren't you afraid of hitting something in all this?" Longford asked, alarmed. It was quite impossible to see.

"Yes and no. I'd say the chances are remote. We'll certainly swing a wide berth around the *Francesca* and just have to hope the river's big enough to accommodate us and any traffic."

The *Mãe de Deus* fought the strong current of the Amazon, moving south, instead of east. Kincaid hoped the compass was accurate. After a mile, he straightened out, heading due east, the current confirming the compass reading. Longford moved to turn on the searchlight, but Kincaid held his arm.

"It doesn't help us in fog this thick, but *they* might notice; we'll be too close. In fact, let's turn out the rest of our lights." So saying, Kincaid pushed the stanchions to AHEAD FULL and covered the binnacle. It was now pitch black, tingled with an undefinable silver, and the *Mãe de Deus* was plunging blind down the Amazon at full speed.

"Harry, this is mad. If we were to hit something now, it would mean our lives, the rubber, everything—"

"Stop babbling. It's our only chance to recover the lead. Providence has handed it to us; it would be ungrateful not to take it."

"But—"

"The Lord helps those who help themselves. Remember Gordon and his Bible."

Longford groaned and covered his eyes, a superfluous gesture under the circumstances. General Gordon, if Longford had understood the story, read his Bible before battle, not during.

Kincaid risked lighting another cigar, but ventured no further comment or consolation.

For two hours they traveled in this nerve-wracking fashion, joined by Iquitos, who reported Dolores to be under control. They found, despite their best efforts not to do so, that they strained their eyes, trying to see.

Abruptly, Kincaid threw the stanchions and all was still. They listened and heard only the creak of their own craft and the lapping of water. Kincaid smiled over the stub of his cigar.

"This is what I call a trim bit of boat."

He drew back the stanchions, plunging them forward once more into the dark.

18

Success agreed with Kincaid. Overtaking the *Francesca* in a blind fog and passing her lifted his spirits as nothing else in months, unless one counted his ambivalent stabs of pleasure when Dolores had drunkenly declared her love for him at her engagement party, or when she had gone to bed with him. But the *Francesca* affair—the "castling," he reminded himself with a smile—was different. He was very like his old self, suddenly, recalling the days when he'd fought with vigor against Berber attacks in the desert and then passed himself off as a chieftain by painting his face blue beneath his burnoose and having himself circumcised.

Still at the wheel, Kincaid stared at the coming day and felt the worst had passed. It was not the sort of confidence he usually allowed himself, but he could not see what could go wrong—unless he was stupid enough to let her seduce him a second time. They would stop for fuel somewhere up ahead, shoot something to eat, and be on their way in no time.

The howler monkey sat before him on the steering wheel, scampering over the spokes like a treadmill to stay in place when he spun it. Don't worry, Carmen, he thought, breakfast will soon be served. But not even the hunger pangs in his stomach, nor the absence of their nonexistent fuel reserve was sufficient to dampen Kincaid's mood. He found himself idly rehearsing the future (another luxury he had learned never to indulge), toying with the chattering monkey and deciding where and how to stay out of sight when they reached Pará early and had to wait for the dreadnought. And what of Dolores? In a rather roundabout fashion of rationalization, Kincaid even managed to find a way not only to forgive her for the trouble she'd caused, but actually to be glad her ingenuity had given him something off which to spark his own nature.

Even the appearance of Longford, who relieved Kincaid's watch, failed to rouse him from his speculations and daydreams. He descended the companionway, carrying the monkey, and poked his head briefly into the engine room where Iquitos, bathed in sweat, was breaking up deckchairs and stuffing their dismembered arms and legs into the furnace. He looked up at Kincaid with an expression at once grave and exhausted. Kincaid nodded. They would stop for fuel, soon.

He went into the Captain's cabin—which he had now appropriated for his own—and treated himself to a cold shower, shaved for the first time in days, and put on his last clean shirt. Then, with Carmen sitting on his shoulder, her tiny hands clutching his hair, he went to pay a call on the charming Senhorita Mendonça, whom they had left in bondage overnight—on his instructions—to prevent any mischief while they slept.

She was still asleep when he entered the fo'c'sle, a tattered silk evening glove wrapped around her mouth, her hands behind her back. Lying on the only remaining wooden berth, she appeared to be quite peaceful. Kincaid contemplated her in this uncharacteristic pose, striking a match against a charred bit of bulkhead and lighting his first cigar of the day. The monkey chattered at the flame and that woke her. She jerked violently, staring wildly about, not remembering, for the moment, where she was. Then her eyes lit on Kincaid and she stopped moving.

"Good morning."

She murmured something behind her gag. Adorable, he thought. He walked to the berth and sat down next to her, flank to flank; she wriggled; he watched until she was up against the bulkhead.

"I'm sorry we have nothing in the way of breakfast to offer you. The fact is we're out of everything." Another muffled response. Kincaid bent over her.

"I love seeing you like this," he whispered, and pulled down her gag, gave her a kiss, and replaced it before she could speak. Then he took pity; enough was enough. He removed the glove.

"You are beneath contempt," she greeted him, all chilly breath, an adder in a poison glade.

"And you are above reproach, which makes us even." He was about to untie her, when footsteps pounded outside the door.

"Harry!" Kincaid left the bonds alone. "Steamship, Harry." Longford stood in the doorway, breathing hard.

Kincaid rose at once, the morning's good humor instantly gone.

"Upstream or down?"

"Down heading up, and they've seen us. Don't forget, we look like the Brazilian Navy."

Kincaid ignored Dolores' snort of derision, replaced the gag, and did a mental pace until he found the direction that led to the light. He opened the locker from which she had borrowed her uniform, and found others.

"Here—" He gestured to Longford. "Put these on. I'm going to see if Mactavish left a hat or a blazer, and put a pair of binoculars around my neck. Do we show much fire damage topside?"

"Some." Longford examined a set of whites that had not been cleaned recently. He left, holding the clothes before him, reluctant to step into the trousers.

Kincaid started out, but his mood had not entirely evaporated. He sat down next to Dolores. When he tried to kiss her again she bit his lip; when he raised the gag she bit his finger. As he left the fo'c'sle, licking his wounds, it occurred to him that, attractive as she was, Dolores' effect was alarmingly similar to that of the piranha.

* * *

The career of Captain João de Villalongeza had seen better days and while he longed for the rigors and manly demands of full-scale war, the warts and fevers of fear also made him glad he had been reduced, even before his twilight years, to demeaning duties as commander of the *Maria Sanchez*, a freighter as sturdy of body as she was uninspired of spirit and design. When Captain de Villalongeza was informed of the starboard appearance of a Navy gunboat, an event that once would have stirred his blood, he now merely grumbled and trudged his way to the bridge of the *Maria Sanchez* and watched as the boat drew near.

Captain de Villalongeza nodded so that his men would assume that ignorance and perplexity were the sole province of those beneath the rank of captain, but he wondered along with them why this gunboat was cruising so close to shore. Vaguely he noticed the absence of guns. Then, across the short distance of murky water that separated them, a voice rang out, and Captain de Villalongeza saw an officer standing on deck, megaphone in hand, his alert military bearing a distinct contrast to de Villalongeza's own easygoing manner and attire. The gunboat captain raised the megaphone and demanded his identity. Captain de Villalongeza lifted his own megaphone to answer.

"The *Maria Sanchez*," he called, serious and of-

ficious. "Bound for Manaus." And when the returning call was to inquire of his cargo, the Captain grinned, a prize gold tooth basking in the
sun, and shouted back: "Three hundred whores!"

A wail rose from below decks and de Villalongeza looked down to see ringed fingers and
painted nails, legs in assorted sizes and shapes en-
cased in tattered silk stockings, a red garter here
and there, soiled silk shoes, and scuffed knees.
Still, the idea of all those whores was something
Captain de Villalongeza felt a man ought to be
proud of, and so he looked across the water at
the other boat and grinned to its captain. The
other commander was not amused, was instead all
business and commenced to call out in detail the
purpose of his mission.

The *São Paulo* (Captain de Villalongeza read
her insignia through his binoculars) was on the
trail of rubber thieves, men who had stolen seeds
and were fleeing downriver. The Captain did not
need to hear any more to comprehend the magni-
tude of the crime. If the seeds were to get out of
Brazil . . . well, there would be no need to bring
three hundred whores to Manaus because there
would no longer be anyone who could pay. Marriage might be the only institution to thrive in
such a situation.

Then Captain de Villalongeza was told that
these same rubber thieves had also stolen the
yacht of Colonel Mendonça to make good their
escape. The rain had thrown the pursuers off
course and it was possible, the *São Paulo*'s captain

said, that the *Francesca* might actually be behind them now, cutting telegraph cables.

Captain de Villalongeza was given a final admonition: There was a government warrant out for the *Francesca.* If he saw her, he was to stop her at all costs.

He heard a scream that he thought came from the other boat, but their whistle sounded and his own whores were shouting flirtations across the water. He saluted in farewell.

Captain João de Villalongeza saw in this encounter the possibility for belated advancement of his own career, or at the very least, of a large reward. He doubled the watch and ordered all hands to keep a weather eye out for the *Francesca.*

* * *

Kincaid tossed off his captain's hat and jacket, and raced below to the fo'c'sle. He flung open the door and looked at Dolores, who had wrested free of her gag and was screaming to no avail. He hung on the sides of the door, breathing hard, swinging in and out, smiling hungrily and with great erotic amusement. Her determination and bravery excited him as no cosmopolitan polish could have.

"I congratulate you. You never say die."

She said nothing, but sat on her haunches, still trussed up, tossing the hair out of her face with a wave of her head. Kincaid approached and untied her.

"You'll be happy to know I'm going ashore in a bit. We're out of fuel as well as food."

"And me?" She knew the request would be denied her.

"Oh, to be sure, you. I wouldn't let you out of my sight. It's not that I don't trust you." He grinned. "It's just that, well, disaster seems to follow in your wake."

Dolores stood up, rubbed her wrists, then slapped his face.

He slapped her back.

*　　*　　*

With Iquitos in the lead and Kincaid and Dolores directly behind, they made their way through dense jungle. Long-stalked plants, bamboo and cane, dipped under the weight of their enormous leaves; elephant ears were so large Iquitos did not cut them down but cut holes through them; roots curved up, shot across the jungle floor and circled back to wind around their own trunks; tangled vines hung down, dropping startling pink blossoms. The jungle floor was covered with dead leaves and plants. Trees were fallen and propped up by other trees, and sunlight shot down in parallel lines. Yellow and green and brown moss covered entire logs.

The monkey was hungry, and, recognizing its natural habitat, it scrambled off Kincaid's shoulder and disappeared into the leafy green, searching for food. Kincaid moved to stop her, then let her go with a stab of regret; he had grown fond of Carmen.

A trumpeter bird shouted out and was answered by a similar call; in the tangle of the jungle the sounds were directionless. Crickets hacked and chattered; insects seemed to penetrate the flesh and pulse through the veins like blood.

Kincaid, Dolores, and Iquitos reached a clearing and the men settled down to work. Iquitos checked the action of the Martini rifles; he looked down the open breeches to be sure that the barrels had not been clogged with the tiny mud nests of the dauber wasps. Satisfied they were in working order, he set the rifles down and pointed to various things that could be done. The machetes were used to cut down small trees and chop them into pieces small enough to be tied, wrapped, and hauled back to the dinghy.

They worked fast, in silence, knowing that every moment spent here was a moment in which their pursuers drew closer. Dolores sat in the shade, and Kincaid glanced at her from time to time. She favored his intermittent looks with an inscrutable one of her own.

Vines as thick as a man's wrist were cut and stuffed into small sacks; the bark of a dead tree that looked alarmingly like a boa's skin was peeled and joined the vines. But the real reason Iquitos had stopped at this particular clearing was the prevalence of the *babussu* palm; the bark burned well and evenly and he knew the tough-shelled

nuts had even been used in locomotives as a sub-
stitute for coal.

They worked without speaking for over two
hours, making periodic trips through the hacked-
out tunnel to pack the dinghy with their new fuel
supply. When the dinghy was filled, one of them
would row to the *Mãe de Deus* and help Longford
unload its precious contents. When Iquitos returned from one of these trips, he saw that Dolores
was gone and immediately called to Kincaid. Kincaid sighed, exhausted, patience and tolerance
gone.

"Let her go."

When the Indian protested, Kincaid stood and
waved the machete. "I said let her go. Let her join
forces with the monkey. She's been in our hair for
five hundred miles, throwing every obstacle she
can in our way. If it weren't for her we'd be in
Pará by now. If she wants to die in the jungle, let
her. At this point it's all the same to me."

Iquitos said nothing, feeling a flicker of an old
loyalty and protectiveness to Dolores, an indebted-
ness to her father. But the newer sense of his
mission took ascendance; he looked toward the
twisted jungle wall into which she had vanished
and did not move.

They worked. Sweat poured down Kincaid's
back and chest as he chopped wood and piled it
into the sacks they had brought. He tried to put
Dolores out of his mind, and it was only when
he thought how well he was doing it that he
realized he was not doing it at all.

He glanced across the clearing at Iquitos. To his surprise, the Indian was not working but standing up, still and alert. Kincaid was about to speak but Iquitos held up a hand, so he listened instead. The sounds were the same to him, the birds, the insects, the shrill cries high in the trees. If anything was unusual, it was that there were fewer sounds.

Kincaid shrugged and bent to his work again when he heard something else, a high, piercing whine, indistinct, far away, but surrounding him, as if the jungle were moaning. And leaping from the distance sharp and close, was her scream.

Kincaid looked up, irritated at the way his alarm had traveled to the secret places of fear in his body. Her scream seemed to explain that other strange whining sound and he shook his head at Iquitos, but the Indian remained rigid, still listening. Kincaid shook his head. He would waste no time being taken in by another of Dolores' tricks.

But she screamed again. The pitch was frantic. Before he could make another resolve to resist her, there came a third shriek and this time doubt gave way to panic. The jungle whine that surrounded them seemed to be coming closer. Kincaid grabbed his rifle and ran out of the clearing into the density of the undergrowth in the direction of her cries. Iquitos took up his own rifle and followed. The screams increased in volume and terror.

And then there was another sound, subtle, felt more than heard at first, as the jungle floor seemed to rumble as if shaken from beneath. The distant whine approached and clarified: Dolores' screams were joined by others; great bellowing animal roars, frenzied cries, trumpeting pain. The entire jungle throbbed with fear. When they broke into the clearing, the screams had become a succession of inhuman trills. They stopped short, rifles dangling uselessly.

Kincaid had heard stories about what he was seeing but had been sure that stories were all they were; it had all been too fantastic, too grotesque and enormous to contemplate as real. But the ants he saw were real and their power awesome. Millions upon millions of these ants, with names as pointed as *rapax, legionis,* and *praedator,* would all at once begin a concerted, militarized move across a wide area of jungle. The ground shook under their march, trees trembled and fell, uprooted, unable to withstand the onslaught. Animals sensed their approach and fled in terror, for the ants were relentless; they destroyed every living thing in their mindless path. Anteaters and birds that fed on ants had no effect whatsoever.

Iguanas and lizards darted across Kincaid's feet, ants firmly dug into their backs. The near-dead body of a pink pelican fell before him, dotted with tiny sores. A huge tortoise crawled by, a hole already eaten through its shell. All manner of animal life ran past them: brown rats the size of small pigs, pigs as large as goats, jaguars and ocelots whose ferocity was extinguished by fear.

All struggled, grunting and howling, toward the river.

Kincaid looked for Dolores, but the sounds were now too loud to distinguish hers, and the sights too changing and violent, until from a fallen log, a hand flailed in the air and he saw that the log was Dolores' squirming body totally covered with the killer ants. As Kincaid made his way to her she tried to rise. Ants fell from her, exposing a face demented with horror. When he saw her eyes, he knew that until that moment she had had no hope.

"Get out of here!" he shouted to the Indian at his side, who stared at Dolores, mesmerized. "Get back to the dinghy!" Kincaid shoved him hard to break the spell, then reached out his arms to the shroud of ants that covered Dolores. Iquitos had a sudden memory that among certain tribes a young man's initiation into the warrior class required him to hold an arm inside a hollow tree filled with these ants.

In another second Kincaid's own body was covered with them, the pain a series of tiny burns, as if sparks of live coal were being thrown at him; the steellike pincers of the ants, bigger than their entire bodies, dug in and stayed. As he half-lifted, half-dragged Dolores, he could hear her screams again and to his horror, he could also hear his own. The frenzied, panicked sounds of the animals was the din of the apocalypse and Kincaid and Dolores ran with it, only their eyes visible, their hands brushing ants away with desperate, useless speed.

As they neared the river, a new sound of pain assailed their ears. The animals, in a last attempt to rid their bodies of the insatiable ants, had flung themselves into the water where the ants died only to be replaced as messengers of doom by the piranha. Kincaid saw the animals meet their deaths, but did not stop running. The sensation was beyond pain: Every bit of exposed flesh was on fire and he counted himself lucky he'd eschewed the short pants and shirt that Longford recommended for the fuel-gathering expedition.

When finally they broke from the jungle, they were unrecognizable as human beings. They looked like a writhing mass, somehow, hideously perambulating toward the river. Animals rushed by covered, pursued by the countless millions who came on in bloody search for a host. Iquitos had waited in the dinghy despite the imminent danger to himself.

Kincaid stumbled forward, Dolores' body jerking and shaking in uncontrolled hysteria next to him. They got to the shore where the sight and sound of pain-crazed animals being devoured by ants or piranha made them quicken their frantic steps. As soon as they reached the dinghy, he threw her inside and Iquitos immediately pushed off toward the *Mãe de Deus*. The ants covered the boat and the last load of fuel and now commenced devouring the Indian as well. He had taken the precaution of dousing himself with water and they slid off him—at first. For all the time it took to row to the boat, they were tearing at their clothes, slapping at the ants, anything to still the tiny stabs of hot pain.

When they reached the yacht they were almost naked, their clothes in shreds from the insistent pincers, eager for flesh. Longford, watching from the bow, knew enough to keep out of the reach of his friends.

"The showers!" he shouted, pointing below. When the three ran past him, he doused the deck behind them.

Kincaid, Dolores, and Iquitos pressed themselves into the captain's shower stall. The water was of sufficient pressure to edge off the ants and after some half-mad moments of flailing and scratching, a time when death seemed almost preferable to the three, the ants were finally dead themselves, lying in glistening piles on the shower floor like barnacles on a rock after a wave.

"Don't let them get to the stuff," Kincaid told Iquitos. His voice was choked and ragged and he knew he'd been screaming. Iquitos covered the floor outside the hothouse with kerosene, stamped his feet on the few stray ants he saw, then ran along the passageway doing the same.

Dolores was staring at the dead ants, her body in a paroxysm of revulsion, a shudder so violent it knocked her off balance. Blood poured down their bodies along rivulets of water. Kincaid held her tightly by the shoulders then ran his fingers through her hair to get rid of the ants caught in the thick mass. He murmured words of encouragement and comfort. The tremors and hysteria passed, draining her strength, and she leaned into his chest, her breathing becoming regular.

When she was calmer, Kincaid tried to edge her away from him. The water had cleaned them, but blood still oozed from innumerable bites. She clung to him. In his excitement, he pushed her away, but she held fast. He lifted her face and her eyes were half-closed. Her nostrils flared, clotted with blood. She tried to speak, drops of blood pink on her lacerated lips. Kincaid longed to lick them and the effort of resistance made him groan. He tried to laugh; she continued to stare. She began kissing the cuts on his face. He pushed her away, anger mounting along with an unbearable animal arousal.

She stared, wide-eyed, a drop of blood seeped from her hairline down her cheek. He touched her hair and pressed an ant between his fingers. She regarded him with glazed eyes. The pain had released in her a violence that came of having borne pain. She pressed herself to him; the points of her breasts blotted his chest with a mixture of their blood. Then she kissed him hard, wondering that such stirrings could take place within her now, here. She saw the confusion in his face, in the half-closed eyes and lines between his brows and strained, tentative smile. He shook his head and backed away when she moved to kiss him again, but the violence was in him too.

With frantic, graceless movements, their hands

limp and useless, they licked the blood from each other's faces, from each other's shoulders and necks. They moaned; their teeth chattered, caught between passion and hysteria. He pushed his face between her legs and came up slick with her blood. And at the end—when the passion demanded a union they were almost afraid to seal— they came together.

* * *

Kincaid did not know how many times Iquitos had called to him but he felt he had suddenly awakened from a dream. Dolores, still in his arms, automatically sought to prevent him from rising, but Iquitos was shrieking now. Pushing her away and grabbing the remnants of his trousers, Kincaid dashed to the companionway.

He emerged topside, looking about, and saw the Indian, standing by the rail, staring over the side, an expression of horror on his rigid features. Uneasily Kincaid walked toward him.

"What is it? Answer me! What—"

No answer was necessary. The Indian could only point, and when Kincaid looked, he thought his heart would stop. Longford, in an effort to rescue the last of the *babussu* nuts, had pulled the dinghy close to the boat and had fallen into it. His body was not moving; covered with ants, holes where his eyes had been, bone showing through the pitted flesh of his hands; his hands which seemed to be imploring mercy or aid. The ants were devouring the rest of him as they watched.

Kincaid said nothing. The silence hung as if the air had gone out of the world. Dolores came on deck; Kincaid did not attempt to shield her from the sight. She gasped and reached out to hold his arm but she did not scream. None of them could take their eyes from Longford's body. To do so would have been to abandon him; they knew that they had to look, to watch, to see it through until the end.

Kincaid looked at the river, at the sky, at the jungle so near to them. Where was the bright promise of the morning now? It seemed a hundred years ago. What did it matter that the *Mãe de Deus* had beaten the *Francesca*? There was no way to beat the Amazon.

Iquitos touched his arm.

"We must get rid of the dinghy."

Kincaid looked at him. "I want to bury him."

Iquitos stared; had he lost his mind? "The ants—"

"I want to bury him."

❈ 19 ❈

As the sun sank tissue-gray and gold over the river, moisture from the air condensed on all surfaces until chairs and poles and all manner of inanimate objects seemed to have sprung pores and were in a damnable sweat. Captain de Villalongeza paced the bridge of the *Maria Sanchez* with accustomed sleepiness. Soon it would be suggested by his first mate, by prearrangement, that he retire to his cabin; the Captain would protest; the first mate would insist, and the Captain would relent, retire, and prepare for a special dispensation from the cargo section, just to loosen the muscles.

When the first officer called his name, Captain de Villalongeza's protest was already half-voiced, but then he opened his eyes and saw what was coming toward them from up river.

"The *Francesca!*" the first officer whispered in amazement. The Captain whipped the binoculars from the officer's hands, snapping the worn neck strap, and peered at the white and gray shape on the purple river.

"And flying her flags! The gall!" he said in

astonishment, his exhilaration mounting. He turned from the sight, dug into his pocket, and rubbed his rosary for the wonderful fortune that was sailing his way.

"Signal them," he ordered his first officer, his voice dark and shaking. The first officer motioned to the second, the second to the third, and the third to the bo'sun; flags were run up, white patches on the glooming sky. The *Francesca* did not stop, ignored them rather and swung out further into the river. The sheer audacity of this move enraged the Captain and spurred him on to further stratagems. He ordered the whistle sounded, to no effect. The *Francesca* ignored the bellow and continued her attempt to circumvent the *Maria Sanchez*.

"Alter course to intercept," the Captain said, trying to contain his excitement. "*Ram them!*" The second officer, after checking with the first, ignored the command. Captain de Villalongeza ran out to the deck, picking up a rifle on the way, and began firing at the *Francesca*. He gloried at the sound of the open blast and the *pchoo* that came several seconds later. I have them, he thought, and mentally erected a statue of himself in the square of his native village. The *Francesca* altered course again, swinging back toward him, and stopped engines alongside the *Maria Sanchez*.

Two men and a woman were standing on the bridge below opposite, all three agitated, and Captain de Villalongeza knew the sweetness of victory. The younger of the two men was holding a megaphone and lifted it to his mouth.

"What in heaven's name do you think you're doing?" he screamed, and Captain de Villalongeza was astonished to hear the arrogance in the thief's voice.

"We have orders to stop this ship!" he shouted back, blown up with self-righteousness and faith. "You are carrying rubber seeds! It is illegal to remove such merchandise from Brazil!" Having stated the unarguable, de Villalongeza watched the older man take the megaphone from the younger.

"Do you know me, Captain?" the old man said in a voice that was anything but contrite. He lowered the megaphone and Captain de Villalongeza stared in disbelief.

"Colonel Mendonça," he whispered, then repeated it at a military shout, trying to recoup the loss with good form.

"*We* are pursuing the rubber thieves!" Colonel Mendonça shouted. "We were delayed in the fog and had to repair a steam governor." He was not impatient or angry as Captain de Villalongeza feared he might be. "Who told you to watch for us?"

"The commander of a navy gunboat," the Captain replied, with the dawning realization that he had been obeying orders, that blame could be strewn at someone else's feet, that he had been and remained in the right. He might yet receive something for his efforts; if not a statue, perhaps a ribbon, a letter, or a handshake from the governor. He did not, at any rate, think he would be shot.

"This commander," the old Colonel shouted after conferring with the younger man after the younger man had conferred with the woman. "What did he look like?"

Here was a poser; de Villalongeza resisted an impulse to remove his hat and scratch his head. The Colonel, seeing him hesitate, did not wait for a reply.

"Did this commander specifically tell you to stop my yacht? He told you to intercept the *Francesca*, did he?"

"Most definitely." De Villalongeza was happy to be clear on that point, the more so as it tended toward his own exoneration.

"Did he tell you where he learned of the rubber theft, or how?"

"He said simply that there was a warrant issued for the *Francesca*."

The Captain could see the old man take down his megaphone, obviously perplexed. To his astonishment, the woman took it from him and held it to her lips.

"Tell us of this gunboat, Captain. You're certain it was a gunboat?"

The question was an affront to all of de Villalongeza's military aspirations and fantasies.

"Quite certain, *senhorita*. It was the regulation

color and had the correct markings on her funnel. The *São Paulo.*"

"Did it have guns?"

The question stunned him, bringing back with a rush and a flash his vague observation, which he had not even bothered to commit to the log; a gunboat without guns.

"Did you hear me, Captain? Did you see deck guns?" The woman's voice was piercing across the water.

"Yes! Yes, I did!"

The three opposite him shifted about, their heads rotated and their hands moved up and down; Captain de Villalongeza hoped he was making a good impression.

"How long ago did you encounter this gunboat, Captain?" Colonel Mendonça asked.

Captain de Villalongeza hesitated again; he wanted to get this right, but he had been so sleepy; and to have to ask his officers in front of Colonel Mendonça would be humiliating and most unseemly. Why had he not bothered to enter the encounter in the log? He never entered anything there.

"Five hours!" he called back and heard the muttered protestations behind him, but it was too late to do anything about them. Besides, he thought, as he watched the old Colonel double over and the *Francesca* pull away, they couldn't do anything about it anyway. No matter what he told them, they were going to go at top speed.

As elements of the armada from Manaus passed him in the wake of the *Francesca*, Captain de Villalongeza's only wish was that he be able to go with them and be there when the battle was waged. Failing that, he would retire to his cabin and tickle one of the whores.

*   *   *

The *Mãe de Deus* clung to the bank by a grappling anchor wrapped around the trunk of a giant palm. Kincaid carried Longford's remains in a blanket onto the blazing white sand. The gruesome package reeked of the kerosene they had used to throw off the ants and reclaim the corpse. Iquitos stood beside the grave he had dug in the sand. He waited anxiously to get underway again and had tried to convince Kincaid, but the pragmatic mercenary was oddly adamant on this point. Iquitos shrugged; what had begun as a single act of rebellion and defiance on his own part had turned into a kind of dream, a dream in which the principal players were himself, Kincaid, Dolores, Longford, and the boat itself, the once-proud *Mãe de Deus*, now scarred and hacked and driven to her limits in a frantic attempt to escape the confines of their nightmare. But standing at the grave, Iquitos knew that none of them would escape. The Amazon would claim them all; the jungle would overgrow their plans as it had overgrown their lives. He watched Kincaid gently lowering Longford's body into the hole. He had liked

the little man; found him unassuming and reliable.
They had had the same motives for trying to steal
the rubber seeds. As for Kincaid, he had never
understood the Yanqui, anyway, and probably
never would. He had supposed him at first to be
a blind opportunist, but he had learned—he was
learning now—that Kincaid had levels beneath
levels. He reminded Iquitos of an onion with its
various layers; but was there anything at the center? He would never learn, he knew; not in a
lifetime of peeling layers away.

Dolores sat beside a single dry bush. She turned
away from the ceremony to face the river, her face
drained of all emotion. She wondered whether her
father would catch them, not sure anymore that
she wanted him to. She was no longer certain of
anything. It seemed she had been living in a series
of worlds and one by one they had exploded. The
myths of her romanticism, the infallibility and
power of her father, the blind loyalty of Iquitos,
Kincaid's tragic aura, and Manaus' traditional and
established social structure with its offhand rationalization for slavery—one by one, like bubbles in
champagne going flat, they had all popped and
vanished. Leaving what? They had left her, now,
hopelessly uncertain. How did she know there
were not more worlds to collapse? How did she
know the present, dreamlike world of the river
was the last? Things had happened she would not
have believed possible if they had been foretold.
She had been unable, despite all her new-found
knowledge and experience, to stifle her love for

Kincaid; nor could she have conceived—until now
—that it was possible for love and hate to exist
simultaneously. If she waited long enough, perhaps one of them would consume the other. She
did not know which result she preferred; she no
longer presumed to know which would be better.
In school, reading Plato, she had learned that the
admission of ignorance was the beginning of true
wisdom. She turned again to the grave, watching
Kincaid fill in the sand. When the rains came and
the river rose—in a week, a month, perhaps later
that same day—the bank would be submerged;
poor Longford's final resting place was to be a
transient one.

Kincaid stared at the grave. His head felt light
and hot in the sun, and the kerosene fumes made
him dizzy. He tried to mumble something, but the
words wouldn't come, only random thoughts. If
anyone had died it should not have been
Longford, a man of peace, who deplored violence,
who had harmed no one. But why had he felt the
need to bury him? Kincaid realized with a startling
rush of clarity, by Longford's grave, that he had
insisted on the burial not because his feelings for
Longford were so great, but because they were
so little. Oh, he had liked the little Englishman;
he had known him for a long time, even felt an affection of sorts for him. But in reality the burial
was an attempt to go through the motions of feeling, as if by doing so he could conjure up the
sense of feeling. He was imitating a human being,
not for anyone's benefit but his own, but imitating,

nonetheless, hoping desperately it might somehow, by some mysterious alchemy, become genuine. His entire existence—restless, nomadic, romantic—he saw now as nothing more than a sustained attempt to flee from his own absence.

Kincaid decided to say nothing; not only did he not believe in the next life; he didn't believe in the present one, either. The best he could do, he decided, was not to burden Longford's soul—if he had one—with hypocrisy.

"May he rest in peace."

He looked up and saw Dolores standing on the little mound of sand across from him. He resisted, as strongly as he had resisted anything in his life, the impulse to throw himself into her arms and sob like a child for his lost humanity.

Dolores looked at him and began to cry. She made no sounds, but tears streamed down her dirty face in rivulets like a miniature Amazon delta. She sank to her knees across from Kincaid by the grave and wept. Minutes passed.

Iquitos paced impatiently by the margin. The *Francesca* would be coming, soon; in his heart he could replicate the pounding of her engines. If they were caught he would be killed; it pained him as much to die and fail in his mission to free his people as it did to reveal his treachery to the Colonel. There was a time in his boyhood when life had seemed like a series of adventures that would never end; his father teaching him to carve a blowgun from a chonta-palm trunk; his mother roasting corn on green twigs that he had gathered for her himself; the smell of that corn, rich and hot; the taste . . .

Something moved in the jungle. Iquitos brushed away the sand flies swarming about his face. He had caught the movement in the periphery of his vision and now turned around and faced it. Kincaid and Dolores, staring at each other across the grave, saw nothing. Iquitos sensed what was coming, but was powerless to prevent it. Everything was ordained; as in dreams. Slowly, as the sounds increased, he felt that his fate was about to be met.

He called Kincaid's name softly and the man looked up. Iquitos stared at him.

"Remember," he said quietly, "that I saved your life. I waited in the dinghy."

Kincaid frowned. "I remember."

"Remember."

Kincaid stood quickly and started to walk toward Iquitos but stopped and turned; it was then that the Indians emerged from the jungle. Dolores saw them, and scrambled up beside Kincaid.

The Indians advanced. There were perhaps thirty of them, very beautiful, with graceful limbs that tapered at the wrists and ankles. Although their skin was dark, many were painted a deep rose color that, as they came closer, turned out not to be paint but some sort of skin disease covering their bodies. The younger members of the tribe had skin that was covered also in fine sand— the sand they stood on, the sand that covered Longford—and their bodies had taken on the texture of velvet. The men wore parrot feathers in their hair and the women wore nothing, but all faces were painted like masks. Their genitals were painted red. They advanced slowly, curiously, with a strange dignity; they had no weapons but for knives slung on the belts of some of the men.

Iquitos whispered, "Do . . . not . . . move."

The Indians approached and, ignoring Iquitos, proceeded to inspect Dolores and Kincaid. They appeared fascinated by the buttons on Kincaid's coat and shirt and on Dolores' borrowed uniform. Dolores endeavored to obey Iquitos' injunction, but could hardly refrain from shaking. If she did not manage to put her mind somewhere else, she knew she would start to scream. Which world was this? Their fingers were picking at her as if her flesh were carrion, and before she was quite aware of it, they had begun to remove her clothes. She cast a desperate glance at Kincaid and saw that they were doing the same to him. He returned her look, his features immobile. The Indians did not appear hostile, they did not seem to want to hurt them; it was all curiosity, its detachment was terrifying.

Kincaid and Dolores stood before them, naked, Dolores' eyes fixed on the ground before her in fear and shame.

The Indians knelt at their feet in two circles and began to lick their skin. They licked everywhere, especially interested in the parts of their bodies that had hair, for they themselves were completely free of it. Dolores felt herself grow faint as two Indians knelt between her legs and inspected her there with their tongues. The examination continued upward, and upon its completion, the attitude of the Indians began to change. They became agitated, alarmed, even frightened, and backed away from Kincaid and Dolores, regarding them with fear and with revulsion. It was then that they spoke for the first time, their voices high and birdlike, chirping sounds that would blend into the jungle the way no other human voice could.

Iquitos turned slowly to Kincaid. "They try to lick away the white paint that covers your body," he explained. "I do not understand their every word. But they are afraid of you; that you have some disease that turns your skin white." The Indians came forward again and surrounded Iquitos. He swallowed and went on. "They are afraid for me. If I stay with you they think I will get this disease and turn white." He almost smiled, then turned and spoke haltingly with the Indians, who answered energetically and all at once. Kincaid knew what was coming before Iquitos turned again. "I must go with them." His voice rang hollow with incredulity, but he knew it was merely a suspicion confirmed; he would never leave the jungle.

With some instinctive idea of forestalling events, Kincaid moved toward him, more naked than the Indians, and absurdly helpless, but Iquitos signaled him back.

"The seeds," he reminded Kincaid urgently. "If you are stopped, the journey has no point. I have no point. He has no point." He jerked his head in the direction of the fresh grave. Baffled and unbelieving, Kincaid hesitated. It was happening so fast. His mind, so facile, so ready to improvise, could not conceive that the event had unfolded, had already completed itself. He needed time and there was no time. Until now there had always been a way out, an alternative, room to maneuver. He stood on the sand, staring, dumb with shock.

"I will rejoin you," Iquitos said in the same hollow tone. "If only my skin were really white," he called to Kincaid, unable to suppress the smile, his eyes filling with tears. "They would leave me then."

The Indians withdrew in an undulating knot toward the jungle, protecting Iquitos with their bodies as Kincaid watched helplessly.

"Remember," Iquitos' voice called out.

"I remember," Kincaid shouted back, choking on the words. "Be careful." The advice sounded pitiful and stupid.

"*Iquitos!*" Dolores' scream tore the sky and she ran toward them, heedless of her nakedness, and tried to reach him. They hurled her back disinterestedly upon the sand. "Iquitos!" She tried again to reach him, already disappearing into the jungle foliage. Again they threw her back. This time she stayed on her knees and didn't move. Kincaid picked up their clothes and walked toward her.

"What did you want to tell him?" he asked, kneeling beside her. She looked at him.

"That I understood."

Kincaid started to help her on with her clothes. When he looked up, they were gone, as if they'd never been.

* * *

The furnace was a ravenous monster whose belly was never filled. Feeling like Sisyphus, Kincaid, stuffed shovelsful of *babussu* nuts into the gaping mouth, cramming the bottomless pit with food. He knocked closed the iron gate and, mopping his neck and chest with the remains of his last shirt, stumbled topside.

The sun promised a day of unrelieved heat, and his energy ebbed. He had had no food in as long as he remembered. He knew they couldn't go on much longer without it, but he was out of ideas.

It exasperated him to know the water beneath teemed with edible fish. They had thrown overboard or burned everything resembling tackle, and even if he could improvise a line, the *Mãe de Deus'* pounding engines and great speed would render fishing impossible. Stopping now was out of the question.

He dragged himself to the wheelhouse and pored over Mactavish's charts, blinking sweat out of his eyes. Obidos, Santarem, and Monte Alegre were part of history. He took his bearings and saw that they were passing a collection of huts identified as Almeirim; a similar collection would appear on the southern bank, Porto de Moz. They were cruising close to the north, staying shy of river traffic, the jungle to their left, a solid wall of trees over fifty feet high. The river was so broad at this point, nearing the delta, that the farther shore could not be seen, merely sensed as a penciling of black on the horizon. If Porto de Moz was there, Kincaid couldn't make it out, even with binoculars. The water was flat and still, despite the current, its depths infinite and remote. The sense of otherworldliness, of isolation in a vast expanse of unknown, would have been complete, were it not for the incessant buzzing of flies and the stultifying heat.

Kincaid leaned against the wheel, exhausted. Below, sitting in the bow, Dolores faced away from him. The angle of her back, the slump of her shoulders, showed her own exhaustion and the despair that had come of her defeat. She had yielded to him as a woman and as an enemy and sat there now, he knew, wondering what was left. Kincaid watched her for a time, then lashed the wheel and went to stand beside her. Below them, river porpoises snorted and bellowed, accompanying them to open sea. He stared at her delicate profile against the lushness of the jungle.

"It appears you will succeed after all. Nothing stops you; not principles, not people."

"I'm sorry."

"Sorry you're destroying my father?"

"Sorry I'm destroying you. You were the one obstacle I couldn't have foreseen."

She turned away. Her attraction for him had no room for such compassion. "You've overcome it as you have everything else."

Kincaid bent his face close to hers. The river rushed by the bow in teasing splashes. Reflected sunlight burned his eyes. He touched her hand, her chin, her cheek. "I haven't overcome it. I've just closed my eyes to it. If I'd left them open, I'd be dead."

Dolores sighed, her head heavy on her neck. She shook it with weariness.

"We'll make Gurupá by moonrise. If you like I'll set you ashore there." She said nothing, but reached up to take his arm. He kissed her. There was little passion in the kiss; they were exhausted and the combat that gave the erotic edge to their desire was absent. But a new understanding, a certain dry trust was communicated.

Kincaid continued to hold her hand for some time, then released it, stumbled back to the wheelhouse and removed the lash. He spun the wheel hard to starboard. The *Mãe de Deus* would traverse the river's huge expanse and then hug the southern shore until Gurupá, following the main channel south around the enormous delta island of Marajó, itself larger than Switzerland, and so to Pará. Somehow at Gurupá, or at Breves, he would stop and get food and replenish his supply of coal or *babussu* nuts. Her jewels would buy him what he needed. He stared at the chart, making sure he understood the route; there was no doubt: to the north of Marajó, around the smaller island of Itapupa, the size of Massachusetts, all was impenetrable delta marsh.

He sagged against the wheel, inert, and stayed there he did not know how long. He looked at his watch and saw that it was two-thirty; two-thirty on a moist, steaming afternoon, cruising across the endless width of the Amazon . . . He must have dozed on his feet, for he was startled by Dolores' cry and found himself blinking. She stood where he had left her, in the bow, but it wasn't until he followed her gaze upriver that he saw.

The *Francesca* was bearing down on them.

Kincaid whirled and stared at the charts; they would never make Gurupá. He spun the wheel to port and headed back for Itapupa. When he looked up, ready to race to the stokehold, Dolores was standing there, holding one of the Martini rifles.

"Help me."

She stared at him, bewildered.

"Help me," he repeated.

"Why?"

He started to babble, saying the first things that came into his mind, watching the *Francesca* loom larger on the horizon out of the corner of his eye. He talked gibberish, spouting morality, ethics, slavery, money, happily-ever-afters. He told her he loved her, he reminded her of Coutard and the life that awaited her if she went back. He promised her the world; he railed at her insensitivity; if the journey downriver had any meaning at all, he shouted, his voice trembling; if Longford and Iquitos' sacrifices were of any importance. . . . She listened without hearing, hypnotized, seeing only his lips move.

"Dolores!"

"Why?"

Kincaid shrugged, slumped. He had run dry. "I can't think of a reason in the world."

She didn't move. Slowly he went toward her; she raised the gun when he came near, but let him take it from her hands. He pulled her past him and propped her up against the wheel, almost collapsing against her back with exhaustion and relief.

"Head for the marshes—" He pointed.

"How will you know what I'll do when you go below?" she asked dully, looking straight ahead. He kissed the back of her hair.

"I trust you."

He left her to steer, depending on her, while he crawled to the companionway and ran below-decks to stoke the boilers with the last of the fuel. He whistled through the speaking tube and told her to throw the stanchions to FULL AHEAD. After a moment's hesitation, bells clanged and the ship began to tremble with the revolutions of the screw.

"Hard port," he commanded through the tube, "head for the marshes!" This time she responded immediately. He bent over the furnace and fed its insatiable jaws like a soul in purgatory. Sweat gleamed on his body, running across his scarred back and chest. His face burned in the furnace's glow, his heart pounded and his muscles ached. He ran back on deck, the *Francesca* was closer, materializing like an apparition. In early middle age, Kincaid felt himself being overtaken by his past. It was disappointing somehow and insubstantial. He noticed her pennants and flags flapping in the wind with gay abandon, as though she were part of a regatta. The next time he came up, he could see marksmen crawling into place on her foredeck with rifles, ready to fire when they came in range. The marshes, by contrast, seemed as far away as heaven, yet he knew they were as lethal as bullets. Strange to hasten so to one's doom; the fitting climax to the dream of his life.

He could almost hear his tendons pulling apart, his heart ready to explode. When his eyes saw Dolores they merely registered her presence. His body operated on a fuel source never before tapped; he was eating up his insides, his energy pumping in a form of self-destruction. He had to go on. Desperation drove him beyond stamina.

The next time he emerged, his legs felt as though they were dragging balls and chains through mud; he couldn't lift his arms. Ahead of them, the island of Itapupa grew out of the late-afternoon mists, and the rain began. As did the riflefire, which shattered the glass of the wheelhouse. Kincaid pulled Dolores down, falling with her.

"They will catch us," she predicted dully, crouching beside him. She would be punished for her disloyalty. Kincaid peeked over the top of the wheel, took a last set of bearings, and tied the lash. He pulled her out of the wheelhouse and along the deck toward the companionway.

"How will we know where we're going?" she protested in the voice of a child.

"It won't make any difference."

The channel narrowed abruptly as they passed land's end and the marshes began, tall grass interspersed with wide intervals of choppy water, and then more and more tall grass, and the jungle closed in on them like a green sky. The river sucked them toward the marshes, and the fragile hollow shell of the *Mãe de Deus* glided high and light and disappeared from view.

* * *

Aboard the *Francesca*, consternation reigned. Mercedes and her brother had ordered the sharpshooters to fire, over the objections of Colonel Mendonça, and in the confusion, some had obeyed. But it was Mendonça who insisted on pursuit when the *Mãe de Deus* vanished in the reeds. The Captain of the *Francesca* wanted to haul off, but Mendonça wouldn't hear of it.

"Are you countermanding my orders?" he gasped, wheezing for breath.

"There is no channel, Colonel," protested the

frightened officer. "The screw will become entangled in the growth. Even they will not make it. The way is impassable."

Mendonça looked wildly, disbelievingly about, rushed panting to the foredeck and, trembling, looked through the binoculars. It was not possible. "Follow them!" he demanded, blood bubbling in his mouth.

Mercedes came up behind him and put a hand on his shoulder. "It's not necessary, Colonel," she tried to explain. "The chase is over. Let us proceed to Pará."

"Never!" He shook her arm off and pushed her aside, stumbling back to the bridge, the blood filling his mouth now. He stopped and looked again at the river, dizzy with despair. It seemed to him now that his life flowed on ahead of him for only a very short way. Behind him was where it all had been: in the jungle, in the river. He had an overwhelming sense suddenly of having lived right to the edge of his life; he had seen his friends and his wives buried; now his daughter. He alone survived, but his journey, like the river itself, was almost over. He sank feebly into a deck chair, doubled up with pain.

Mercedes watched for some moments, but made no move to help him. When she had realized the *Mãe de Deus* had beaten them into the marshes, that she would not be permitted to witness her revenge, she had found herself momentarily allied with the old man; she wanted to pursue, to pursue at all costs, even if it meant tearing off the bottom of the *Francesca*'s hull, twisting off the screw and dying in the muck with Kincaid.

But she thought better of it. She restrained herself. She listened to the Captain's protestations. Always get the advice of experts, her father had taught her. Mercedes was above all a practical person, a businesswoman. And while emotionally it was anticlimactic and unsatisfying not to see Kincaid's destruction with her own eyes, she reflected that it wasn't really necessary. He had, in fact, done her a favor, killing the girl as well as himself, and killing the old man in his crazed progress after them, in his frantic, desperate efforts to overtake. She smiled. It was not quite the vengeance she had envisioned, but she would be philosophical.

"Stop engines," she commanded. Her brother came over and stared at the huddled figure in the deck chair, taking his sister's hand like a child. They owned the Amazon now. The *Francesca*, with her dying owner, headed south for Pará.

*   *   *

Kincaid unlocked the door of the hothouse and accustomed his eyes to the dark. He picked up a rubber seed, oily and brown and smelling of the jungle, and he laughed softly to think of the trouble this small thing had caused, the disaster it had provoked. He wondered fleetingly if this journey had been merely a series of tests that were aimed to prove him worthy of taking the rubber; or if it was instead a saga of punishment for a life of questionable value. He rubbed the seed against his lips and put it in his pocket for some kind of luck, then went back on deck. He put his arm around Dolores and they watched, ignoring the wheel, drifting with the choked current, forgetting the engines. The boat glided erratically through the tall grasses that clutched at them like tentacles. Alligators joined them to swim alongside for a few yards and then submerged with their guilty secrets. The sun was going down, the sky so vast it was dark, raining on one side, light on the other. They had come a thousand miles together on this river. He held her tightly, wondering what the future would be, powerless to affect it. It was the end of the Amazon.

EPILOGUE

It was the end of many things. Colonel Mendonça died before the *Francesca* reached Pará.
The Coutards saw to it that he was returned in
state to the city he had helped build, and they
gave him a funeral the likes of which the Southern
hemisphere had never seen. The community
mourned as well the abduction of Mendonça's
daughter, and a fund was even set aside to employ
a network of international detectives to locate her;
but the fund ran dry without results, and no one
but a frightened old sister of the Colonel continued to pay the detectives. They took her money
then, as a matter of course, but did nothing.

Several months later the news came back to
Manaus that the rubber seedlets had made the
voyage to England successfully, surviving the
long crossing and the transplantation in the elaborate hothouses of the Royal Geographic Society.
Samples of the rubber seedlings and of various
Brazilian soils made a popular tourist display in
the main halls of the Society, mounted on marble
columns, housed in small glass cylinders just as
soil had been exhibited in the great American
Centennial exposition, some years earlier. Manaus

felt there was no cause for immediate panic, and indeed the results of the theft seemed to have no impact at all. The rubber kings were even wont to speculate on the exertions caused by the theft of the seedlings, when after all, what had actually happened? Nothing, so far as they were concerned. The price of rubber remained the same; went up, even.

Mercedes Coutard might have understood, might even have taken steps at that late date, but she died giving birth to a baby girl; her master plan to rule Amazonas fell into the hands of Pierre Coutard, and from there it was only a short fall to the whorehouses. Even that did not last; Coutard fell prey to the syphilis he had lived with for years. Finally, nothing human or handsome left of him, he was carted off to a luxurious madhouse and remained there until his demise.

Iquitos was never seen or heard from again.

But Manaus itself continued to flourish. Costs of rubber escalated wildly as the rubber kings followed the plan laid out by the Coutards of continued monopolistic price-heightening. The world came begging, and as the century ended and the automobile showed its fierce potential, the prices of Amazon rubber went even higher. The idea of five tires for every automobile and the concept of automobile production accelerating until, as Ford promised, every family would own one, was enough to quadruple the price of rubber. Mendonça had been right. Slavery was officially abolished in 1888, but its practical effects were barely

felt in the jungle. How else were the growers to
get their rubber? And besides, the Indians would
starve without their jobs in the *estradas*. Or so
went the logic of the new millionaires. Life in
Manaus went up a dizzying spiral of the most bizarre wealth a city had ever seen. The London
Times reported that of the richest cities in the
world, Manaus ranked fifth. This was cause for
celebration and for renewed vigor: Manaus
would ascend that list; it would become the richest city in the world, the first. New estates were
built, mansions such as only exist in dreams. They
would out-do the Vanderbilts and the Astors, the
Carnegies and the Rockefellers. Automobiles appeared on the streets, and took the place of the
regal carriages of the previous century.

The Royal Geographic Society became in
time a joke in the memories of those older citizens, those who had lived through the great panic.
It was an easy task to ignore the shipment of tiny
rubber trees from the Society's hothouses to the
soil of Ceylon and Malaya, places that seemed
barbaric to the rich of Manaus, if they had heard
of them at all. No, there was nothing to worry
about. There were new whores and new
horses and more champagne and the highest con-
sumption of diamonds in the world. It was a
new century; there were untold rubber trees left
to drain.

And then, quite abruptly, almost arbitrarily, it
ended. But there was nothing really arbitrary

about it. The stolen seeds had taken root and flourished. And while Manaus, besotted with itself, had pursued extravagance upon extravagance, importing dizzier and giddier follies— during all this time, ten thousand miles away, the seeds had been growing.

In 1905 the transplanted *hevea brasiliensis* of Harry Kincaid produced its first harvest. In contrast to the wildly confident Manaus price of three dollars per pound, Malay rubber could be and was produced for less than nine cents. It was the end. In Manaus, panic filled the streets. Lines outside the Booth Steamship Company formed, women queuing up for hours, for days, desperate to leave their dazzling metropolis, unable to use the banknotes and currency that inflation had rendered worthless. They tossed emeralds and rubies and their precious diamonds on the steamship office's worn and greasy counters. Once the jewels were gone, other, perhaps not more precious but certainly more personal, items were put out for bargaining.

The stage of the Teatro do Amazonas was dark with slithery shadows. Lizards darted over the balconies of gold leaf; hornbacked armadillos scuttled across the red velvet seats; snakes slipped along the crystal chandeliers; spores developed in the wet heat; vines grew from the wings.

Bankruptcies were as common as *babussu* nuts. The Bank of Amazonas printed the forms in quadruplicate and dealt them out like losing hands of cards. Millionaires metamorphosed abruptly into paupers; yachts were confiscated, mansions lost. The parties were over. Celebration gave way to mourning; the cakewalk bowed to the dirge. As servants lost their homes they took to the streets. Unused to the jungle many of them had never seen, it was impossible for them to return to it. They foraged in roving bands, pillaged for money, for food, for anything to stay alive. Child prostitution rose along with venereal disease and suicide. Suffering and despair were the final rewards of the avarice that had made Manaus what it was.

All that is known for certain about Harry Kincaid and Dolores Mendonça is that they reached the sea and their rendezvous and sailed to England together on the *H.M.S. Achilles*, speaking little to each other or anyone else; that they officiated at the unloading of the rubber seeds when the *Achilles* docked at Liverpool; that they signed their names to several sets of bills of lading and a receipt for nine thousand pounds, sterling; that they walked from the Liverpool docks to the streets, where they got into a carriage; that the carriage bore them to the railroad station; and that they boarded a train for London. When the train arrived in London, the welcoming committee from the Royal Geographic Society was perplexed to discover that neither Kincaid nor the woman was on board. The committee waited through several arrivals that day and the next. Then it gave up and devoted its energies to the original task of getting the rubber seeds to Ceylon and Malaya.

Rumors concerning the fates of Harry Kincaid and Dolores Mendonça started, flourished, faded, and died.

ABOUT THE AUTHORS

NICHOLAS MEYER is the author of two major bestsellers, *The Seven-Per-Cent Solution* and *The West End Horror*. In 1975, he received the Golden Dagger from the Crime Writers Association of England and a Playboy Fiction Award. He has been nominated for numerous prizes, among them an Academy Award. His home is Los Angeles, California, although he is a native New Yorker.

BARRY JAY KAPLAN has published a dozen romances and gothics under various pen names and has just completed a new novel that was three years in the writing. He lives in New York City.

RELAX!
SIT DOWN
and Catch Up On Your Reading!

☐	11877	**HOLOCAUST** by Gerald Green	$2.25
☐	11260	**THE CHANCELLOR MANUSCRIPT** by Robert Ludlum	$2.25
☐	10077	**TRINITY** by Leon Uris	$2.75
☐	2300	**THE MONEYCHANGERS** by Arthur Hailey	$1.95
☐	12550	**THE MEDITERRANEAN CAPER** by Clive Cussler	$2.25
☐	11469	**AN EXCHANGE OF EAGLES** by Owen Sela	$2.25
☐	2600	**RAGTIME** by E. L. Doctorow	$2.25
☐	11428	**FAIRYTALES** by Cynthia Freeman	$2.25
☐	11966	**THE ODESSA FILE** by Frederick Forsyth	$2.25
☐	11557	**BLOOD RED ROSES** by Elizabeth B. Coker	$2.25
☐	11708	**JAWS 2** by Hank Searls	$2.25
☐	12490	**TINKER, TAILOR, SOLDIER, SPY** by John Le Carre	$2.50
☐	11929	**THE DOGS OF WAR** by Frederick Forsyth	$2.25
☐	10526	**INDIA ALLEN** by Elizabeth B. Coker	$1.95
☐	12489	**THE HARRAD EXPERIMENT** by Robert Rimmer	$2.25
☐	11767	**IMPERIAL 109** by Richard Doyle	$2.50
☐	10500	**DOLORES** by Jacqueline Susann	$1.95
☐	11601	**THE LOVE MACHINE** by Jacqueline Susann	$2.25
☐	11886	**PROFESSOR OF DESIRE** by Philip Roth	$2.50
☐	10857	**THE DAY OF THE JACKAL** by Frederick Forsyth	$1.95
☐	11952	**DRAGONARD** by Rupert Gilchrist	$1.95
☐	11331	**THE HAIGERLOCH PROJECT** by Ib Melchior	$2.25
☐	11330	**THE BEGGARS ARE COMING** by Mary Loos	$1.95

Buy them at your local bookstore or use this handy coupon for ordering:

Bantam Book Catalog

Here's your up-to-the-minute listing of over 1,400 titles by your favorite authors.

This illustrated, large format catalog gives a description of each title. For your convenience, it is divided into categories in fiction and non-fiction—gothics, science fiction, westerns, mysteries, cookbooks, mysticism and occult, biographies, history, family living, health, psychology, art.

So don't delay—take advantage of this special opportunity to increase your reading pleasure.

Just send us your name and address and 50¢ (to help defray postage and handling costs).

BANTAM BOOKS, INC.
Dept. FC, 414 East Golf Road, Des Plaines, Ill. 60016

Mr./Mrs./Miss_____
(please print)

Address_____

City_____State_____Zip_____

Do you know someone who enjoys books? Just give us their names and addresses and we'll send them a catalog too!

_____

Mr./Mrs./Miss_____

Address_____

City_____State_____Zip_____

_____

Mr./Mrs./Miss_____

Address_____

City_____State_____Zip_____

FC—9/76